Class No. F Acc No. C/178403

Author: Ward, L Loc:

LEABHARLANN
CHONDAE AN CHABHAIN

11 JUN 2005
-6 NOV 2007
-5 JUN 2011

1. This book may be kept three weeks. It is to be returned on / before the last date stamped below.
2. A fine of 25c will be
part of week a book is

F / C178403

24 AUG 2005

OUTSIDE Valentine

A NOVEL

LIZA WARD

CHATTO & WINDUS
London

Many of the events fictionalised in *Outside Valentine* are based on actual characters and circumstances surrounding the murders committed by Charles Starkweather in Nebraska in 1958

Published by Chatto & Windus 2005

First published in the United States of America by Henry Holt in 2004
2 4 6 8 10 9 7 5 3 1

Copyright © 2004 by Liza Ward

Liza Ward has asserted her right under the Copyright, Designs and Patents Act 1988 to be identified as the author of this work.

This book is sold subject to the condition that it shall not, by way of trade or otherwise, be lent, resold, hired out, or otherwise circulated without the publisher's prior consent in any form of binding or cover other than that in which it is published and without a similar condition including this condition being imposed on the subsequent purchaser

First published in Great Britain in 2003 by
Chatto & Windus
Random House, 20 Vauxhall Bridge Road,
London SW1V 2SA

Random House Australia (Pty) Limited
20 Alfred Street, Milsons Point, Sydney,
New South Wales 2061, Australia

Random House New Zealand Limited
18 Poland Road, Glenfield,
Auckland 10, New Zealand

Random House (Pty) Limited
Endulini, 5A Jubilee Road, Parktown 2193, South Africa

The Random House Group Limited Reg. No. 954009
www.randomhouse.co.uk

A CIP catalogue record for this book
is available from the British Library

ISBN 0 7011 7803 5

Papers used by Random House are natural, recyclable products made from wood grown in sustainable forests; the manufacturing processes conform to the environmental regulations of the country of origin

Printed and bound in Great Britain by
Clays Ltd, St Ives plc

CAVAN COUNTY LIBRARY
ACC No. C/178403
CLASS NO. F
INVOICE NO 6247 HF
PRICE €12-64

For my mother and father

OUTSIDE VALENTINE

CAVAN COUNTY LIBRARY

CHAPTER ONE

1991

In my dream, the snow was falling all across my old Nebraska. The minister had come to tell me about my parents. A spot of blood appeared on his collar, and then another, and through the sheet I felt the coldness of his hand.

In the moment before opening my eyes, I was a boy in my bed again with the duck painting hanging over it, my mother calling up the stairs. Her voice brought a moment of incredible relief, but coming back to my life as it is, the emptiness almost made me cry out. Everything was just as I'd left it the night before: the empty cocktail glass, the book about the Roman shipwreck, the thick curtains gathered on either side of the window like two ball skirts trapped in a stiff-armed dance.

I wandered down the hall through the pale dawn light, a grown man in his pajamas searching for his mother's voice. But the apartment was quiet with all its doors shut against me, Susan and the children tucked securely behind them. I put my hand on the brass knob of the bedroom door, tempted to turn it and push it open just to see how my wife looked, fast asleep with her hair fanned out over the pillow, her eye mask in place. In the past, it had comforted me to wake up in our bed and put my palm where her body had been, knowing she hadn't gone far. But we no longer lived that way. Tom

Osborne, our orange cat, eyed me suspiciously from the top of the bookshelf.

As the sun came up over the East River, I was on my way, and all that morning I hid in my office, staring at the walls, knowing I was supposed to be doing things. But I couldn't quite remember what they were, and when my assistant, Francesca, came in, I'd smile, quickly open a book, or wrinkle my brow at a stack of papers I barely recognized. No appointments were marked on the calendar, though one could never be completely sure what that meant. Francesca and I both tended to write things down on envelopes or stick-ums, which we always managed to lose. We could often be found wearing pink rubber gloves, fishing through trash cans for elusive telephone numbers or dates.

"Ah, here we go!" she'd cry at the start of one of our crazed goose chases, as if she were dragging me onto the dance floor. Actually, I loved our wild searches; in fact, these days they seemed to be all that was keeping the office alive. Calls were few, appointments rare. Nobody wanted to buy, and most of the time it would have been easy to disappear, to walk over to the Met or just pay a visit to Jon Mondratti, who, like clockwork, would uncork the libations. Unfortunately, there was always the danger of falling in love with something at Mondratti's, where it is easy to lose oneself in the red rooms at the top of that dark stairwell. I liked to run my fingers across the antique Tabriz carpets, carried across oceans in enormous sheaves, or drift among the scroll-backed Dutch Rococo chairs and nineteenth-century paintings from distant and altogether more beautiful times.

Mondratti's oil sketch of a tiger, a Delacroix, has always been an obsession of mine. The animal seems to luxuriate in the shade of a rock shelf, the light playing over those sensuous stripes. There is something so human in its eyes. Sometimes I'd sit there for an hour or so, just fantasizing, trying to come up with a way to afford it. It didn't matter what else was falling down around me, what other responsibilities I hadn't met. At certain moments, my need for that painting was all that seemed important, and I would have sacrificed anything to have it. You see, I could no longer be trusted around beautiful things and my weakness was apparent. Suddenly everyone had realized I was missing something.

AFTER FRANCESCA LEFT THE GALLERY, I CREPT INTO THE SILENT SHOWROOM AND lay down in the center of the floor. Through my sport coat, I could feel the cool marble on my back. The humidifier hummed and the buses screeched down Fifth Avenue. I could smell the past on all my works of art, as if it were drifting through the large glass cases. Some pieces had been buried in the ground for centuries; others had lined forgotten tombs. I would have to part with all these objects someday. That was the heartbreaking nature of my work. I held history in my hand for one brief moment and tried to give it a price no one would ever pay. I didn't ever want to let go.

When the phone rang, it was Susan.

"You're still there, Lowell," she said. "When are you coming home?"

"In a minute," I said, holding a groan in my throat and fighting the urge to disappear. "I'm making a sale."

THE WHOLE APARTMENT WAS IN SHADOWS. SUSAN STOOD AT THE END OF THE hall by her bedroom in her bathrobe, though it was just early evening. My wife has a talent for going to sleep every time she is upset—a rare gift. In deep sleep she dreams incredible stories; when we were younger, and living year round in Port Saugus, she would tell them to me if I brought her tea and rubbed her feet. The house Susan had inherited from her uncle was a quiet place. Fog from the river softened everything.

"What did you sell?" Susan asked, putting her hands on her hips.

I didn't answer, just shrugged my shoulders as she came into the foyer, unfolded a piece of paper, and held it out for me. The insignia at the top of the page looked familiar. "It was addressed to you," she said, "but I opened it anyway because I could tell it was a bill, and if you haven't noticed that's what I take care of around here. Somebody's got to maintain some sort of normal order."

Ignoring her, I walked straight into the living room to pour myself a drink. When I turned around I could see her still standing by the front door, looking wounded.

"You can't brush this off," she said, as if it were some sort of cancer scare. "It's a statement about a safe-deposit box at a bank near Port Saugus. We owe them three thousand dollars. That's years of unpaid rent." She sat down on the couch and leaned her elbows on her knees, holding the bill by her fingertips. "What's in it, Lowell?"

I just shook my head. I couldn't remember what I'd put in that box all those years ago. For so long, I'd been wanting the whole business, the past really, to just go away.

My wife pretended to study the bill further, as if she could pry some truth from it. Then, gathering her courage, she finally spoke. "I'm the one who keeps everything running around here. And I'm tired of it." Sitting in her white robe among the dark velvet cushions, Susan looked less sturdy than usual; it was as if she were drowning in all that softness, an object in need of fundamental restoration.

My wife melting away in her nightgown was something I didn't like to see. I drained my drink and put it down on the table. We were both, suddenly, getting older, and lately I had noticed something different about her shoulders. They were curving like the old ladies I used to see at church in Lincoln. Life was hurrying past us now. Our son, Hank, was about to leave for college, and Mary, it seemed, already had one foot out the door to follow. Susan and I had been together for some twenty-odd years, and I'd never been completely sure about marrying her, or risking love, which at times felt so uncomfortable. But she had a way of stepping in and I had a way of going along.

I grabbed at the bill.

"This is unbelievable. I don't even know if we *can* pay it," said my wife, resting her forehead in her hand.

"Not that there's any point."

"Well, I'll never sell Port Saugus no matter how bad things get," Susan countered. She tried to meet my eyes but I didn't look up. "It could be something of value, you know," she said. "Something you wouldn't want to lose."

"Why does it matter so much to you?"

"Because, Lowe," she said softly, "it seems to matter so much to *you.*"

I made myself another drink, eyeing my wife's reflection in the mirror behind the bar as the bourbon snaked over the rocks. "Listen here," I said to her. "There isn't a goddamn thing in that box."

CHAPTER TWO

1957

When I am half asleep and everything is dark, ghosts rise out of the prairie and swim across my eyes. The girl crawls up from the storm cellar with glass in her knee. She peers at me and her fists are clenched. She cries, "Caril Ann, where is my math book?" There is no sense telling that girl in my mind where those schoolbooks got to, pages blowing, by the side of a road in Bennet, Nebraska. And of course Roe Street is always standing in the door of the outhouse with his belt in his hand and a hole in his head, blaming me for all that Charlie did.

I do not call these *dreams* because dreams are something you wish to have happened. Everyone knows how I never wished any of it. It was not my fault. From the very beginning it was never my fault, not even the skipping of school. People act a certain way when they are treated wrong, and I had already done the eighth grade. It was wrong of Roe to try and send me back.

The first day I saw Charlie behind our new house with his .22 in his hand, there was a whisper of the way things would go. I was not supposed to be hiding in the trees, crying for everything gone wrong. I was supposed to be in school, my legs tucked up under the same old desk, my face turning red for not knowing the answers Mrs. Kramer asked because she knew I could not get them right. I was crying because Roe had chased me away from the house for not minding him. He knew I was hiding out, but he could not do a thing about it and still get to work. I was making my own laws; Roe had drove me to it. I showed him this. I threw Roe's rules back in his face.

BEFORE SHE MARRIED ROE AND GAVE BIRTH TO BETTY SUE, MOTHER WOULD let me spend all day on the couch eating Sugar Daddies, if I wanted. Now I was to clean my room, go to school, and mind Roe in whatever I did. This was not hardly fair. Life is a give-and-take and I had nothing to show for it. We were living in a new house and I had a bigger room, that's true, but it was still a run-down place with a latrine out back, mounds of dirt in front, and weeds that grew up over the porch and about strangled it.

When Roe came in my room without knocking to see was I ready for school, I was wearing nothing but my pink kimono with a red sketch of Chinese women dancing over it and panties underneath. I was brushing my hair with good strong strokes. The kimono was a gift my true father had sent Mother from Kansas City after the Korean wars were done. It made her sick to wear so she had given it to me. She wished he was lying shot in a ditch. She said this when she opened the box. For thinking these nasty thoughts, she did not deserve his gifts and I had told her so. She looked at me then, with her eyes all pinched, and shook her head. She said, "What do you care, Caril Ann? I don't see nothing in this box for *you*."

I was brushing my hair in the mirror, biding my own time, when the door smacked open. Roe was standing with his Watson Brothers shirt tucked in his pants and ready to go.

My robe was opened a bit. His brown eyes were mad and hard. He stared me up-down like he couldn't believe a girl wouldn't want to repeat the damn eighth grade. I hadn't even turned around, but I could see it all, beyond my own face in the mirror, and Betty Sue past the doorjamb, skidding over the floor in a sagging diaper, chewing on the corner of a box under the kitchen table. I didn't so much as put my hairbrush down. I did not show I cared about him standing there.

I just brushed, like I learned to in a magazine. To me, he was just some old man who had married my mother a second time.

"You're not ready," Roe said, as if he needed to.

"Oh," I said. I smoothed my hair behind my ears like everything was simple. "I'm not going." My heart beat hard. I could feel it in my chest, and a warm wind stirring up from the opened window behind my bed kind of kissed my ears.

Roe slapped the wall, and the plaster and yellow paint chips flaked all over the floor. I turned around and faced him straight on.

"Goddamn it," he said. "Get in the car right now, Caril Ann."

I knew better than to step an inch closer or to get in his car. It was a beat-up old Ford with split seams inside that smelled of dog. I stayed right where I was by the mirror.

Mother appeared behind him, her face in the space between his shoulder and head. I pleaded my eyes at her, as if Roe wasn't there, as if this room was a place where only me and her existed, as if everything was back to how it was before Roe came stomping into our house and rattling his cage. I said to her, "I don't want to go with him." But it was no good. Her eyes were all torn up and tired. She put one hand on Roe's shoulder, the other on her hip. She shaked her head. "Lord, what did I do?" she said.

"Nothing," I said. I slit my eyes in Roe's direction. "It's him who's made all the problems for us."

Mother's face went mean. She wagged her finger at me. "Wise up, Caril Ann," she said. "Don't be kicking the gift horse."

"I'll deal with her," Roe went on, shutting the door on Mother's face.

Betty Sue was crying in the kitchen, which was nothing new; I mean, she cried by the hour and that was just what we needed out in this place on the edge of town. She cried when she got left alone too long. She cried when she messed something up no one could fix, like my poster of Frankie Avalon, which she scribbled red pen over and nobody said a word. I mean, I was the one who should have been crying, with all this pushiness.

Roe stood in front of me, stealing all the air. It was hot. The sun made squares on the floor. They shifted and danced with the shapes of leaves. The boards were sticky under my toes from some pop I had spilled and just let dry. Roe Street unbuckled his belt like he was making to whip me, though he had never done it before and I wasn't scared.

Roe came closer and the belt looped from his hand like a crazy eight. "Caril Ann," he said, looking ape as I'd ever seen him, no matter how bad I'd been. The purple was crawling up under the bristles of his hair.

"I'm not going anywhere dressed like this," I said, putting my hands on my hips and sticking my bare knee a ways out from between the folds of silk. There I was, a lady in the middle of his ugly mess.

"Do as I say, Caril Ann; mind me and do as I say."

"Yes, Roe," I said. I flipped my hair behind my shoulder for him to tell just how much I did not mean it, so then he lunged at me, pulling my arm for sassing him and yanking me around the room. He held my one shoulder in the palm of his hand with his fingers digging in my skin and shook. He held me like this but did not use the belt. He smelled of sweat and the soap Mother used to wash his shirts. There were red spots on his cheeks. I did not know what I should do to win this and not get whipped.

I pulled away, back to the wall, but it was no good. Roe tugged the collar of my kimono, scrunching up the silk in his fist. I could not move for fearing the cloth would rip. Another robe like this was not an easy thing to find, so I hooked my thumb under the sash and pulled a little. I felt the silk slide away from my skin with a tickle and goose bumps rise on my white skin. The kimono fell around my sides. I stood there with my panties loose around my middle for being so worn. I could not believe it. I stared up in his face a moment. "Look what you did, Roe," I said.

Roe let go my arm and left off the whipping. The belt dropped like a snake that was shot in the head. "Cover yourself and get ready for school," he said. "You're going." But he did not sound so sure. He closed the door softly, like everything was suddenly fine.

I stood there a moment, still as salt. It was so hot in the room I could not breathe. The tree outside my window went calm, like somebody took the air away. All night its branches had scratched at the screen and I laid in bed straight as a pin, wondering what was up.

I started to cry, hugging my daddy's kimono around me. I do not know why I cried when I had basically won this thing. I still don't know, but sometimes I don't understand why I do the things I do. It is the great mystery of my independent self. Maybe it was for not wanting to go to school ever. Maybe it was because I did not want a part of this world where people like Roe tell me to do things and I am to mind them unconditioned of how I feel about it. Everyone in the world is behind bars.

So I picked up my sketchbook and my pencils, scattered over the floor and in the cracks between the boards, and placed each one in the box. Then I pulled up on the screen, threw my legs over the sill, and thrust myself out the window, landing my bare feet in the dirt.

I sprinted quick as a whip across the yard and behind the outhouse that smelled heavy and sick in the late-summer heat. My heart never raced so hard for being bad. The sun beat down on the brown yard like there never would be another drop of rain. Beyond it, a sprinkle of trees fringed the cornfield.

As I ran, I could hear Nig whipping around on the chain, smelling me near. I could hear Mother on the porch, realizing I had gone. It was skinning her alive. "Caril Ann!" she screamed. But I did not stop.

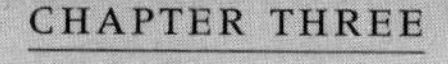

CHAPTER THREE

1959

I was ten years old in Chicago when I first heard of the Starkweather killings. Upstairs in the study, I sat by the radio with a candy bar in my hand and listened. The reports reminded me of *Gunsmoke* or *The Inner Sanctum.* Authorities combed the state of Nebraska. Reckless lovers were on the run. Was the Fugate girl a victim or an accomplice? What had Starkweather been like as a child? "Can you remember who he was before this tragedy unfolded?" the radio asked. "He got picked on in kindergarten," one of his brothers said. "They called him Little Red." I had a certain affection for him because of that. For a while it was Charlie who had my sympathy in this story.

Then we moved to Lincoln. My mother became more agitated. Things started to change. And when I heard about the boy just a few blocks away who'd been orphaned because of Starkweather, I lost any feeling I had for Little Red. It was that boy left alone I couldn't seem to get off my mind. I always imagined him wandering on his own. Don't all children worry about finding themselves left alone? I always did, even before my mother got restless. I always knew somehow I would wind up without her.

. . .

IT WAS LATE JUNE OF 1959, THE DAY BEFORE STARKWEATHER WAS TO BE ELECtrocuted, when my mother went out and bought the Studebaker Golden Hawk. Teenagers gathered around the Nebraska State Penitentiary, waiting for the lights to dim and 2200 blue volts to go slamming through the murderer's body. I'd been watching those kids strut up and down across the television screen from the safety of our parlor. They were defiantly hanging off the hoods of cars, slugging beer, their eyes fixed on the prison windows for some sign of Starkweather's passing.

When Lucille, our housekeeper, cried my name, I catapulted off the love seat and charged through the foyer, worried that the execution had already happened. Lucille was standing at the window in the bright green kitchen, wiping her dark hands on her apron as she watched a gold car pull up the drive. My mother was behind the wheel, honking and waving, her scarf billowing out behind her. Lucille placed her warm palms on my shoulder. "Lord, what your momma got herself into this time? Daddy gonna have himself a fit." I pictured my father with a red face, pounding the desk that had once been his father's or yanking at his tie. It was the only sort of fit I could imagine him having, in the safety of his study, far from my mother's gaze.

Mother charged into the kitchen through the garage door, swinging the car keys around the tip of her finger. Her nails were fire-engine red. I hadn't ever seen them with polish. The kitchen was filled with the scent of mint brownies, her favorite, but she did not seem to notice. She was flying, and we were just a few things left adrift in her wake.

"Girls," she said, "come on." She tugged us through the kitchen and into the cool garage. The brand new car sat ticking in the empty spot beside the dusty Chevrolet we'd driven from Chicago to Lincoln the summer before, when my grandfather had died suddenly, leaving Capital Steel and the house to my father.

My mother opened the driver-side door. "Meet the Studebaker Limited-Production Nineteen Fifty-seven Golden Hawk Four Hundred," she said. "Without even a scratch." The car was solid gold with cream-colored tail fins and a white leather interior. My mother put her hand on the hot hood and stared at Lucille. "So what do you think?"

Lucille shook her head. "You don't wanna know what I think, Mrs. Hurst."

"I do so," said my mother. "I always want to know what you think, Lucille. It's very important to me." My mother was always saying these sorts of things. I think she got them from plays. Whenever my mother bought new clothes from Miller and Paine on my father's credit, she pulled Lucille up the pink-carpeted staircase. I'd watch as Mother held dresses with tags still attached up against Lucille, parading her proudly in front of the mirror. "Don't you look lovely!" she would cry. Or "That color complements your dark complexion so well. I don't want it, after all. You keep it!"

Lucille never seemed to object, but afterward she would sit in my room and brush my hair while I cracked bubble gum and listened to *Gunsmoke* and we would laugh. Nothing my mother did ever seemed quite real.

Now here we were, the three of us, standing around the gold car as if it were some sort of fiery comet dropped from the sky. "Folks gonna talk," Lucille said cautiously, circling the Studebaker. "You don't do anything halfway, do you?"

"Of course I don't." My mother clenched her fists. "I saw it in the sun off the Cornhusker Highway. I had to have it right then. I've never felt this crazy before about anything."

"*I* love it, Mother," I offered. "I think it's beautiful."

My mother turned to me but never really looked. "Well, get in then Puggy," she said. "We're going for a ride."

Trotting around the front of the car, I opened the passenger door. My mother climbed slowly inside, watching me, and then suddenly stuck her palm out, freezing me where I stood, my hand wrapped around the chrome door handle.

"Take off your shoes, please," she said. "God knows where you've been."

Like a good girl, I shed my saddle shoes and climbed in beside her. The white leather was warm with the late June sun and smooth as the inside of a shell. My mother fixed her scarf in the rearview mirror. When she turned the key in the ignition, the car rumbled to life, and my mother inched it out of the garage. A ray of sun caught the face of her watch and splashed over the dash. My mother was small and neat, with black hair and smooth tan skin. The turned-up nose so unfortunate on my own face lent hers a sprightly charm.

I hugged my arm around the flesh hanging over the waist of my skirt and tried to suck in as my mother jammed her foot on the accelerator and the car launched backward. I saw Lucille lift her hands to her face. I heard a honking horn. I turned around. My father was just then coming in the drive, but my mother failed to see him, and the back of the Golden Hawk Studebaker rammed right into the front fender of my father's Packard.

My father got out, slamming the car door, silently inspecting his broken headlight. He approached my mother's window slowly, as if he were trapping a wild beast, and then bent down and peered inside the car. "What's this about, pet?" He was trying to seem calm and open-minded. His blue eyes were wide and his brow was raised. It made me want to giggle. Beads of moisture clung to his temples.

"What does it look like? I bought a car," my mother said, staring straight ahead. "I needed one."

My father shook his head in disbelief. He was leaning his elbows on the door. "Why would you do that?"

"I'm tired of being surrounded by your father's things." My mother sighed. "Dead this, dead that. I want my *own* things."

My father's face turned red. "I don't understand why you would do this without talking it over." He paused. "It's like you're sneaking around, Ann. Why would you do that?"

"This whole town's ready to pop." My mother shrugged her shoulders. "I got the itch."

"I can't believe it," said my father, mopping his brow with his handkerchief. "This whole thing would be amusing if you weren't my wife." He smacked the side of the car. "Do you think money grows on trees, Ann? Is that what you think?" My father leaned his head through the window. "Tell me how much this boat cost."

My mother was boiling up. Her knuckles were white and her eyes were hot and wicked.

"Tell me how much." My father was exasperated. "It's not even a family car, for Christ's sake." His tie had dropped over the edge of the window.

My mother grabbed the tie in her fist and tugged hard. My father's head lurched forward. "You ruin everything," she snapped. "You're so ungrateful!"

A storm of shock passed over my father's face. Then his features went blank. He pulled back his head, straightened his tie, and went inside to pour himself a drink.

BEFORE DINNER, I HEARD MY FATHER SPEAKING ON THE TELEPHONE TO SOMEONE about the execution: "And how is that poor boy who lost his parents?" I wanted to ask my father what he'd heard about the boy when he hung up the phone, but I could tell by the look on his face that he wasn't in the mood to waste time with me.

My mother lay on the living room floor, her bare feet propped on the arm of the couch, a glass of wine in her hand, her hair spread out over the Oriental rug. Even at dinner, after Lucille had gone home, my parents didn't really speak to each other. They just raced through the motions of sitting down, and before I'd even started eating they were back on the patio, getting drunk in the uncomfortable silence that all Lincoln shared that night. Each household held its breath and waited for the lights to dim—which would never actually happen, my father assured us, though everyone else said the electrocution would have this effect. I wanted to know what was happening, but my father wouldn't let me turn on the newscasts.

"It's nothing to get excited about," he said, coming through the French doors from the darkened living room with another drink in his hand. "I want you to understand that, Puggy. It's not some holiday." My father patted me on the head. It was my favorite thing he did, though I hated their nickname for me. It made me feel like the fat aunt visiting the glamorous couple. I never quite understood how I had come to be their child.

He sat back down heavily in his chair. The candles were burning low on the slate table, and the fireflies winked at me in little sparks from the dark bed of the rhododendrons. "It's a time to mourn the lives that were lost," my father said, swirling the ice around in his glass. He peered into the bottom of his drink and took a long sip. "It's time to applaud the efficiency of American justice." I pictured blue electricity coursing through wires in the basement of the penitentiary, while the boy sat in his living room waiting for someone to come home.

My mother snorted and poured herself more wine. "You didn't even know the dead people," she said to my father. "Don't pretend to be involved." The bottle of wine was almost empty. Her eyes were wet and flashy, burning with life. Outside, the leaves rustled excitedly in the ancient trees along Van Dorn Street.

My father would not let it rest. "We're all involved. These were people our friends knew, people my father knew," he said. "It was a senseless killing." He looked down at his hands, folded tightly around his glass. My mother's hair was glistening over her shoulders. She shook it dangerously close to the flame and looked at my father. He pulled the candle to him, out of her reach. It left a splatter of wax that I started to pick at.

"Let's turn on all the lights in this spooky old house and just see what happens," said my mother, suddenly transformed. She clapped her hands. "Let's do something. I want to celebrate something." Her voice was heavy and thick. She started toward the French doors, stumbling in the dark. My father, of course, was waiting. He caught her around the waist, picked her up, and carried her into the living room. I stood by the bookcase, watching in the dark.

"Turn on the lights!" said my mother. She swung her legs violently. Her heel caught one of the china frogs on the end table and knocked it to the ground. It smashed to pieces. My father held her tight until she stopped struggling. "I'm so sorry," she said finally, starting to cry.

"I never liked that thing much," my father whispered. He wasn't angry anymore. He kissed her on the ear.

"Turn on the lights, please," she sobbed.

"I *can't* turn on the lights," he said. "I might drop you. Then you'd run away and I'd be all alone." My father cradled her head. Stepping over the china fragments, he carried her through the shadows and up the stairs to bed.

Nobody told me when to go to sleep that night. Everything was quiet. I stared out the windows at the streetlights on Van Dorn, sniffing the cork from my mother's bottle of wine. I imagined that I had lost my parents. I imagined that I had lost everything. I walked around the house in the dark. On the television there was only static. I stumbled over furniture and thought of my grandfather's ghost, of the way Lucille had found him in the living room armchair, dead from a heart attack, the newspaper folded neatly over his knee, the ice not yet melted in his drink. His cigarette smoke still lingered in our heavy curtains. I buried my face in the folds and inhaled, hoping for some secret knowledge, a whisper perhaps, from the world where Starkweather was going.

THE NEXT MORNING, I SAT AT THE KITCHEN TABLE COUNTING OUT PENNY candy money that Lucille had given me for helping with housework. Arranging the coins in bright piles, I added up how much I would be able to buy. Lucille was cleaning the oven. My mother stood at the counter with the *Lincoln Journal Star* open in front of her, reading the details of the execution out loud. Her back was to me. Charles Starkweather had been electrocuted at 12:04 A.M. Two graves were being dug—one in the Wyuka Cemetery and another nearby—one for the murderer and one for the doctor who had declared him dead and then died from a heart attack right in the execution chamber. I wondered if Starkweather's power reached beyond the grave. "Imagine!" my mother said. "Don't you find the world tied together by such strange ironies, Lucille?"

"I don't know about that." Lucille stuck her arm into the back of the oven and scrubbed. "What I do know is the *house* looks like it got electrocuted last night."

I giggled. I couldn't help it.

My mother turned to me. She eyed the change on the table suspiciously, then reached over and brushed the nickels and dimes into her palm. The silver clinked against the back of her rings. "It's summer," she said to me. "Why don't you do something, Puggy? Why don't you get out of the house? You're starting to look pasty. You could go for a swim at the country club. It's an awful place, but at least you could get some exercise. You can't just sit around the house all day eating candy."

I thought of tanned limbs splashing in aqua water just down the street. Floral umbrellas blowing in the breeze, the sound of tennis balls crisply smacking rackets.

"I think we've got some mysterious blood in our veins," my mother announced. "You can tell by my coloring. You take that into consideration the next time you go to that country club." Then, returning to the newspaper, she buried herself in the pages and forgot all about me. I narrowed my eyes and stuck my tongue out at her, but of course she couldn't see. Her face was hidden behind the front-page photo: the oak-plank electric chair against a blank wall, looking no more significant than a piece of patio furniture. It was the headline that caught my eye. I tried to read it backward: It said MASS MURDERER DECLARED DEAD; NEBRASKA HAS ITS WAY. I wondered if there was anything about the boy hidden somewhere inside that story. Maybe he had been interviewed about his feelings. Or maybe someone had kindly sent him away from all this.

When my mother took off in the Studebaker, I grabbed a mint brownie and the newspaper and went up to my room. A bee hit the screen. The morning light was still soft and new. I spread the pages out on the floor. Sometimes my mother just took up so much space. I took a bite of brownie and brushed crumbs off the pages. In section A10 there was a recap of *the bloody trail* Charles Starkweather and Caril Ann Fugate had left across the state of Nebraska, with pictures of all the people they had killed. They all stared out from the page like actors in the theater program I had found on the front table after one of my parents' late nights back in Chicago: *A Doll's House*. The people looked so happy, so certain about the future, it was hard to believe they were dead.

Charlie and Caril Ann were sitting on somebody's couch looking happiest of all. He had his arm around her shoulder and his head cocked to one side. Her pretty brown hair was brushed over one shoulder, and her eyes twinkled like she'd just finished laughing. They looked all tangled up in each other. I wondered if *I'd* ever find someone to love. I was tangled up alone.

CHAPTER FOUR

1991

I woke up in the spare bedroom that night, surprised to find my wife lying beside me, staring from across the mattress, her hands folded under her cheek and her eyes shining in the night glow from the window. "How long have you been here?" I said. I felt almost violated at the thought of her creeping around without my knowledge.

"Something's happened," she answered.

"What?" I shook myself awake and sat up, reaching out to touch her shoulder, but Susan rolled over and faced the wall. She was crying now. "What happened?" I asked. I was tired, maybe still a little drunk, but she had my attention. Squinting at the curves of her bare white shoulders against the soft amber light of the city, I thought of Hank and Mary, who were barely children anymore. I thought of the gallery and all the precious objects I had collected. "Susan." I traced my finger down her spine, trying to prepare for one of those dreaded midnight moments, because bad things do happen, though you spend most of your life trying to convince your children that everything will be all right.

"Why do you touch me like a cactus?" My wife rolled over again and looked at me, tears gleaming on her cheeks.

I pulled my hand back and sat up against the headboard. "I just want to know what's wrong. Did something bad happen, Susan?" I tried to act gentle, as if I were speaking to a child.

"Yes, in my head," she said. "I was just lying there alone and everything fell apart. I have no one to talk to. I'm going to miss Hank. Then she'll go."

I turned on the light and squinted at her. "What exactly is the problem?"

Her eyes were red and sad, and she looked at me like she expected something. "My mother didn't even know she was pregnant with me until my father saw a bulge in her stomach while she was running through a sprinkler." Susan paused. "Isn't that horrible? It never even occurred to her. It was a big joke between them, the fact that she didn't know. Did you realize that about me?"

"God, Susan," I said, kicking the covers off my legs. "Is that it?" I felt angry and manipulated, but I laughed it off. I had heard this sort of thing before.

"You don't take me seriously," she said. "You don't even try to act concerned. You think I'm a nag because I want you to deal with things. Like that box."

"Enough about the box," I said, getting out of bed. "You can't just bulldoze in here in the middle of the night and expect me to absorb your mood." I walked out of the room and closed the door behind me. In the living room, I leaned my elbows on the mantelpiece and tried to rub the grit out of my eyes. It would have been easy to go back to bed, to listen to Susan, to reassure her that I loved her, to go through all the motions that seemed to work for other people. Years ago at the altar, we had been asked by those in charge of the ceremony to accept each other in spite of our weaknesses, to love each other in sickness and in health, and at the time it had seemed normal to promise these things. I had had no sense of myself. She was somewhere to go.

LATER I STOOD OUTSIDE THE BEDROOM DOOR, KNOWING IT WAS AS SIMPLE AS turning the knob. I could hear her crying, yet something inside me refused to budge. I felt like I was twelve years old again, and our housekeeper had caught me shooting squirrels out of trees with a BB gun. A few years later, at Moira's funeral, I had just sat there picturing the way that woman had looked at me—like I was responsible for all the grief and suffering of the world.

Down the hall I detected the dull hum of Mary's stereo, which upset me. She should have been asleep. I got the uneasy feeling she'd been listening to my argument with Susan through the wall. I went into the living room and stayed up all night, rehanging the paintings in my pajamas, trying to remind myself that my marriage hadn't always been this way.

The August we moved to Port Saugus, my wife had slept naked with all the windows open. One hot night she had awakened suddenly and stood up, skin white in the moonlight. I watched her at the window, concern edging across her face. Somehow Bucky and Binx, our new beagles, had dug a hole in the dirt underneath the wire of their pen, and she had caught sight of their little puppy bodies staggering across the moonlit yard. Before I could move, Susan had run outside. Still naked, she chased the dogs all the way across the lawn to the edge of the neighbor's place, her rear end rippling as she ran, her long hair flying like a hippie's. The neighbor's lights had snapped on, illuminating her beautiful body, as she dove to the ground on her hands and knees, grabbing for one tiny leg. She rescued both of them then, parading proudly back across the lawn with a spotted body cradled underneath each ample breast. That night I had stood at the window laughing, half amazed at my wife's intuition, her determination, her shamelessness. But all these years later, stomping around in the middle of the night, rehanging Captain Yardley's yellowed watercolors, I just wanted to erase her from my mind. I treasured the late night quiet, the sense of the rest of New York sleeping. I thought of Binx and Bucky beneath an oak tree, their bodies turned to tiny skeletons in the soil, and of my parents, buried for over thirty years now. I could barely even remember where.

WHEN I TOOK HANK TO COLLEGE THREE DAYS LATER, I PROMISED MY WIFE I'd stop at the bank near Port Saugus and pay the absurd amount of money to get whatever was inside that ridiculous safe-deposit box. I'd tried to convince her that I wouldn't find anything, but it wasn't good enough. She was relentless and I wanted to end the dispute. Pressing a brass key into my palm, she closed my fist around it, saying, "It was on your old key ring in the file drawer. I can't imagine what else it's for."

"Well, we'll give it a try," I said.

"Thank you," she said, her fingers tracing my knuckles. "I know it isn't easy."

Leaning forward, I kissed her on the mouth, although I was angry. "I know it isn't easy" may be my least favorite phrase. But she looked so sad, and in a way I understood. At one point we had had our dreams, and now it all seemed so different, as if all the good parts were over.

After the doorman had helped us pack up the car, and Susan and Mary stood waving at the curb, I realized I'd completely forgotten the key. "Wave to your mother," I said to Hank quickly, as if that would change things. I suppose I could have gone back upstairs for the key, but I convinced myself that the bank would open the box for me and find nothing to plague us or auction off. Anyway, I was helping out, performing my fatherly duty, taking care of Hank's move in the hopes of making Susan's life a little easier. On the highway I let Hank listen to any radio station he wanted, and when he drove too fast I just ignored it. I didn't really care for the music, but it hid the fact that we had so little to say.

At a bar in the middle of New York State, halfway between home and the college, I bought my son a beer, and we ate peanuts, throwing the shells on the floor. Hank asked, "Are you and Mom happy?"

I looked into my drink, trying to hide my discomfort. "Well, yes," I said. "We're very content. Why do you ask?"

"Because you don't *seem* that happy."

"You know, Hank, your mother can be difficult, but that doesn't make her any less appealing."

He looked at me as if I weren't quite right and muttered, "Mom's not *that* difficult."

At school, I carried his lamps, skis, and books through the cinderblock halls and up four flights of stairs. I tried to help him arrange the room. But he had his own ideas and seemed ready for me to get going. Before heading out, I gave him a present I'd been saving, rolled up in some old clothes in the trunk. It was a Zulu ceremonial club, a symbol of manhood, but when he just looked at it, uncertain, I slipped him a fifty, hoping to end the awkwardness. Then the bottom dropped out of a box I'd forgotten to reinforce, a container full of things his mother thought he needed: a tissue dispenser, ceramic bookends he'd made in fourth grade, and a picture of Hank and Mary each holding a struggling beagle, standing together under the oak tree in Port Saugus. The glass over the photograph had shattered but I carefully removed the photo, putting it in my breast pocket and promising to find another frame, a better frame, maybe even get it engraved. When Hank shrugged, I caught a glimpse of what Susan saw in me and suddenly felt ashamed.

I got home late, after Susan had gone to bed, and left early before she rose, jotting down a quick note and leaving it on the kitchen table for her to find. *Nothing in the box,* it said. I had never lied to Susan so blatantly before, but I told myself there was no harm done. It would be easier for everyone. I stole out of the apartment as the dawn light was easing through the windows and made certain the door latch caught softly, telling myself I was being considerate as I always tried to be.

AT THE GALLERY, FRANCESCA SPILLED HER COFFEE AND LET OUT A STRING OF Italian curses as the postal worker tossed down a new stack of bills. Every time the telephone rang I was relieved to find it wasn't Susan. But of course I knew she was waiting and I had no idea what to say.

That night, as I walked down Fifth Avenue, the sky began to clear. It felt like an omen. The evening sun cut through the leaves, casting an emerald halo over the sidewalk. As the soft lights went on in the windows around me, and happy strangers in safe marriages drifted through their lives, I found myself thinking about the times when Susan and I had still slept beside each other, wondering if it wasn't possible after all to try again.

• • •

A YEAR AGO, AFTER OUR LAST FAMILY TRIP TO PORT SAUGUS AND BEFORE I started sleeping in the spare bedroom, I took to hiding myself there in the evenings. The room became a sort of sanctuary; no one ever knocked or tried to interrupt. Usually, I just sat there reading, occasionally glancing over at the windows across the street. My neighbors and their quiet comings and goings, their seemingly comforting routines, had always soothed me in a strange way.

One night as I sat watching, the boy's room just across the way lit up and a woman stepped in front of a poster of a big green crayon, holding her son in her arms. He had his head on her shoulder, his small foot dangling just below her hip. Perhaps he'd fallen asleep on the couch or put his head down on a restaurant table. Perhaps his parents had just let him keep on dreaming. I hadn't been able to look away, though the mother's face remained a mystery, clouded by rain.

I could have sworn a moment of understanding passed between us, though I suppose she couldn't see me sitting in the darkness. It was in the way she'd cradled her elbows in her hands after she put down the child, then moved her palms up and down her arms, rubbing off the chill I, too, was experiencing before reaching up suddenly and pulling the drapes closed.

"So this is what you do in here?"

I turned around to find Susan standing behind me, her back against the door frame, white as a ghost in her nightgown.

"It's not what you think."

"How do you know what I think? You never ask."

"I was watching the storm." I could have explained it better, how something about the sleeping boy had made me want to go back to the moment when our own children were little and trusting, before they'd started to call everything into question. But that sort of effort always came out sounding convoluted. It exhausted me; Susan wanted everything explained. It was like she wanted to get inside me and poke around.

"I thought you were probably wishing you had a different life," she said bitterly. Then she closed the door behind her, bolting an invisible latch, sealing us into our separate lives. I didn't go back to our bed after that, and she didn't ask me to.

We never talked about the change in sleeping arrangements, and when the children asked, Susan blamed it on concrete things: my snoring, the way I kept her awake by rubbing my feet together like a grasshopper. Over time, we began to believe in these invented explanations ourselves.

"HOW ABOUT A KISS, SUSAN," I SAID, WHEN I GOT BACK HOME.

She stood in the hall with her arms folded under her breasts as if she'd been waiting for me, wearing those pig slippers the children had given her for Christmas one year, with the beady little eyes and ears. She'd put them on immediately and we'd all laughed so hard our sides split. "So the key fit?" she said.

I nodded, warily.

"And the box was empty?"

"That's what I told you," I said.

"Are you sure, because if you're not you should say so now."

I stared at my feet.

"You didn't even go," said my wife, opening her fist and showing me the key. "You couldn't even do that much."

"I forgot," I said.

"Bullshit, Lowell! You had every intention of forgetting. And then you *lied*."

"Oh, come on, Susan. Will you lighten up? It's a box." I went into the spare room, put my briefcase on the bed, and splashed some water on my face. Then I went into the living room to make myself a drink. A stiff one, with lots of bourbon.

"Oh, wonderful. Does that make it easier?" my wife said. She leaned back into the couch and propped her slippers on the ottoman so that the pig eyes were staring straight at me. "You're so predictable."

"Susan." I laughed. "I'm not paying three thousand dollars for a safe-deposit box full of jack shit."

"Lowe, I think you know what's in that box. Admit it."

"I already told you I don't know."

"You don't know anything. You forget everything. You forget where your feet are. I always have to pick up the pieces, and you can't even remember I'm alive!"

"I don't have to listen to this," I said, although I sat right down in my chair anyway.

Susan took out a crumpled pack of cigarettes from her bathrobe pocket and lit one.

"When did you start doing that again?" I said.

"Today," she answered. "I was so depressed about your lie, I went to Dr. Davis. He told me to do something good for myself, something I enjoy, and I've always enjoyed this, really. He told me to be honest. And honestly, my smoking years were the happiest of my life."

"I'd rather you didn't smoke in the apartment." I would have rather she not smoke at all. Smoking would kill her. I pictured myself at her bedside, sucking fluid from her lungs with some strange sort of mechanical bellows, the children creeping around in the shadows, shutting doors more softly than children should have to. Except they were grown.

"There are several things I'd rather *you* didn't do," my wife said icily. She sucked in deeply on her cigarette and let out a slow stream of smoke.

"Where's Mary?" I asked.

"At Jack's," my wife answered.

"A boyfriend?"

"A friend who's a boy." She looked at me sadly and shook her head. "You don't know anything about us, do you? You never really bothered."

Maybe I didn't want to know. I'd been thinking a lot about Francesca lately, about how she never criticized. She accepted me for my eccentricities, even found them amusing.

"You know," I said, "I've been telling Francesca not to open my mail for years. She listens to me because she trusts and respects me."

"Is that what you want? Someone who listens to everything you say?" my wife asked, staring at me with her eyes narrowed, her elbow resting on her knee, the smoke from her cigarette curling up around her head. "Because you don't really say *anything*. You just go on repeating the same things over and over, like I'm someone you see once a year at a cocktail party."

"Nobody respects me," I said. "That's what I want."

"Do you respect *me*?" My wife waited for an answer.

"Just take off those slippers, OK?" This was all I could manage.

"I have tried so hard to draw you out, to make you happy. It's always been about you, as they say," she went on, violently stubbing out her cigarette.

The bourbon rose up, stinging the inside of my throat, making me wince. "Now what the hell do you mean by that?" I said.

My wife went quiet, the angry red in her cheeks draining to a shade so pale she suddenly became a girl again, standing in that snowy garden. I couldn't bear to remember her that way, so long ago.

"I wanted to take care of you because you were so alone and I was alone too. I never thought about what *I* needed. Now I'm asking for something back."

"What makes you think I was alone?" I said.

She looked down at her hands and bit her lip, which meant she thought she knew me better than I could know myself.

"What exactly do you need?"

"I've told you so many times it's not worth repeating." She got up from the couch and started toward the foyer. I knew she was going to bed.

At the doorway she stopped, turned around, and stood there looking at me as a last orange beam of sunlight cut across the room. "I've always been good for you," she said. "In spite of what you believe, I want what's best. We have to go forward now. We have to."

I heard her slippers padding away, and then the creak of her bedroom door.

Upstairs, I could hear Butterfield, the Dempseys' lapdog, skitting back and forth across the floor. I went to the picture window and looked out over Central Park, at the leaves in the gathering dusk, picturing them turning yellow and wondering if we would be here in this same place when it happened again next year. I tried to imagine myself anywhere else but packed into this box of an apartment. Even in the near darkness, I could see straight down through the leaves into the park, to the zoo where I knew the polar bears would be swimming slow laps in their murky green pool as the city churned around them.

I stayed up late, thinking about my son, wondering how much better he was faring without us. Sometimes, it seemed, leaving home was what saved a person. Home could be so complicated. I ate cold chicken out of the icebox without using a plate, ripping the meat off the bone with my teeth. I pored over *Das Wrack,* borrowed from the Institute of Fine Arts library, staining the jacket with greasy fingers and wondering if I'd have to pay a fine. Did they still do that? Gradually I drank too much, and Susan did not reappear.

Hours later, as I came out of the bathroom, I noticed my daughter leaning against the living room door frame with the cat in her arms. For a moment I didn't recognize her. I didn't recognize anything. I was stunned. "You startled me," I said, grasping the edge of the bathroom door and hiding my drink on the sink behind me. It had always been this way between us. She was often troubled, but whenever I tried to get her to speak up about what the problem was, she'd slam the door or tell me nothing was wrong.

"What are you doing, Dad?" Mary hissed, in a whisper that was more judgmental than conspiratorial. Standing there against the backdrop of the dark hall, she looked like a Velázquez, her hair coming loose from her braid and Tom Osborne's orange tail twitching beneath her chin. I had no idea how long she'd been standing there.

"Waiting up," I said, closing the bathroom door behind me. "You're supposed to be home already."

"Were you drinking in there?" my daughter said, setting Tom down on the floor. She narrowed her eyes and twisted the tip of her braid around her finger.

"No," I said. "Don't turn this around. Listen, sixteen is too young to be out past midnight with a boy."

My daughter stared at me. "What do you think I've been doing?"

"I have no idea." I shrugged my shoulders. "Honestly, I have no idea what anyone's doing around here. You women are pretty goddamned self-absorbed and secretive."

"What are you saying?"

I watched the cat twirl its tail around her leg.

"Just don't grow up too fast."

"I can't wait to grow up," she said. "I can't wait to get out of here!"

"Tell me why," I said, trying to grab her arm. But she pulled away. "I want to know why."

"You're drunk," she said, as she melted back down the dark hall with Tom Osborne at her heels. "It's so embarrassing." In spite of my anger, I wanted to follow her, to sit down on the edge of the twin bed and reach out for the hand I had helped create, but then what would I say exactly, *Don't leave us alone*?

In the spare bedroom, I sat down in the chair and closed my eyes, straining to hear a sound from my wife's room. I tried to imagine what she was dreaming as clearly as I'd once been able to in Port Saugus, when we'd lingered in bed together in the mornings before the children woke up and she described every vivid image and physical sensation that had gone through her head the night before. *She'd been walking over the river and she'd felt the coldness on the soles of her feet. The whole world was buried in snow. The oceans were frozen. Her mother had driven her car across the Bering Strait.* Her stories always chased away the fragments of memories that came to me in the night. Back then, I had never dreamed about the minister or my parents.

Putting my hands together in front of my forehead, I made a sort of steeple out of my fingers, and leaned my elbows on my knees. Something wet slipped down the edge of my thumb, and when I drew my hands away from my face I realized I'd been crying.

I TRIED TO LEAVE EARLY BEFORE SUSAN GOT UP. THEN I PUT THE SAFE-DEPOSIT box key in my pocket. Maybe I'd use it. Maybe I'd throw it in the river. I guess I didn't quite know what was going to happen. But Susan found me in the foyer as I unlocked the door. She stood in her nightgown, its white hem brushing the Oriental rug. She seemed so young and innocent, standing there without the faintest idea what I was up to. "Where are you going?" she said, without the least bit of suspicion. She rubbed her eyes in the gray light.

I thrust the suitcase into the hall, and answered, "I'm claiming the safe-deposit box, like you wanted."

"Well, part of being married, Lowe, is doing what the other person wants," she said, covering her mouth to hide a yawn. "Life is a give-and-take."

CHAPTER FIVE

1957

I headed out between rows of corn going brown from no rain. I ran down the paths, my knees lifting out between the silk, the sweat sliding down my back. The drier husks stinged and tore my arms, but I ran fast as I could, sheltered in the stalks.

I made for the cool shadows of the cottonwoods on the edge of the field, gnarled and gray in the sun. The leaves danced like yellow pennies in hot little fingers. I could hear Mother screaming on the porch and Betty Sue starting to cry. I went toward the trees like I knew I'd be offered something. It was like I already knew the tree house would be there. It was a shadow in the back of my mind maybe, a hand reaching out.

There were boards in the tallest tree laid to make a floor and a splintered roof above it. The sun shined down through the cracks, winking at me to come on up. I was not surprised by the broken ladder: one board nailed above another, climbing up the trunk. I placed my feet on the rungs like I knew they would hold me and did not fear to fall, though the wood twisted where my toes dug and tore at the bark. The sketchbook tucked under my arm made the climbing hard, and my robe fell open a bit. But the tree was not so very high. The boards wiggled and creaked with my weight when I thrust myself up into its arms and then down on the floor, where I hung my legs over. I rested my feet on a branch and breathed hard. I peered down at my toes and the leaf shadows over them. They felt some part different from myself. My feet were dusty and bleeding where the corn had stripped them. Way off I could see Nig by his tree, a little black speck, beating his tail in the dirt and rattling his chain. The screen door slammed. Roe's car started up and my heart lifted in my dry throat. Everything went tight, even though I knew he had gave up. Everybody gives up when it comes to me.

I was lying back on the boards, my hands behind my head, staring at a blade of blue through the gaps in the roof. I had been sketching things in my book from my mind all morning long: Nig's pointed little face with the one ear down where the stiff part had broke and I had tried to tape it; a clump of blue flowers; my own hand thin against the wood, with a thread of blood around the thumbnail.

When a stick broke on the ground, I sat up straight. My heart jumped up. I tucked my legs under my robe and tried to make myself small against the trunk of the tree. I listened close. I imagined Roe coming back from work early with his belt in his hand, or Mother having called the truant officers on me and them hunting me down all over the neighborhood. She would feel sorry for it later when everybody knew how misbehaved I was. She would blame it on herself for marrying Roe and giving her heart away so cheap. I held my breath. I had a gentle sense of something coming. I wasn't scared. Around me, nothing breathed.

After a spell of waiting, I could not help myself or keep still another moment. I peeked over the edge of the floor, so quiet with trying not to make a sound. My legs were flat out behind me. My knuckles gripped at the edge of the floor.

That's when I saw Charlie below me, the leaves making quarter shadows over the red of his hair. My visitor was slinking through the shadows beneath the cottonwoods, thinking himself alone. I saw him first, through the branches, but he did not see me. I had no idea how long he had been there, weaving around the trunks of our trees with the .22 cocked, listening to the sounds in the brush. He had been so quiet. My heart caught in my throat.

The bright sun glinted off the gun's metal barrel that was pointed toward the brush where pheasants nested and ate on the corn. The light shined off everything and filled it with a hardness. Charlie was small and wiry as a cow dog with his ears sticking out his head. From where I lay flat on the floor, I thought him to be young and not fully grown, just a boy, standing at the base of the tree, hunting, playing a man. I was not afraid. I could never imagine in that moment that he would change my life.

It filled me with a secret thrill for the boy not knowing himself to be watched. It gave me a power. I imagined all the animals watching the hunter, and how silly he must seem, to rattle around with a gun, while they buried themselves safe in the beady-eyed blackness, still as stone. But when he heard me take a breath, Charlie swung that gun around so fast and pointed it up in my face, lining his eye down the barrel. I did not hide behind the boards or press my body against the trunk. I stared right back at his turned-up face through the leaves, not breathing, not moving a muscle. His face was sharp. His gaze was so far off. All of a sudden, it seemed like the joke was on me. So I tried and showed how I was nothing but a girl, not doing a thing wrong but sitting in the tree. I tried a smile. But he didn't look back at me with any expression of niceness. He stood below, the barrel turned up. He did not take the gun off me. He kept it there.

Suddenly, it did not matter. I did not care what happened to my life. It hit me with a flash how none of it mattered. I didn't care if everything ended right there with some crazy boy shooting me out of a cottonwood tree in my own backyard. Everyone would feel sorry for it, sorry for chasing me away and making me repeat the eighth grade.

I sat straight up then and shoved my legs over the boards. I balled up my fist and jammed it in front my face. I shook it at him.

He did not make to fire. I gathered the kimono around my thighs and stared right down at him. "Go on," I said. "Shoot me, you want to so badly—you ape-shit nuthouse. I don't care." I lifted up the silk and showed him my panties.

Charlie took his face away from the barrel then. His cheeks went red as if I had slapped him. He lowered the gun and shook his head. He stood there looking up. He speculated me like a person, like he couldn't believe it. I felt ashamed in that instant, for what I was wearing.

"Quit acting like a whore," he said finally.

I covered myself, feeling silly then, to be left in a situation such as this. I cinched myself back on the floor so he could not see my body, so he could not see what sort of a girl I was.

It was quiet. I didn't know what to say.

"What do you mean, pointing that thing at me?" I called at him. I did not look down. I tried to sound sure, like I had never done a stupid thing like show him my underwear, and how it was old and worn.

Charlie didn't say a word. I couldn't tell if he had left. It filled me with some kind of panic.

I peeked over the edge. I couldn't help to look. He was standing there, staring up. I tried to make my face seem mean. "You're trespassing," I said.

"You're the one trespassing." Charlie's voice was hard, though his face did not look mad. "It's my tree house. I built it." He nodded his head like he could tell I was surprised, like he could tell I was ashamed having showed him all I did. His face was all of a sudden kind. The gun rested down by his side. I could not say a word. I just sat there, my mouth hanging open. I was lonely, maybe, from being in the tree.

"Well, you should have did a better job," I said. "Everything's crooked and falling down up here." I stood. The boards wiggled under my feet. I crossed my arms over my chest, but I could not help to smile. Charlie's eyes were deep green. They seemed to twinkle at me with little secrets. His face was half in the shadows.

He looked up at me, standing in my kimono. "What are you"—he laughed—"some kind of crazy-assed Jap?"

I could not help laughing too. I laughed so hard I cried. It came in a deep relief to my tired heart. I could not offer Charlie a word but my laughing. I didn't need to. In those moments we both understood it: how the whole world had gone and drug us together. The sun shined brighter for it. The roof of my house was washed in gold. The sky seemed bluer than you could ever imagine.

CHAPTER SIX

1962

We lived on the south side of Lincoln, where tall shady trees lined the streets and the houses were old and grand, keeping secrets behind smooth flawless drapes. The cars in driveways were always shiny. Women in aprons swept the front steps, and when the sun set you could smell dinner cooking. Lucille kept my grandfather's house looking like everyone else's, pristine and sparkling, but she wasn't fooling anyone. My mother was brusque and fidgety. My father often went to parties alone and was the first to leave. He didn't want to be away from her for too long. But she seemed not to care whether or not he was there. She settled down behind thousand-page novels, disappearing to places where her life became less real and my father and I were the illusion.

At school, the walls were bright and the flat sun fell in through the big windows. Girls who had friends giggled and linked arms, but the ghost of Starkweather haunted us. When he was fourteen like me, he had been a student at Irving. He had changed that place. Sometimes I would get the strange feeling that I was sitting at a desk where he had once sat, waiting for someone to take me by the hand and pull me into some different place where everything mattered a little more. Because of Starkweather, teachers treated us carefully. They were more attentive to our needs, looking for warning signs and quick to sound the alarm when someone displayed evidence of a violent temper. Everyone stepped softly except for Miss Winter, our physical education teacher. In her calisthenics class it was survival of the fittest, and I was anything but that.

She would stand over us with a whistle and force us to do sit-ups with partners, while the boys climbed ropes and hurled balls at each other's chests on the other side of the gymnasium curtain. I always got stuck with Cora Lessing. When I held down her feet, she'd groan and haul herself toward me like some sort of beached sea creature, her red hair spraying over the mat in every direction. Her eyes were a dim, desperate blue, like the washed-up bottle glass I used to find on the shores of Lake Michigan. I tried to avoid her. I didn't want anyone to think we were friends. In Lincoln, I was an outsider from Chicago, an oddball whose mother had quickly developed a reputation for behavior unbecoming a lady. Or so I imagined. I tried not to care that no one spoke to me—anywhere, really. When Cora and I got paired up, I'd put on a sour expression, hoping it would show I was destined for better things.

The other girls were long-limbed, brassy, big-toothed Nebraskans who, at the age of fourteen, could have easily passed for high school seniors. My mother, who had a name for everything, called their kind of Lincoln women "cobs," because of their flaxen hair and those straight teeth that seemed specially designed to row a cob of corn. "Cobs," she'd complain to my father after one of the rare times she went to a party at the country club. "Nothing but cobs. Did you see how they stared at me? Ha."

"They just thought you were beautiful," my father would say.

But he was wrong. Everyone knew we weren't quite normal, and I was tired of it.

One day when we were supposed to play volleyball, I was early for gym. I always tried to change into my shorts before the other girls came down. I didn't want to be naked in front of them. I knew what wasn't right about the way I looked.

I thought I was alone in the locker room, but then a toilet flushed and Cora Lessing came out of a stall, wiping her hands on her shorts as if she thought that was sufficient. Digging around in my locker, I pretended to look for my other tennis shoe. When she sat down on the bench, I could feel her watching me. "I guess we'll be the last ones picked for teams again," she said finally. Her misery suddenly invigorated me. I wanted to slap her.

Instead, I turned around and stared, but she just sat there with her hands on her pink knees, looking up at me with big liquid eyes, and it seemed to me that everything depended on separating myself from her weaknesses. My heart was skipping. "No, Cora, *you'll* be the last one picked," I said, slamming my locker door and leaving her alone, sitting on the bench.

AT DINNER THAT NIGHT, THERE WERE FRESH PEONIES ON THE TABLE, MY mother's favorite. Lucille had been filling the house with flowers all week and Mother had been taking them out of the water and putting them in her hair. It made me sad to think of the flowers wasted in my mother's hair, their petals dropping as she trailed up and down the stairs like Miss Hawaii.

My father carefully poured my mother more wine while she picked at her food. "We need to discuss something," he said to her suddenly, and I brightened, sensing the possibility of something more dramatic than usual. Maybe we were going to discuss me, my troubles, the problem I was on my way to becoming. My mother put down her fork and lifted a blossom out of the vase. She looked at me, but I didn't look back. I knew what was coming. She was going to offer the latest version of her madwoman act so that everyone would think only about her.

"Olie called me at the office," my father said, looking so innocent I wanted to cry. "He says the elms in front need to come down before it gets too cold." I felt like throwing something, breaking out of this boredom.

"Why?" my mother said.

"Because they have the Dutch elm, Ann."

"They don't *look* sick," she said, shooting him a wounded look that I didn't find convincing.

"He told you months ago."

"I don't remember." My mother crossed her arms and put them on the table. Of course she was lying. She was always lying, always denying things. My uncle had told me she sometimes had troubles with the truth, and I believed everything he said about her. He had been the one to tell me about her first marriage. "You know, we all hide things. Mother's not perfect," he had said once. Then he frowned as if it was the idea of her imperfection that disturbed him particularly. Apparently, when she was twenty, she'd run off with a man named Nils who gambled away all the money she had inherited. The marriage lasted two months. My uncle tracked her down in a hotel outside Erie, Pennsylvania, to find her sitting backward on the bed in her slip, staring straight in front of her, studying the headboard as if it were a map of the world. When he told me the story, I knew exactly the look he was describing. She looked that way when something took place that wasn't in the script, the only times you could believe she wasn't acting.

"Olie said you and he went out to the driveway last May and took a look at the leaves," my father said. "He showed you where they were turning brown."

"*I* didn't see any brown," my mother said. "Besides, it's autumn, and everything's brown."

"Do they *have* to come down?" I asked.

"No, Puggy, probably not. He just wants to control everything," she said. "Your father always wants to look like he's in control."

For months, elms had been coming down all over Lincoln. The buzz of chain saws had filled the summer, and all the buildings looked lost, as if suffering from amnesia. My father sighed. "It's not as if I *want* them cut down," he explained.

"If anyone tries, I'll chain myself to the roots. I'll scream like a banshee," my mother said.

"Well, we wouldn't want *that.*"

My mother raised one eyebrow. "What *would* you want?"

"For you to let them do it," my father said, digging into his pot roast.

"No, Thatcher, I mean really. What do you really want? What do you *desire*?" My mother's dark eyes bore into his blue ones.

"Sometimes I feel like you don't have any idea. Sometimes I feel like that's what's wrong with this whole place. Everyone tries to look happy, but they've been doing what they're supposed to for so long, they can't remember what they really wanted."

I thought she was trying to make him forget about the trees, but believed he would go along with her game in an effort to make *her* forget. That way each could think the other had won. But then things turned into less of a game.

My father folded his napkin and tucked it beside his plate. "I'll tell you what, Ann. I want to make you happy. I've been trying pretty damn hard for quite some time."

For a moment my mother looked stunned. "Really," she said finally, and then she sort of laughed. "We could have an intellectual discussion. You could read *Lady Chatterley's Lover.*" I couldn't remember my father ever having read anything besides the paper. "It's about a bored woman who commits an indiscretion with the gamekeeper because he's more real and simple in what he desires than her proper husband—who doesn't *have* any desires."

My father looked lost.

"I know what *I* want," I said, to remind them I was sitting right there.

"What's that, Puggy?" my father said.

"More potatoes."

"Now that's something I can understand," my father said. He reached for my plate, but my mother put her hand on his arm.

"There won't be any leftovers for Lucille," she said. "Besides, you don't need any more food, Puggy. I know how many brownies you had before dinner. Lucille shouldn't indulge you. You eat so many sweets and then you brush the sink instead of your teeth. I'm amazed you haven't lost your capacity to chew."

Unthinkable words danced a little jig on my tongue, but I kept them inside. Sometimes I wanted to do the craziest things—like stand up and scream or strip off my clothes and run out into the street and French-kiss the first person I could find.

"That's enough," my father said, but I was already on my way, pumping my legs up the stairs. I could hear them downstairs, bickering. Before long, they'd be laughing like everything was just fine. I imagined my parents chasing each other around the dining room table like planets orbiting the sun, drawn to each other by some inexplicable force. I brushed my teeth three times and took out the article about the Starkweather killings I'd kept secreted away for so long. I turned the worn pages and studied the protective way Charlie had his arm around Caril Ann. Their bodies leaned in toward each other. They were all smiles. No hint of how true love was going to make them crazy.

THE NEXT DAY I PRETENDED TO BE SICK, WHICH WAS USUALLY EASY. I WENT TO the downstairs toilet and spat out water. My father would tell me to go back to bed, and my mother would say something like, "Why don't we all stay in bed? Nothing would be any different."

But this time Lucille came into the bathroom, put her hand on my shoulder, and turned me around. "You don't smell like sick."

"I *am* sick." I looked down at my feet.

Lucille shook her head. "I don't think so."

"I *can't* go to school."

"Susan, you can't check out 'cause you hate it."

"This once?" I pleaded. "Don't tell Daddy."

When Lucille's brown eyes turned sad, I knew she wouldn't tell him.

I WAS IN MY ROOM LISTENING TO A SAM COOKE SONG AND EATING A Charleston Chew that Lucille had left for me when I heard sounds. I reached over and turned down the radio. My mother was screeching as if someone were tearing out her fingernails. Getting out of bed, I crept down the hall toward my parents' open door. Clothes were flung over the light pink carpet, stockings draped the vanity table. My mother was pulling out everything from the dressing room and the bureau drawers.

Lucille stood by the window with her arms crossed over her starched apron, shaking her head. Outside, the oak tree shivered, tickling red leaves against the pane. My mother put her palm down on the vanity table. I could see her face, the black waves of hair shielding her sharp features as if she had planned it to fall that way. "I can't believe this!" my mother sobbed.

"I'm sorry, Mrs. Hurst," Lucille said, but she stayed where she was by the window.

"What happened?" I said.

"You ask her!" My mother pointed at Lucille. "She's moving to Detroit! She's leaving me!" I kept quiet. Seizing the opportunity to put herself at the center of everything, my mother flopped down on the bed with her feet hanging off and covered her face with a pillow the way she had the Christmas before, when she complained that my father hadn't gotten her anything personal.

"Why are you leaving?" I said to Lucille, stepping farther into the room. My mother was silent behind her pillow.

"I'm going back where I'm from," Lucille said. "My daughter lives there. She just had a baby."

My mother removed the pillow from her face and stared vacantly at the ceiling. "You're from here, Lucille," she said. "Don't try to pretend you're from anywhere else. If you stay in any one place long enough, it becomes where you're from, and there isn't anything you can do about it. I'm almost starting to be from here no matter how much I hate it. Who would have thought *Nebraska*? Who would have thought I'd be *dull*?"

A silk camisole slid off the top of the bureau and fluttered to the floor.

"I don't know about dull," said Lucille, shaking her head.

"Don't tell me how I am unless you're prepared to listen to how *you* are." My mother sat up and covered her mouth, as if keeping something inside she knew shouldn't be said. I wondered why she never felt the need to restrain herself when it came to me.

Lucille sighed, bent over, and started picking up clothes and folding them slowly against her apron. When her skin got dry, the brown knuckles turned chalky like the streaks in her hair. Her hands would catch on silk, the tablecloth, even my cotton nightgown when she rubbed my back, whispering all the little things she could remember about my grandfather. Lucille's words were like photographs. Sometimes I could feel him breathing or smell his cigarettes just behind the wall. I used to sit in the living room armchair where he had died of a heart attack and close my eyes, leaning my head against the side of the chair, trying to imagine what it felt like to die. "Crazy child," Lucille had said once, when she came in to dust. "You shouldn't go around practicing to be dead. They don't give prizes."

MY MOTHER SHIMMIED OFF THE BED AND STOOD UP. AN AUTUMN WIND BEAT the side of the house. "I thought we were friends," she said to Lucille.

"I thought so too," Lucille said.

"You've given up the right to think that."

"That's too bad." Lucille shook her head.

"Will you come back and visit?" I asked, but my mother didn't give Lucille a chance to answer.

"Of course she won't. Why would anyone ever come back here?"

I thought about all the children I had known when we lived in Chicago. At one time, I could never imagine *not* knowing them. Now I had no idea what those little girls looked like or who they had become. The world could change because of one person's decision to do something, but I had a feeling I would never be the one to decide anything.

Charles Starkweather had decided to kill Mr. and Mrs. Bowman four years ago because he said his girlfriend had wanted him to. Now people locked their doors and worried about their own children turning into monsters. Now the Bowmans' son had no parents. He still lived in the white house on South 24th Street where it had all happened, not far from where we lived now. Some of his relatives had moved in to help him.

Thinking about my own mother dying, the peonies, the consoling words people would offer, I wanted to kneel down beside her and put my head in her lap and tell her I loved her, even though I wasn't at all sure I did. But my mother stood up suddenly and turned to Lucille. "Look, I've made a mess. I don't mean to be so horrible. I'm sorry, I'm just heartbroken." She walked toward me, still looking at the floor. She passed me in the doorway. I brushed my fingers across my mother's arm, but she didn't feel it.

THE FOLLOWING WEEK LUCILLE LEFT AND MY MOTHER STAYED IN HER ROOM, not making a sound. Outside, men in green jackets cut down the elms, which were ancient and beautiful and gave the streets in our part of town a sense of belonging. Lined with stumps, the driveway looked shocked. Our house seemed lost, its yellow paint cracked like a tired old face. There were no sweets in the kitchen, and my bed was still unmade when I'd get back into it at night. I missed the Charleston Chews Lucille always left for me beneath the dust ruffle. Suddenly I didn't have any clean clothes. Sometimes I'd come home from school almost expecting to find Lucille mopping the kitchen floor or standing at the foot of the stairs with her hands on her hips, shaking her head because everything had gone to pot. She would have laughed about how lost we were, and suddenly everything wouldn't have seemed so hopeless.

One afternoon, I went into the living room to watch television and all the curtains were lying in large tan heaps on the rug like slaughtered animals. The house was silent. Flecks of dust sparkled in the dim afternoon sunlight. I could hear my breath. I didn't go up to my mother's room to ask what had happened. I watched myself in the tall gilt mirror, a figure moving far away out of the corner of someone's eye. I could pass through a room without changing a thing, not even the air. I waited for my father to get home from work. I sat at the foot of the stairs and just stayed there as the sun set and the house got dark.

"Look what she did," I said, as my father came through the door, but he just sighed. He made himself a drink without saying a word. Then he got out the ladder, and I handed up the heavy fabric, while he threaded the brass rings back along the rods.

I overheard my parents talking about it later. They were in the kitchen. I was doing homework at the dining room table, trying to remember the Pythagorean theorem. "What came over you?" my father wanted to know. She didn't like the drapes. They made her feel trapped. I was so tired of hearing about the way *she* felt. The bouquet on the side table had wilted and turned brown. I took my pencil between my thumb and forefinger and knocked over the vase with the pink nub of the eraser. There wasn't any water left. A rain of dried petals sprayed over the rug. Those petals seemed to sum up the change that had come over our lives. After Lucille left. Before the snow.

I WENT UP TO MY ROOM AND GOT OUT THAT OLD NEWSPAPER CLIPPING. I unfolded the article by the soft glow from the lamp with the pink shade I'd had for as long as I could remember and studied the victims' faces. I don't know what I was expecting to see—a high school pin, a piece of jewelry, some little detail that would say *This was me, the type of person I was.* But there wasn't anything about those photos I hadn't noticed before. Caril Ann still grinned and Starkweather looked proud. Those pictures weren't enough.

On my way home from school the next day, I didn't turn right on Van Dorn. I walked past our street and went up South 24th where the Bowmans and their maid had been murdered. I wanted to see what the house looked like after all this time. I was a detective, the only one who hadn't given up on the case. Stealing a glance over the fence at the spotless windows, that perfect white paint, those carefully clipped bushes on either side of the front door, I felt shut out, and I wanted so badly to crawl inside.

If I had been there at the time, in the thick of it all, I would have understood that pain. I wished I'd lived in Lincoln when Starkweather and his girlfriend were driving around killing everyone. I tried to imagine what that had been like, citizens forming vigilante posses, torches burning through the night. It would have been a time worth remembering my whole life long.

Red leaves drifted onto the sidewalk. I tried to see through the walls, to the awful heart of the mystery. I pictured Mr. and Mrs. Bowman lying dead with their arms around each other even though I knew their bodies hadn't been found that way. He had been just inside the door. She had been tied up somewhere. I had never even seen the Bowman boy, but I wanted to ask him how it felt to lose your parents and be lord of the manor like that all of a sudden, to sit in the stiff-backed chairs feeling so desperate and alone, listening for the ghosts. Maybe the Bowman boy got drunk and covered his ears every night to shut out the past, the way my mother tried to shut out other things. I told myself he was the sort of person I'd have something to say to, someone who needed caring for.

When I turned around to go, Cora Lessing stood glaring at me with one hand on the neighbor's gate. I had no idea how long she'd been there, watching me. I pretended I wasn't surprised to see her, like I was just on my way home from somewhere. The wind blew red hair across her wide pale face. She looked wild, almost, among the falling leaves. She had hated me since that day in school when I had hurt her. I could see it in the way she stood. I didn't really blame her. "I know what you're doing!" she said sourly.

"I'm not *doing* anything." I held my canvas bag to my chest.

"They don't like it when people stare. That's what you're doing."

"How do you know?" I said.

"I live next door." I turned to look. Cora's was a gray-shingled house with a wide front porch. It was ordinary in every way and yet special in being so near to a tragic place. Those windows must have seen such terrible things. I wondered how much Cora knew about the day when it had happened. It was my duty to find out. I was on a covert mission, under cover. I smiled.

Cora looked down at her feet. She opened the gate and closed it behind her and started up the path to her front door.

"Wait," I said. "I need to ask you something," though I couldn't think of any sort of question. It was too late. She kept walking and didn't look back. The wind picked up and blew my skirt against my knees, and I felt a strange sense of guilt for the way I had treated her. I hugged my arms around myself and started for home, and when I got to our block I walked softly, as if I could creep up on an unfolding secret.

My mother was standing by the window, just inside the front door, with her hands on her hips. She must have been watching me pick my way down the path. When I put my key in the lock, she pulled me inside quickly and slammed the door behind me, as if the cold air had bitten her. She was wearing her blue dress with the brass buttons, her white pumps, her fire-red lipstick.

"Where are you going?" I said.

"Nowhere." Outside, it was getting dark. All the lights in the house were off. My mother grabbed the wool sleeve of my peacoat and pulled me through the foyer into the living room, which was stuffy and silent. Heavy shadows draped the furniture. "How was school?" my mother asked.

"The same as always," I said.

"Your hair's a mess," she added, taking me by the shoulders and holding me away from her as if looking at me for the first time. "Do you always walk around like that? Want me to brush it for you?"

"No," I said. "It's all right."

"Why not?" She frowned and pushed my hair back behind my ear and looked me in the eyes.

I didn't answer her.

"Let's listen to records and redo the living room." My mother walked over to the phonograph. "Now that Lucille's gone we can do what we want with this old place. I've got lots of ideas."

"I like it how it is," I said.

My mother put on my Chubby Checker record, which meant she'd been digging around in my room.

When she turned around and put her hand on the back of my grandfather's chair, I noticed she wasn't wearing her wedding ring.

"Where did you get that record?" I asked her.

"I'm only trying to talk to you. You don't have to be so rude," she said, staring into my face. "I'm always making an effort and no one's ever returning it."

"Why aren't you wearing your ring?" I said.

My mother put her hands on her hips. "I'm changing my look. I'm doing the Twist." She came over to me where I stood by the bookcase and grabbed me by the arm. I pulled away from her. Later, I wished I'd gone along with her, my mother and I doing the Twist all over the living room. It would have been something to remember.

"Hey," she said. "Let's break all the old furniture by accident so your father will have to get all new furniture. It'll be our own things then." Her eyes were sparkling in the dim light.

I shook my head. "You'll make Daddy angry."

"Thank God!" my mother cried. "At least someone besides me would be angry in this house."

I thought of Starkweather's face sitting in my drawer, that proud smirk. "*I'm* angry," I said, but I'm not sure she heard me, because suddenly she sat down and put her hand over her heart and took a deep breath. "Oh," she said, and started to cry. I thought I could see the tears falling into her lap. "God," she sobbed, and looked up at me with her brow wrinkled and her beautiful gypsy eyes blurred with red. I didn't know what I was supposed to do.

"Do *you* know who I am?" she said. "Do you have any idea?"

"My mother?" But maybe it wasn't even true. Maybe that explained it.

"Sometimes I don't feel like one. I don't feel like anything."

I couldn't think of another thing to say, so I just stood there pulling a knot out of my hair.

"I'm so alone in this big house," she went on, opening and closing her fist. "No one gives me a chance. No one ever really does. It's true."

She was letting me know I was part of the problem. I couldn't help failing her. I imagined my uncle finding my mother alone in the Erie, Pennsylvania, hotel room on the bed in her slip. I imagined he had sat there staring at her back, too shocked to touch her or say anything because he couldn't tell whether she had become herself in that hotel room, alone, or the opposite of herself. My mother seemed to me then like someone who could drag the whole world down around her, someone like Starkweather. She could swallow everyone and everything.

On the other side of the garden, the sun came out from behind its blanket of clouds, shining through the branches of our one remaining elm. My pupils shrank in the light. All the dark color turned white.

"I have to go do something," I said, turning my back on her. I marched upstairs, closed my bedroom door, pressed my ear to the white wood, and listened. But there wasn't a sound anywhere in the house. Only the cars sliding past on Van Dorn, quick and soft as whispers.

BEFORE MY FATHER GOT HOME, MY MOTHER WENT UP TO HER BEDROOM AND made as if she'd never left it. I tried to fix my hair the way I thought my mother might like it, in a folded-over bun at the nape of my neck like Lucille used to do for me. The hairs were sticking out everywhere. I couldn't get it right. Later, after my father had come downstairs, I knocked on her door anyway. "Go to the country club and get a hamburger or something," she said from behind the door. "And leave me out of it. You can tell your father that!"

I found my father at his desk with his elbows on the stained blotter, still wearing his tie, twirling a pencil between his fingers, the lime in his untouched drink floating along the rim of the crystal glass. He hadn't changed a thing in the study since the death of my grandfather. Even the files in the drawers were the same; he had picked up right where his father left off. When I saw him at his desk like this, not doing anything, or out on the garden bench, bracing his feet against the elm tree as the dusk came on, I assumed he was thinking about my mother. He seemed more passionate about her than anything else in the world.

When I cleared my throat, my father looked up, startled. "These figures won't add up," he said, putting the pencil down and shaking his head.

"Mother says to go to the club without her. Just us. We can get hamburgers."

My father sat there looking puzzled for a moment. "She hates the living room couch," he said. "She wants to drag it into the garage and burn it. She called me out of a meeting today to say she was going to do it all by herself." He looked at me. "I hope *you* understand the value of a buck."

I nodded my head. I felt that my father was speaking to me as if I were an adult, looking to me for an answer. I moved up close to the desk and put my fingers on the smooth surface. I didn't speak for a moment. "She's not wearing her ring," I said.

My father sighed and loosened his tie. "Oh, she's just dancing her dance." But his face didn't tell me he believed that.

His face told me he thought we were in trouble, and maybe we really were. Maybe she wasn't just acting, trying for my father's attention. Maybe it was real. I pictured my mother holding a gun to her head as bitter tears poured down her face. They'd have a picture of her in the paper just like the murder victims. *Yes,* I would say when all the people asked, *we're hanging in there.* I took a breath. "She's gone wacko, Daddy."

"Watch your mouth," my father snapped, rapping his knuckles on the desk and staring at me like he couldn't believe what I had said. "I can't have you talking that way about your mother. She's upset about Lucille. You need to understand that. And your mother and I are a team."

Tears tickled my cheeks as I closed my eyes, trying to trap them beneath my lids.

My father didn't say anything more for a moment. I could hear his chair squeaking as he leaned back. The leather sighed. When I opened my eyes, he was looking at me with his forehead wrinkled and his arms folded over his chest. "Come here, Puggy," he said, patting his knee. I went over and sat down on his lap, my feet touching the floor. He put his arms around me and kissed the back of my head. I'll always remember the smell of his embrace: aftershave and, more faintly, the few sips of gin he'd taken of his after-work gimlet. "She's fed up with me," he said. "That's all."

WHEN WE CAME HOME FROM THE COUNTRY CLUB THAT NIGHT, EVERY ROOM IN the house was dark. We stepped into the shadowed foyer, flicked on the light, and wiped our feet on the mat. My mother was sitting halfway up the stairs in her bathrobe, waiting for us with her hands folded over her knees. I almost didn't see her.

My parents stared at each other in uncomfortable silence.

"What's this all about?" my father said. "Why are you sitting here in the dark, Ann? You locked me out."

"Don't be harsh, Thatcher," she snapped. She pressed her nose into a tissue clutched in her fist and snaked her other hand along the banister. Her fingertips traced the ridges in the cherry wood. "You don't love me, do you?" she said.

I waited for my father to tell her how I was the one who felt unloved. I waited for him to say that maybe she should think a little about her daughter. But he didn't.

"You're not wearing your ring," he said instead. I went to hang my coat in the closet.

"We need new furniture. I'm suffocating. Everything's even more dead without the trees. I need to be taken on a vacation. To a forest," she said. "You don't know how upset I am about those trees." Everything was about what *she* needed. It took so much work to love her.

My father looked down at his hands. "Next time Capital builds a bridge."

"What do you mean?"

Everything was silent for a moment, but there was money in the air.

"Are we *poor*?" I whispered, but nobody answered.

My mother narrowed her eyes at my father. "Did you let Lucille go, Thatcher? Tell me."

My father didn't say anything.

"Did you fire her?"

"No," he said. "Calm down." But he wouldn't look at her.

My mother started down the stairs, but she had been drinking. She tripped and came toward us suddenly, sliding on her back down the remaining steps. I wanted to yell. My brain tingled at the thought of broken bones, my mother's head smacking the banister.

She landed at the bottom of the stairs with her silk robe up around her hips, exposing her underwear. In the still moment before she covered herself, I could see her thighs threaded with spider veins, blue shadows beneath dry skin. She tugged the robe down.

My father went over to her and tried to help her up but she wouldn't let him.

My mother was crying. She got on her hands and knees and pulled herself up by the banister.

"You've had too much to drink," my father said, touching her on the shoulder.

"Leave me alone!" my mother sobbed.

"Ann."

"You fired her, Thatcher."

"I didn't *fire* anyone. Why do you insist on that?"

"My sense tells me so."

"We don't have any money. Did you sense that?"

"You fired her."

"I wouldn't *fire* her."

"I feel all wrong."

"About us?"

"I'm always alone. I thought things would be different," she sobbed. "This isn't the way I pictured it. Any of it."

I went into my father's study. I sat down at his desk and looked out the window at the jagged outline of the neighbors' trees. The sky was dark. I thought about the day my father pulled our Chevrolet crammed with suitcases into the driveway, and my mother didn't want to get out of the car. It was hot, mid-July, and the air hung thick. My grandfather's house was closed up and silent as if holding his death behind the shutters. The roses along the driveway had dropped petals onto the dusty gravel. Everything was scorched. My mother just sat there shaking her head as the car cooled down. "It's not like I remember," she said to my father. "It's even worse."

I HEARD MY FATHER'S HEAVY FOOTSTEPS ON THE STAIRS ABOVE THE STUDY. They paused on the landing and faded away, and then I couldn't hear a sound. When I went into the foyer, my mother had pulled a chair up beside the telephone table. Her back was to me. She held the white receiver up to her ear. The curled wire dangled over the floor. A small circle of light fell over her shoulders. "You're not listening," she whispered into the telephone.

CHAPTER SEVEN

1957

Me and Charlie started going together, and it seemed in the beginning like it never would end. He found me waiting in the tree like a present all wrapped up, and I didn't have so much as a choice to look the other way.

I was always thinking about the world, and all the flatness that lay between me and it, and the television tapped me hints through invisible wires, and everybody's pictures were always smiling in magazines. But that was the closest I could get to where I wanted to be. When I found Charlie, it was like he was the only thing I could see for miles around on that dry hot prairie.

When he climbed up in the tree house, Charlie didn't so much as look at me. He didn't say a word, not even his name. He just laid on his back stiff as a board, like something electric that wasn't plugged in, his eyes wide open. I got all jumpy wondering what it was he decided wasn't right. I thought he was disappointed on account of my panties maybe, and how I showed him they were no account. My sister Barbara had got all new ones when she married Rodney, and one day she spread them out on the bed for me to look at, saying panties like these were the secret to men's hearts.

"Sorry," I said to Charlie.

"How come?"

I tried to think of a reason, but there wasn't a thing I could come up with to make me sound smart. "I don't have anything to say. I'm not a talker," I said, even though *he* should have been the one trying to get things going.

Charlie cleared his throat and kept his eyes on the sky like he was waiting for something to fall. "Not-a-Talker, huh? That your Indian name?"

I sat up, then, and pointed my finger at the .22. "Then you're Shoots-Without-Looking." It just came out. He grinned then, on account of me being so funny like that, out of the blue. It was one of those lucky things you couldn't ever plan, like capturing the shadow of a cloud when your pencil hadn't meant to do anything except doodle around.

"I got a friend from Pine Ridge, and he wouldn't like you calling me that," Charlie said, but I could tell he was only teasing.

"Who's your friend?" I said.

"Jonny Magpie. We got an understanding." Charlie sounded tough the way he said it, like a cowboy or an outlaw, and it gave me a secret thrill, me being there in the tree beside him, hiding out, like some girl he stole from a town with no laws. He rolled over on his side and looked right at me, with his eyes half closed like he just woke up. Only later I knew it was for needing the glasses, not on account of my face being so bright.

I smiled real sweet and almost reached out and touched him. "What's your understanding?" I didn't even know his name yet.

"You're just a bitty girl," he said, and shaked his head. "I ain't even gonna bother trying."

"I'm not," I said, but a wind took my voice away and shivered the tree. My heart shivered right back with it. A cloud covered the light, and just like that it all washed over me again. I thought of Mother and Roe and how they didn't ever listen, and how no one at school thought I'd turn out right. There I was all over again, biting my lip, staring hard at the sky so as not to cry.

"What's wrong?" Charlie wanted to know. I could see the sun burning through the cloud, more like a moon than anything else. It gave me a strange feeling all of a sudden, like looking through the other side of a picture, where everything was put backward or upside-down.

"I'm not dumb," I said.

Charlie's eyes went soft. They could change like the sky. It was nothing I'd ever be able to draw. They changed too fast. "I know you ain't dumb." He held out his hand like he was making to touch my cheek, but then he tucked it back behind him. "I didn't mean anything," he said, and swallowed hard, kind of. "I don't want you to think bad of me."

"Why do you care what I think?"

Charlie didn't answer. He sat up, took a yellow leaf off his arm that had come free in the wind, and got to pulling it apart. Everything was going so fast around us, like it was all caught up in a funnel. "You got a boyfriend?" he said.

My heart kicked up. He didn't have a ring or a letter jacket, and I wondered what he could give me. "Not right now," I said, like he caught me on a good day.

"You *ever* had one?"

I could only think of Kenny, who was ugly and tried to follow me home and grabbed me once behind the gym. I said, "One time, but not for very long."

"Well, I don't like him anyhow."

I couldn't help but smile over this. I didn't like Kenny either. "Tell me the understanding you got with Jonny Magpie," I said.

"It's just that Jonny don't want white people telling him what to do, and I don't want no one telling me when and where to haul my trash."

"Would you do what *I* told you?" I said. I pushed my knee out a little from between the kimono, but Charlie didn't see.

"It ain't fair for a man to tell another one how to live," he said. "Jonny Magpie and me, we want to live our own way."

"Why do you think I'm up here?" I said. "I want to live my own way too."

Charlie grinned and laid on his side with his elbow holding up his head so he could keep on looking at me. I looked right back. He said, "Maybe."

"Maybe what?" I wondered if he was thinking about kissing me, but he never so much as touched my pinkie.

"Maybe you and me got an understanding, then," he said, and my heart got warm, on account of never having had an understanding with anyone.

Then Charlie told me the things I'd been thinking all along, I just hadn't been sure enough to know them. Like that rules were only one person's way of looking at things, and that the white men took all the plains from the Indians and then pretended to act nice by giving them back only the crap-ass pieces and making them stay there. "The Sioux're gonna get back up in those saddles sometime soon," Charlie said, "and then the whole world better look out."

"Who told you that?" I said.

"Who do you think?" Charlie told me there was a kind of fight in the two of us and people like Jonny Magpie and James Dean, who wouldn't just lay down and take it from anyone.

He talked about *us* like we were part of the same thing. "It's so easy to fall in love," I said, looking right at him.

Charlie laughed at me. "Those ain't even your words."

"I *like* Buddy Holly."

"He's a candy-ass. Someone needs to bust him up."

"I don't think so."

"Who cares what you think?"

Charlie just sat there chewing on his lip and scratching his head. Then he spat on his shirt, picked up the gun, and got to shining it like it was the last thing on earth. The whole sky just dropped away with the sun. The branches rattled like a bag of bones being shaked, and I hugged my shoulders to keep warm.

"Don't be sore," Charlie said, laying down the gun, his face all scrunched up like he really did mean it. "Come here."

"Just 'cause someone else said it, doesn't mean it isn't true," I said, but I wasn't really sore.

"Come here," Charlie said again, and slid up next to me. He put his arm around me, and I leaned my head back on his neck. I could feel his pulse like something wild, like a little animal. "You're so tiny," he said. "I get scared the wind'll squish you."

We sat like that for a while, still as salt, like something would break if we so much as moved a finger.

THE WIND HAD KICKED UP AND WHISPERED IN THE CORN WHEN I SNEAKED ON through, and it seemed like all those husks were telling me not to take another step. But there was not a thing for me to do right then but go on back the way I had came and take whatever Roe and Mother threw my way. I didn't have anything else just then but a little hope of Charlie loving me, like a tiny rock in the middle of an empty field.

I thought I'd sneak on through my bedroom window the same way I came out, as if I never had left, but someone had closed the window and bolted the sill, and no matter how I pushed I couldn't lift it. There wasn't any choice but to go around front. I went real slow around the side of the house and walked right up to the porch. There was Mother in the doorway bouncing Betty Sue up and down in her arms. Betty Sue was too old to get bounced, or even held like that; it was only going to make her more of a baby. She'd be in high school one day and still wearing a diaper, the way things were going. I mean, I could see it coming. I mean, it was just *stupid.*

Mother dropped open her mouth and stared at me like she couldn't believe I showed up again after I had run away like that, like she almost hoped I never would come back. I hugged my sketchbook and looked down at my feet that were scratched and bleeding from all my running. I didn't even feel it. "Where you been?" Mother said, biting her lip.

I didn't answer.

"Where, Caril Ann? You tell me."

"School."

"Like that? Don't you lie to me!"

"I tried to get a lift," I said.

"You tell me the truth!"

"That *is* the truth." Then I kicked a stone, and hurt my toe, and turned around to hide my wince. I squinted out at the road and a slip of sky far off turning green with weather.

"You look at me when I talk to you!" Mother yelled.

So I turned back around.

"I don't know if I should thank God or shake my fist," Mother said, and she started to cry. She held Betty Sue's head against her neck like things would all be fine if she just kept her special baby near. "You're going nowhere fast," she said.

I snuffled a laugh, but a kind of sob came out instead. Mother looked so embarrassed of me and afraid. It was like everything inside me was going to do the opposite, and here I was feeling sorry for Mother, her being all hung up with a baby and an old man who always hobbled around rattling his cage, when I was the one everyone should feel sorry for. "I hate it here," I said.

"You don't understand what you got," Mother said.

"Oh, I understand." I went in my room and slammed the door and pushed the chair against it, but no one so much as tried to get in. I listened all through supper to Roe and Mother in the kitchen talk about tying me up and throwing me in the trunk if that's what it took to get me where I needed to be. But somehow it made no difference anymore. Everything looked better to me now I had Charlie to think about.

I LAY IN BED LATER, KICKING AROUND SO MUCH I COULDN'T SLEEP, THINKING about a magazine I read. When you trust someone, it said, you love someone. I realized then, I never trusted Roe or Mother, but for some strange reason I already trusted Charlie. Love is not necessarily made out of blood, and anyway Roe and me didn't have so much as a drop the same between us. I imagined love made out of different colored silk squares sewed together with stitches you can't see.

A magic man pulled a scarf like this from his pocket a while back at the Lincoln County Fair. He kept pulling and pulling and it kept on coming out like a never-ending river running into the bright red sky. I knew it had to be a trick, though. It had to end somewhere because everything ends. When I narrowed my eyes at the magic man, he looked me in the face and winked to tell me I was not just some dumb girl with scuffed-up baton boots who had to repeat the eighth grade, but an important person like his own self, who understood how everything in the world all went down. And then there was a last orange square and he flurried his fingers into a puff of smoke, and when the smoke cleared his hands were empty, his pockets hanging, and it was as if all those colors had never been.

I woke in the night like a shot and threw off the covers. I sat up in bed straight as a pin, but everything looked different. Maybe it was a different day, a hundred years later with people from Mars and everyone dead, and here I was in a world where everything had changed right around me while I was sleeping. The clouds were gone, and a moon was hanging so full and bright it made shadows and cast the mirror in silver. My sketchbook was open on the floor, and a picture I had done of a cottonwood rose up from the crease of it. I tried to figure out the time, but there was no way of knowing, really.

Then I heard something. My heart pounded like nails, and I thought *Who's there?* I rubbed my eyes. The whole thing seemed like a dream, only I wasn't sleeping. And then maybe I even said it out loud—"Who's there?"—because just as I was thinking it, someone tapped out an answer. *Tap-tap.* It came from the window. I wasn't so much scared as nervous maybe, not ready for whatever was coming. My mouth felt thick. I got out of bed and went to the window and squinted out into the dark; I could see something right there, some animal, but I couldn't tell what. It had ears and a tongue and shiny eyes, and then it all came together. There was my dog's face peering at me through the glass. I rubbed my eyes to see was I dreaming after all, and a shape rose up out of the dark. There was Charlie holding my dog in his arms like a baby and bending his little paw back and forth so it looked like a person waving. I snuffled a laugh. I couldn't believe it. He had gone and got Nig off the chain, and I hadn't heard so much as a bark. I pushed hard, and the window creaked open. I brushed a flake of paint off my elbow. "What are you doing here?" I said, real soft on account of Roe and Mother sleeping in the very next room.

"I don't know. I had a dream and I couldn't sleep. I gotta talk to you." Charlie's voice was full of something, about to burst.

Nig tinkled his collar and reached his head back and licked Charlie's neck, and Charlie let out a laugh. "Hush," I whispered.

"Come on out and play with us," Chuck said.

"What are we going to play?"

"We'll walk some. Right, boy?" he said, giving the dog a shake like he was supposed to answer. Nig didn't so much as wiggle, and he could be a slippery little fellow.

"Hush," I said.

"Then come on."

"I'll think about it," I said, but I was only pretending. I got my kimono off the peg and put it over my nightdress. Charlie crouched down on one knee and reached up his hand, and I pushed both feet out the window and stepped down onto his thigh like something in a movie.

"Don't you got any other clothes?" he whispered.

"Don't complain."

"I ain't complaining."

EVERYTHING LOOKED SOFT AND SILVER LIKE COBWEBS IN A WORLD OF GHOSTS. A million stars twinkled all at once. I knew that some of these weren't stars at all but bigger, more important things like planets. "What makes them wink? The sun's a star, and it doesn't wink," I said, and turned my head so I was staring at his ear.

"It ain't a star, silly. It's a ball of fire." Charlie leaned me up against the chicken coop and pushed his lips to mine. His mouth was hot and hungry and all over me, and I had never known what it was to feel that way. I wanted to give my whole self up right then, just melt into his skin. But Barbara said you had to make boys wait, so just before I fell all the way in I let go. I ran into the corn. It was just a game. I didn't want to be anywhere else but with Charlie. My heart lifted up and I had the feeling it was always going to be me and Charlie here underneath these same stars and all the planets turning.

I went this way and that until somehow I got doubled back behind Charlie, and there I was just watching him fumble around, calling my name. He was a good hunter, but he was not so good at hunting me.

Nig's collar jingled close by with a happy silver sound. I thought about how we were all three of us free. It was so easy. All you had to do was climb out a window. I sneaked out from behind and put my palms over Charlie's eyes. His whole body jumped like a scared little boy.

"It's only me," I said.

"Why'd you run? Did I go too fast?"

I shaked my head. "I was only fooling."

He grabbed my arm. "I wanted to show you something."

We went together back between the trees.

"I've seen it here," I said.

"Not like this."

Charlie took my hand when we walked, and I looked up at the branches. You could only see their shapes black against the lighter sky, gnarled up like some old person's fist. There were shadows on the ground, and when a breeze came it seemed like the whole world moved together in one single dream.

"How'd you know it was my window, Chuck?" I asked.

He kind of laughed and squeezed my arm. "'Cause it used to be *my* window."

"You used to live there?"

"I did. Me and my brothers and Ma and Gus."

"Who's Gus?"

"My old man. We're Starkweathers."

Starkweather. It was a name that belonged here with me, in the woods, in the middle of the night. I wanted to say I loved him right then, but I didn't want to get it wrong. So I just walked beside him.

There were tiny glitters coming up out of nowhere among the trees and moving all around us: rabbit eyes. The rabbits were chewing on things, the grass maybe, and when we came near they stared like flashbulbs, then scurried away to hide in the brush. A whole family lived under a woodpile, Charlie said, and there was a field beyond on someone else's land where they all went to meet at night.

"How do you know?"

"I've seen 'em."

"Did you hunt them?"

"Not there," he said. "If I went and did that, they'd never come back."

An owl hooted somewhere close by like it was telling us a warning. My skin got bumps and I hugged my arms around myself, but it was not for being scared. I felt like I was looking into a far-off place. Me and Charlie were invisible ghosts with see-through hands, floating all over the world without so much as a care what other people did.

"You ever seen an owl tree?" Chuck said.

"I don't know," I said, and he pulled me past the ladder to the farthest tree along the fence. I could see there was only a sprinkle of leaves on the branches, which meant it was dying, and a hole in the trunk where the owl lived. I wondered what the owl would do when the tree got too tired to stand up on its own anymore.

We crouched down in the roots and Charlie showed me all the things the owl had left behind: the tiny jaws of mice that still had teeth, hunks of fur, a skeleton of something bigger, a baby prairie dog, and all the feathers the owl had dropped for so much ruffling around. The bones were white. The feathers shined. I held a jaw in my hand and felt how smooth it was, trying to remember it just right so I'd be able to put it down later in my sketchbook. It was a crazy thing how all these perfect bits had been in the stomach of a bird once.

"What happened when they died?" I said.

"I don't know. I used to get all hanged up about it."

I petted his hair and got to wondering why he was ever scared of the dark to begin with. We kneeled down in the chucked-up bones and got to kissing again. Charlie leaned against the tree trunk and I sat across his lap, staring up through the branches at the moon, that seemed to me then like a bit of bone itself. I wanted to stay like that with Charlie under the owl tree forever. But it couldn't last forever.

We had to go back. We got Nig and slipped back between the trees. The house was sleeping and everything was dark. When Charlie took me to the window, he tried to go back through with me. "It was my room. I wanna see it," he whispered.

"Only for a minute," I said. "Only if you're quiet." It didn't seem right to let him in so quick, but I couldn't help it, he wanted to so bad.

When Charlie stepped through, he didn't so much as look around. He just got into bed and I got beside him. He put his head to my head, and we held each other real silent in the dark, listening to the sound of our hearts together. "You gotta go," I whispered, even though I didn't want him to. "I'll get in trouble."

"Whatta you care about trouble?" He put his mouth on my mouth so I couldn't answer. He got to kissing my neck, and my ear, and my whole body shaked with trying to stay still. Somehow the robe came off and everything else, and I was laying there naked in his arms. His fingers felt everywhere, tiny lights waking up new parts, and it all rushed forward. And all of a sudden, there wasn't a choice but to keep on going. The smell of everything secret rose up around him. Every muscle quaked with trying to be still. He was over me and pushing in, and then his body went crazy, like a bird cupped in your hand, trying to break free.

And then it all went quiet. Charlie sighed. I put my head on his chest and listened to his heart slow down after all that rushing.

"You ever did that before?" he whispered.

"No," I said.

"Did it hurt?"

"No," I said.

"I hope you liked it the way I did."

"You better go," I said, though I couldn't think about him ever being anywhere else.

"How come?"

"I'll get in trouble."

"What kind? Your old man gonna beat you?"

"He's not my true father," I said, "but he thinks he is."

"He ever hit you?"

"Not really," I whispered, wishing I could say yes to show how bad Roe was. But I wasn't going to lie to Charlie.

Inside of a minute, I had fell asleep. When I woke up, the sky was light, and Charlie was gone, and someone was beating down the door on account of the chair still propped against it. I rolled out of bed, put on my clothes, and got ready for school, on account of nothing being so bad now that Charlie cared enough to see me through it.

THINGS WENT LIKE THIS FOR A WHILE: I WOULD CUT OUT OF SCHOOL AND MEET Charlie at the tree house beyond the corn. That's where I drew all the different parts of him and fell in love with them one by one till they added up to something. I hung my drawings up in the tree until the wind took them down. I didn't care where they blew. I signed every one. Charlie and me would lay in the branches and pet each other's hair until Roe found us and said I couldn't go with Charlie anymore. But that wasn't going to stop us. When I told Charlie, he kicked at the tires of his Ford and said how nobody thought he was any good. I pressed my palm to his greased-up ducktail and looked him in the flint-green eyes, saying "Me neither, Chuck, nobody sees my true self except you."

"That's how come I love you so much." And Charlie put his head on my lap and looked up at me, chewing on a blade of grass like he was chewing on a piece of me. He touched my breasts and said, "And these bitty things. I love them too." And the leaves in the trees shimmied around on the branches like they were all talking at once.

CHAPTER EIGHT

1962

I crept downstairs, still wearing my nightgown. The house was silent as I pulled back the living room curtains. Taking my grandfather's leather-bound atlas off the bookshelf, I sat down on the floor in a patch of sunlight behind the couch where no one would see me. I sifted through countries, looking for our own. I wanted to count how many states lay between Nebraska and New York, where my uncle lived. Tracing my finger along the green edge of the Great Plains, I pressed my thumb into the blue of Lake Michigan. I wondered if it was him my mother had called, and how long it would take him to travel through six states.

My grandfather had circled places on the map where Capital Steel had constructed bridges. In a yellowed clipping that fell out of the book, I read that in Fort Madison, Iowa, two construction workers had died building a bridge across the Mississippi. In the atlas, my grandfather had marked the spot with carefully shaded pencil crosses, scrawling their names in the margin as if he had been haunted by responsibility. The names were long and Russian, with several syllables I could not decipher. In Council Bluffs, a bridge over the Missouri connected Iowa to Nebraska. The lead-gray circles were smudged with fingerprints. I imagined steel against steel glittering in the autumn sun as my uncle sped over wide muddy rivers on his way to rescue my mother from whatever it was she couldn't stand about our life.

In the kitchen, my mother startled me. She was staring out the window, already waiting, I guessed, and I started to panic. She didn't turn around when I opened the icebox door. I put the jar of milk down on the counter heavily and fumbled around in the cupboard for a box of cereal, even though I knew there wasn't any left. "What are you waiting for?" I said finally.

My mother turned around and faced me. She wasn't wearing any makeup. She didn't look ready to go anywhere. I wondered if she'd been up all night. "Not waiting," she said. "Wishing."

"How long does it take to drive from New York to Lincoln?" I asked.

"How would I know?"

Then she turned around and unlatched the window and pulled it open. My mother just stood there, breathing in the air like she wasn't cold at all. She folded her arms on the windowsill and pressed her nose against the screen. Standing behind my mother, I wanted to touch her, rest my head on her shoulder, put some part of myself near to remind her I was still there. It seemed like we should need each other.

Moving up beside her, in front of the window, I touched my fingertips to the collar of her shirt. "Mother?" I whispered, but she didn't seem to notice. She kept staring through the screen. I opened my mouth to speak, but then I couldn't remember what I'd wanted to say. A cold wind blew my cotton nightgown back against my skin. My hair tickled my neck like fingertips.

Out the window I could see the driveway lined with rhododendron bushes and the elm stumps. When I was little and we had come to visit, I would follow the trail of my grandfather's cigar smoke out the back door and down the driveway into the summer shade of the leaves. The breeze tickled shadows in the tire marks. The roses always bloomed. Somehow, the thick hum of the insects and the fingers of my grandfather's smoke had made the whole world seem ancient and wise.

• • •

MY MOTHER SPENT THE WEEKEND STARING OUT WINDOWS, WAITING FOR HER brother to come whisk her away to some bright grander place. I was sure of it. This was my secret. I held it inside. My father spent hours on the bench in the garden, reading the newspaper, though the fall air was cold. He drank coffee with brandy instead of cream. I'd seen him go into his study twice without looking at me and heard the clink of the crystal decanter against the side of his mug. Red leaves fluttered down through the light, and he kept shaking them off the crease in his newspaper. Finally, he put the paper down and raked the whole garden. He gathered the leaves in garbage bags and loaded them into the trunk of the Chevy. He drove off and didn't come back for a long time.

I wanted desperately to talk to Lucille. She seemed like the only person who had ever listened. I thought about writing out what I would say: *Lucille, Mother needs you. The situation is dire. She's drinking herself to death. She took all the tranquilizers. She's going to slash her wrists and stick them under the faucet. She's planning to jump off the roof of the Cornhusker Hotel. If you ever cared about anything, you'll come back now.*

I thought about where my mother might keep Lucille's daughter's telephone number in Detroit. Creeping down the hall, my stocking feet sunk into the thick beige carpet. Pausing by the stairwell, I listened for a sound, but there was nothing. My parents' bedroom door was open, and I slipped inside. It was dark and shadowy, cluttered like I'd never seen it. Dirty button-down shirts were piled in the corner waiting to be dry-cleaned. The bed wasn't made. Stockings and bras exploded from the bureau drawers, as if someone had been caught emptying them out and had just run away.

I went over to my mother's nightstand and opened the drawer. There was an eye mask to keep out the sunlight. A package of wax earplugs. A Sucrets box full of hairpins that I had never noticed my mother wearing. At her vanity table, I rummaged around in her makeup drawer, through little pots of pink paint that said Chanel on the lid, powder and brushes, lipsticks, brown pencils and black pencils, mascara. I didn't know what to do with any of it. Beauty seemed like a house I hadn't been invited to. It had to be constructed carefully, controlled, and I thought I was the kind of person whose hands would always be too shaky to ever pull it off.

Opening my mother's jewelry box, I took out her engagement ring and slipped it on, surprised at how perfectly it fit. Holding my finger up to the light, I looked deep into the diamond sitting like a sparkling eye in a delicate square of black enamel. Sometimes it felt like my mother's heart was a diamond. Glittering and hard, meant to be admired.

The telephone number was tucked into the lid of the ring case, scrawled in black pen on a folded piece of stationery. I didn't recognize the area code, but I knew I had stumbled upon something mysterious and important. It seemed right that my mother would keep the telephone number in a special place like that. Lucille was close to her heart. I sat down on the edge of the bed and dialed, then quickly put back the receiver on the cradle, then dialed again. I waited while it rang and told myself, "No fooling, this is your duty."

"Hello?" a man said, sleepily.

Surprised, I didn't say anything back.

"Hello?"

"Who am I calling?" I said.

"Who is *this*?"

"Does Lucille Leopold work there?" My voice sounded nervous and small.

"Excuse me?"

"Uncle—"

"You've—"

I placed the black receiver back on the stand and twisted off my mother's ring. My chest fluttered. I had been so close to falling into another skin. Slipping the number into my pocket, I quietly left the room just as my father was coming up the stairs with one shirttail untucked, the buttons open at his neck.

"Hello there," he said, breathing heavily, as if the stairs had taken everything out of him. "It's hot. Stuffy in here, don't you think?" He seemed so helpless, so feeble in that moment, trying to pretend like everything was fine.

"I guess," I said.

"I'm opening some windows to make a cross flow."

"Do you need any help?" I called after him, but he didn't answer, so I went to my room and shut the door. I put the telephone number in my bureau drawer with the Starkweather story hidden under my cutouts of Frankie Avalon surfing at Venice Beach and Fabian behind the scenes during the making of *Five Weeks in a Balloon.* That was the way it worked. You hid something precious in an unexpected place. My uncle had told me that my grandmother had traveled everywhere with her jewels in a brown paper bag so no one would think to steal them, but she confused the bag with her lunch on a train in Italy. When she went to put on her emeralds for an important evening, she found nothing but stale bread.

THINGS WERE GOING TO STRAIGHTEN OUT, I WAS CONVINCED. THEY HAD TO. I started putting more time into my appearance before going to school, not that it made too much difference. I smoothed my long hair down over my cheeks to hide the roundness and tucked in my blouses. No more little-girl nonsense. I convinced myself I was losing weight without Lucille around. Hidden safely within my peacoat on the way to school, I was conscious of each step I took, each hair that blew across my cheek, every delicate pang of hunger that told me I was one inch closer to a comforting emptiness.

I ate sparingly in the cafeteria, but by the time school let out the hunger was always like a jackknife, and on my way home everything rushed too quickly around me. The white houses on Van Dorn Street looked shocked by Big Red football banners, and it was all I could do to reach the soda fountain at the pharmacy without fainting. I'd sink down gratefully on a stool and buy a vanilla milkshake with the change I'd picked from my parents' coat pockets in the hall closet, and finish up with a bagful of candy. Then I'd feel terrible about what I'd done, like I'd always be on the outside of everything.

On my way home one afternoon, I did a strange thing, which I'd been thinking about for a while. I went up South 24th Street with the intention of presenting Cora with some sort of peace offering. I felt bad for what I'd done and bad for her. I wondered if she thought about how easily it could have been her dead on the floor in a pool of blood instead of the Bowmans. People said it all over town: *What lovely people the Bowmans were.*

I emptied my pockets of Mary Janes, which I was sure Cora liked, but at the last moment I put them in the Bowmans' mailbox instead of hers. My hands were shaking. I couldn't believe what I had done, but I didn't take them back. It was an important message, a secret signal to the boy whom I imagined living all alone in the big house where normal people were scared to visit.

All through dinner I couldn't sit still. The Bowman boy was my Boo Radley, only handsome, a beautiful combination of those sad faces in the newspaper reports, those pictures of his parents who looked so perfect and attentive. I had often thought that if Mrs. Bowman had been my mother our lives might not have felt so strange.

Later, I grabbed my coat and tiptoed out the kitchen door and through the shadowy garage. The inside of my nose ached with cold. I buried my hands deep in my pockets. The moon sat like a plate on a table of glittering knife points, and strange shapes bloomed from the rhododendrons. I stood on our frozen lawn looking back at the house. There wasn't any motion or warmth. Only the television flickered behind the living room drapes like faraway heat lightning.

A few minutes later, I found myself standing outside the Bowmans' house. The windows were illuminated on the ground floor. The outdoor light winked, a long-awaited beacon. The house looked warm and safe. No one would ever have been able to guess such horrible things had once happened there. Cora's house was the dark one. The windows gaped like deep black mouths.

I opened the mailbox and held my breath when the hinge squeaked. I stuck my hand inside, just to see. Nothing—the candy was gone. My fingers were stiff with cold inside my mittens. A dog barked, and I jumped. When it barked again, sharp and insistent, hollow with cold, I turned on my heel and hurried home.

I came around the side of our own house, and my parents' bedroom light was on. Looking up between the branches of the oak tree, I could see my mother, her arms folded on the sill, her eyes turned to the sky, as if she were trying to find another universe. I remember how warm the squares of light looked in the other houses on our street during that time, how each window was a satin treasure box, containing a safe little world.

MY FATHER WAS STANDING OVER THE SINK DRYING THE DISHES WHEN I OPENED the back door. "Where have you been, young lady?" he said.

I felt giddy. "Lying in the grass looking up at the stars," I said. "Trying to find the Big Dipper."

"Just because your mother has stepped out to lunch doesn't mean everything else goes haywire around here," my father said. "The rules are the rules."

"Have you been fighting again?"

He picked up a plate and ran a dish towel over the surface. Then he sighed and leaned an elbow on the counter and studied my face. "What can I do, Susan? What do you need?"

I thought about it for a moment, and then I realized I didn't know what it was I wanted or needed. I wanted to look different, I wanted to *be* different, but these weren't things he could do anything about. He never did the things he promised anyway. "I want a hula hoop," I said.

"A what?"

"Never mind." I went upstairs, opened my bureau drawer, and moved aside the cutouts and the article about the electrocution. I took out the telephone number and unfolded it. I stared at it, trying to figure out if it was my mother's handwriting or if someone had slipped it to her across a bar, but I couldn't remember what her numbers looked like, only her decadent script swooping across the page.

IN CALISTHENICS I MADE A POINT OF STANDING NEXT TO CORA. "HI," I SAID, but she wouldn't look at me. She shrugged her shoulders and stared down at the tips of her dirty tennis shoes until Miss Winter blew her whistle and we all had to run from the red line to the blue line and then back again.

That afternoon, I followed Cora past my street, up South 24th, half a block behind so she wouldn't see me, so I could think about what to say. I didn't want to go home until my father got there. I didn't want to have to be the one to tell him my mother had left with my uncle or that strange man on the telephone. I didn't want to find the note beside her wedding ring on the kitchen table, the closet and drawers empty of her belongings. I wondered if my father would cry when he saw there wasn't a trace of her, if he'd be strong in front of me or angry.

I stood behind one of the last elms that still remained, old, gnarled, and twisting out of the sidewalk. Leaning up against the rough trunk, I watched Cora open the gate. The hem of her camel-colored coat disappeared behind the side of the sprawling house. A blue pickup truck with white lettering on the side pulled out of the Bowmans' driveway, but I could see it wasn't anything to get excited about. The bed of the truck was full of tree limbs. A man sat behind the wheel wearing a baseball cap. He stared straight ahead as he turned past me. I waited another minute before walking boldly up the path. I stood there with my finger extended and rang Cora Lessing's doorbell.

I could hear footsteps, and then the door opened and a skinny little boy with red hair and a catcher's mitt on one hand stood there frowning at me. He put the mitt in front of his nose and sniffed it.

"Hi," I said. "Is Cora home?"

"Who wants to know?"

"I'm a friend from school."

"I don't believe you. My sister doesn't have any friends." He opened the door farther, stepping back, and I went inside, taking advantage of the moment. The hall was light and airy. I stood beneath a chandelier made of colored glass that cast shapes on the ceiling. A staticky radio played somewhere far off, announcing a voice from another part of the world.

"Where is she?" I said.

"Out looking for the cat. I boomeranged pop tops at him yesterday, so he ran away. I hate the cat." He wrinkled his nose and scratched his head with the mitt and sat down on the stairs. "I hate my sister, too."

I didn't know what to say, so I just nodded and looked at the floor. The wood was shiny and waxy, the kind you could skate over in your stocking feet or see your reflection in. "Maybe I should come back," I said, but then Cora appeared, unbuttoning her camel coat. She stopped in the doorway and squinted her pale eyes at me. Then she looked at her brother. "I still couldn't find Cinders, Toby. You are in so much trouble now."

The boy stuck out his tongue and darted up the stairs. Cora waited for me to say something.

"I'm sorry about your cat," I said.

She just stared at me.

"I came to talk to you." My voice sounded smaller than I wanted it to. I didn't feel so sure of myself anymore. I picked a hangnail. The radio jabbered upstairs, some sort of interview. I could hear questions being asked, and then a pause before someone answered. I remembered Starkweather's brother interviewed on the radio before the execution. It felt like so many years ago. Who would have thought I'd end up so close to it all? "I'm sorry I wasn't nice to you that time in the locker room," I said quickly. "I didn't mean it."

Cora didn't look at me. She unbuttoned her coat and opened a closet door. "I didn't notice. I don't even know what you're talking about," she said, but her voice sounded like she did know, like she hated me.

"I hope we can be friends," I said.

"You never wanted to be friends before I caught you staring at the neighbor's house."

"I didn't come to stare at the neighbor's house. I came to say I'm sorry," I said.

"It's never as simple as that," Cora said. She went over to the front door, held it open, and shot me a smug look with her pale blue eyes. A gust of wind ripped through the hall and a door slammed shut, making us both jump. The chandelier chimed. The white wall swirled with color. Then the air went still.

"I feel bad," I said.

"I doubt it. Only *poets* and *artists* identify." She wrinkled her nose like someone else had told her to say this, and she wasn't sure exactly what it meant. "I can't talk about it anymore. I have things to do," she said.

But I didn't want to go home. I had the urge to undo it all, to unravel my life right then and there and stitch it back together in a different way. People started over all the time. The Bowmans' son had started over after the death of his parents. Or maybe he hadn't been able to. You can't start over if you haven't faced what came before. Maybe Cora had looked through the fence and seen him crying in the rose garden. No one to dry his tears. *I would catch them in my hands.*

"Please," I said. "Let me stay."

She gave me a bitter look.

I stepped out into the cold air. "I'm going to look for your cat," I said. The radio upstairs crackled, and my heart jumped. Someone had twisted the volume the wrong way. Cora closed the door.

I stood on the porch for a moment, thinking about what to do. Dark clouds gathered in the sky. The air smelled of winter. I knelt down in the barren flowerbed and peered under the porch. "Come here, Cinders," I said, but nothing happened. I wasn't even sure you were supposed to call a cat the way you did a dog. We'd never had any pets. I went around the side of the house and looked up into the branches of the trees. I didn't see anything except a clear view of the Bowmans' house, behind a low white fence that couldn't have kept anyone out. I felt my throat catch and my pulse quicken, being so close to a mystery. But I also felt small, like a dried leaf in a breeze, helplessly going wherever the wind felt like taking me. The air bit my cheeks, but I didn't care. I buried my hands deep in my pockets and kept myself from looking over the fence. I imagined Cora watching me from an upstairs window, testing my loyalty.

The front of the Lessings' house had made it seem like any other in Lincoln, contained on its neat little plot of land, but when I went around to the back there were a million places someone could hide. The garden unfolded before me, wild and unexpected, larger than I could have possibly imagined. Toward the back was a stand of small trees, and stepping between the spindly trunks I felt more at ease. I had a perfect view of the Bowmans' garden. I ran my hand along the points of the picket fence and swirled a pile of dried leaves around with my foot, as if the cat could somehow be hiding in there. But I didn't really care. I peered over the fence into what reminded me of a secret grotto where forbidden lovers met. There was a small fish pool, with a stone statue of an angel balancing on one foot, pointing a trumpet up toward the sky. I imagined Charles Starkweather and Caril Ann Fugate sitting down with their guns propped up against the side of the bench, blood on their shirts, staring into the pool, thinking about all the terrible things they'd done for love. It had been cold then too, the dead of winter, with snow instead of leaves everywhere, and I pictured their hearts like two frozen boxes slamming against each other. Everything had been white.

As if the sky had read my mind, the first flurries of snow swirled through the trees. I tried to see where the flakes hit the ground, whether the snow was melting or sticking, but the wind wouldn't let it settle. Then I caught sight of what looked like the twitch of a tail twisting around the base of the stone fountain. It was the only reason I needed. I didn't think twice. I just climbed over the fence and slipped into the garden.

I fixed my eyes on whatever it was and tried not to breathe. My pulse thudded in my ears. My feet crunched over the brittle grass. I stepped carefully forward into the circle of gravel, where those murderers must once have stepped, trying not to scare it away. I crept up to the frozen pool and called the cat. My voice sounded shrill and uncertain. The tail twitched and flipped behind the statue. The metal end of something hit stone.

A woman emerged from behind some bushes, pulling the end of the black hose toward her. I backed up, but it was too late. She'd already seen me.

"Well, I never—" She broke off suddenly, dropping the hose and putting one hand over her heart. I could see rings flashing beneath the wool sleeve of her coat, her earlobes sagging with the weight of pearls. "I never, never, never was so startled," she said. "What are you doing here?"

"I'm a friend of Cora from next door," I explained. "We were looking for her cat. I thought I saw Cinders, but I guess it was just the hose. I'm sorry." I could feel my face going red. Had she been the one to find my Mary Janes?

"Who are you?"

"I'm the Hurst girl," I said, tucking my chin into my collar. I was surprised at myself. I'd been on the verge of lying.

"What?"

I turned up my face and looked straight into her hard beautiful eyes. "Susan Hurst," I said, using my full name.

"Well, I'm sorry to say I haven't seen a cat. If I do, though, I'll let them know." She picked up the hose again and started winding it awkwardly over her arm.

I turned to go. "Sorry," I said, looking back over my shoulder, but she'd already disappeared behind the hedge. The snowflakes were falling more heavily now, collecting on the trumpet of the stone angel. The pool was frozen, and the orange ghosts of goldfish drifted beneath the surface.

By the time I got home, a delicate trace of snow had cupped in the rhododendrons. A silence had crept over the street, and our house was like a tomb. Something felt missing, and I went through the gray rooms searching for my mother.

CHAPTER NINE

1991

I spent the whole drive upstate trying not to think about the safe-deposit box or my family, just imagining myself relaxing with a drink and a good book, listening to the sound of the cool gray river which ran by the house. I hadn't been there in ages.

Zipping up the New York State Thruway, I tried to smile though there wasn't anyone to see. But that key to the safe-deposit box burned a hole in my pocket, and I couldn't get comfortable. My wife had made the whole thing into a terrible burden.

I took back roads through Dutchess County, drawing out the day as raindrops spattered the windshield and yellow leaves spun down onto the wet road. I flew through Balmville and Ulster Park, feeling like I'd never look back, but before I knew it I found myself standing in the basement of the First National Bank, holding the key in my hand and staring at the bronze door of deposit box 342.

"You know, I'm not really sure there's anything inside," I said to the attendant.

"It's your box—you should know," the attendant said.

"In fact, I don't even remember ever having been here before. It could be the wrong key."

"Well, your signature checks out, so—" He turned his key in the first lock.

"Listen—um, could you step back just a bit?" I said, but the attendant just loomed there, unnerving me considerably, as I took the brass key between my fingers and pressed it into the brass lock. I almost hoped my key wouldn't fit. But it clicked in the lock and turned easily.

After a moment's hesitation, I reached in. My fingers stumbled over something. I felt my heart lurch as I drew out a container the size of a shoebox. There it was, heavy in my hands, the cardboard so old and cracked I thought it might break. I didn't want to know what was inside, but I remembered holding that box one day long ago. And for some strange reason, it hit me right then, standing in the basement vault of that goddamn bank: I really *was* leaving Susan. I had no intention of ever going back.

My fingers shook as I paid the bill, signed an order to end the rental, and tucked the box under my coat to hide it from the rain.

DRIVING TOWARD PORT SAUGUS WITH THE BOX ON THE SEAT BESIDE ME, I TRIED to come up with a plan for the gallery. Francesca needed to be called. I'd have to trust her to pack things up. I could run my business from the country, until I came up with a better plan. A little anxious, despite the soothing rhythm of my windshield wipers, the only thing I wanted was a glass of bourbon. I'd drink as much as I could keep down, and there would be no one to tell me to stop. The rain shaded the road in charcoal and saturated the first fall leaves with color. So this was freedom, this gray meandering through silent oaks and maples.

At an approaching intersection, a hitchhiker wearing a plastic bag as a raincoat held up a smeared sign that said UTICA, and I wondered for a moment what made him so desperate to get there. I thought of picking him up and delivering him far beyond his destination, of driving and driving until we were far from anyone who remembered our names. In some strange city where all lost men eventually turned up, I would simply hand him the box, say, "All yours, chief," clap him on the back, and speed away into the fog. I wouldn't ever have to look inside that box if I didn't want to.

When I paused for the stoplight, the hitchhiker stepped off the curb and put out his thumb. I rolled down my window to be polite, and he bent over, leaning his elbow inside. He was no more than a boy, my son's age perhaps, yet he seemed to lack the energy of anything approximating youth. I could smell nicotine on him, and the mustiness of damp, unwashed clothing.

"You goin' my way?" he said.

"Unfortunately, I'm not," I said, feeling his gaze passing over the box. "But I thought I might be able to deposit you at a more promising intersection."

"What's *that* s-supposed to mean?"

"Well, it doesn't look very promising around here. There's not much traffic, son."

"If you haven't noticed, nothing's very promising around here." He took his elbow off the window and glared at me as if I were responsible for this. Something about him unnerved me. His eyes looked restless.

"I'm sorry about that," I said. "Anyway, good luck to you." And I put my foot on the gas, leaving him scowling on the empty road in the glow of the blinking stoplight.

I couldn't shake the uneasy feeling he had inspired. I imagined a macabre scene from one of those movies Hank watched, a moment where I opened the box to find a bone, a human hand secreted away, unnoticed for years. I remembered a trip we'd taken when I was a boy, so my father could see the Inca ruins at Ingapirca. Terrible rainstorms had plagued us and we never got to the site, but one afternoon when my mother was resting in the hotel room, my father had taken me to a museum full of shrunken heads on sticks. I'd begged and begged and finally he had bought me a curio head with real hair and eyelashes, nestled in a balsa-wood coffin with a string through its nose. Back at home, the head had scared me, and one night my mother had made a great ceremony of gathering us together in the living room, taking it by the neck, and tossing it into the fire. I allowed myself to remember her face; she was laughing in the firelight, but I could not manage to summon up how it was she sounded.

Turning right onto Flint Rock Road, I pulled into the parking lot of the Duck Goose Diner and put the box in the trunk because I didn't want to think about it anymore. There weren't any other cars in the parking lot. Thursday afternoon, and the world was tucked away, hidden from the storm. A blue neon OPEN sign blinked softly in the diner window, and I could make out a solitary individual sitting in its glow, wearing a John Deere hat and quietly eating his meal.

Opening the door of the Duck Goose, I walked up to the register and slapped my hands on the counter. A waitress came out of the kitchen with her hands on her hips and frowned. I wanted those hips to be slim. I wanted her rear to be heart-shaped, her lips to be full; after all, these were my first hours of freedom. But this woman wasn't much of an inspiration.

"I used to live here," I told her. "My kids and I used to come here for pie."

"Right," she said. "So then you—what, moved down to Westchester so you could take the train to the city?"

I laughed it off. "No, I'm just a poor guy with no place to go."

The man in the booth coughed loudly and I tried not to look at him. The waitress started wiping down the counter, wearing what I thought might be a smirk.

"So, do you still have that nice fresh-baked apple pie?"

"Only cherry," she said.

"OK, then."

"Does that mean you want it?"

"You bet," I said, getting tired of the whole exchange. I picked up the sports page, just hoping to tune her out. This was precisely the sort of thing my wife couldn't stand.

The pie was store-bought, one of those sticky-sweet frozen things, but I ate it anyway, even tipped the waitress for good measure. I always tip too much.

On my way out, I passed the pay phone and got the sudden urge to call Hank—tell him how proud I was, that I missed him already. This was the sort of spontaneous expression of feeling people admired. So I went back to the car, got my address book, came back in, and nervously attempted to shove a rather ridiculous amount of change into the phone for my call.

"Henry," I said, as the waitress eyed me suspiciously from behind the counter, perhaps annoyed that she couldn't monitor my conversation through the glass door. I turned my back on her. "It's Dad."

"Hey, Dad." I could hear somebody talking in the background, maybe his roommate, maybe a group of new friends.

"How's school?" I said.

"Fine, I guess."

"And are you having a good time?"

"I guess so."

"Well, your old man is in a rather unexpected place at the moment. Want to hazard a guess?"

"Saudi Arabia?"

"Ha. Might as well be. The Duck Goose Diner," I said. "Remember? Near Port Saugus."

"No."

"We used to come here after Little League for fresh apple pie because your mother never cooked."

He said nothing.

"They don't have that pie anymore," I went on. "Guess time leaves no stone unturned. But you loved that pie."

"Dad?"

"Listen, I could come up tomorrow and take you and some of your new friends out for pizza."

"It's not Little League, Dad," he said. "Where's Mom?"

"No idea." Suddenly I felt terribly uncomfortable. Looking over my shoulder, I saw the waitress eyeing me suspiciously, as if I was on the run from the law or had just thrown my wife into the river. "Is this a bad time?" I asked Hank.

"I just saw you."

"Are you with a girl?"

"Jesus Christ, Dad."

"Remember not to unveil the ceremonial club too soon, son."

"There's this thing on the quad. I'm late."

"I'm so proud—" I tried to add, but he was gone, and I stood for a moment with the receiver in my hand, not sure what to do next. I wondered suddenly if I'd been any use to my children at all. Now that I'd left Susan, would my children ever want to see me again? How hard could it be for them to say goodbye to someone who had never really been there? Of course, I *had* been there in certain ways. But then things became more complicated. My business required so much. And now Hank had left home. Soon Mary would, too, and there was no way for Susan and me to go on together in the same hopeful spirit with which our lives had begun. I thought of the apartment, its empty rooms, the thick quiet that had grown between us.

SUSAN INHERITED THE HOUSE IN PORT SAUGUS FROM HER UNCLE IN 1972. IN 1973, after I finished my dissertation on Nero's Golden Palace and just before Susan had discovered she was pregnant, we moved in. We spent months picking through Douglas's belongings together, making numerous trips to Goodwill and the dump as Susan's stomach grew. The puppies got into everything. The roof had to be patched. The plan was to turn the barn into a showroom for the objects I had begun to collect with the money left to me. The floor needed work, and the walls required even more repair. There was a lot to be done, and I stepped up to the plate: I found myself doing things I never thought possible, even pulling them off with flair. I sanded the barn floor myself and painted it a color called London Fog. I turned the baby's room into a sky by covering it with robin's-egg blue and cutting foam into the shapes of clouds, which I'd dip in white paint and then stamp on the ceiling. Several times Susan appeared on the threshold looking pleased, laughing when white drops of paint landed in my hair. "It really is a sky," she said once. "Bird droppings and all." Later, I admit I lost interest. But in those days I wanted a home different from the one I'd grown up in. More artistic and relaxed, not so grand. I was convinced that an easy, comfortable place could help make things right.

Susan's uncle Douglas had been in ill health for years, and junk had piled up around the place. Susan went through it frantically, with a sort of crazed energy, as if she'd lost something valuable there long ago. When I noticed this and asked about it, she told me she was trying to discover the person her mysterious uncle had been. She said she'd always imagined so many things about him. But that didn't explain the urgency. She seemed so driven. I realized it had to do with her mother, whom Susan refused to discuss. All she wanted to talk about was Douglas, who had paid for her education. "Without him," she always said, "I would have had very little, really. He was close to my mother, but he isolated himself from everything else. It seems like he was hiding here."

One evening I found martini glasses and champagne flutes as thin as paper tucked up on a top shelf of a cabinet, probably left over from a time when Douglas had entertained. I drove into town for champagne, cleaned out two flutes with my shirttail, and surprised Susan. She had been so happy, like a little girl finally allowed to do something she had always dreamed about. We clinked glasses to what my memory has labeled that winter's first snow. Then I picked her up and carried her over the threshold the way I'd forgotten to when we were first married. These kinds of things, these little things—conventions, really—have always made my wife unreasonably happy.

As the weeks passed, she continued her furious hunt; in a bureau drawer she found a boxful of unsent letters addressed to a man named Downs in Oxford, Mississippi. I was varnishing the barn floor when she appeared in the doorway holding one. "I need you to stop what you're doing and listen to this," she said softly. I turned off the clunking space heater and did what she asked.

"Dear Michael," she read to me.

> "I cannot believe that I find myself this old. A woman comes now every day to bring me my meals. But as soon as she leaves I make my way outside and throw everything into the mulch. It is a long trip; every step feels like a journey, but I use the side of the house for support. Do you remember my view of the river? You always seemed to enjoy it when you came, though I was sure you had seen so many more beautiful places. My trip to Biloxi to see you was special for me—one of the things I will always remember. I barely recognize my

own hands as I write these words. They are shaking and almost useless, but they are eager to write, Michael, that I have never stopped thinking of you."

Susan buried her face in my flannel shirt and started to cry. I held her close, felt the swell of her belly between us, but could not really pretend to be as moved as she was.

"I've decided to mail the letters," she said. "I think Michael Downs would want to have them. Who wouldn't want a love letter?"

I didn't know what to say. Susan's obstetrician had warned me about mood swings. He had told me to be patient. "You're just upset," I said. "Go inside and lie down, and I'll make you some lemon tea."

"Are you saying I shouldn't mail it?" My wife pulled away from me.

That seemed so personal and intrusive. "I think it would be best not to get involved," I said. "He may not have wanted to mail any of them."

"Maybe he didn't have any stamps."

"Sweetheart, please be reasonable. The woman who brought him food would have brought him stamps," I said, though I suppose, in another way, I wasn't being reasonable myself. The smell of the varnish was getting to me, and I couldn't stop thinking about all the strange things that might have gone on. I have always appreciated a man's discretion about his personal life. Perhaps Douglas also felt that there were certain things in this world that need not be discussed. Perhaps it was this silence that had kept him alone.

Susan looked up at me with tears on her lashes, her lip quivering, and said, "It's sad, don't you think?"

"I don't know, Susan. If your uncle was throwing away his food, maybe he wanted to die. Maybe this Downs is a no-good sort of fellow. It doesn't seem worth getting upset about."

"Don't you see? My uncle loved this man. There's an entire life right here in this letter!" She stormed outside and slammed the door. Through the window, I watched her sit down on the back steps of the house, bury the letter in her coat pocket, and light a cigarette. My lovely wife with a pencil in her pulled-back hair. She wanted everyone to have someone; that was her idea of happiness. I felt she was going to somehow hurt the baby by getting upset, so I went out and sat down beside her.

She wiped a tear away with her sleeve, and said, "It looks gray to *me*."

"What does?"

"The river."

"I'm sorry," I said, touching the edge of her dark wool coat. And then I took her hand and kissed it. "I'll try not to be so cold." And I did try. For all those years, I watched my every sentence, trying to convince them all that I had moved forward, that love for me wasn't connected to a terrible kind of pain.

THERE WAS WATER EVERYWHERE THAT FIRST SPRING IN PORT SAUGUS. WE FELL asleep at night to the rhythm of raindrops hitting tin pots in the hallway. Often, it wasn't the storms that woke us but our beagles howling at the thunder, discovering for the first time that they were hounds. It rained constantly, the gray river swelled, and inside Susan our son floated in tranquillity. Hank was born with his thumb in his mouth, and we had no idea about the days, weeks, and months of mind games and bottles of bitters we would go through, trying to get him to stop. His thumb stayed shriveled and soggy for years, leaving its little wet mark like a rabbit print on everything he touched, a reminder of the rain.

It must have been a month before Hank was born, late March, when Susan first brought up what we would tell our child about my parents. I was lying there in the dawn light watching her enormous stomach rise and fall with the deep rhythm of sleep. Behind her through the picture window I could see gray clouds and a fringe of trees on the other side of the river. I had felt separate from every living thing for so long, and at that moment I thought it could all change. I didn't want to be that way anymore. Sliding up close to Susan, I touched her stomach with the palm of my hand. She opened her eyes slowly and I smiled. "What were you dreaming?" I said.

"I wasn't asleep."

"Are you sure?" I ran my finger over the ridge of her distended navel hidden beneath the nightgown. I was glad it was hidden, and yet it stimulated a sort of sexual curiosity in me. There was something so base, so animal about her shape, exaggerated like an ancient, female idol. I wanted to make love to her but was afraid of hurting something.

"Guess what I was doing?" she said, and went on without waiting for me to try. "Attempting subliminal communication with the baby."

I chuckled. "You make it sound like some sort of space alien."

"Let's hope not," she said, and let out a slow yawn.

"Did you learn anything about it?" I wanted to know.

"No, but I learned something about myself."

"Did the baby tell you how profoundly odd its father thinks you are?"

She smiled and shook her head. "I was just thinking about coming here and going through all these old things. I mean, the whole time I knew what I was looking for. I knew why it was so important to me." She stopped for a moment and put both hands on her stomach, and I could see her fingers twitch as the baby kicked. "This whole time I've been looking for something of my mother's," she said.

"We found pictures. That was nice."

"I wanted more than that."

"Yes," I said, "I guess you did." I reached out to brush a strand of hair out of her face, but she caught my hand and held it to her chest.

"We're going to have to do a lot of explaining to this child, Lowell. We're going to have to make it feel safe."

"What exactly do you mean?"

"I think you know what I mean." And of course I did, I just wasn't sure it warranted a discussion. How was that going to change anything? Before I'd left my parents that last time for boarding school, I had always felt safe in their house. But that feeling had only made the loss more devastating when it came.

"We've got years," I said, sitting up and throwing back the covers and putting my feet on the floor. I just couldn't imagine how it would ever be possible to explain such incomprehensible things to a child.

"I know it's difficult, but I think we should start considering it," she said. "Maybe even talk to someone."

"I really can't consider it right now," I said, with a bit more heat than I had intended. "I have to pick out lighting fixtures, and someone needs to call Dick Cassidy about the drainpipe."

"Of course," she said. "It's overwhelming."

I stood up and went downstairs to let out the dogs.

CHAPTER TEN

1958

How it started was just how anything else starts. Mother and Roe were at Barbara's for lunch, and I was supposed to be watching Betty Sue, only I was watching the window instead, waiting for Charlie. I had let in the dog and was petting him on the couch. It was too cold to leave Nig outside, even though that was the rule. No dogs in the house! Roe said. What did I care? When Roe was at work Mother wouldn't care if Nig so much as pulled up a chair and joined us for dinner.

Winter had come on overnight in a gray burst, kicking up snow and wind to blow against the house. Air made it through cracks, like pieces of glass that scraped at my skin, and the whole world groaned with loneliness. I was cold on account of wearing the skirt, because I had just stole Roe's razor and shaved my legs and I wanted Charlie to see. It was the first time I had did this, and it didn't go very well. I wasn't sure of the bones and the shapes and which way you should move the blade. I cut myself in the kitchen sink, and left the spill of blood on the counter, and the drops on the floor, to show Charlie how it hurt to be beautiful.

Betty Sue waddled out in a sagging diaper. She needed a change, but I did not want any part of it. The more you changed her, the more she'd go on thinking it was just fine to do it wherever she wanted. I went on playing with Nig's ear like I didn't even see her. His head was asleep in my lap. "Who dhat?" she said, hiding her sticky little face behind one hand.

"If you're not going to talk correct," I said, "you can just quit talking altogether."

"Who dhat?"

"You know damn well who I am."

Nig sat up and cocked his head with one ear up and the other down, broke from being shaked too hard, and there was Charlie's red Ford pulling in. He slammed the door and swaggered up in his leather jacket, pausing on the step like he knew himself to be watched. Betty Sue followed me to the door.

"Who dhat?" she said.

"It's me, Charlie," Charlie said.

"She's playing dumb." I took his hand.

"Maybe she's not playing."

I pulled his arm and drug him over to the couch and pushed him down. His leather squeaked. Then I sat beside him. There were water drops on his glasses so I took them off and cleaned them on my shirt and put them back on his squinty little face. A smile creeped up over the edge of his frown. "What?" I said.

"Damn snow on my leather." Charlie brushed his shoulders.

"Why'd you wear it then?" I snuffled my nose in his ear.

"Quit it," he said. "That tickles."

I threw my bare legs up on his lap and leaned my hair back over the arm of the couch and just let it hang there. Betty Sue chased the dog into Mother and Roe's room. Charlie ran his hand up and down my leg. I thought about saving the dog. Charlie's fingers caught at the cut. "What happened?" he said.

"I shaved for you. Blood's all over the kitchen."

"Well, you shouldn't have did that. You had better clean it up," Charlie said. "Put on some pants."

I took my legs off him and crossed my arms over my chest. I blew air out through my cheeks like it was a heavy burden I held to make him happy, getting heavier every minute like a snowball rolling bigger and bigger until it gets so big it could crush a person.

"Don't be sore at me, Caril Ann," Charlie said. He sneaked his arm around my shoulder and put his lips to my neck, and just like that I wasn't sore. My eyes closed for the rush. "There ain't any reason to be sore," Charlie whispered. His voice tickled my skin. "It's not your fault you can't see what's coming. I like your smell."

"*Like*?" I said.

"I *love* your smell."

"What do I smell like?"

"I don't know." He reached my hand over to his pocket. "Feel this," he said. And I pulled out a twenty. I took it between my fingers and stretched it tight and breathed in the green smell.

"Are we going to Vegas?" I said.

"We're going for steak."

"It's the middle of the day."

"You gotta eat sometime."

"Well, I can't bring Betty Sue along, can I? She'll spoil our romantic time."

Charlie made to cover my mouth with the front of his hand. "Come on, chickie, stop your cheeping," but I didn't laugh. I had to eat sometime, but nobody cared about that. Only Charlie cared to do nice things for me. Mother and Roe only told me all I *couldn't* do. And now Charlie and me had to sneak around because Roe went and made not seeing Charlie a rule too. It wasn't fair.

I shrugged away. "I can't leave the baby."

"It ain't *your* baby. Not even your full sister."

I rolled my eyes at him to say I didn't have time for his reasons, but inside, my heart got full for Charlie treating me like a queen.

"All right," Charlie said, standing up and fussing with the collar of his jacket. "I'm just gonna sit and have a steak by my own self and tell the waitress I love her instead of you." He kicked the edge of the rug with the tip of his boot.

"That's not nice," I said. I wanted to kiss him.

"Don't you love me like we talked about?"

I got up and kissed him on the end of his nose. He was sad things weren't turning out like he thought. He could be that way, like a little boy. I wanted to make it better for him. "If you let me drive, I'll love you." I squeezed him tight. It was a game with us, but not so much a game to me. Charlie never would let me drive. He said, for one, I would be a woman in a couple of years and everyone knew they couldn't drive, and for two, I spent too much time goggling at him to ever look at the road. But Charlie didn't laugh now. I could feel his arms squeeze back, and how there was a kind of sadness in the way he held on like I was the last piece of straw in a great gust of wind.

He pulled free and went to the window and got lost in staring at ice on the road. I could tell he was thinking bad thoughts about how the world wasn't any good to him.

"Chuck," I said.

He ran his finger on the crack and looked over his shoulder at me. "It makes me mad how they go and say I can't see you. Who do they think I am, some no-good dumb-ass trash hauler, Caril Ann? I don't gotta listen. And neither do you."

"*I'm* not listening." I put my arms around Charlie's neck and buried my face in the smell of his jacket. "*They* never once took me for a steak," I said into the wrinkle of it. "There's nobody to give me steak but you."

I went and put Betty Sue in her crib. "Be good," I said. "Go to sleep," but she wouldn't quit crying. I fixed her diaper and bounced her around and made her a hat from a piece of newspaper that was laying on the floor half under the bed. I thought it was a nice thing to do and so did Betty Sue. She mashed it in her hand and pushed it down over her eyes and popped her finger in her mouth and stood watching me through the bars of the crib. "Don't say anything," I whispered, and closed the door real soft like I was trying not to wake her up.

I could see Charlie through the window, already outside, sitting up on the hood of his car and waiting for me to come along. He tapped his foot on the fender and hugged himself for the cold. Everything, as far as I could see from the window, was gray and dead. The neighbor's house covered in plastic to keep out the wind, the rusted out icebox, the no-good tire laying out front under a hunk of snow. Charlie's hair was the only brightness I could find and I followed it out, like a glint of light in a dark cave. You have to take good things like lights in the dark and steak when they come your way.

Charlie opened the passenger door for me, but I shrugged up my shoulders like I didn't even see. I walked around to the driver seat and slid myself in behind the wheel.

"We're not going anywhere like that," Charlie said.

"Give me the keys."

"You're fourteen. You ain't allowed to drive."

"So? I'm not allowed to see you either."

"It's different," he said.

"Who do you think I am? Don't you trust me?" I pressed my foot up and down on the pedal.

"You want steak or not?" Charlie looked hard at the ground 'cause he couldn't look at me. "Move over or don't move over."

"I won't," I said, but I slid over anyway 'cause I had already decided to go, and I was hungry, besides. What else was there to do? Charlie could be this way when it came to cars. He was the only one at Capital Race Track who wouldn't bow down. Still, I thought he should bow down to me.

He put his hand on my knee and said he was sorry, and I forgot in the meantime about how he didn't trust me and how in that case it couldn't be love.

CHARLIE SAID HE LIKED HOW THE WAITRESS TREATED HIM RESPECTFUL, NOT even asking him for so much as proof when he ordered a beer despite of sitting across from a baby like me. I brought him down, he said. I made him look fifteen even though he was really nineteen, but I also made him look lucky. What I really wanted to say was *You look young 'cause you're barely pushing five-foot-four*. But I bit my tongue and pretended to smile. I understood all the things that could be said but shouldn't. You should love someone for all that they are, even the weak parts. I was trying my best. I just sat there sipping pop, staring out the window of Hanger's. A lady bundled up good tucked her little girl into the backseat of a car, and across the way black bags stuck over the gas pumps blew in the wind.

There was a light on a chain over our table with a shade made out of dark glass, and it cast Charlie's hair in a glow. I squinted my eyes so his hair was like fire, not the hard kind of fire but the kind that would melt my heart. I ate a steak the size of my head, and the bread kept on coming so I ate that too. "I'm fat up to here," I said, putting my hand to my throat.

"You couldn't ever be," Charlie said. "You're so tiny, that steak would break you clear in two before it made you fat."

I rolled my eyes and ordered a slice of fudge cake with whip cream on top. Charlie got another beer. I closed my eyes for the sweetness of the dessert. I made the whip cream into shapes and a tower. "I could eat this forever until I floated away," I said.

"No, you couldn't." Charlie stared at me like there was a piece of chocolate stuck on the corner of my mouth. "You couldn't die from eating whip cream."

"Who said anything about dying?"

"You said floating." Charlie shrugged like that was answer enough and leaned his head back on the red leather bench. "I wish I had twenties around all the time so I could spend every last one on you." He took a sip of beer and closed his eyes, and when he opened them again he was smiling. "Caril?"

"What?"

"If you wanted something bad enough, I'd spend the night in the gutter for it. I'd do whatever."

"Don't sleep in the gutter, Chuck," I said. "Don't be crazy," and all of a sudden I did not want to ask where he had got this first twenty.

"I'm not crazy," Charlie said. "I love you."

I thought about Betty Sue with her leg stuck half over the crib with trying to climb out, and how she could fall that way and hit her head on the floor, and how everything would be my fault for not watching her right.

I pushed the rest of the cake away. "If you loved me, you'd let me drive your car, but you don't. You don't trust me."

Charlie looked at me like I'd slapped him clear across the face. His cheeks went red. Maybe it was from the beer. Then he reached in his pocket. "I do too love you," he said, and he gave me the keys. "It ain't right to let you drive my wheels, though, so don't tell. Everyone'd call me a pansy."

"You're not a pansy, Chuck. I love you," I said. "I love you more than Frankie Avalon. I love you more than the whole wide world." And I jingled the keys around my finger with a bright silver sound.

I MADE A LEFT TURN OUT OF HANGER'S, AND WENT REAL CAREFUL DOWN O Street, barely poking my foot to the pedal. There were not so very many cars on the road, and no one was coming, so I went straight through a stop sign. It didn't make any sense, but Charlie got mad. "You gotta stop anyhow," he said.

"How come?"

"They'll throw you in jail."

"Who?" I said. "I don't see anyone."

"They come out of wherever and bust you up."

"OK," I said, checking the mirror.

The gas and the brakes and the wheel. That was all there was to it. The metal on metal, and all the simple things you did that made everything come out right on the road. It was a wonder how something so filled up with power could be so easy. I felt the wheel and the way the sounds from the engine jiggled up through my arms and into my jaw and tossed my teeth together like flints. For a minute I did not think to look at Charlie beside me. I was too busy looking at the road. But I could tell he was nervous. There was a string of tenseness and I could feel it twang. I didn't need to look. Soon we left the buildings behind, and I kicked it in and barreled out of town. I rolled down the window so I could feel the wind rip my hair, but it was too cold, so I had to roll it back up, and when I leaned over, the car leaned too. "Watch it!" Charlie said.

"Can we turn down that road where they found the body?"

"What for?" Charlie said, leaning forward to play with the radio. But it was more commercials, so he gave up and shut it off.

"So I could practice driving more."

"There isn't time. I got a mind to do some hunting before your folks come back," Charlie said, and I knew he meant to kill some of the rabbits who lived out in a pile of logs under the cottonwoods.

"Please don't kill the rabbits," I said.

"I'll only get one."

"What if it's married?"

"Rabbits don't get married," Charlie said, and kissed me on the cheek. I pressed my foot to the floor, but a blue truck with one headlight was coming the other way, and I slowed down on account of the road looking tight. The tires squealed over a crust of ice and it all fell out from under me like that half-broke chair in school when my skirt went up and everyone laughed. The truck stopped. The road wheezed and the wheel shook and Charlie was yelling at me not to brake, but I broke anyway, and it was the last choice I ever made.

CHAPTER ELEVEN

1962

I drifted through the still house, already knowing I wouldn't find my mother. The rooms had that deep quiet of something missing. When I went upstairs and opened her bureau, I found the red drawer liner staring up at me. In the dressing room, clothes still hung in neat rows, but they weren't the sorts of things she would ever need. She'd taken her long black coat, so I guessed she planned on going out somewhere nice. Dresses with delicate beading were wrapped in plastic that touched the floor, and shawls embroidered with South American designs remained stacked on the shelf beside handbags I'd never seen her use. I felt so lost when I saw her yellow pillbox hat, just waiting there, left alone on one of the shelves where she'd removed other more essential items. I started pulling things off the shelves. Downstairs, I rummaged through the coat closet, as if by some miracle I could find her hiding there.

When I checked the garage, I found she'd also taken the Studebaker. No one had come for her; she'd left on her own. But that didn't make me feel any better. I stepped into the spot where the car should have been, stared down into a black pool of oil, and clutched my arms around myself to keep out the cold. I could see my breath, and the sharp shape of rakes hanging from the far wall made me feel like crying. Above the row of tools, gray flakes fluttered against the dirty windowpane. I walked out the side door, sat down on one of the elm stumps, and waited for my father to come home from work. We were on our own now.

WHEN I SAW MY FATHER'S CAR TURNING IN, I RACED TO MEET HIM. HE REACHED over and opened the passenger side door, and light flooded the warm interior of the car. "Get out of the cold, just for a minute," he said. "You shouldn't be standing out here."

"She's gone," I said, gripping the edge of the window, eyeing the thin layer of snow over everything. I suddenly realized that my mother had really left. What kind of girl could cause such a thing—a mother who left without a thought or a note or a goodbye?

I went around the front of the car and got in beside my father, as he guided the car down the remaining portion of the drive. I didn't look at his face because I didn't want to see what I knew he had to be feeling. When the snow melted off my hair and trickled down my forehead, I caught the drops with the sleeve of my coat. "All Mother's things are gone," I said. "And her car, Daddy."

"More space for this one," my father said, patting the wheel of the Packard. "No reason for you to kill yourself in the cold." He got out and opened the garage door, his trench coat spreading like a bat wing in the headlights.

I felt like I barely knew him. He never told stories, and most of the time it seemed he only spoke to her. He only looked at her. She was all that mattered. I didn't know what was going to happen now. I was cold and wet. There wasn't a soul in the world I could claim to know well, no one who wouldn't shrug their shoulders and roll their eyes if I just lay down in the snow and gave up. Life wasn't like this for the cobs at school. Only for the Bowman boy whose parents had been killed, and Cora maybe, whose own brother had told me he hated her. Some of us just hadn't turned out right. It didn't seem at all fair.

My father got back in and parked the Packard in the Studebaker's spot. When we filed into the silent kitchen, I started to cry. I didn't even try to hold it back. I told myself it wasn't because of my mother, and yet for years afterward I would be left wondering what I had done to make her go.

"I'm always making everyone cry," my father said. " I'm not sure exactly how I do it. Am I such a terrible man?"

I just couldn't imagine our lives. I didn't think I could fill her shoes.

"I got you one of those hoops," he said. "With pink stripes."

"Where is it?"

"In the trunk."

"You don't understand what I'm trying to tell you," I said. "Mother's things are gone. She left us. I was only trying to let you know."

"Oh, no, Puggy," my father said. "She wouldn't do that." He took off his hat, put it on the table, and started making a drink. "Didn't she tell you? She went to Kansas City to visit a college friend. There's no reason to be upset."

"Who'd she go visit?" I asked.

"What's-her-name. One of those panty-raid girls." He filled his glass with ice. "Somebody-or-other Kimball. She'll be back."

WE SAT IN THE LIVING ROOM WATCHING THE NEWS AND WAITING FOR THE POT to boil. I was trying to make spaghetti as the newscasters told the world about the storm and the two high-wire circus performers who had plummeted to their deaths. Snow was falling heavily all over the Midwest. They were predicting up to a foot in some regions of Nebraska and Kansas. Travel advisories were in effect. It seemed like everything was happening at once.

My father took his feet off the ottoman and set his drink on the end table beside my grandmother's collection of ceramic frogs. He leaned forward, his arms on his knees, as we studied the laced pattern of snowflakes on the television screen decorating our section of the map. "What time did she leave?" He checked his watch.

"I don't know." I wanted to tell him it didn't matter. We had never been enough for her. Why couldn't he see that?

My father stared out at Van Dorn as if the hooded glaze of

streetlights might tell him something. "Well, they didn't mention a storm in Missouri." He sighed.

"But the snowflakes were covering it." I could tell he was worried, and I wanted to show him I was worried too. I took a ruler off the letter desk, opened the French doors, and pressed the ruler into the snow to test how many inches had fallen. When I was a little girl in Chicago, there had been a blizzard the day after my parents' annual New Year's party. Some of the guests who had passed out in the spare rooms or on couches were trapped, and my mother made them mimosas. My father and I had closed ourselves in the library to watch the snow. He had pretended to pull a quarter out of my ear, and I had screamed, thinking everything inside me had turned to silver. "Things could be worse," he'd said. "Some people only produce pennies," which had made me even more upset. I remember his face looking preoccupied as he sat me down and went through how he'd done the trick. Then we put on our boots and ventured outside. We walked through the hushed city streets hand in hand, making guesses about how much new snow was falling. Later my father had plunged a yardstick into the snow.

"Three inches, Daddy," I said, stepping back into the living room and closing the door behind me. "Do you think she's all right?"

"Of course. She's probably already in Kansas City." My father turned off the television and sat back down. "I've been thinking." He drummed his finger on the side of his head. "About getting a new couch. She'd like that, don't you think?"

I shrugged.

"Oh, yes." He slapped his hand across his thigh. "She definitely would." Then he lay down and put one of the old couch cushions over his face and sighed into the crease of it.

Watching him lying there so helpless, I wanted everything back the way it had been. I wanted Lucille to brush my hair and smooth everything over. I wanted some kind of order in our lives like normal people had.

"What are you doing?" I said.

My father didn't answer.

• • •

UPSTAIRS, I OPENED MY BUREAU DRAWER AND UNFOLDED THE TELEPHONE number I'd found in my mother's jewelry box, repeating the digits over and over to myself as if I might lose it on the way to my parents' room. I crept softly inside. Wandering through the dark, I ran my fingers over the bedspread, the base of the lamp, the cool glass surface of my mother's vanity table. I smelled all her glamorous scents. In the mirror, my face glowed pale blue in the snow light.

Moving the telephone off the nightstand, I threaded the cord into my mother's dressing room, turned on the light, and closed the door. Crouching in a plastic curtain of my mother's bagged dresses, I dialed the number, then let it ring for a long time.

"Hello?" he said, finally.

"Hello." My hands were shaking. "Listen. You don't know me, but . . . I'm calling to see if my mother's there."

"Well, that all depends on who your mother is," he said slowly, and laughed as if it was some sort of joke.

"Ann Peyton Hurst."

A pause followed, as if the phone had gone dead. I brushed a bit of plastic off my face and cinched forward on my knees. "Hello?"

"How did you get this number?"

"I found it."

"Who *is* this?"

"This is her daughter. Who's this?"

"Nils Ivers. Maybe you haven't heard of me. Your mother was an Ivers once. For about two months."

"I really need to get in touch with her," I said. "There's a blizzard."

"Well, there isn't any snow *here.* " He paused. "Is she leaving someone else now?"

I didn't say anything.

"Where are *you*?" he said.

I didn't answer for a second. "Lincoln, Nebraska," I said finally. "Where all those murders happened." I hoped that might impress him. I thought of him as a man who might like a story like that.

"Well, you're on the line with LA, sugar. This is a long-distance call."

"That doesn't matter," I said suddenly. "We're rolling in money."

"Sounds nice. How old are you?"

I paused. Fourteen was too young. "Seventeen," I told him.

"I bet you're beautiful."

"Everyone says so." I felt like my mouth was moving without my mind telling it what to say.

"I bet you look just like her."

"I do," I lied. "People can't believe it. We wear the same clothes," I said, eyeing her yellow pillbox hat. It was the strangest feeling, I felt like a puppet with someone else pulling the strings.

"You sound like quite a sparkler. A real Roman candle. Have you ever thought about the movies? I always thought your mother should be in the movies."

"Sometimes," I said. "But I'm more interested in other things."

"Like what?"

"Horses and stuff. Listen, I can't talk anymore. I have to go," I said.

"What's the rush? Is it an emergency? Has she gotten herself into trouble again?"

"What kind of trouble?"

"She hasn't tried to harm herself?"

I felt a new kind of fear creeping in. I no longer knew what to say.

"Don't worry." He tried to reassure me. "I'm sure she hasn't. She knows she's her own best investment."

"I'm tying up the line."

"Ahhh," he said. "I get it. Your boyfriend. He give you his jacket?"

"He told me he'd call," I said. "I have to go."

"Wait," he said quickly. "People thought I didn't love her. They were wrong. I did."

I hung up the phone and leaned my head back against the wall and counted the dresses my mother had left behind. My heart was thumping so hard I thought it might break my chest. Downstairs, the spaghetti pot was boiling over.

• • •

MORE THAN A FOOT OF SNOW FELL DURING THE NIGHT, AND THE FOLLOWING day it kept on coming. Shapes in the garden dulled, then changed, leaving alien imprints on living room walls like the last sigh of a sinking ship. The morning *Star* didn't arrive until evening. On the radio, the voices of Lincoln expressed concern about the roads and announced long lists of canceled or postponed events. Time had stopped as the snow piled up. From the window, it was hard to see the street. The yard was a long white cape that would have looked nice with my mother's hair.

My father worked in his study with the door shut, but I couldn't imagine what he was doing. It didn't seem like anyone could possibly be working. Everything normal had stopped. Putting on my boots, I forced my way down the drive. The snow was almost up to my knees, and it was hard to pick up my feet. I imagined how the elms would have looked, all glistening. The tops of the rhododendrons swelled like bubbles trapped on a frozen surface. When I opened the mailbox, the metal door creaked with cold. Snow tumbled off the top, a tiny avalanche—nothing inside. I watched the lights of a plow round the corner with the steadiness of a tank coming to rescue Lincoln from an invading army. Bring provisions! I imagined the neighbors screaming. No one had a voice. The world wouldn't listen. In my fantasy, everyone had lost someone, and my mother was just one more memory hidden beneath so much snow. Emergency conditions, I told myself. My father was as silent as the hushed winter world.

Stories are easier to imagine in a snowstorm. It doesn't really matter what is true and what isn't when it's just one mind thinking alone. I wrote this down on a pad of paper and read it over and over to myself. It made me feel brilliant. I became so excited by what I'd written that I wanted to tell my father. I waited outside his study door until he finally opened it.

"You startled me!" he said, as I shoved the paper at him without explanation. He held it out at a distance, squinting down at my writing because he wasn't wearing his reading glasses. "'It doesn't really matter . . . what's true and what isn't true,'" my father read slowly, "'when it's just one mind thinking about something alone.'" He seemed to consider this for a moment. Then he nodded and raised his eyebrows. "Where did you get that idea?"

"From my head," I said. Suddenly all kinds of things were going on there. It didn't seem so horrible, the idea of my father and I being trapped here together. I could cook for him, iron his shirts, dance with him when he got lonely. I had taken a dance lesson once.

"I'm impressed, Susan. That's intelligent." He handed the paper back to me. "You've got a point. I don't agree with it, though."

"Why?"

"Because I believe in fact. A fact is a fact. I'm a rational thinker," he said. "Drives your mother crazy."

I hoped he wasn't going to start talking about her. I hoped she wasn't truly crazy, the kind that made you want to hurt yourself. But I didn't think that was possible. She loved herself too much.

We ate what we could find in the cupboards, canned foods collecting dust on the shelves left over from the days when my grandfather had been alive. I tried to take over, make progress, but I found myself imagining stories trapped inside cans for years, denting aluminum with angry little shouts and the need to be heard. When the lids were opened, swollen metal sighed with relief.

I found canned peaches. My father and I ate them with forks right out of the can. "It's funny," he said, between bites. "I was just remembering the time my sister Portia tried to bury herself in the snow and then yelled for someone to come and dig her out. I'd entirely forgotten until now."

"Why did she try to bury herself?" I asked.

"It had to do with a story our mother told us about our grandparents," my father said. "There was a terrible blizzard in McCook. Your great-grandparents, Elsa and Hans, were recently married and had just come from Sweden. They barely knew anyone in Nebraska, and they barely knew each other."

"Why did they get married if they barely knew each other?"

"Oh, I don't know, it was different then. " My father frowned. "Marriage wasn't always about love."

"How about with Elsa and Hans?"

"Not at first. Several feet of snow fell, trapping them inside with no food for days and nothing to keep them warm. My mother always said the snow forced them to endure an entire lifetime in one week. And only then did they fall in love. Mother always said it was love that kept them alive. Neither could bear to watch the other die. So they lived—for a long time, anyway."

"How did they keep each other alive with love?" I wanted to know.

My father shrugged. "Oh, I don't know, it's just a story your grandmother liked to tell in an effort to point out the positive. It was the Depression. Things were hard." He took a bite of peach and frowned. He had told me before about how it had been. Good men who had lost jobs lined up downtown in the hopes of laying their hands on a government shovel. My grandfather had always paid my father to dig out the driveway, but during those difficult years, he hired men, the first three needy strangers who came to the back door looking for any kind of work. "Our friends the Johannsons lost everything," my father said. He leaned his chin on his hand and looked out at the snow. "I think Portia went a little crazy. It had snowed day after day. After I dug her out of the flower bed, she wrote love notes to some boy and scattered them all over the house. I'd find her by the front door staring out the little window, waiting for someone to come rescue her."

"Why did the story make Aunt Portia do all that?" I asked my father.

"I don't know," he said. "Maybe she just wanted to be saved."

"From what?"

"Well, don't we all want that in some way?" my father said.

I wanted to know what it was he wanted to be saved from.

"From humanity, Susan. There's too much brutality and unfairness in the world. People do horrible things to hurt each other."

"Like Starkweather," I said.

"And Hitler. And all the Communists." But we both knew what

we were really talking about. Loving my mother had scratched us raw, and that only made us want to be more tender.

THERE WAS NO SCHOOL THE NEXT DAY. MY FATHER WENT TO WORK, AND I WAS left all alone to wander the house. I took an old album off the bookcase and opened it to a photograph of my father and Aunt Portia standing on either side of the elm tree in the garden. My father looked about my age. His face was smooth without the creases of worrying, and one of his arms looped around the back of the trunk, the hand reaching out to pull my aunt's long auburn braid. My aunt's eyes were piercing. She stared directly at the camera without smiling, unaware of what her brother was about to do. The elm looked tall and stately, as if it could never die, and there was no hint of my father's coming back to the very same house to fill his father's shoes, or that my mother would leave him just before a crippling blizzard in November of 1962. There was no hint of plumpness in Aunt Portia's features, or Uncle Freddy, or the three unremarkable children she would bear him. Portia and Thatcher were names that held the promise of Victorian love affairs. What had they dreamed of in their beds at night?

Out the window the snow had stopped, but the world was still hushed under its spell. It seemed to me like everything would be frozen forever. I put on an Everly Brothers record and my mind wandered through the big blank day, reeling from fantasies involving Portia's mysterious love to those where the Bowmans' son took my face in his hands and kissed my lips in a bedroom where Starkweather and Fugate had made love and murdered, all in the same breath. The boy spoke sweet words to me with the voice of my mother's first husband: *You're a real Roman candle.*

I don't know why I wanted to hear that man's voice again, but I did. It wasn't just that I wanted him to tell me something more about my mother, about the different ways she might try to harm herself. I wanted him to tell me something shocking, something that had more to do with me. I went into the foyer and sat down at the telephone table, dialing the number I had committed to memory.

He answered right away.

"Hello," I said. "It's me again. Susan."

"Well, hello, honey. Find your mother yet?"

"That's why I'm calling."

"That hurts. I thought you'd call because you missed me. Do you?"

"I don't know. Do you miss *her*?" I said.

I could hear him fumbling with something, a pot or a dish. "No." Nils sighed.

"Is that because she's with you?"

"No," he said, chuckling. "You're pretty sharp. But she's not the type to come crawling back, is she?"

"Why are you home in the middle of the day? Don't you work?"

"What are you, a detective? Why are you home from school?"

"It's a snow day."

"Hmmm," he said. "Can your boyfriend make it to come and visit, or are you all alone?"

"He isn't allowed over. It's against my father's rules."

"I bet you break the rules sometimes, though, don't you? Your mother sure did." Nils laughed.

"You mean when she ran away with you?"

"And other times. Never mind. What's he like, your boyfriend?"

"Well, he's very strong. He's faced a lot of tragedy, and that's what I've been trying to help him through."

"How do you do that?"

I paused. "He's tough in front of everyone, but when he's with me he whispers all the things he's secretly scared of. I just let him cry it all out," I said. "Sometimes he cries so much my hair gets wet with his tears."

"What color is your hair?"

"Black."

"Like your mother's?"

"Yes."

"What else do you do with your boyfriend to help him through?"

"We take walks," I said.

"That can't be it," Nils said. "Boys want more than walks. It's why they waste time taking walks to begin with."

I didn't know what to say anymore, so I just sat there with the receiver to my ear, but I couldn't hang up.

"Anybody there?" he said softly, as if he was afraid of waking me. He spoke in that same hushed voice, like he was trying to imagine or remember a particular moment. "Tell me, did he take your virginity, Susan?"

I hung up the phone.

All at once, Nils was right there inside me, seeing the things I saw, feeling what I felt, twisting it all around. He could move through wires and tangle up my heart. There wasn't any space between Los Angeles and Lincoln, Nebraska. Distance and time came together at a broken stoplight, and my mother and I and Nils were all crashing into each other head-on.

The ring of the telephone broke the stillness, and my heart flipped over. It jangled my nerves. It rang and rang: three, four times. I ran to the living room and covered my ears with the couch cushions and mashed my lips up against the arm. Nils could do anything. He had lost my mother's money. He had made her crazy. He had done something horrible to her, something unforgivable; I knew that now. That was why she did the things she did to us.

After the phone stopped ringing, I went up to my parents' bedroom and started in. I emptied out drawers and ran my fingers along the cracks looking for false bottoms containing secret stashes of love letters. I poked my fingers into cold dark holes and pried apart hinges. I took out the insoles in heels and dumped the contents of purses on the dressing room floor. When I found nothing, I sat on my knees staring in amazement at the mess I had made. The room looked burglarized. I left it that way and went downstairs and opened the drawers in the letter desk where my mother kept addresses. I sifted through stacks of postcards from people I had never heard of, but none were from Nils.

A shaft of sunlight spilled into the living room and then disappeared behind a cloud, leaving a shimmer of dust in its wake. And when the telephone rang for the second time, it was a sign. I watched my hand pass over the rotary, my fingers wrap around the receiver.

The cold line tickled my arm. It was the only thing I could feel. "Hello?" I said.

"Susan?"

"Yeah?"

"It's Cora. I forgive you."

THE CAT WAS FROZEN SOLID, STUCK ON ITS HIND LEGS, ITS CLAWS TANGLED IN the mesh of the Lessings' screen door. A layer of snow had fallen over the poor animal's black fur. Beneath a white dome piled high like a Klan hood, the green eyes were glassy, opaque with frost.

Cora and I stood on the back steps, staring at the cat in disbelief. "I thought you'd want to see it," she said, wiping tear streaks off her round cheeks. "He didn't think it was safe to come home until it was too late. You're the first person I called."

"Thanks," I said, sounding more insincere than I had wanted to. I watched my breath float up in the sunlight like a cloud of dust and then returned my eyes to the cat.

"What do I do with him?" Cora said.

"What about your parents?"

"Poppy's away on business. Mummy's working up in the studio. She's in an artistic fugue."

"Is she an artist?"

"Well, Mummy's working in new mediums. She collects feathers and makes sculptures. But it's not that. I don't want to upset her. She's been upset for a while, really." Cora looked down at the cat again and sniffled into her glove. "It's not like I can bury him. I can't even touch him. Toby won't come out of his room. He's put something against the door so I can't get in."

I stole a glance over my shoulder at the Bowmans' house. A light was on in an upstairs window, but I couldn't see anyone inside. I imagined the woman from the garden removing her jewels, sitting down on her knees in the very spot where the bodies had been found, putting her face in her hands. Because of the snow, she couldn't go out. The snow made her remember everything. Her memories were probably spinning so fast now that she couldn't control them. Everything that had happened there was flooding into her mind.

"I'll touch him," I said to Cora, crouching down on my knees and knocking the dome of snow off the cat's head. I had never touched anything dead before. But I wasn't really touching death, I assured myself. There my fingers were, inside a glove, reaching out for snow and ice. "He almost doesn't look real," I said. "It's like wax."

"He's real to me," Cora said. "He's Cinders. He sleeps on my pillow. He was waiting all night in a blizzard for me to let him inside, wondering what he'd done to deserve this. I should have left the door open."

"In a blizzard?" I put my hand on her shoulder because that's what I figured a friend should do. "There wasn't anything you could do. It's your brother's fault for chasing him off."

Her pale eyes narrowed bitterly beneath the edge of a striped knit hat. "I guess," she said.

We decided to build a sepulchre in the snow, where the cat could be kept until the earth softened or Mr. Lessing came back from his business trip with a better idea. It's what people did in the "hinterland," Cora said, when the ground was too frozen for burial. We fashioned a hut out of snow in the back of the garden beside the stand of trees, with a mouth just wide enough for the cat's body.

I told her my great-grandparents were snowed in without food, that they had survived on the plains of Nebraska against impossible odds by keeping each other warm with their love.

"That sounds made up," Cora said, sitting back in the snow to catch her breath. She'd stopped crying. "Nobody can keep each other warm with love. Unless you mean by doing it."

"That's not what I mean," I said. "I think people in love can keep each other alive just by the power of feeling." When I was twelve, I'd snuck downstairs one night and watched my parents dance around the living room in the middle of the night. They had seemed so in love to me then, as if they were holding each other up with love, like they'd crumble without it.

"How do you know?" Cora said.

"I just do." I pretended to concentrate on fortifying a wall, but I could see her looking at me.

"Who is he?" Cora said. "The one you love."

"Nobody you know." A wind sent a fresh storm swirling down from tree limbs. Snowflakes shimmered like crystal in the bright sun, beautiful little pinpricks that made you squint your eyes. I imagined the Bowmans' son watching me from an upstairs window in the neighboring house. I wondered if it was possible to love someone you had never met.

We got up and walked back to the house in our own footprints without speaking a word. Together, Cora and I freed the frozen cat from the mesh screen and carried him back through the tunnel of snow to the sepulchre. Cinders's legs stuck out like branches. The whiskers were stiff and clear, brittle as burnt sugar. One snapped against my coat when I lifted him. I was afraid of where our hands and breath made prints of warmth. In places we had touched, the layer of ice melted away to reveal wet black fur beneath. We reached the edge of the trees and set the cat down in the snow. "Toby should be doing this," Cora said. Her voice was breaking again.

"Don't worry," I assured her. "We'll make him pay." I liked the sound of those words in my mouth. They were powerful, like Dr. No or John Wayne in *The Alamo.*

"You'll help me?"

"Sure," I said. "I'm your friend." I picked up the cat again to prove my point, starting to guide it into the chamber as best I could. After that, I started packing snow into the hole without a second thought.

The sun was sinking low behind the trees, casting emaciated shadow trunks in the snow.

"Since we're friends now, I have to tell you something," Cora said, looking over at me. I waited to hear what she'd say. "I don't have any other friends."

"That's okay. I don't either. And my mother's left us. She thinks my father fired the housekeeper without telling her, but that was only an excuse. She's always wanted to leave. I think she has a secret lover."

Cora gathered a bit of snow off the sepulchre and pressed it to her cheek. When she took her hand away, an angry red splotch stayed behind as if the cold had burned her.

"I'm making a wish," she said. "I wish things were different. I wish I had Cinders. What do you wish?"

"I don't have any wishes." I stared up into the frost-covered branches. "I'm a rational thinker."

"Everyone has wishes." Cora took off her mitten. She leaned forward, and carved CINDERS into the side of the sepulchre.

"I want someone to love me," I admitted finally.

"I thought someone did."

"No. Not really."

"Me too," Cora said. "I want that too."

WHEN I GOT HOME, MY MOTHER'S BELONGINGS WERE STILL SCATTERED EVERYwhere. Her brown coat with the fur collar lay draped over the chair in the foyer, the belt trailing on the rug. Upstairs, I knew, shoes and shirts and wrinkled skirts spilled out of her closet, as if she'd been frantically looking for something when the bomb struck. One high heel teetered at the top of the staircase right where I'd left it. Strange shapes fluttered along the walls in spotty sunlight. Everything looked caught, frozen underwater. I was lost, stuck between worlds, diving for treasure in a sunken ship.

"Hello," I called, to see if anyone was there. "Hello?" The house was silent.

I went into the living room. Sharp light cut through the French doors like a thousand diamonds and, feeling the sudden urge to let in some air, I swung them open. An icy wind tore straight through the garden and into the living room. My mother's note cards blew off the letter desk and circled on a sudden gust before coming to rest on the Oriental rug in the moment of stillness that followed. I shut the doors.

Warm again, I lay down in the scatter of white cards. I could almost see them cramped with words: *Meet me by the elms; I'll be swinging from the branches.* I closed my eyes. I was here. It was just *me,* falling into a half dream with no one to wake me up.

Outside, icicles broke free of gutters, piercing the hedges like sparking arrows. Snow shuddered past the windows in sudden bursts of flour, burying everything. There was no sense of time or place.

Somewhere deep below, the boiler pumped. Knitting needles tapped the radiators, and my grandfather's ghost stared into the night as Hans and Elsa dug through decades of snow. Before long, I saw the pale blue illumination of a beautiful dream.

A terrible blizzard hit McCook, Nebraska, early that first spring. Snow kept on falling for days. Even before kissing like newlyweds were supposed to, Elsa and Hans scurried down the ladder and looked out the window in the hopes that the storm had passed while they'd been asleep. But one day they woke up to find there wasn't any morning. Snow had covered the windows and buried the house almost entirely. In the barn, a calf had died of cold trying to nurse from its mother's frozen udder. An icicle had formed around her tail. But Hans couldn't get to the animals. He and Elsa had nothing left. Their stomachs groaned with hunger. They drank melted snow for water. Hans and Elsa lay in bed under blankets holding each other, but they never slept. They lost track of time, living by the light of candles and lanterns, waiting for the sod roof Hans had just finished to buckle beneath the weight of snow and freeze them on the bed where they lay, clutching each other like two twins foot to forehead in a womb. Each assumed the other to be asleep and thought, I don't want to die beside this stranger. I am completely alone.

When Elsa peeked at her husband through half-closed lids, she saw a face that was blank with sleep and knew Hans was dreaming about her hair. After all, it was the only reason he had married her. And when Hans wrapped his arms around his wife and touched a golden strand with the tip of his finger, he felt like he was touching an impossible emptiness. He had heard somewhere about woman's intuition and wondered how it was that this girl could spend the last moments of her life asleep, never telling him what would happen. It was selfish.

Somewhere in the middle of a day after what seemed like years, a fierce wind shook the house and a piece of the roof fell in. Hans grabbed Elsa's hair in his fist. "What's going to happen?" he screamed.

"Let go!" she cried, and pushed him away. "How should I know? You're the man. You do something."

Hans stared down at the piece of sod. "But what?" he said, reaching out again for the beacon of her hair.

Elsa slapped his hand away and climbed down the ladder to the room below. Sweeping her fingers over surfaces, she opened and closed drawers in the dark until finally she felt the cold metal shears. Anger burned her heart with a fire, and she wasn't chilled or hungry anymore.

"Don't try to go outside or anything," Hans said, coming down the ladder. "You'll only drown in snow."

"That isn't possible," she said, as she lifted her arms above and behind her. "You can't drown in snow. You suffocate." Her nightgown spread out like wings, her golden hair caught for a moment in candlelight. Hans saw how long and beautiful it was, surprised by waves every now and then, like sudden rapids in a river. And then he saw the scissors. "Don't be stupid," he said.

"I'm not. I'm being smart." Elsa held out the curtain of her hair.

Hans tried to imagine what his father would have done. His father had been a sergeant. "I am your husband, Elsa," he said. " I command you not to cut your hair."

Elsa brought the shears to her scalp. Golden hair fell in piles. Hans pushed his chest against her nose. Elbows met jaws, met knees, met teeth. Hans grabbed. Elsa bit. Loose hair caught like corn silk in the corner of mouths. Scissors sliced skin. Hans stepped back and pressed the cut with his thumb. Elsa covered her mouth with her hand, and stared at the hair on the floor between them and the drop of her husband's blood that had fallen. Then Elsa tasted blood in Hans's mouth. The horse bucked, and Hans bit his tongue.

She knew what he'd been wondering. How fast had his father ridden before falling on that field outside Stockholm? Hans's mother claimed he'd gone down fighting, but Hans couldn't quite bring himself to believe. He'd found the box beneath the bed with the uniform, the mustard stain, the holes in the back of the coat where the bullets had gone in. Hans was thinking how no one else's father had fallen in battle. It wasn't fair.

And then Hans, too, fell. Elsa could smell it: the leather, the sweat, the dung, as rocks in the road rose up to meet him. She felt the pebble bury in his scalp and found the jagged white scar with his fingers, only they weren't just his fingers, they were his father's fingers, and they were her fingers.

"Hans," she said. "I'm sorry I cut you."

"You didn't," Hans said.

"I did."

"Really," he said. "I didn't notice." There was a bump in Elsa's nose he had never noticed, and a dimple where the right cheek met the smooth rise of lips, and in the premature crease in her forehead from too much frowning, he found the first boy Elsa had kissed. He'd lured her behind the crates in her parents' storeroom with stories of spiders having babies. But Elsa knew that spiders did not "have" babies. "They're not babies," she'd said, bending down. "They're not even spiders," and then he'd grabbed her. His lips had been like cardboard—Hans could feel them—his spit like the glue Elsa had used to fix the button eyes on her Mookey doll after the dog had bitten them off. Hans could feel that glue and Elsa's disappointment, the frown when the buttons wouldn't stick. "You should have sewn them on," Hans said.

"I suppose." Elsa pressed a rag to his finger to stop the bleeding. Hans liked the smell of her ear. He liked it so much he couldn't let his breath go. He kept breathing in and in until his face turned blue. "Stop," Elsa said quietly. "I'm afraid you'll die."

"What are you most afraid of?"

"You, Hans."

"Don't be."

"What makes you feel most alone?"

"You, Elsa."

"Not anymore, though."

"No. Not anymore."

Elsa touched Hans's jawbone, and Hans ran his fingers through the scruff on Elsa's scalp. The hair was patchy and ragged, but it felt to Hans like a field of wheat. Hans's jaw was smooth in Elsa's hand, like the graceful bones in a wing. Hans traced the outline of ribs beneath Elsa's nightgown. "This one points out in a funny direction," he said.

Elsa found the scar on his scalp. She laughed. "You're losing your hair."

"Come on, Elsa, let me touch it more."

"Hands," Elsa said in English. "I'm going to call you Hands."

Hans and Elsa lay intertwined on the floor like two figures petrified in lava. Their breathing slowed. Crystals formed in the creases of smiles. But soon a pick scraped wood outside as snow fell away, and each felt the other's heart stir.

Hans and Elsa blinked in confusion and covered their eyes to keep out the sudden light. Men stood in the doorway, holding shovels and lanterns, their mouths hanging open like woodpecker holes. Ice had collected in their beards. To Hans and Elsa, it could have been any moment in history. The men could have been Vikings on a frozen shore or explorers discovering a secret cave. It could have been the ice age.

The men put their hands over their hearts and cried for joy. "It's been so hard. So many are dead. But you're alive. You're alive!"

"Oh," Hans said, stretching and yawning, peering at the men through half-closed lids. "I forgot."

"Yes, remember?" Elsa said, rubbing sleep out of her eyes. "We were going to die."

I wanted my great-grandparents' story to be real, just the way I had dreamed it. I vowed to make it real, even if it took me my whole life.

CHAPTER TWELVE

1958

We spun out, turning in circles and circles in front of the truck. Everything went ape from that point on. I saw the rusted-out bumper, and the headlight winking close enough to almost hit. Charlie and me were frozen inside the car as it turned around and around, never stopping until suddenly it did stop, with its nose in a mound of dirt and snow about twenty feet off from the truck. There was an old man behind the wheel I could see, with a plaid hat pulled down, and a mouth that was twisted up on one side like somebody smacked it with a pan. He started up the truck and went by, shaking his head like it was all a nasty trick I had played. I watched the rusted blue disappear into gray. The quiet felt like something shoved down my throat. I gagged because suddenly I was scared things were going to turn out all wrong.

I put my head in Charlie's jacket and started to cry.

"I'll kill him," Charlie said. "Next time I see that truck, I'll follow it and follow it and run it off the road."

"I'm sorry." I sniffled.

"If he ain't dead then, I'll hit him on the head with the goddamn jack."

"I'm sorry I skidded the car."

"Hey." Charlie held me away from him and looked in my face.

"There's no sense crying. It ain't your fault you didn't know any better. That's how come you got me."

"I don't know anything." I sniffled. Then he put his lips on mine and kissed like he never had kissed before, like he was trying to dig out a deeper part of me. His whole body went up against my body. My head pushed into the window, and I traced my fingers over the ridge in his pants.

"I love you," I said.

"I love you so much I can't love anything else. You're the only thing I don't hate."

"Me too."

Charlie went to the trunk and got out the chains. It took more than an hour for us to get out of that ditch. A ghost moon hung somewhere in the clouds. The air got colder, and everything snapped.

ROE'S CAR WAS PULLED IN AND ALL THE LIGHTS WERE ON. IT WAS A GOOD thing there wasn't any doctor's car because it would mean something had happened to Betty Sue. There was nothing to do but face it. I thought I could never be in trouble worse than this, and though Roe had never used the belt before he had reason enough to use it now. Nig was back on the chain and barking at the sound of Charlie's car. "We could turn around," Charlie said.

"Where would we go?" There was nowhere we could go with no money and Charlie back living with his folks on account of quitting the garbage route.

"We could sleep in the car."

"It's cold, Chuck."

"I'll go in with you," Charlie said.

"I can't decide if that's worse or better."

"It can't get any worse," said Charlie. He shut off the car. Roe was out on the porch. I could see his body black in the light of the door and how his shoulders were hunkered, mean and hard against it. I could tell he was already ape. I thought I could see he was holding the belt. Charlie and me got out of the car. Charlie put his arm around my shoulder and helped me walk to the porch. Roe met us halfway. He didn't say a word. He just grabbed Charlie by the back of his leather and drug him toward the car. Charlie dug in his heels, but it wasn't any good. Roe was bigger than him, and stronger maybe. Roe pushed him down. Charlie slipped his cowboy boots on the ice and went falling in the driveway, hitting his head on the side of the car. My heart jumped. "Don't push him."

"Don't come around here ever, you little piss-ant punk, or I'll get the police on you," Roe shouted. "I already told you once you had no warning,"

"I don't care," was all Charlie could say. "I don't care."

Roe pulled me up the steps and slammed the door behind us, and Charlie disappeared in the cold dark night.

There was bright light all around. Nothing looked as I had ever seen it. I could hear Betty Sue off crying, and how Mother was trying to make her stop with the radio Charlie had got me. It was not Betty Sue's to listen to. It sounded very far away, like part of a different life.

"You are in a world of trouble," Roe said. "I tried to do all I could for you, and now I can't do anymore. I give up! You're not mine to sweat over, either. Betty might be dead on account of you putting yourself before anything else. Whose blood is it on the floor?"

"You got it wrong," I said. "I was only gone for a second. She scratched me!"

"Don't you sass me." He started shaking me then by my coat collar. I thought this time Roe might really hit me. He was angry enough to. I'd never seen him this angry. His face went so red it was purple. I slipped out of my coat. Roe was left just holding the hood in his hand like he was stupid, standing there in the middle of the floor. I set off into the kitchen. Mother was sitting at the table, with Betty Sue crying on her knee. She looked up when I came in and shaked her head at me like she'd never seen anything so disgusting as her own daughter wanting her help. She reached over and turned off the radio.

"Betty Sue cut me with the scissors," I said.

"How could you?"

"How could *she*?"

Mother didn't believe a word I said. I could see it in her face.

"Noooooo," Betty Sue cried.

"*Wah, wah, wah!* Shut up, why don't you?" I yelled. I had nothing to lose. I could see my dark blood dried up on the light kitchen floor, the color of rust, like the inside of me had just curled up and fell out.

"Caril!" Mother said. "I had to check Betty all over to see she wasn't hurt!" I stared at the floor.

Roe did not make to touch me anymore. He came into the kitchen and tossed a rag at my head and got to making a sandwich, only he was banging things open and shut and throwing the mustard and ham on the bread like he was throwing pieces of me. I just stood there with the rag in my hand.

"Caril!" Mother said again.

"She can't see that boy," Roe said, like this was a new thing. "And she doesn't mind what I say. I got no idea where she came from."

"I can't look at you. Go to your room!" Mother said.

"I didn't do a thing."

"Go! And stay there till hell gets icy!"

"It ain't her fault." Everyone jumped and we all turned, like we were part of the same thing. There was Charlie taking up the kitchen door.

"Get out!" Roe said.

"Just listen," Charlie said.

"You don't got one thing worth hearing. Now go!"

But Charlie wasn't going anywhere.

Roe picked up the kitchen knife and held it at Charlie, and Charlie lifted the .22 that was hidden behind his leg. "Don't point that thing at me," Roe said.

"It ain't loaded."

Roe came at him with the knife. Charlie's whole face squeezed up, and just like that: a bang. Everything is frozen but moving forward even so. The knife clinks to the floor. There is a hole in Roe's head and his eyes don't see. He just lays by the table, and I do not know what is my blood and what is his anymore because it has gone and sprayed all over like a bucket of paint. There is a funny smell like somebody has gone to the bathroom right there in the kitchen. I feel my own pants to make sure it isn't me, and I look at Charlie to make sure it isn't him. He looks like a deer on a cold wet night, just realizing the road's a road, and he's standing in the middle with a tractor trailer bearing down. I watch his eyes blink open and shut. I want to say, *I still love you,* but just like the deer, the look dies. His chin curls to his chest like he's trying to swallow. His face goes hard, and it never looks back. Mother is screaming and holding Betty Sue against her.

We can put him in the ground, I want to say. But she won't stop screaming.

"Listen here," Charlie says, but nobody's listening. "Listen."

She's making a break for the back door, but her hand can't catch the screen. There are moths on the other side. Moths in winter. She tries again, but there is another bang, and for a second I do not know if it is the screen or the gun. Mother falls half inside the door with her skirt up on top of Betty Sue. Betty is screaming and howling because Mother fell on her, and I am screaming, "Shut up! Shut up, shut up, shut up!" I don't feel anything. I just want no more screaming. I reach down and pull her out from under Mother. There is blood coming out of Mother's mouth and nothing on her face to tell where she has gone. *She has forgot all about everything.* And just like that, I no longer have a mother.

Betty's diaper is off and pee is running down her leg and she's crawling for Charlie, still screaming. There is blood in her little blond curls. I reach over and catch her heel. Her head goes forward. She makes a funny sound. Then Charlie sticks the knife in her neck.

"Don't," I say.

"It's too late," says Charlie.

"Don't."

I went in the living room, turned on the television, and laid down on the couch to watch Ed Sullivan and a new singer I never heard of talk about being a star. I didn't even know it was Sunday. I didn't even know it was P.M. Everything smelled rotten, like cabbage, and for a while the smell seemed stuck inside of me. Charlie came over, took the tip of my boot in his fingers, and shook it gentle back and forth. "You're OK. Want anything?"

"No," I said. "That steak. It wasn't cooked good. It was all red inside." Then everything spinned around, and I leaned over. I threw up right there in front of his feet.

WHEN CHARLIE WAS DONE WITH THE CLEANING, HE LAID DOWN ON THE COUCH with his eyes wide opened and stared at the ceiling. His eyes were wet in the corners. I could see them shining in the light, and I thought maybe he was crying. I went and put on my coat and got the flashlight from under the bed that used to be Roe and Mother's. I had Betty's newspaper hat crammed in my pocket.

"Where are you going?" Charlie said, sitting up with his hair all spiky.

"I'm saying goodbye."

"There's no sense doing that. We're together in this one, Caril Ann. Don't you see how much I trust you? You have to trust me too."

"I'm not going anywhere," I said. "I'm saying goodbye to Mother."

"What for? She can't say anything back."

I let the back door slam behind me and crunched my feet across the yard. There was no light but my flashlight, not a sketch of moon behind the clouds, or one point of a star anywhere I could see. I opened the door to the chicken coop and scrunched myself inside. It still smelled like chickens even though we had never put any chickens in it. I shone the light around, looking for Mother. My breath plumed out in the cold like a tiny ghost.

Charlie had put her up on one of the shelves wrapped in a rug. I unwrapped a corner. I put my hand on her. The skin was cold. It felt nothing like her anymore, but a rock or a stick or a leaf that could just carry away on the wind like it had never been at all. I found her hair and touched it gentle, and then reached my fist around and pulled out a tuft. I could hear the ripping and the silence on the other end of the rip that was death.

I tucked the hair inside Betty's newspaper hat and went back into the night. I ran between the husks of corn that were dead and rattly with cold. My boots banged across the snow. It felt like the earth underneath me went on forever. Frosted air ripped my throat like glass that was shattered. I thrust myself between the trunks of the trees. They looked so thin. Nowhere was there a sound. My flashlight bounced from trunk to trunk until I found the one with the ladder that went up to the tree house Charlie made. I found the rotted place where one of the boards had come free and made a hole in the trunk. I hollowed a little more out with the butt of the flashlight.

In science, a teacher told us how every tree in the Nebraska State Forest was planted by men. Before people knew anything about science they explained the world by legends. Back then she said the cottonwoods were called shiver trees on account of their dancing leaves all chattering in a wind. *Shhhhiiver treees,* the teacher said, like the room was cold. The trees could cure fevers if you knew what to do. It was said that if a woman took a lock of hair or a clipping of nail, put it away inside the bark, let the tree's skin grow over, and walked back careful, with her head down, not talking, after a short time the sickness would vanish like it had never been.

I found the hollow in the bark with my fingers and shoved in the paper and my mother's hair. I climbed up the ladder. I put my cold head back on the cold, cold boards and closed my eyes. I was in the car again, turning on a slip of ice with the old man shaking his fist. Everything creaked. A wind shivered the branches and I shivered with it. The sky cracked with the cold.

I could hear Charlie's feet coming up through the trees. I never was so cold. I turned off the flashlight and laid very still, trying not to make a sound.

"Caril, you up there?" Charlie's voice drifted up from the ground.

I didn't say anything.

"Caril?" His voice cracked.

I took a breath. "Yes, Chuck," I said, real soft, so he might barely make it out. "I'm here."

CHAPTER THIRTEEN

1962

When I woke up, the sky was dark and I was still on the living room floor. I could hear my father's keys in the front door. I sat up suddenly, and looked around at my mother's note cards scattered over the carpet. Books had been yanked from the shelves, exploding haphazardly onto the floor. Upstairs, my parents' room was still in shambles, my mother's clothes ripped from the shelves.

As soon as I saw my father's face, my face fell too. I felt like a big disappointment to him. "Were there any calls?" he wanted to know, setting his briefcase heavily down on the chair by the door. He didn't even say hello. He didn't wipe the snow off his feet. Dark spots of moisture pooled around his galoshes, and he tracked footprints from the door to the coat closet.

Shrugging my shoulders, I stared at my shoes. I kept my distance, leaning back against the banister by the door to the bathroom. But he didn't go into the living room or notice anything out of order. He knew she wasn't coming back now. I saw it sinking in.

"Well, were there?"

"I don't know," I said.

"What do you mean, you don't know?"

"I wasn't here."

"Where were you?"

"At a friend's."

"What friend? You can't just come and go without telling me."

"Daddy," I said, "don't worry. I'm not going anywhere. I'm not like Mother. I'm staying here with you."

My father looked at me like he might just suddenly go to pieces. I shrank back as he passed me, shaking his head on his way into the study. He slammed the door.

It was over with Mother. Why couldn't he see? We had never really been a family. She had never really been a wife or a mother. She was just someone who made other people love her, people who weren't as beautiful or special as she was.

I went into the living room and started straightening the books and stacking the note cards on the letter desk. It was a lost cause, though, and I eventually gave up. Outside, all along Van Dorn Street, snowdrifts were piled high, and I could see the lights in the big old houses where lovely people lived with beautiful things that never left their shelves.

BY THE TIME MY FATHER DISCOVERED MOTHER'S THINGS OUT OF ORDER, I WAS already in bed. He knocked on the door and stuck his head inside before I could answer. The string at the waist of his pajamas wasn't tied right, and I caught a glimpse of the tuft of hair between his legs. I turned away, embarrassed. He was coming apart. Everything was breaking up around us, and wherever Mother was she didn't care. She never wanted me around, and that wasn't just because she hated Nebraska. When we went to department stores in Chicago, I had tried to keep up with her, had wanted to walk with her as she shopped for all the clothes she would ever wear. But she always just left me by the perfume counter, waiting.

"Puggy." My father sighed. "I'm too tired to ask. When I get home from work tomorrow night, I expect your mother's things to be lovingly folded and arranged in their proper order. I want to pretend this never happened."

"Yes, Daddy," I said, and then—barely whispering—"Do you think she left because of me?"

But he had already closed the door.

I couldn't sleep that night. I kept thinking of my father trying to find peace in the middle of all that mess in their room. I uprooted my sheets with my feet and then had to get out of bed and tuck them back in. Moonlight on the snow washed an electric-blue light over the blankets, and every time I tried to shut my eyes my mind would spin with the horrible possibility of living inside these same walls forever, alone with my father, who would always be waiting for my mother. So much of my life had already been spent waiting for one of them to treat me like their daughter, someone they were in charge of. I didn't want to wait for anything anymore.

In the middle of the night, I turned on the light and crept into the dark hallway. This old house never slept; even at night it seemed alive. Old books with leather spines spilled out stories, and the past seemed so close. Downstairs, my grandfather was on his hands and knees picking bits of china frog out of the carpet. Behind the closed door of my parents' bedroom, I imagined my father running his finger up and down the smooth silk of my mother's stocking. I wanted to protect my father. I put my ear to his bedroom door, but everything was quiet.

Downstairs, I pulled the chair up to the telephone table. I had no idea what time it was, but it didn't matter. Nils Ivers was certainly a night owl, the kind who spent his evenings in smoke-filled rooms watching showgirls in feather bodices kicking their legs up. Picking up the telephone, I dialed.

After several rings he answered.

"It's Susan," I began.

"It's very late, isn't it?"

"Well, I have something to tell you."

"Let me guess. You miss me?"

"She's back. I thought you should know."

He paused, and I imagined words caught in his throat. "Well, I was sure I'd never hear from *you* again," he said.

"Why?"

"I thought I'd scared you."

"Nothing scares me."

"I can see that. What are you doing?"

I took a breath. There wasn't a sound. It felt like the whole world was listening. "Reading *Lady Chatterley's Lover,*" I said. "I'm in bed with a cigarette. They're right down the hall."

"That's dangerous. Don't fall asleep." He laughed. "What are they doing?"

"Who?"

"Mother and Father."

"I don't know what they're doing. They're locked in the bedroom," I said.

I decided he was probably trying to picture what might be going on behind my parents' closed door. I hoped he was picturing something intimate. My mother's cheek against my father's chest, my father's fingers tracing the sharp ridges of her feline spine.

"Nils," I said.

"I'm listening."

"They're really in love. She's not going to leave him. She would never—"

"Don't believe your eyes," he interrupted. "Don't believe everything you see. Ann doesn't like getting what she wants. She's crazy. She likes to be stepped on and—"

"Don't say that." I hated him. I wanted him gone. "Don't call here."

"You're the one calling me, sugar."

I hung up the phone and went into the living room, where everything was still, a different world. Nothing looked familiar anymore. I picked up one of the cushions, running my finger along the seam. Unzipping the cover, I reached inside, and pulled out a handful of feathers. I kneaded the silky tendrils, feeling the soft crunch of wheatlike spines. Then I opened my fist and blew. The white cloud of feathers fluttered down around my legs in the dark. I strained my ears to hear the new language of our broken order.

STARKWEATHER'S WORDS WERE BROKEN AND JUMBLED, LIKE EVERYTHING ELSE around me. I sat on the iced-over bleachers by the track, instead of eating lunch the next day, and read an old issue of *Parade* that contained an interview with Starkweather on death row. Kids were always passing it around school.

What made you do it?

Things started out right, and then they went bad.

How did things go bad?

I had the hope of any youngster. Those woods behind our house was a whole world where my brothers and me would play. But then I got picked on the first day of school, when I had to stand up and say what I did in the forest.

And what happened when you stood up in front of the class?

There wasn't any words I could think of to use. Everyone laughed.

And this caused you to go out and kill eleven people?

Well, yup. See, there ain't no point pointing fingers.

Who else would you blame?

Her. She helped.

Caril Ann Fugate?

She gave me a chance. No one ever gave me a chance.

There was a picture of Starkweather behind bars on his prison cot, leaning back against the wall of his cell, running his tongue over his top lip. He looked sure of himself and well put together. He looked like someone who'd been given every chance in the world.

I thought of my mother, crying on the living room couch while I stood there watching in the hard winter light. *No one gives me a chance.* What kind of a chance had she ever given me?

Ever since I could remember, she was trying to push me out of the house: camps, archery, music, none of which I was any good at. "I'm giving you a chance to shine," she'd say. Her last attempt was dancing lessons. She always admired everything graceful.

• • •

MY MOTHER HAD FOUND AN AD IN THE CLASSIFIEDS FOR PRIVATE DANCING instruction with Len Silverman. It was the week after Starkweather's execution. She drove me to my first lesson in the Studebaker Golden Hawk 400, taking the long way past Wyuka Cemetery. People had come from miles away to stare at the freshly turned earth by Starkweather's grave. They paid money for autographs his father had collected. People stared at my mother's car as if she were part of all the excitement. So she had waved and honked, rolling her eyes as we barreled down R Street.

"You're nervous," she said. "Why are you nervous? I can tell you're nervous. You're shredding your nails." My mother grabbed my hand and pulled it away from my mouth. "You're always chewing on something."

When we pulled up along the curb beside Len Silverman's, she told me to go ring the bell. I remember her looking clean and neat, unaffected by the heat.

"You're not coming with me?" I asked.

"Don't be silly. You're a big girl," my mother said. A tall lean man with blond curly hair was suddenly beckoning me forward. My mother waved at Len, blew me a kiss, and drove away.

He closed the door behind me, and the rest of the sunny world slipped away. All the shades in the living room were drawn.

"What's it so dark for?" I said.

"Fred likes it that way." Len steered me toward a bright fish tank bubbling in a corner of the darkened living room. One blue fish drifted in circles around a pink ceramic castle.

"That's Fred Astaire, the Siamese fighting fish. Fred is antisocial. No Ginger Rogers for this guy."

Touching my finger to the clear glass of the tank, I pretended to study Fred carefully, but out of the corner of my eye I could see Len, his face swimming in the shadows of a magnified aquatic plant. Fred's flippers hung limp in the water, swaying softly in an invisible current, like the billowy silk sleeve of Len's electric-blue shirt. When

Len sprinkled some flakes into the tank, the fish drifted effortlessly upward and lipped the surface of the water.

"Well," he said. "Shall we start?"

My heart fluttered as I remembered a story about a little girl with white kid gloves who walked straight into the jaws of a tiger. I felt for the first time as if I were playing a role in something as dramatic as what Starkweather had done. Little girl disappears in the heartland. Last seen dancing her heart out. Irresponsible parent to blame.

As if pulled by a string I followed him out of the darkness, through the bright kitchen, and into the studio. Len put his hands on my shoulders but held me away from him as he tapped one shiny shoe to an imaginary beat. "Come on. Relax," he said. "You're all wound up. Have you ever had dancing lessons before?"

I shook my head. I wanted his hands off me. At the same time, I wanted his hands on me so I could feel even worse. I wanted to give up. I wanted to disappear.

Len looked into my eyes. "It's so important to believe in yourself, honey, not only in dancing but in life." He took one hand off my shoulder and lifted my chin away from my chest. "Head up. That's the first step. You have grace inside of you. Believe in that." Len stepped away from me and started toward the phonograph. Then he came back. "I needed one last look at you." He paused. "I'm used to teaching ladies with their best years behind them. Has anyone ever told you how lovely you are?"

I had never thought of myself as lovely. Len placed the needle on the record. *You don't remember me, but I remember you,* Little Anthony sang mournfully. *T'was not so long ago you broke my heart in two.* He swooped toward me and tried to grab my hand. I pulled it away.

"You're just too beautiful." Len sighed.

I wrinkled my nose at him. I asked, "Where's the bathroom?"

On my way back to the studio, I stopped at the icebox. Half-finished bottles of wine lined the side shelves. I thought of my mother then, of the way she wandered restlessly through rooms as if she didn't care about anything or notice anyone. I thought how strange it was that people loved her, because she seemed not to need them. Perhaps it was that easy to be loved. Perhaps not caring was her secret.

Gingerly lifting a bottle of wine from the side shelf, I pulled out the cork and winced at the popping sound. I listened for trouble, but Little Anthony's voice drifted softly from the studio. I lifted the bottle to my lips and sipped cautiously.

Len was sorting through his record collection. I came up behind him. "Did you find everything OK, Puggy?" he asked.

"I did," I said, giving him a secret look and batting my eyelashes. "Did you know my parents call me Puggy because of my nose?" I wanted him to tell me something nice about my nose. No one ever had.

"Well, you're not so shy after all," said Len. "Want to learn the cha-cha?"

I held my hands behind my back and looked at the floor as Len put on some Latin music and moved his hips. Sidling toward me, he put his hands on my shoulders. I followed Len's lead, stiffly at first. I stomped my feet. I watched the floor. I stepped on his toes but he seemed not to notice. But then I let myself go. I lifted my chin. It wasn't so hard to do whatever he did. Before I knew it, the beat was in my blood. It made sense: cha-cha-cha. I wanted a flower to hold in my teeth. I wanted to spin across our living room carpet while my parents watched, shocked into silence by my sudden transformation.

"You're a natural!" Len cried. "One, two, cha-cha-cha." Len's feet guided me like strings. We cha-cha'd from one end of the studio to the other. One step blended into the next until I was moving my feet to my own separate beat.

"One day I'm going to be watching you on *American Bandstand.*" Len said. "Justine Carelli's history. You'll be dancing with Bob Clayton. I'm sure of it. I can't wait to tell your mother."

"Don't tell her," I whispered. "Don't tell my mother anything."

The needle fumbled over the vinyl. The music started again. I stood on my tiptoes and threw my arms around Len's shoulders. I pressed my lips to his neck.

Len snatched himself away as if I had burned him. He held me at arm's length. He shook his head and looked into my eyes. "Baby, baby," he said, "where are you headed?"

The tears streamed down my cheeks and I couldn't stop them. "When is my mother coming?" I cried.

"Oh, sweetie," Len said sadly. "Your mother doesn't have time to pick you up today. *I'm* driving you home."

In the car, Len patted my knee. He said, "Darling, don't be angry. It's all my fault. I'm not used to working with children." But I didn't feel like a child anymore. I huddled against the door, not saying a word, staring out the windshield through my tears, tracing the painted line on the blinding asphalt until we reached the manicured lawns of the south side.

I got my mother in trouble for all this. When my father came home from work, he found me just sitting there, gazing at the rhododendrons. "What's going on?" He shook me by the shoulders.

"Len left me in the driveway," I said.

"Who's Len?"

I didn't answer.

"Where's Mother?"

He marched me through the garage and into the kitchen.

"Look what I found," he said, as my mother came through the door from the hallway, holding a glass of iced tea in her hand.

I remembered wishing she would drop her glass. I wanted her to burst into tears or throw her arms around me, but she just stood there with her nice new haircut curling around her ears, sipping her iced tea. "Where have you been, Puggy?" She placed her palms behind her and clutched the edge of the counter. She shifted her feet in her clean white pumps. "I was worried," she said. "You were supposed to be back already. Weren't you?" My mother looked at her watch.

"Back from where, Ann? And who's Len?" my father demanded.

"Oh, relax. He had an ad in the paper"—my mother rolled her eyes—"for dancing lessons."

"Where? At his house?" My father crossed his arms.

"Don't take that tone with me, Thatcher!" my mother snapped. "It's not civil." She turned to me. "Why are you crying, baby?"

"I don't feel well," I said.

"Are you sick?"

"I swear to God." My father shook his head. "If you left her with some stranger, Ann, with everything that's happened, I don't know what I'll do."

"Stop preaching!" My mother stomped her foot in her high-heeled shoe. "Oh, Thatcher, listen to yourself. I can't listen to you anymore."

My father turned me around and looked me in the face. "Did this Len touch you, Susan? Did he hug you too tight?"

I wiped my tears away with my sleeve. "No, Daddy," I said. "Why would anyone want to do that?"

That night I woke up with a start to the sound of music drifting under my door, got up, and stepped tentatively into the hall. I started down the soft carpeted stairs, sliding my hand along the banister with a mounting sense of dread. It occurred to me my parents might have killed each other because nobody had woken me up for dinner. My heart flipped over at the thought. Crazier things had happened. My grandfather had died in the living room of a heart attack one April evening as he sat quietly reading the paper. Starkweather and Fugate demanded pancakes from Mrs. Bowman while law enforcement was setting up roadblocks at the other end of the state. In Chicago, eighty-seven little girls died on the top floor of Our Lady of the Angels School while fire truck 85 was mistakenly directed to Our Lady of the Angels Church.

Following the slow gentle sound of the music, I peered around the living room doorway. My mother was wearing her white nightgown and my father was in his pajamas. Their hands were clasped, their bodies intertwined. The song drifted out from the old phonograph. My father was turning my mother around slowly. They passed lightly through the shadows and gracefully circled my grandfather's heavy furniture. My father was looking down at my mother as if he had never seen anything so beautiful. Her cheek was pressed to his shoulder, her eyes closed as if lost in a dream.

I wondered what had awakened my parents, or if they had even gone to sleep. Had they sat up in bed in the middle of the night stricken with love or rocked by the urge to forgive? I couldn't imagine what had happened to make them feel this way. Standing in my bathrobe, I watched from the darkness with my hand on the edge of the foyer wall. Bitter tears stung my eyes because I didn't understand. They had each other, and nothing had ever looked so sweet. Every time my parents fought, I'd remember their dance as some kind of truth. They'd always be together. They'd always find a way through. But I wasn't sure anymore. I really thought it was over.

THE BELL RANG, ANNOUNCING THE END OF LUNCH PERIOD, AND I LEFT THE cold metal bleachers behind and headed for History. I couldn't pay attention to the lesson on westward expansion. All that moving and charting of new territory made me think too much of everything my mother had so easily left behind.

I couldn't go back to our empty house alone with all those memories, so I asked Cora to come along. She said she'd help me clean up my mother's mess of things because we were friends, and friends helped each other out. When we slipped through the front door of my house, I was embarrassed by how old and dark the foyer was, how worn out and tired the carpeting seemed in comparison with the Lessings' shining wood floors. Even the air felt heavier here.

We started with my parents' room, tucking Mother's clothes back into drawers. Cora found her black shoes with the large rhinestones and tried them on. She wrapped a Spanish scarf around her head and pretended to tell my future, which made me laugh. It sounded so hopeful, so full of love. She told me my mother was coming back. For a moment I almost believed her.

When we were straightening up the living room, Cora found a pack of half-finished cigarettes in the side-table drawer. I knew they'd been there for a long time, left over from my grandfather, maybe.

"Have you ever smoked before?" I asked Cora.

"Uh-huh," she said. "My cousin Simone is a rebel. I'm her rebel-in-training. You?"

"No," I said.

"I didn't think so," Cora said. "You don't seem like much of a rebel."

"Well, you're wrong about that," I said, wishing she'd heard me on the phone with Nils. "I'm going out to have a smoke." I'd taken note before of a correlation between slenderness and cigarettes. Audrey Hepburn smoked throughout *Breakfast at Tiffany's*. I couldn't remember her eating a morsel.

Cora followed me out through the French doors into the garden. We traipsed through the snow, sat down on the bench beneath the only elm tree that was still alive, and lit each other's cigarettes. I closed my eyes and held my grandfather's smoke in my mouth, trying to develop a taste for it. Then I let it go and watched the gray cloud float up into the light-blue evening sky.

"I'm broken up about my cat," Cora said. "That's why I'm smoking. It's how people cope with grief." A gray cone of ash fell away from my cigarette and danced on a little wind.

"I'm sorry," I said.

Cora stubbed out her cigarette in the snow and tucked the butt into her coat pocket. I did the same. We sat there for a while in silence, listening to the crisp echo of a neighbor's shovel digging in snow. Cora's cheeks were flushed with cold. I dug a hole around the bench leg with the tip of my boot and thought about Starkweather standing up in front of the class with nothing to say. I didn't want to feel so alone. I wanted to reach out to her.

"I've been talking to my mother's first husband on the phone," I said.

"What for?"

"I'm trying to figure out where she went." But I knew it hadn't been as simple as that.

"I don't think she left for good. She would have taken those sparkly shoes."

"She's crazy," I said. "She's always been crazy."

Cora frowned and kicked the snow with her boot. She burrowed her hands deep in her pockets. "People think Mummy's crazy," she said.

"Why?"

"It's only because they don't know her. She's crazy with guilt, even though it wasn't her fault. She thought for a long time she could have stopped it from happening."

"Stopped what?" I said, trying to hide my eagerness.

Cora rested her neck against the back of the bench and crossed her arms over her chest, staring up into the frost-covered branches. Maybe it was my half confession that made Cora tell me, but I knew it was mostly the snow, because I hadn't earned that story, not yet anyway, and it's quite possible I never did.

Mrs. Bowman had visited Cora's mother on the very day her fate was sealed. It was a week before her death, right around the time that Charles Starkweather lifted his .22 and shot Caril Ann Fugate's stepfather point-blank in the temple.

Mrs. Bowman hadn't been in the habit of calling, Cora explained. Society ladies and artists didn't mix. They had different opinions about the way things should be. For instance, it was strange to the Lessings how the Bowmans sent a fruitcake through the mail every Christmas when they could have easily delivered it themselves. And Mrs. Bowman apparently hadn't liked the wild way the Lessings left their garden. Occasionally, she'd offer polite suggestions over the fence that began with "You know . . ." and once she'd gone so far as to recommend her own gardener. But she meant well, it was obvious to anyone. Though hardly beautiful, she had gracious old-fashioned manners, and her crepe suits were well tailored. On that day, however, Cora thought something about her seemed out of place. It was as if the polish on Mrs. Bowman's smile had worn thin.

"I hope it's not a bad time," she said when she arrived, giving Cora a warm look and handing Mrs. Lessing a tray of muffins. It was, in fact, a bad time. Mrs. Lessing had been in the middle of painting; there was gesso under her fingernails and blue paint on her shoes. But she didn't want to be rude. She welcomed Mrs. Bowman in, took the muffins, and hung her coat in the closet. "Thank you," Mrs. Lessing said.

"Don't thank me, thank the housekeeper." Mrs. Bowman laughed quickly. "I'm a disaster in the kitchen. If it wasn't for Moira, the boys would have left me long ago."

Mrs. Lessing led her into the living room, offered her a seat, and then sat down across from her, with the muffin tray resting awkwardly on her knees. Cora lingered in the doorway, running her stocking foot back and forth across the smooth wood floor.

"I didn't mean to barge in, but it occurred to me how funny it was I'd never paid you a visit in—what, how many years is it now, Corrine?"

"Eleven."

"Has it been that long? I'm a terrible neighbor." Mrs. Bowman looked sadly around the room, taking a long glance at Cora and Toby's old school pictures framed on the wall. "You know, lately everything keeps reminding me of how old I'm getting. Do you ever feel that way?"

"Oh, yes," said Mrs. Lessing. She put the muffin tray on the coffee table.

"Suddenly, I have a teenager. He came home from school for the holidays and I could see the change. He wouldn't talk to me. He was all puffed up like a little man."

"He's away at school?"

"At Choate. In Connecticut. He went back last week. It's just Arthur and me now, and the dog," said Mrs. Bowman. "And Moira, but she can't hear and doesn't speak much, and our house sometimes feels so big and quiet. Some afternoons seem to go on forever with just the sound of the clocks and no one roaring in from school."

"I forgot to offer you something," Cora's mother said.

Mrs. Bowman told her not to bother, she was just happy to talk.

There was something lonely about her neighbor, and Mrs. Lessing found herself sympathizing. She leaned back in her chair, admiring the rings on Mrs. Bowman's fingers. "They're beautiful," she said. Mrs. Bowman handed her one with a large pearl surrounded by diamonds. She tried it on.

Cora came into the room and pried a muffin out of the tray.

"Shall we get you a plate, dear?" Mrs. Bowman said, starting to rise as if she were obligated.

"It's all right," Cora's mother said.

"You're an artist, so tell me," Mrs. Bowman said. "Is the ring *really* beautiful or just gaudy? I've always kind of wondered."

"It has a nice design," said Cora's mother, holding her hand out in front of her.

They started talking about art. Mrs. Bowman was well educated in that department, and in several other departments, it seemed. She supported several musicians in the area and was on the board of the University Museum. She'd always dreamed of being artistic. Mrs. Lessing talked about her own work, her painting of the sandhill crane with one foot raised picking at a mound of dirt, and the landscape of grasslands she particularly liked, with the homesteader cabin.

"Can I see them?" Mrs. Bowman asked.

"I don't show them to anyone," Mrs. Lessing said. "They're not ready to be seen."

"Will something be ready to be seen next week?" she wanted to know. There was going to be an auction to benefit the Historical Society. A painting of the sand hills would be perfect.

Mrs. Lessing agreed to show her neighbor something, Cora said, which was a rarity. So she locked herself in the attic for days, because she felt she didn't have anything good enough. She painted a picture of a turbulent sky, with thunderstorms casting shadows on rolling hills of sand and a flock of geese tossed in the wind. Outside, the world was up in arms. They'd discovered the bodies of Caril Ann's family and an old farmer outside Lincoln, but Cora remembered her mother paid little attention. She just kept on working.

The week went by and the painting was done, and Mrs. Lessing made tea, and sat waiting in the living room for Mrs. Bowman to arrive. Around this time, law enforcement unearthed the bodies of two missing teenagers from a storm cellar near Bennet.

Cora's mother kept walking out onto the porch and looking over at the Bowmans' house. It seemed to be sleeping peacefully, still as glass behind drawn shades. Perhaps Mrs. Bowman had forgotten.

Finally she got up the courage to call. Mrs. Bowman answered and said that, yes, in fact, she *had* forgotten. But she wasn't feeling well. A headache, actually, but she'd stop by another time. She *did* sound strained, or perhaps just busy, like she didn't have the time. The more Cora's mother thought about it, the more annoyed she got. After all that work. . . .

When they found the bodies, Cora's mother tried to pull out her hair. *I'm sorry, I won't be able to make it. Another time,* she scribbled in white across the thunderous sky she'd painted for Jeanette Bowman. "How could you have known from those words? Be reasonable," Mr. Lessing pleaded at night behind the closed bedroom door. "Please listen."

But why, that particular time, on that particular day? I should have known something was wrong. Mrs. Lessing stopped painting. She hadn't painted since. She collected feathers, made halos and wings, and sat in the attic room that Cora's father had made into a studio, staring out at the snow. Cora said it was like her mother had gone away too. She didn't know if she'd ever come back.

I stared up at the sky, not knowing what to say. The blue went on and on forever. Starkweather's trail kept getting wider. I could see how Mrs. Lessing felt. I knew what it was like to feel responsible for something that couldn't be changed.

It's OK, I know the story, I'd say to the Bowman boy, taking his hand in mine and looking into his eyes.

"Cora," I said. "I'm so sorry." I squeezed her mitten-clad hand.

"It's OK," she said, and smiled. Small points of color rose on her cheeks. I leaned my head on her shoulder, trying to replace one touch with another.

CHAPTER FOURTEEN

1991

I pulled into our driveway in Port Saugus and parked the car around the side of the house so no one would think to drop by and ask where we'd been. Nothing looked the same. The weeds had grown up high around the porch, and the roof had gone green with lichen. Gray shingles littered the ground around the converted barn, and a thick fog was coming up from the river, erasing everything with it. I left the cardboard box on the porch and made my way through the wet grass to the oak tree where our beagles were buried, the little tags we'd left around their necks far beneath a blanket of yellowed leaves, their skeletons choked by hungry roots. I peered around the side of the barn, looking for any trace of our artist neighbor Jane, who was always good for an argument over a glass of bourbon. But her house had been painted a strange purplish color, and the Fiat wasn't in the driveway. In the past, Jane had been closer to Susan, but I always looked forward to seeing her. Judging from the paint job, however, I assumed she'd picked up quietly and moved on. I was almost relieved. I didn't want to think of her watching the house lights go on or imagining all the reasons why I might be here alone.

I hadn't planned on setting foot in the converted barn. Over the years I'd grown to hate it even more than I had once loved it. It had become a sort of dumping ground for all the things Susan and I couldn't find a place for. But it looked to me like the roof had been damaged: a large branch had been ripped off the tallest maple, perhaps in one of August's more violent electrical storms. Apparently Dick Cassidy, whom we paid to look in on the place, hadn't been doing his job.

Reaching under the planter near the front of the barn, I got the key out and opened the door. Everything smelled damp and neglected. The fallen branch had made a large hole in the roof, and rain had collected at the foot of the ladder. I could hear the slow music of drops spilling from the hayloft to the floor, but furniture from the old house in Lincoln was hard to make out in the flat light. I stepped between the rows, blundering through screens of invisible cobwebs, and ran my hands over the dropcloths and plastic covers, feeling for moisture. Everything was still dry, though coated in a thick layer of dust.

My mother would not have been pleased to see her treasures so neglected, but there were just too many to sort through. Carefully selecting furniture had been one of her favorite pastimes. She knew people who combed estate auctions and phoned her when they found just the right thing. When she couldn't make it herself, my mother would enter her bid and spend all day waiting by the telephone eating petits fours with a startled look on her face. I had thought it laughable, even strange, until I'd offered my first bid at auction many years later and found myself remembering these little things; the way she'd sigh, study her sleeves, or straighten seams when something special, something she'd really wanted, had slipped through her hands.

Locating my toolbox, I pulled a sheet of plastic off a bookshelf and awkwardly climbed the ladder to the hayloft, as the quick shape of a swallow darted between the broken boards. I stood there on the wet floor of the loft, examining the damage. It wasn't so bad. Once I'd cleared away some of the brittle branches, the hole would be easy enough to fix: I'd cover it temporarily with plastic and make arrangements to get it repaired the next day. Simple enough. But no chore is ever as simple as it seems. Sawing off the last difficult branches, I found a bird's nest balancing on the rafter, the skeletons of four baby barn swallows nestled in the bottom, like prehistoric fossils my father and I had once found in the surface of a rock so many years ago on the Box Butte plain.

I stared at the few remaining feathers clinging to the inside of the mud nest like the last leaves on a branch, wondering what the plight of these helpless creatures had been. Disease, starvation, neglect? It was impossible to tell. I couldn't bring myself to disturb the little tomb, so I stretched the tarp quickly over the hole in the roof and nailed it in place. I had just turned to go when something thudded against the plastic, leaving a spray of feathers in its wake.

Once, twice, three more times, this bird tried to break through before stunning herself or finally giving up. I touched a small puncture left by her impact and thought about my wife's persistence. She had tried so many times to guide us toward a normal life where everything was out on the table. Susan seemed to have grown into someone more self-possessed than I had—and more driven. She spent hours and hours going over the children's homework, monitoring their progress, encouraging them in every way possible. Night after night she had sat with Hank at the dining room table, correcting his college admissions essays. Soon it would be Mary's turn; Susan had bought her all the latest college guides and test preparation booklets, which still sat in a pile by the door to her room. Mary's lack of interest never seemed to discourage Susan. She had always been determined to give them everything a mother could provide.

I thought about how devastating it would be for her if I never came back. Early in our marriage she mooned constantly over an old Sam Cooke song she used to love: *My baby done gone away and left me.* She sang it over and over, secure in the knowledge that I never would go. Standing there in the gloom surrounded by all my mother's furniture, I felt so guilty about what I was thinking of doing that I almost decided to drive back. Yet stepping out onto the lawn, and looking up at the old tired house, with all that flaking paint, I thought about the starts Susan and I had made over the years and how each one had seemed more like an end.

. . .

IT HAD BEEN A LITTLE MORE THAN A YEAR SINCE WE'D COME HERE to PORT Saugus, bumping around in the tight halls trying to avoid each other. The children had sat outside on the cement wall overlooking the river, their heads hanging like prisoners. When it got dark, they drove us out of rooms by turning up the radio so loud I couldn't think. Susan filled her time with walks along the river and trips to the library, while I attempted to caulk windows or visit stoneyards and antiques shops. I hadn't actually wanted to be there: We'd scheduled the trip around the arrival of a truck bearing my parents' furniture, which my uncle had returned to me after the death of his wife, Clara, my mother's sister. I just wanted to sell everything, but Susan insisted on going through it together, deciding what to keep out and what to store away. She wanted things kept in good condition for the children. "Think of what it will mean to them someday," she kept repeating, though they didn't know my parents, or have any connection to that past. On the day the shipment arrived, I was off seeing a client who kept a house in the Catskills. When I came home in the early evening, Susan was frustrated but trying not to show it. My timing, in her eyes, was too impeccable.

"I could have used your *input,*" she said, dicing a garlic clove with an unnecessary amount of vigor. The kitchen was unbearably hot, and I wiped my brow on my sleeve. I had postponed my trip to the client's twice in an effort to accommodate her. But I tried to keep the peace.

"Ah," I said. "A lot of stuff?"

"A fair amount."

"I'm sorry I wasn't here to help."

"I picked out some nice pieces and had the boys put them in the living room. The rest they left in a horrible jumble in the barn." I followed her down the hall and into the living room with a knot of dread in my stomach.

By the window, I recognized the armchair embroidered with bees that had once been my father's favorite. There was also a mahogany side table, and my mother's grand piano, which now dominated the entire living room. I turned my back on everything and took a deep breath, trying to collect myself. I could still see my mother sitting on that bench, her fingers fumbling over the keys as she desperately tried to turn sound into music. She had always failed.

"That's my mother's piano," I said.

"Did she play?"

I didn't answer because I couldn't actually remember if she'd ever completed a song.

Susan came up and hugged me from behind, but I just stood there with my arms at my sides. "I know it doesn't look quite right here," she said, stepping away and tracing her finger over the smooth black lid of the piano.

"Then what possessed you to put it in the house? None of us even play and the kids have no interest now."

"It's a beautiful piano."

"We have no use for a piano," I said, aware of how stiff and ungrateful I sounded, "no matter how beautiful."

She sighed and closed her eyes, trying to gather patience, then opened them slowly and said, "All right, we'll get rid of it. We'll use the money for the college fund."

But it was the last week of our vacation, and I just didn't want any more chores or responsibilities. I spent time making notes in the kitchen about what needed to be done when I returned to the gallery. I rarely went into the living room, but whenever I did, I noticed the children stepping around the piano carefully. No one had dared open the lid, and I had a feeling that conversations had occurred to which I had not been privy. My life had been filled with a certain amount of this—things that couldn't be said around me.

All that month it was hot. Susan and I slept with a fan in the window to pull cool air in off the river, but that last night it was so sticky I couldn't sleep. I poured myself a bourbon and slipped out the back door, letting the screen close softly, hoping the river might offer a bit of breeze. It was a brilliant evening. Stars littered the sky like the lights of some vast distant city, and for a moment I felt at peace with all things. I remembered mounting the steps of the Acropolis in graduate school, and the relief I had experienced gazing up at the Parthenon for the first time, at that perfect ancient symmetry. The chaos and smog of Athens had disappeared beneath me. The rightness of the building silenced my head, as the sound of the river did that night.

Inside the house, though, I could hear the children whispering in the dark.

"Do you think he sat in that chair?" Hank said.

"Who?"

"Him. Starkweather."

"I don't know," Mary said. "It gives me this funny feeling, like I'm about to cry when I think about it. But it's like I'm proud, too, of this horrible thing that happened, and I hate myself when I tell people about it, like I think it makes me special."

A breeze moved through the leaves, and Hank murmured something I couldn't make out. I heard the swirl of water down by the riverbank.

"I've done that too," Hank said. "I've told people."

"Not like I did. He hates me."

"Dad doesn't hate you," Hank said. "He doesn't think like that."

"How do *you* know how he thinks?"

Perhaps it was the bourbon, I don't know, but suddenly I saw it all so clearly. How could they expect to understand what I couldn't understand myself? I wanted to hold my children, put their heads against my chest the way I never had been able to, comfort them as so many other more competent fathers would have done. But I couldn't just walk in there and start talking about what had happened to their grandparents. To me, it had always felt like something to be ashamed of. I knew it had changed me, and yet I couldn't remember who I'd been before.

When they were younger and the time had come for me to speak about the past, I hadn't been prepared. After school one day, Hank wanted to know where my parents were. They had been writing letters in class, and several children had written to their grandparents. "What about Grandpa Bowman," I asked. "Did you write to him?" I don't know why I asked. The words had come out of nowhere. Hank, of course, had never known him and seemed mystified by my question. Grandpa Bowman, of course, was long dead and buried.

"Where is he?" Hank wanted to know.

I explained to him that all living things die, sometimes without warning. I didn't get into it any more than that.

"Was it snowing when they died?" he asked.

How could he have known? "Yes," I said. "It was so quiet and cold."

CHAPTER FIFTEEN

1962

For two weeks following the blizzard, the temperatures stayed frigid. Cora and I were ice queens, and beneath the white blanket that stretched over Lincoln everything was silent. People had drawn inward and no one was watching; we could become whoever we wanted to be. My mother had left behind some sweaters that still smelled of her perfume, so I started to wear them. I was not eating much and could fit two fingers between my red plaid skirt and my waist. Cora gathered her hair in a careful braid, tying a colorful ribbon around the end. Instead of going to Van Dorn Pharmacy after school for treats, we hid in places where no one could find us and smoked the rest of my grandfather's cigarettes. Pleased by our secret rebellion, we watched our smoke curl up into the huge white sky and examined the frozen world: the ice-coated branches that looked like bird talons, the huge snowdrifts sculpted by wind.

Marching across untouched surfaces behind the country club, we pierced the sparkling crust with our high winter boots, knowing it wouldn't always be this way. Things were going to have to change. This was a strange, hushed interlude, and when we separated outside Cora's gate just before dusk, I'd linger for a moment, watching her walk up the porch steps, hoping to be asked inside. I didn't want to go home to my father, who kept pretending that everything was fine. But Cora had homework and she was driven about it. She was already planning her class schedule at Radcliffe, while all I could think of was the Bowmans' son alone in that house and Mrs. Lessing, her ruined paintings and her troubled heart.

I TOLD CORA I WANTED TO VISIT MY GRANDFATHER'S GRAVE TO REMEMBER him better, but even then I knew that wasn't the only reason why I wanted to go to Wyuka Cemetery. I'd been to my grandfather's grave twice, and I remembered that it was by a tree not so far from the R Street entrance where Starkweather was buried. My parents and I had gone once after the funeral to visit my grandfather, only my mother hadn't been very interested. She'd stood for a moment by the grave and then told us she was going off for a walk. When she came back fifteen minutes later, her eyes bitten by frost, my father had asked whom she'd visited.

She'd looked away and kicked at the gravel with a high-heeled shoe. Her hair was tied up, swinging like a girl's, but her expression was careful. "I wanted to see Starkweather," she said finally.

My father had dropped his arms at his sides. "Why in God's good name?"

She had sort of laughed then and thrust her hands in her pocket. "Maybe I don't believe in the same God you do."

"What's that supposed to mean?"

"Whatever it is I believe in doesn't mind my trying to understand. It doesn't take note."

"There's nothing about it to understand," my father had said.

"The people who wanted to put that Fugate girl to death didn't try to understand."

"And why should they?"

"She was *fourteen,* Thatcher."

My father shook his head.

"You've got your way of going about things," Mother had said, "and I've got mine." She'd pulled the collar of her red spring coat close around her neck and trailed behind us on the way back to the car, as if she wasn't really sure she wanted to come along. I'd wanted to stay back and walk beside her and talk more about Caril Ann Fugate. I would have asked her why she thought the girl went along for the ride and whether or not it had anything to do with love. I'd felt such a part of my mother then; we shared a need to understand something. But I kept up with my father's brusque angry strides as if what she'd said hadn't interested me. I remembered how afraid I was to look behind me and find she'd disappeared.

My mother had seemed to know herself then, and when Cora and I stood by the front gate to the cemetery, I couldn't help thinking I was somehow closer to understanding why she had left. We bought a little holiday wreath at the chapel near the O Street entrance and started up the plowed lane past the Home of the Friendless, where people without families were laid to rest. I wondered if my mother would end up in one of those places or if I would. You never could tell. We made our way, stumbling between the stones, toward two tall pines twisting in the wind, but my grandfather wasn't where I thought he'd be, and we got all turned around. "Why are we here if you don't know what you're looking for?" Cora said finally, throwing up her hands in exasperation. "Why didn't you ask for a map?"

"It's around here somewhere," I said, trying to sound certain. "It's by those two trees. I know it."

"Maybe it's covered up in snow," she said. I tried to remember which direction my mother had gone when she'd left my father and me to visit Starkweather.

"No, it's big and white. There's an angel on it. My grandmother's there. My father will be, and my mother's supposed to be too. Maybe that's why she left. She didn't want to die here. With all of us."

Cora sort of laughed. "She wanted to be buried somewhere else?"

I hadn't meant it to be funny but I laughed anyway, though it didn't seem right to be laughing in a cemetery. We searched for a little bit longer, staring down at cold stone names imagining who those people had been, how they had died. We found a tiny baby named Rose and a ten-year-old named Matthew Macalaster who had died in 1933.

We were about to give up on my grandfather when a man in a heavy coat came tramping toward us, breaking a trail between the trees. He looked up as he passed and met my eyes for a moment, nodding his head in acknowledgment. There was something familiar about that face, its strong jaw, the orange hair. He could have been eighteen or thirty-five; it was impossible to tell. I smiled and stared down at my hands. He stopped not far from where we stood and got down on his knees beside a large granite tombstone. He took off his glove, brushed it over the inscription, and placed two sprigs of holly in the snow. He hesitated before rising. Perhaps he was praying. Then he got to his feet and started off toward the R Street entrance.

After he'd disappeared out of sight, I went forward toward the headstone, hoping for some hint.

"Where are you going?" Cora said, following behind me.

"It could be my grandfather," I said, even though I knew that wasn't possible. I knelt down in the snow and tried to read the names on the large stone, but I couldn't make them out. We had to dig a bit. We had to brush more ice away and scratch with our fingers: ARTHUR BOWMAN, JEANETTE BOWMAN, REST IN PEACE. Of course their birth dates were different. He was four years older. But the date of death, January 28, 1958, was the same. Here they were, buried beside each other, those people I had thought about so many times, their bones becoming this very earth upon which I stood.

I closed my eyes for a moment. There wasn't any blood or breath inside me. I took off my glove and ran my fingers along the names, feeling my purpose, my connection grow. The lines in those names were so rigid and cold. I wanted to give them life. Tears were gathering in the corners of my eyes.

"Did you know they were here?" Cora said. I'd almost forgotten about her.

I shook my head. "Did *you*?"

"No," she said. "I wonder if my mother does."

"Was he their son?" I said, touching a sprig of holly the man had left, feeling a point prick my skin, hoping I would shed a little drop of blood.

"Who?"

"That guy."

"Lowell?"

"Yes. Lowell." *Lowell Bowman.* I said his name over and over to myself.

"That wasn't Lowell," Cora said, getting to her feet.

"But he looked sort of familiar." I tried to hide my disappointment. I wanted to stay by that grave for a while.

And then something dawned on me. That strong jaw, the orange hair. They had called Starkweather "Little Red." I could hear his brother speaking on the radio like it was yesterday. A chill rattled my spine.

I propped my grandfather's wreath beside the holly and stood up. "Where's Starkweather buried?" I said.

"Why do you want to know?"

"Don't question me."

"Why can't I question you?"

I didn't have an answer. I just took off toward the R Street entrance with Cora at my heels. It wasn't long before we stumbled upon it. Someone had dug out that flat rectangle from the snow. We could read the words. They were simply carved: CHARLES STARKWEATHER and the dates of his birth and execution, and REST IN PEACE. Not so different really from any other gravestone. There were fresh footprints leading up to the grave and a sprig of holly, just as I'd suspected. I thought of Starkweather's proud look in the newspaper clipping. He'd had four brothers, but I had never wondered about how it must have felt to share the bones, the hair, the same blood of a person who caused such terrible pain. I wanted to chase down the brother who had left the holly and ask him why he thought Charlie's life had gone so terribly wrong.

WE WALKED HOME IN SILENCE AS THE SUNLIGHT DIMMED. AS WE NEARED Cora's house, a black car pulled into the Bowmans' driveway, spinning for a moment on the ice before disappearing behind the house. I wasn't able to make out the driver. "See you tomorrow," Cora said, catching me watching.

I put my hand on the iron fence in an effort to keep her from leaving. The wind tinkled the frozen branches of the elm tree and lifted our hair. "What if someone follows me home?" I said. I didn't need to explain any further than that. I knew we were both thinking about Starkweather.

Cora shrugged. "You can come inside," she said, and it was easy to follow her. Maybe she understood that I was lonesome. It was something I should have given her credit for. You should never betray the people who actually try to understand.

Cora and I shed our boots on a square of newspaper by the door, skating in our stocking feet down the hall, through the living room, and into the kitchen. Mrs. Lessing was standing at the sink, but she didn't seem to be doing anything. She was just staring out the window. Her gray hair was tied in a bun. Her dress had little flowers. Even from behind I could tell she was nothing like I'd imagined her to be. She was small and hunched over, insignificant and ordinary against the backdrop of the bright white kitchen. We lingered in the doorway for a moment. Perhaps Cora was afraid to disturb her. "Mummy," she said finally. Mrs. Lessing jumped and turned around, her hand at her throat.

"I'm sorry to disturb you," I said.

"I don't know what came over me. I just floated off somewhere," Mrs. Lessing said.

"This is Susan Hurst. She helped me with Cinders."

"Of course." Mrs. Lessing wiped her hands on her apron. "Thank you. We've been so sad. We loved Cinders." A bit of soapsuds clung to her collarbone. I wanted to brush it away. Mrs. Lessing asked if she could make us anything.

"You don't need to go to any trouble," I said. I didn't feel I could possibly eat.

"Yes, you do," Cora said. "We're having Fluff." She went to the icebox and took out the jar, and Mrs. Lessing popped two pieces of Wonder Bread in the toaster. I wasn't allowed to eat Wonder Bread at home. My parents didn't even know what Marshmallow Fluff was.

"Can I help with anything?" I said.

"You're the guest," Mrs. Lessing said, shaking her head. She took two plates out of the cupboard and got out a knife. I noticed how long and pale her hands were, like the translucent pearly stones I had once found on the shore of Lake Michigan. The toast popped, and she cut it into halves. The kitchen smelled warm and sweet, like things mothers were supposed to make.

Mrs. Lessing frowned. When she opened her mouth to speak, the words seemed caught. "It's so terrible to think of Cinders clawing at the door all night. We just wanted to make a nice home for him," she said finally.

The bow on her apron was coming untied. I wanted to fix it. "You didn't *know,* Mrs. Lessing," I said. "It wasn't anyone's fault."

"I'm not so sure," she said.

Cora gave me a hard look and pinched my arm. I followed her through the living room and into the sunroom, where silk flowers sat on top of a bookshelf that held a stack of board games in bright boxes. Stuffed ducks and decoys swam in a phalanx across the painted wood floor. White feathers floated like dust in the fading light, as if the snow had somehow found its way inside. One wall was almost entirely made out of windows that looked out on the side garden and, beyond it, the Bowmans' house, all those rooms just out of reach. I tried to notice other things.

"Why did you pinch me?" I said.

"You're a bull in a china shop." Cora set the jar of Fluff and the toast down on a glass table and pulled out a chair.

"I didn't mean to be. I was just trying to make her feel better," I said.

"Nothing can make her feel better."

I pictured Mrs. Lessing sitting in a wheelchair by an alpine lake, holding her face up to the sun and sighing deeply. Had she stood at the windows in the sunroom looking out at the Bowmans' house on the day Mrs. Bowman failed to show up? Had she wondered about all those drawn shades?

We sat down at the table and painted our toast with thick white marshmallow. "Where's your brother?" I said.

"Hiding in his room," Cora said, between mouthfuls. "I told him that cat's going to follow him around trying to scratch his eyes out until it gets a proper burial."

"You know that's not true," I said, taking a bite of toast smothered in Fluff. It was so good, so nice to eat something someone had made correctly. I thought of Lucille, who had always made everything so perfectly.

Cora shrugged. "You never know. It might be true."

"If that's true, the souls of murdered people must wander around all the time," I said. I could see the Bowmans' house from where I sat, still and white beneath a thick blanket of snow not so different from their headstones. I imagined Starkweather and his victims coming across each other on dark cold nights in the cemetery. Those graves had been so close. It didn't seem right.

"Not if they had a proper burial."

"What about Starkweather?"

She paused with a piece of toast in her hand. "He had a proper burial." She looked down at it and took a bite. "Too proper."

"What were you doing when it happened?" I said.

"When what happened?"

"The murders."

Cora shrugged. "I can't remember."

"You must remember."

"No, Susan, I don't. We don't want to remember."

"So you just forget?"

"If it wasn't for Mummy, it might never have happened."

"You mean, if she'd stopped it from happening?"

"No. I mean it would be easier to forget."

"But it *did* happen. They're your memories too. There must have been reporters asking questions."

"Nobody asked me anything."

"Who lives there now with Lowell?" I asked.

"Mrs. Bowman's sister Clara and her husband. The Pritchards."

"Do you like them?"

"I don't know. I don't really think about them."

Why didn't she want to share this? I was so frustrated. I tried to hide it by thinking about other things. "Remember when I told you I called my mother's ex-husband to find out where he was?" I said.

She nodded.

"Well, I think he's in love with me. He thinks I'm just like my mother."

"Are you?"

I shook my head.

"Then why do you think he's in love with you?" Cora put her elbows on the table and leaned her face on her hands.

"I don't just think it, I know it," I said. "Sometimes I feel like I know people I've never met."

"Sometimes I just know things too," Cora said. "Sometimes I know what people are thinking."

"What am I thinking?"

She narrowed her eyes and bit her lip like she was about to accuse me of something. "You're thinking about the murders."

"I'm not," I lied.

"Then what?" she said, shooting me a suspicious look.

"I'm thinking how lost my father is without my mother," I said.

"Are *you* lost too?"

"No. I know which way I'm going," I said, which sounded false, like something from a movie. We sat in silence. I wanted someone to speak, but I couldn't think of anything to say. Outside, it looked like more snow was on the way and I wondered where I belonged. I wondered if the Bowmans' son was somewhere inside his house, thinking about where *he* belonged, too.

I stared out the window at the bleached world shivering beneath the pale blue sky. A white winter bird picked grains out of a feeder.

"Do you think you'd ever let a man take everything he wanted?" Cora said after a time. "Like the man on the telephone?"

I thought of Nils taking my body, crushing me in his arms. But if someone like Lowell wanted to do it with me, I thought I might after a long time—if it would help him. I remembered the slippery electric-blue silk of the dancing teacher's shirt against my cheek, the feeling inside me when we danced, and then when Len pushed me away. If I was ever going to be kissed, I'd have to wait for it to happen. "No, I never would," I said.

"Do you think anyone would ever want to with me?" She searched me with desperate eyes, wanting me to tell her things would be all right.

"Of course," I said, quickly, but I didn't really know.

The sky faded, and stars emerged. A light went on in the Bowmans' living room. Cora looked at me and raised one eyebrow. What seemed like no more than a game to her was something so real to me. We crept closer and pressed our noses to the cold glass. The Bowmans' windows were large, and you could see everything: couches, side tables, tall antique lamps. There must have been paintings and mirrors I couldn't make out. But I could see other things, right into the past. The articles had said Mrs. Bowman had been forced to make pancakes for the murderers while they cut out newspaper clippings of themselves, as if they wanted to keep a record of their terrible crimes for a scrapbook. Had they sat on that couch or in those chairs? Caril Ann had eaten a box of chocolates. If she'd dropped the wrappers on the floor, some might still be there. Every room held reminders of people who no longer lived. I wanted to see deeper inside; I wanted to look in on every room, as if it were a doll's house.

Mrs. Pritchard stepped in front of the window with her arms full of rolls of bright paper and sat down at a table. We watched her through a set of Mr. Lessing's birding binoculars. She sat stiffly in her chair, probably measuring boxes, cutting ribbon. After a while she put her head in her hands and sat there completely still. I didn't think she would be crying. I remembered her standing in the garden, harsh and beautiful. What sort of woman would want to live in a house where her sister had been murdered? A house remembered everything, held everything. Even though she had lived in it only a short time, my mother had left so much of herself in our house. We couldn't escape her fragrance or the disorder she always left behind.

Later, in Cora's room, we tried to see into upstairs windows, but everything was dark. I knew Lowell was somewhere inside those walls, feeling alone and frightened. I tried to imagine his heart beating beside mine.

"I don't think we should do this," Cora said.

"I know," I said, disappointed. "I guess it isn't right."

"You know something, though?"

I shook my head.

"I'm glad you're here. I never thought I'd have a friend," Cora said.

I felt bad because I hadn't been thinking about her. I didn't know what to say, so I looked down at my hands and said nothing.

WE RESOLVED THAT EVENING NEVER TO SPY ON THE NEIGHBORS AGAIN. WE knew it was wrong to feel entitled to witness other people's lives that way. It was a sort of burglary. We knew that, but as time went on and Cora lost interest, it grew harder and harder for me to stop when I came over. I got to know the Pritchards, as I watched through the windows. They had guests over one Sunday for dinner, and everybody kissed on both cheeks, even the minister. They drank martinis, the real thing. Mr. and Mrs. Pritchard fought, but no one ever cried. Instead of crying, Mrs. Pritchard scattered newspapers and stood with her hands on her hips, her mouth moving like a silent movie. Mr. Pritchard shook his head and went into the garden and lit a cigar. Upstairs, Mrs. Pritchard kept a sequined ball gown on a dressmaker's dummy. I'd seen it glittering valentine red in the half light of an open closet, but when she stepped into the living room one evening to show Mr. Prichard after all these years how the dress still fit, I found it more orange than it had seemed, like a soft sunset, or the embers of a slow burning fire. I couldn't tear my eyes away.

MEN DELIVERED A NEW BURGUNDY COUCH TO OUR HOUSE AND HAULED MY grandfather's brown one away. The truck skidded on the ice and had to be pulled out with a chain. But my father didn't complain about the overtime. Though Capital Steel didn't have any contracts to build bridges, my father had talked to my mother on the phone, and he wasn't going to get upset about a few extra dollars. Her scattered phone calls gave him a sort of false optimism. "She'll be back soon," he told me, after the truck had been hauled away.

"When?"

"Whenever." And my father shrugged like it made no difference. He no longer mentioned Kansas City. "But when she does get here, the couch will be waiting," he said, sounding content.

"Did she ask to speak to me?" I said.

"It was late. I didn't want to wake you up."

One night the phone woke me and I crept into the hall, trying to figure out who it was. I could hear my father insisting, protesting, behind his closed door. He said nothing about it to me the next day, but the Sunday following Mother's call, he spent all day on the new couch, sweeping his palms back and forth over the arms, his face caved in like one of the old cushions.

I went upstairs and took out the clipping and stared at Mr. and Mrs. Bowman's smiling faces. I thought about their bodies buried for the rest of time in the same dark earth as the man who killed them. All night long the wind would howl. It was dry and cold and unforgiving.

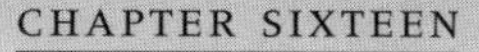

CHAPTER SIXTEEN

1958

I wanted to get somewhere, leave Nebraska, hide all our footprints under snow, but Charlie said he had a mind to double back to Lincoln since everyone was looking for us everyplace else. They were hunting a Ford, but by this time we were already driving a Chevy. Soon it was going to be something else, something better. You had to play games with the lawmen. But the games were easy, like the demolition derby. It was all about not bowing down and thinking one step ahead till it was metal and engines sparking and steel ripping up the road.

"It's gonna be them who break down first?" I asked, hoping he'd sound sure when he answered back.

"Well, we got this far."

"Where did we get to?"

"We're together, ain't we?"

"I guess," I said. But I thought we were headed someplace else.

We had spent the night in the car on the corner of Van Dorn and some other street. I can't remember which. I didn't know this part of town. It was cold, and I could not sleep for remembering what Charlie did to the dead girl. He had done in the old man before that, but it wasn't like this one. Every time my eyes closed and my head fell over to one side, Charlie moved and I thought he was trying to leave me. I could not stop thinking how easy he could leave me with nothing else at all, not even him.

I did not like the way Charlie had put down the gun and then raised it up again, like he wasn't sure about killing her. He was so sure about the other ones. Not that I wanted him to kill her. I did not want him to kill any of them. It had all just started and I couldn't get it to stop.

"Please," she had said shivering, creasing up her forehead, as I held the flashlight on her face. She put out her hands, begging, and he fired and I tell you that by the time I heard this shot any thrill was gone. She dropped soft to the floor and crawled in the corner. Just curled up in a ball like a hit deer that runs away to die on the side of the road. Charlie went outside to get the boy.

Her name was Carol, same as me, just spelled different. I saw it in her math book, but I did not feel right about calling her by it. The girl was laying on her side. I put my palm up to her nose, and there wasn't any breath. The cellar was dark and smelled of straw and the earth. I felt like I was buried beside her.

She was a girl who did not get left back and probably never missed a day of school in her whole life. I thought of the teen angel song, because the girl looked like she was one. A checked hairband slipped down over her forehead, and a locket pooled in a gold pile by her half-opened mouth, like her heart had slipped out when it stopped beating and then froze up small like something in a story. The heart said *Daddy's Girl,* and there was a picture inside to prove it. There was also a diamond on her finger to say she was somebody else's girl, too. I folded her finger under so Charlie wouldn't think to take the ring and give it to me. He would do that, give me things and talk like it was just the thing for me even though it was someone else's and he hadn't even picked it out.

The cellar door clanged open and Charlie pushed the boy through and drug him down the steps. I turned out the flashlight. "What'd you do that for?" Charlie said.

"I don't want to see."

"Well, turn it back on."

"I don't want to see anymore."

"Come on, ain't you gonna help?"

"What am I supposed to do?"

"Go outside and cover the blood."

"With what?"

"I don't know, *you* think, Caril. I'm tired of thinking for the both of us."

"OK," I said, but I did not feel OK. I turned on the flashlight, and went outside, and crouched down on the snow, and got to turning it over, making it white again. It was hard work, with being so icy and no gloves. I gave up and went back down.

At first I didn't see him, only the boy laid out, then a little flash of silver: Charlie's eyeglasses catching the light. The boy was hunched in the corner beside the killed girl. Her stockings were half off, dress pulled up over her face. Charlie had his hand on her leg.

My heart went spinning like a wheel in a ditch. "Chuck. Leave her be. Pull up *my* dress."

He sat up and squinted his eye like he had just woke up in the middle of the night. "Come here," he said. "It ain't what you think."

But I didn't. I didn't feel that I had feet anymore to follow him, but just a heart that was broke and in the dark. I went outside. The stars squinted down. A cloud was over the moon, but I could still see dark spots where the boy had coughed out blood in the snow. I did not hug myself for the cold but hung my arms dead at my sides and let the wind take me, because nothing else ever would.

Charlie's feet stomped up the stairs. "Come on," he said. "Don't be sore. You know I still love you." I walked away from the cellar mouth. Charlie's feet crunched after me.

I looked out at the road, but there was nothing else I could see anywhere, not a ripple of a hill or a bush. I felt like I was standing on the tip of the world, looking out over the edge into emptiness. It was the thickest black I had ever seen. Then the world swirled around and the moon broke free, and the ground was washed in a million stars. I could see the boy's car resting by the side of the road, and frost on the windshield like somebody breathing. But nobody was breathing. An owl hooted, and there was Charlie.

"I never was with another girl but you. I only wanted a look."

"Why?"

"Because I never was with another girl. I wanted to see another girl before I died."

"What about Peg?" She was his girl before me.

"It's just something you say. I never did. There's just you. Nobody loves like me and you."

"How do you know?"

"I just know. Like I know this whole thing ain't gonna pan out for me."

NOW WE WERE DRIVING REAL SLOW THROUGH THE RICH PART OF TOWN, WITH the big old trees and the gardens and the black cars, and at one end of the neighborhood was the club where people who had money smoked cigars and jiggled around in little white carts. Charlie told me we weren't going to kill any of them. We were just going to pick out a house big enough for us to get lost in and hide out for a day, eating the food and rolling around in the beds, bigger than anything we ever laid in before. I didn't want to roll around. I just wanted to sleep and wake up in another place and time.

"You pick the place," Charlie said. "Pick a house you like."

"I like every one."

"Pick your favorite."

"I don't have a favorite."

"Come on."

We drove around and around the same streets, and everything washed in a blur. People pulled cars out of driveways on their way to work and fixed their ties behind windshields, thinking nothing bad could ever happen, not to them. *Not you, no, not you.* The houses were gray and white with brick ones breaking them up every so often. Branches swished and fences rolled out like long white ropes.

Charlie bumped me on the shoulder. "What's it gonna be?" he said.

"What'll we do with the people?" I said.

"They better not cause any trouble, is all." Charlie looked over at me. I put my forehead against the window's cold and closed my eyes. I tried to think what trouble the boy and girl in Bennet had caused. They had only stopped to give us a lift. Somehow it had turned into trouble, only I couldn't figure out when.

"How can you pick when you're sleeping," Charlie said.

I opened my eyes. "I'm not," I said.

It was a brick house painted white, with a big old tree in the middle of a circle drive out front and another drive that disappeared down the side of the house. I told Charlie I picked it for the fenced flower garden with a white gate, and for the screened-in porch, because I have always wanted to eat in a screened-in porch on a summer night. But really I just chose it on account of being made to choose, which is not really a choice no matter how you see it.

Charlie waited at a stop sign for a milk truck to go on, then turned into the drive real slow, without a signal. "This is it," said Charlie. "Our dream house." But his face wasn't smiling. He rolled down the window to listen for sounds. He didn't want any surprises. The air gusted. The branches swung with a heaviness. There was gravel under the tires and ice chunks from half-melted puddles. A stone popped the fender and a pine tree creaked. Charlie parked the car alongside the garage and got out real slow, holding the gun in one hand and barely tapping the door shut with the other, so as not to make a sound. He put his hand out to motion I should stay behind.

Charlie tucked the gun in the back of his blue jeans. He patted his hair and disappeared around the side of the garage. Watching him from the back, he did not look like a person who wanted to cause trouble, but a little boy with bowed legs you could trip easy and send to the ground. It was his face that told you different. There wasn't anybody going to knock him down.

I listened hard, but I could not hear a sound for the wind. Everything was gray, and soon it started to snow. Big fat flakes that cried down the windshield. Charlie stuck his head around the side of the house and waved his hand for me to come along. Then he was gone again. There was nothing left for me to hope, so I got out of the car. I thought about running. But I did not have anything anymore to run back to. I went up the back steps and opened the screen.

A LADY STOOD IN THE KITCHEN DOORWAY WITH A LITTLE BLACK DOG HIDING behind her feet. A fine lady with sad soft eyes and money in the bank. Charlie had the gun on her. She had her hand on her heart, thinking who was I, coming in, and I closed the door soft, trying not to scare anyone. The little dog got to yapping and snarling from behind her shoes. She picked it up and said, "No, Queenie," and the thing went quiet. Her fancy ring twinkled, a pearl surrounded by diamonds. It looked so big it could break her finger. There was the bracelet, too, like a gold rope with little stones sliding down her arm.

A girl was off to one side with her white apron on, moving her lips around like she was trying to spit something out. I could smell the coffee she must have been getting ready on the stove. Cream and sugar laid out on the table like it was for a king. A house full of party smells, so warm inside. Who would have expected people like us? On the cover of the paper on the table was a picture taken of me and Charlie sitting on the couch, ten thousand years back before this all got going.

The fine lady looked from the paper back to Charlie.

"You got it," he said.

The lady petted the dog's head over and over.

"Do as I say and nobody gets hurt," Charlie said.

"What would you like us to do?" she said.

Charlie waved the gun at the apron girl. "Make us something to eat." The girl didn't move.

"You have any directions now, you give them to me," the lady said. "She can't hear. It doesn't mean she isn't minding what you say. You have to talk so she can see your lips or she won't understand."

Charlie frowned. "What happened to her?"

"She's deaf."

"Yeah?" He shook his head, and flopped down in the chair. "All the money in the world and you hire a girl can't take orders. Man, oh, man." He laughed. "How much you pay her?"

The lady did not let on she was afraid. "Moira's a good girl," she said.

"I bet."

I gave him a look. There wasn't any reason to be wise. We were the ones putting *her* out.

"You hungry?" he said to me.

"I guess." I couldn't tell if I was or not. I just wanted to fall asleep somewhere.

"How about pancakes?"

I shrugged.

"They're her favorite," he told the lady, like she should care. Charlie waved the .22 at the maid. "Make us pancakes," he said.

The maid didn't get the idea. She was in a panic with her hand on her forehead and I could see she was breathing deep on account of her shoulders going up and down. The lady put the dog on the floor, real slow, and went over to the stove and talked in the maid's face. "Moira, you go finish the dusting. There's nothing to be scared of. They say they aren't going to hurt us."

"Just so you know, that ain't definite." Charlie leaned back in the chair and threw his feet up on the table. "She better stick to the dusting, is all." He shaked open the paper and held it up in front of his face, then peeked over the edge at me. "Look."

I didn't want to look.

"We're famous."

"I already saw," I said. The lady opened a cupboard and got out a bowl and went to the icebox. The dog skittered in circles.

"Come here, doggy," I said. "Come to Caril."

"That ain't any dog," Charlie laughed. "It's a fly on shit."

The lady closed the icebox and cracked two eggs in the bowl. "She's a poodle."

"Nobody asked."

The lady got to stirring up the bowl. The pancakes were from a mix. "My grandma has a poodle," I said.

Charlie gave me a look back fast. He knew my grandma had no such thing. "Go make sure that maid ain't up to anything funny," he said, handing me his knife. Then he went back to staring at the paper. I had no idea what I would do if I did find her trying something. I knew what Charlie would want me to do; stick the knife in her back. It would all be quiet. It wouldn't make a sound.

But the maid was not up to anything funny after all. She was in the very next room, polishing a long dark dinner table with a lemony wax. She looked so calm making those big circles, like she was in another scene altogether. So far off, someplace I wouldn't have minding being. Her back was to me, and she did not turn around on account of being deaf. There was a pitcher of red flowers in the middle of the table, and I went around the other side from her, to take one out. When I did this, the maid jumped clear out of her skin and made a noise like gagging. Her black curls shaked on account of her whole body shaking. Her skin was very white. I put the flower to my nose, but it did not smell like anything. It was winter. I held it out across the table. "Here," I said, but she wouldn't take it. She stood dumb with the rag in her hand, like the flower was a gun and I had it pointed. I hid the knife behind my back to show I would never use it.

"I'm not the one to be scared of," I said. "But I can talk to Charlie. He listens to me." She looked at me, blank as a chalkboard. I wanted to tell her how there hadn't been any choice for me, but there was no explaining to a deaf girl.

I dropped the flower and smashed it around with the heel of my boot. The petals spread like a fan of cards in a trick, and in the middle was the heart, smeared out over the rug in a gold dust.

I motioned for the maid to pull down the shades, and she got to doing it right away—yank, yank—like I was the new lady of the house and she might get fired. Dark red curtains blocked the gray world. But I did not want to be the lady of this house even though I had chose it, and there were all the things I would ever want inside. Eight chairs for all the guests. A crystal chandelier with little places for candles left over from times gone by. A bowl of perfect-colored fruit made out of glass. It all looked right, but suddenly it was not on account of me and Charlie. He said he didn't want things to turn out bloody this time. I tried to believe him. But something always sent him ape.

The maid went into the hall and got to cleaning the glass over a painting of a girl in a blue dress with her hand on the back of a chair. Everything in the painting was very dark, except for the hair; that was blond. It was straight hair like me but heavier and thicker, and all over prettier, though Charlie used to say I was the prettiest thing he ever saw. I did not feel that way anymore. I felt ugly, and there was hole in my stomach the size of the moon.

My feet walked over to the big piano. The lid of the piano was held open, so you could see all the hammers inside that jumped when you hit the keys. I thought of the girl in a coffin with the lid open that way, and all the people coming from miles around to say *How pretty she is* or *What a pity it had to end up this way.* I was not sure Charlie had pulled her dress back down. If he didn't, then everyone would know how I wasn't enough for him. Nothing was, of course.

I laid on the couch and tried not to think. I put the knife on the table beside a row of cards left over from Christmas, even though Christmas was already a month past. I picked one up. On the outside was a picture of a big man dressed like Santa on the steps of a fancy house, and four heads poking out behind him. There was the mother, and three little boys wearing pointy green hats. Each person was smiling hard to say there was no happier family in all the world.

Dear Arthur, Jeanette, and Lowell—

Season's Greetings from all of us at the North Pole,

Jim, Bonnie, Jonny, Gavin, and Tommy Reynolds. Can't wait to see you this summer at the lake!!!! Santa says he ordered Lowe a new water ski.

It was the ones with names that would not leave me. I would imagine them to be babies wrapped in blankets handed to mothers who were choosing names. *You are Bobby,* or *August,* or *Grace,* or *Betty Sue.*

When Mother had the baby, she was closed in the room forever and no one would let me see. "It's too ugly," Barbara had said, "and you're not old enough." But she had no idea what ugly things I *would* see.

I had caught a peek of Mother on the bed with her head pushing up from the pillows—pushing and pushing, with the veins in her neck standing out in wires, and groans that split her clear in two. This was in the old house on Belmont with no place else to go, so I had sat down at the table across from Roe and slitted my eyes at him.

"Ouch," I said. "See what you did?"

"Well, it ain't like you came out of nowhere," Roe said. "Don't forget. There was somebody had to do this for you." As if he had no idea who it was.

CHARLIE CAME UP BEHIND AND LEANED HIS ARMS ON THE BACK OF THE couch. "What's that?" he said.

I closed the card. "They go to a lake."

"Who?"

"The people that live here."

"There ain't any lake around."

"Maybe they take an airplane."

Charlie shaked his head and flopped down beside me. He put the gun on the table. "Now, why do you take an airplane to a lake when you can take an airplane to the ocean?"

"I don't know, Chuck. Maybe they like the lake."

"Who likes lakes?"

"Me."

"Come on, Caril Ann, you never even been to a lake."

"How do you know?"

"I know every bit of you." Then Charlie kissed me on the forehead like it was a cute thing that I never went anywhere and now never would. He kissed me on the mouth, but I didn't kiss back.

"Chuck," I said. "Did you fix her dress?"

"Huh?"

"Did you pull up the stockings?"

"Forget it. It ain't like she's gonna catch cold."

"It's not that."

"Well, what?"

"Everybody'll go around saying you don't love me."

"I told you I was only looking," Charlie said. "There ain't a person in this goddamn world gonna make a mistake about the way I feel. Everyone knows." Charlie put his hands around the back of my neck and kissed it. "Look what all I did to show it," he whispered. "I love you."

THE LADY SERVED US PANCAKES IN THE LIBRARY 'CAUSE THAT'S WHERE CHARlie said he wanted to eat. She brought the food and her hands were shaking. It was the maid who set everything else on the red cloth in front of us. When she was done, Charlie took her by the apron and shoved her into the closet. It happened fast, in one wink, and when the girl tried to scream nothing came out, and for a split second I thought I had went and lost my hearing too. The lady swallowed hard and fluttered her fingers along the bracelet, twisting it around and around. The shiny stones twinkled.

"What did you do that for?" I said.

"I want someone can hear what I say. I don't trust her." Charlie took a bite and looked at me. "Ain't you gonna eat something? I had these made special for you."

"I need syrup," I said, but to tell the truth I did not feel like eating. The books on the shelves gave off a funny old smell and out the window there was not a thing but miles of white. The whole world looked to be floating in the middle of a cloud. The furniture tilted. If you fell out the window you'd fall and fall and keep on falling till your cheek smacked the ground somewhere and everything went black.

There were little sounds from the closet. The maid was crying. Charlie rolled his eyes and puffed out his cheeks and cut through his pancakes sharp and straight, like a man who always knew just what he was doing.

The lady reached me the syrup and put it beside my plate, her gold bracelet shining in the lamp. She caught me looking and took it off, showed me where to hook it. There was perfume on her neck I could smell, not from a drugstore but a place downtown like Miller and Paine with different counters and pretty girls who stood behind them wearing name tags. The lady's fingers shaked, and the bracelet slid to the red cloth. She did not take her eyes off Charlie. "You can keep it," she said, like she really did not care.

"Thank you," I said, real polite. It was the prettiest thing I ever put on.

I poured the syrup but could not get down the bites. The bracelet tickled my arm. The clock ticked on the bookshelf. The maid made a noise like somebody was trying to shove a pillow down her throat, and Charlie put his elbows on the table and covered his ears. She kicked her feet on the door. Charlie shook his head. "What's she trying to pull?"

This was how it started. I could feel it all coming apart. I emptied my mouth into the napkin.

"How come she can't shut up?"

"She can't hear herself," the lady said. "She's afraid of the dark." I tried to imagine what it was to be her, locked in a place with no sound and no light.

"She ain't ever gonna shut up."

"Really, she will if you let her out," the lady said.

"What are you saying?"

"We'll do what you want."

"What do you think?" Charlie said, looking at me. "What should I want?" but I could tell he didn't care what I thought. He had already made up his mind.

"I don't know. Let her out," I said.

Charlie picked up the knife. "Oh, *I'll* let her out." He got up and pulled the maid out of the closet. Her head jerked. "No, no," it seemed like she was trying to say. She put her hands over her face and tried to pull away, but it was no good. Charlie drug her out of the room.

The lady put her knuckle up to her teeth and stood there with her face all pale, her fingers shaking. The clock ticked. I looked down at the pancakes but still did not feel like eating. I fiddled the bracelet around my wrist, and went to the window and peeked out from the edge of the curtain, but there was nothing anywhere worth looking at. I pulled the curtain closed. The lady breathed. The clock ticked. I didn't want to hear it anymore.

"Where's the lake?" I said.

"In Minnesota."

"How do you get there?"

"We drive."

"How come you don't take an airplane?"

"It's not that far—and we do it as a family. It's nice," she said, and bit her lip. I knew what she was thinking: *Would she ever see the lake again?* I didn't think so.

She started cleaning up the dishes, stacking plates on the tray and glasses. She piled up the knives and forks and napkins like there was nothing else worth doing in all the world but this. The whole time I was watching her rings, the pearl on her finger and the wedding band. I always thought I would like to have a ring like this when I got married, not just gold but with tiny diamonds to light it up.

Mother did not have so much as a band to say she was married, but I supposed it never mattered. She just stayed around the house all day, with Betty Sue hanging off her hip, looking old on account of loving Roe and having no money to buy fancy skin creams. Before Roe, I sat around, painting my toes red to match the Chinese writing on my kimono, and if I wanted to look at a magazine in the middle of dinner, that was A-OK with Mother. She'd sit down beside me and stare at it too, and she'd go on about how the stories weren't real life and I shouldn't think so.

The lady finished loading the tray, and then picked it up, but the whole thing fell through her hands and I thought she was just going to break down in tears. Dishes clattered. I jumped clear out of my skin. The dog skittered. Pancakes, plates, glasses, spoons: It all went rolling. There was syrup on her night gown and she kneeled down in the mess of it and put her hands on her knees like she couldn't think what piece to pick up first. There was the dog snacking on the butter stick, and the old clock ticking, and the maid's heart beating in Charlie's hands.

I could see the knuckles holding her knees, touching bone, thinking, *This is soft, this is me, this is hard, this is real. What if this is all there is?* Her ring sparkled shiny on the dark blue sky of her dress. I felt sick. There wasn't any air. I went over and cracked the window. Here I was, a girl with no mother to speak of, standing at the window of a house she had chose. I thought of the wind ripping Mother's hair, and how I would never know where to find her ever again. *There she was running, and there was the shot. There was the bullet singing into her dream.* The lady reached over and picked up a piece of a broken glass and put it on the tray. She closed her eyes and leaned her hands on the floor. "What's he doing to Moira?"

I couldn't say.

IN A LITTLE WHILE, THE TELEPHONE RANG AND BOTH OF US JUMPED. THE LADY looked at me to ask what she should do. I didn't know. Then Charlie was there to answer for me. "I thought you said there wasn't anyone going to call."

Ring.

"How should she know?" I said.

Ring.

"Whose side are you on?"

Ring.

"Yours, Chuck."

Ring.

The lady stood up. Charlie cocked the gun. "Get it, like always," he said. "And nothing funny. I can kill you if I want. If you say one word." The lady picked up the telephone. "Hello," she said, and listened for what seemed like too long of a space. "Yes—I'd forgotten." She looked at Charlie. He nodded at her to keep on going. His wrist was shaking. He was in a panic. "A headache," she said. ". . . No, it's fine. I was just resting." She rubbed the ring with her thumb. It twirled around and around. Bright diamonds went to smooth silver back to diamonds. "Another time . . . Goodbye." She hung up the phone and sat down in a chair. Charlie breathed deep and lowered the gun. "Who was it?"

"A friend."

"Did she think anything?"

The lady shook her head. "I'm sorry," she said.

Charlie seemed to believe her. "Where's the TV at?" he said.

"In the den off the foyer."

"Where's that?"

"Off the front hall with the staircase." She looked down at her dress and touched the syrup and rubbed the stick between her fingers. "May I go upstairs and change my clothes?"

Charlie thought about it. "Well, don't try anything funny. Don't forget who's boss." His voice broke on the words. He did not sound like the boss, but a boy out back with a boomerang trying to shoot a squirrel down out of a tree. I wanted to put my head against him and ask if it would be all right to cut the losses at the maid, maybe lift a little money, and head on home to eat peanut butter out of the jar and hear about how much he loved me. But I was never going back home. I knew that much. Home was over for Caril Ann Fugate by then.

THE LADY DID NOT CHANGE HER CLOTHES. SHE DID NOT SO MUCH AS TAKE OFF her shoes. She sat down on the edge of the bed, with the sheets all twisted and dents still in the pillow from two people sleeping. She had the dog in her lap and petted its head over and over. I had the knife in my hand, but I did not know how I would ever use it. The lady laid on her side, curled up her legs, and put her hands together under her head. "What clothes do you want to put on?" I said.

She didn't answer. She just laid there, still as stone, like she wasn't even breathing.

The dog paced back and forth on the edge of the bed with his tail flipping like a rabbit foot, trying to muster a jump to the floor.

I did not know what I should say or do to make her move. There was a picture on top of the dresser, of the lady with her husband's arm around her and what looked to be their boy between them, happy as you please. I put down the knife and picked the picture up. The boy grinned with sleepy eyes and heavy lashes and held the poodle under the front legs so its stomach peeked out at the camera. The boy had the husband's brown hair without the gray sides, and the little dent in the chin, but there was something familiar, something he got from the lady in his face. I turned the picture over and went to the window. A pine tree squeaked in the wind with a little old voice, crying tears against the window. Down below, I saw gray puddles in white pockets of snow. The dog collar tinkled, and paws swished the rug.

"Can you bring me that picture?" the lady said.

I went over to the bed and put the frame in her hands. Her eyes did not look at me. Her lips worked around. "He killed Moira, didn't he?" she said.

"Oh, he probably just tied her up," I said.

"He killed her."

"How do you know?"

She didn't answer. She closed her eyes and then opened them again and let out a sigh. "I'm not waking up," she said. "I'm not dreaming. Will you touch my arm?"

"Why?" I said.

"Because God forgives."

"But I didn't do anything bad for God to forgive."

"I believe you."

"I didn't have so much as a choice."

"I believe you," she said.

"I never did a thing wrong."

"You just loved him."

"I love him, and he loves me. He loves me so much, it makes him crazy."

"If he loved you, he wouldn't do this."

"Charlie loves me," I said.

"Your mother loves you."

"She's dead. She can't love me," I said.

"Maybe she loves you from Heaven."

"Maybe," I said, even though I knew there wasn't a chance. I reached out and touched the lady. Her sleeve was soft and warm and alive. The bracelet shivered down my arm.

"I'm Jeanette," the lady said. She moved the picture up closer to her face. "That's my husband, Arthur, and that's Lowell. He's your age."

"Where is he?"

"Away."

"Did you send him to the lake?"

"We sent him to school—he's my baby."

I did not want to hear about any babies, or all the work that went into having them. It seemed an awful lot of effort for things to turn out this way. You gave somebody life and a name, always risking it might go bad.

"I thought I could never love a person more than Arthur," the lady said. "Then I had our son, and I held him for the first time and he yawned, and I knew. *This is Lowell, this is love.*" Her voice was coming out fast from nowhere, and her words fell over each other one on top of the other—*bam bam bam*—like she'd been thinking about saying this her whole life long. "There isn't any love like that. No matter what he does, or who he becomes, I will always love him." She took a breath. "Like your mother. She loves you."

"I don't have a mother."

She put her face in her hands. "Save me."

Her hairdo was crooked, dented in. I felt sick. I wanted her to stop. The hole in my stomach kept growing till it swallowed me up and burned in my throat. The syrup was rising. I picked up the knife to make her be quiet, but I could tell in her face she knew I never would use it.

"Make him stop," she said, and pleaded her eyes at me.

"I can't," I said. "I don't have a choice."

"There's *always* a choice." The lady was kidding herself.

"It's too late for a choice." I turned my back.

"Jesus says it's never too late."

But as far as I could tell, Jesus was not talking anymore. Jesus was dead, nailed up on the cross, and that was a pretty bad way to go itself. I thought about taking the bracelet off. It made me sorry to think of her giving me something, when there wasn't a thing in the world I could give back. I didn't want her whispers left behind like all the other voices I have heard. But I couldn't take it off. You had to take good things when they came along. It was too pretty, and I had never owned something so pretty. "You're supposed to change your clothes," I said.

The lady got up and went to the bureau, and opened a drawer. I could see her whole body was shaking, but her eyes weren't crying. She watched me in the mirror. "If you're not going to help me, then at least let me try to help myself," she said.

"How can *I* help you?"

"Don't kill his father. Don't kill my husband."

"I'm not the one to ask. I never killed anyone," I said. I couldn't look at her anymore. I already knew how it was going to turn out.

I walked into the boy's room, with the Big Red posters and the trophy of a gold boy in a funny hat swinging a stick at a ball, and a case of tin soldiers trapped on the wall. There was some piece of stone that looked all chipped up from a long-ago place. I wondered why he would want to keep it. I laid down on his bed, closed my eyes, and tried to sleep. The pillow was covered with dog smell, but I didn't care. It was a beautiful room of someone alive who was happy to be that way. Inside my head there were stars I could see, blue shapes in my lids, mouths opening and closing, tongues curled up, and Charlie's hands feeling every part of me, skin to blood to bone, to all the tiny dreams that run through my veins. My head swirled down, down, in the slow part of a storm. The rain ripped up Betty Sue's newspaper hat. The wind took Mother's hair.

Then there were Charlie's steps coming up, one, two, three, four, five, six, seven, and her steps going back—till he canceled them out. The dog yelped. Later I would know it was a lamp that fell. Somebody's foot tripped the cord, a whole body tumbled, the air drained out fast. I could hear the dog crying on account of its neck, and *shush, shush, shush*—Roe on the roof sanding red paint.

WHEN HE FOUND ME SLEEPING IN THE BOY'S ROOM, CHARLIE JUST ABOUT cried. His eyes pinched up and his face went red. He said the lady had tried to kill him on account of me going to sleep. I did not say I had only been trying to sleep. "How'd she try to kill you?" I said, but Charlie couldn't answer. He didn't want to talk.

"I didn't want to kill her, but she made me do it."

"You always had a mind to kill her."

"No, Caril. It didn't start out like that. I didn't start out with a mind to kill anyone. Everyone just treated me bad."

"OK, Chuck, I believe you," I said. "I don't treat you bad."

"I don't know." He looked at me funny and went downstairs to look at the newspapers again. He just kept picking them up.

BLACK WAS COMING ON, CRACKING TREES WITH COLD, AND THEY WERE LOOKING for us everywhere, but we were frozen in the quietest place. The house was dark. Nothing breathed. The whole world felt to be covered in ice. It was my job to wait for the man. He would be coming home from work. Charlie had a mind to set off in the family's car. It would be a nice car, he said, nicer than any I'd ever been in before.

I sat on the couch arm with my back up straight so I couldn't go to sleep, but I got too tired. It was late. I didn't think he was coming after all. I went back upstairs and tried to get the dog out from under the bed in the boy's room. I waved the box of chocolates I had found in the cupboard around on the floor because a box of chocolates is what I would need to get me out from under a bed. "Come here, doggy," I said. "Come to Caril, it's OK." But it was not OK and he would not come out. He was hunkered up against the wall, mewling in pain, so I sat there in the middle of the rug eating all the chocolates myself, staying near, watching him like a secret, leaving one behind in case he changed his mind.

I felt sick and started to cry for not being any use to her. I wanted her boy to have something to come back to. I thought about Nig with no one to love him. I put the leftover chocolate under the edge of the bed and reached up to turn off the light. And then there were the headlights I could see coming down the drive to say that her husband was home now, two more bright scared eyes.

I tiptoed down the hall. "Chuck," I said, but he already knew. He was waiting by the door in the dark. I leaned back up against the wall by the fallen-over lamp and sat down in the crunch of it. My arms were around my knees, my eyes shut, though there was nothing to see.

It is black. It is only black. There is a breath stuck in my chest. The door throws open—"Jeanette?"—and the shadow of the light flicks on, and Charlie's waiting. There is a silence. A surprise of motion. There is the shot. Going in and coming out the other side. The sound of something glass exploding. There is the smoke. And Charlie's footsteps. And static in my eyes from where I rub too hard, making shapes like bruises—a dog—a tree—a hand—a brain. There isn't any sound. I peek down over the railing, and there is a man. There is a pool of blood becoming the carpet. There are his hands. They are at his throat. His tie is loose. His eyes are closed. His lips are moving. I creep downstairs to hear the secret: "Jeanette . . . Jean." He is whispering her name.

CHAPTER SEVENTEEN

1991

In the cluttered rooms of our past, all was just as we'd left it the summer before, and yet everything had changed as places do when they are empty for too long. Moving the box to the hall table, I went into the living room, lifted the sheet off the piano, and sat down on the bench, touching my fingers to the cold white keys. But the instrument was in need of tuning, and I could remember only a fragment of a song I had played as a child, a simple string of chords about dancing Cossacks. I went to the liquor cabinet, not sure if I'd find anything there or what I'd do if I didn't. But there was a bit of scotch left over in the bottle, so I poured myself a drink, sat down on the couch, and stared out the window. I narrowed my eyes, blending color and shape so the lawn bled seamlessly into the river. Jane had painted something like that once. A large rectangular canvas, strips of color and texture marking the place where the land stopped and the water began. It was unsettling—to think that she had moved away, quietly slipping out without a whisper. I knew how easy it could be.

I tried to remember the last time I had seen Jane: She was picking tomatoes in her yellow sun hat. I'd stood there for a moment with my hand on the side of the warm barn wall, watching her through the trees. I thought of Susan standing in the dawn light, the hem of her nightgown brushing the rug, and wondered if I'd always remember her that way. The first time Susan and I had visited Jane, we drank bourbon out of mason jars by candlelight, pretending not to see the children playing their spy games around the edge of the kitchen door frame. Jane's coffee table was made out of stacked crates. The cushions on the living room chairs were losing their stuffing. Yet I had noticed a striking sense of order in Jane's work, large canvases whose symmetrical composition seemed to guide the eye from wall to wall as if each separate painting were part of a synchronized pattern of breath. You could cut a path through the clutter by following those shapes. At one point Jane had come up quietly behind me, touching my arm, and I had felt a connection there, a sort of jolt. Later that night, when the children were safely in bed, I had followed Susan's shadow up the dark staircase with Jane's paintings fresh in my mind and made furious love to her, bracing my arm against the wall to keep the headboard from knocking.

There had been a glitter in my wife's eyes that night; she was full of ideas, and when she got an idea she never failed to see it to fruition. So I wasn't surprised when she and the children came back from Kingston with a ridiculous amount of art supplies. In the following weeks the mud room became their studio. Susan plastered the walls with their crude drawings of the house, the dogs, Jane's horse, Mistletoe. Jane was a constant presence, advising the children and growing closer to Susan. I always tried to keep a distance, not wanting to interfere. Once, when I'd felt completely lost, I had ended up on her doorstep seeking some sort of comfort, and she gave me a glass of bourbon and talked to me as a dear friend would have. She had helped bring me back to the world.

Sitting on the couch now, facing the river, I wondered what Susan was doing, whether she was missing Hank the way my mother had missed me that last fall when I'd gone away to school. Was she listening for the sound of her son's key in the door as my mother had listened for my steps on the path? I was suddenly struck hard by our loneliness, by the idea that it shouldn't have had to be this way.

I got up to refill my glass of scotch. There was a knock on the back door, and I almost jumped. Jane was standing on the steps, peering in.

I felt guilty, as if my thoughts had prompted the visit. She waved tentatively when I started toward her, trying not to appear too startled.

"I saw you coming across the lawn a little while ago," she said, stepping into the living room as soon as I opened the door. "I thought you were on your way to say hello, but then you disappeared." The rain had dampened her silver hair. When a drop slid from her temple down the hard line of her jaw, I almost reached out to catch it.

"How have you been?" I said, feeling as if I'd been caught doing something shameful.

She looked older than she had the year before. Beneath the heavy wrinkled lids, her eyes were soft and a little troubled. I wondered for a moment if Susan had called and asked her to check to see if I was at the house. "I've been all right," she said. "I've been wondering about you and Susan, though."

I stopped myself from telling her I'd just been thinking about her. "It's been too long," I said instead, going no further. My hands didn't feel steady, and the ice in my drink chimed against the side of the glass as I offered her a seat. "We don't come here much anymore."

"Yes. You both sort of disappeared." She smiled and arranged herself carefully on the couch. "But then, so did I. Is Susan here?"

"She's at home."

"I've missed her. How is she?"

"Wonderful," I said, with a sort of forced exuberance.

Jane gave me a puzzled look and stared at her hands, twisting a silver band up and down the length of her finger. It was a wedding ring, which came as a shock. She hadn't ever seemed to need anyone.

"I thought you might have moved away," I said, after an awkward silence. "The house is an odd shade. NQOC," I added with a smile. "You know, Not Quite Our Color." It was a stupid quip, but I thought it might produce a laugh.

"Renters," she said. "I went to Brazil. I told them they could do what they wanted. They were starting a new life, and really I was past caring."

I went into the kitchen and poured her the rest of the scotch, feeling a mild panic set in. The mood had changed. She was less spirited than I had ever seen her. "Did you go there to paint?" I said, handing her the drink. Her hard angles looked softer in the fading light.

She shook her head, took a few sips as if it were a dose of medicine, and set the glass on the coffee table, lacing her fingers together and making a cradle for her thigh the way she often had when we were deep in discussion.

"How things have flipped," she said suddenly. "Remember that time when you came to me?"

"Is that what you're doing now? Are you coming to *me*?" I said.

"I don't know, Lowell." She smiled and picked up her drink again.

"Because I doubt I can offer much."

"It's certainly easier not to." She looked away from me, taking a message pad from the coffee table and beginning to draw: dark lines and heavy shadows from which the flat leaves of tropical plants emerged. I closed my eyes and listened to the quick scratching of the pencil.

"I was just now thinking about you," I confessed suddenly, sipping my drink and frowning at how banal it sounded. I stood up and went to the window, pretending to study the river for a moment, then resettled on the couch next to Jane. The weight of the drink in my hand, and the coming dusk made it easier to get closer, to offer what wasn't asked of me.

"What's happened?" I said, almost reaching out to touch her shoulder.

"I got married," she said, holding up her left hand for me to see.

"That'll do it."

She smiled. "I fell in love with him a long time ago, but then he left."

I asked her where he'd gone.

"Brazil: to live on an island and paint banana leaves." She shrugged her shoulders and rested her arm on the back of the couch.

"Banana leaves?"

"Love is blind, right?" She almost laughed but then her smile drifted away. "There must have been more of a reason than banana leaves. But I didn't want to know about it. Artists are selfish."

"Don't they have to be?"

"No, don't think so, actually." She finished her drink. I was still savoring mine, conscious of the fact that the bottle was empty. "When Alistair called, it was raining like today," she said. "I was just lying on the couch waiting for something to happen. He told me he was very sick and scared of dying. I hadn't spoken to him in more than ten years but, however ridiculous, I didn't even have to think twice; I just packed my things and went to be with him."

"I wouldn't have thought you'd do something like that," I said. But then, it may well have been the right decision. To go back.

"We were married after I got there. It was foolish, but he wanted to. We lived in a beautiful little shack with saloon doors, like something on a postcard," Jane said. "It was strange. All that sunlight and hot air, so much deceptive beauty, and those bottles of pills on the nightstand. He wouldn't put on the caps tightly, and when he'd reach for them they'd go spilling everywhere. I'd wake up to that sound thinking my childhood dog was chasing a ball across the wood floor."

"How strange," I said.

"Yes, it *is* strange how the past comes back," she said. For a brief moment, my dream returned to me, the minister's hands, my mother's voice.

We sat there in silence as the light changed and I felt as if I could almost hear the river.

"It was so hard to take," she told me suddenly. "Not long before the end, I started in on the pills myself."

"That's all right, don't you think?" I said, trying to reassure her. "We've all done something like that at one time or another."

"I don't know," she said, shaking her head. "I could have been stronger." During the afternoons, when he slept, she'd walk along the rocks where hordes of sea turtles sunned themselves like gray old men. The horizon was reassuring, and after the pills kicked in, she didn't have to feel anything. The shadows from palms spread across the golden sand like soft fingers; that was how she described them. She got used to feeling soft and calm.

One day Jane slipped and fell on some seaweed and almost stayed there, almost let the tide take her. "But when I got back, he kept grabbing my arm," she said. His energy, his desire to live, passed through her like a shock.

I imagined my parents' final moments. My mother in her nightgown, my father feeling the startling cold of the rifle at his temple, wondering if she was gone already. When I went home, they gave me pills to sleep, but every morning the dark clouds rolled in again. Sometimes it seemed, as the years passed, that the only compensation for the living world, where things changed, were beautiful objects that stood the test of time.

As a teenager, I had started a collection in the basement of the house in Lincoln. There were drawers of fossils and arrowheads, fragments of Sioux pottery meticulously labeled. Aunt Clara had tried to pull me out of the darkness and into the sunshine, to no avail. Late at night I'd heard her talking to Uncle Philip when she thought I was in bed. "Remember how much he liked to dance at Jeanette's parties? He's just not the same."

"I don't know how you can expect him to let go of what happened when he's still living here," my uncle had said.

"We *talked* about it, Phil. We decided it was best."

The basement was my fortress away from all of them. My collection was about putting everything in a specific order so it made a particular sense. Here were the first amphibians embedded in rock when the water dried up into plains. Here was the Pueblo arrowhead from Bandolier State Park. The remnants of the first American people, and then the later finds, the pearl-handled knife I had discovered wedged beneath the foundation of a homesteader cabin off the road just north of Alliance. "Used for scalping?" I had asked.

My father had laughed. "More likely for spreading butter."

I felt Jane's hand on my knee and opened my eyes, half-expecting to find Susan beside me. "I came back with his paintings," she told me. "I can't even look at them."

I didn't know what she wanted me to tell her.

She tightened her hold and said, "The reason I came here was I want to know how you got through what happened to your family."

I stared at her a moment, trying to imagine the way she might see me. But I hadn't gotten through it, not really. I almost told her then about the box I couldn't open and how my marriage had splintered apart.

Instead, I put my arms around Jane and pulled her to me. She seemed almost to have been expecting it. Our cheeks moved past each other, touching lightly, and I felt the soft folds of her skin, smelled the liquor on her breath, and wondered what Susan would say. I stared down at the turquoise stone around her neck. It was veined with dark threads. I pressed it against her skin and studied the red mark it left behind.

"It's amazing that you and Susan found each other," she said softly, fingering the stone. "Your sort of love seems special."

I bowed my head, feeling small and selfish. "You think so?"

"I do." Her gaze drifted past me, out to the river, and I knew she was thinking about another place.

LATER, AFTER JANE HAD GONE, I MOUNTED THE STAIRS WITHOUT LOOKING AT the family portrait she had painted of us, though I could feel all those eyes watching me. I went into Mary's room and lay down on the floor with my arms tucked under my head. Rain pecked at the window. Staring up at the pastoral clouds floating on the blue ceiling, I tried to reach a quieter place. But behind every thought was the fact that I had left Susan alone, that our children were growing up, that life seemed to be ebbing away.

I started thinking about the boy in Hank's first grade class who died, and how I'd left Susan to deal with everything. One morning the child wouldn't wake up. The paramedics had found the mother early Saturday, pacing in front of the window with the rigid body in her arms and pounding his back in an effort to revive him. But it was too late. The autopsy failed to provide any answers.

The boy, Adrian, had spent a day at our house playing Wiffle ball with Hank earlier that spring. I had spent the afternoon pitching while Mary, jabbering, scampered around on her tiny legs, her dark hair streaming out behind her. When the ball went astray she had chased after it, bearing it back slowly across the lawn in both hands, as if she were the leader of some sort of important medieval procession. I remember how Hank threw down his bat and stamped his foot, complaining about how his sister was slowing down the game, and how kind this little boy was in comparison, clapping each time Mary retrieved the ball.

"Don't clap. She's ruining everything," Hank said, kicking the grass with his sneaker.

Perhaps it was the anger, the frustration in him, I don't know, but when I pitched a slow lob to my six-year-old son, he spread his legs sideways over the plate, cocked the bat, and hit that ball like a pro. As the white globe slowly arced across the sky, I was amazed at my son's strength and suddenly envious of all he had in store. "That's it, sport!" I said, clenching my teeth so hard I thought they might crack. The wind carried the plastic ball out to the right, and it spiraled down over the river, disappearing out of sight behind the cement wall, and for a moment, everything had seemed caught in time, my son's bright future as unquestionable as the assurance with which he'd taken his first real swing.

The little boy, the visitor, had clapped his hands and grinned. He knew he would never hit a ball like that but he didn't seem to mind. We kept Adrian for the rest of that day while his mother worked at the library. He picked at his grilled cheese and sat in the living room staring out the window. His skin was so fair, and his hair so light, he seemed almost like an exoskeleton with nothing inside, a remnant that might blow away in a light wind. It was easy to forget he was there.

When his mother finally came, we found him in the living room dancing with Mary to a tinny song on one of her little plastic records. They were two little adults, my daughter blushing shyly and this strange boy staring straight in front of him like some little Victorian lord. He held my daughter's hands in his and guided her in small circles across the living room rug, and it was this image to which my mind kept returning the evening the first grade teacher called to tell us what had happened.

• • •

I ADMIT I WITHDREW AFTER THAT. I WANTED NO PART OF THE PARENT MEETING, though Susan dragged me along. I told her I'd stay home with the children, but she handed them over to Jane and demanded that I play my part. We stuffed ourselves in rows of tiny desks beside long-faced parents speaking in hushed tones. *Adrian Wells, which one was he? Poor boy, how did it happen?*

Miss Mackey, Danielle, who could not have been much older than twenty-five, stood at the front of the room looking small and perfect, her blue eyes large and wet with confusion and sorrow. She seemed not to know what to say, and yet somehow, rather than being annoyed by her befuddlement, I couldn't stop staring at the fine contour of her shoulders beneath the thin straps of her dress, at the thick silver tag chain from Tiffany's settled in the delicate cleft where her neck met her collarbone. I admired the strength in her little arms, the fine definition of muscle as she went over and opened a window to let in the cool air of the late-spring evening. There was something sweet on the breeze, a scent of flowers that I thought had come from the yard, but when she brushed back between the rows, I realized it was the smell of Miss Mackey herself, some floral perfume, perhaps, or a milky lotion.

What was discussed or decided upon I really can't remember, but when the parents stood around afterward in tight clusters, I examined the children's baskets of art supplies and toys, trying to shake the memory of how pleased the boy had been to be dancing with my daughter. I picked at familiar traces of Elmer's glue on the art tables and sifted through a fruit basket of plastic bears in primary colors. I lined them up in a little row on the shelf. "What's wrong with this picture?" I said to Susan, when she came up behind me.

She stared at me a moment as if to say, *What's right?*

"Look at the ears. See how chewed they are?" I said. "More like bats than bears, don't you think? Dog toys. It's no wonder Hank can't get his thumb out of his mouth."

"Are you worried about germs?"

"Not exactly," I said.

"Then what? Miss Mackey?" she said hopefully, pressing her fingers into my open palm, as we stepped out into the warm evening and made our way across the parking lot and slipped once again into the safety of our old wood-paneled Buick. "Are you worried about her not being experienced enough to handle the situation?"

"She reminds me of a dogwood blossom," I said suddenly, without thinking, and started the car.

Susan leaned back into the seat, stared out at the road as if she were the one driving, and took a sharp breath. "If you mean too delicate to withstand a change in temperature," she said quickly, "I see your point." There was an excitement in the way she rolled down the window, a sort of desperate edge I couldn't understand. She stuck her head out into the night and let the wind catch her hair, then pulled it out of her eyes and tossed herself back against the seat. "Lowell?"

"Yes, dear?" I said, putting my hand on her knee like an actor in a play. I fought the urge to say something devastating, something that would wound her; I don't know why.

"I know it's wrong to want to kiss you at a time like this, but I want to kiss you anyway," Susan said with great urgency, taking my hand off her knee and pressing my fingers to her lips as if she thought I would slip away.

When I traced my finger up the inside of Susan's thigh, I was thinking about Miss Mackey's milky lotion. How old we must have looked to her, how far from where she was. My face was gaunter than it should have been. My stubble was flecked with gray, and part of my dinner had landed on my shirt. "What's gotten you so excited?" I said to Susan, though I almost didn't want to know.

She pressed her hot face into my neck, perhaps in an effort to pull me back from the comfortable place to which I was disappearing, and whispered, "We're dealing with the hard things so well together, don't you think?"

I nodded my head. I didn't want to contradict her. It was a beautiful night. The moon was full, and along the road by the baseball field two pairs of yellow eyes in the tall grass watched our passing.

. . .

NO MORE THAN A WEEK LATER, I WOKE UP IN DARKNESS TO FIND THE BED COLD and empty beside me. The night felt unsettled, and rather than hide my head beneath the quilt, I put my feet on the floor and stepped into the dark hall. A bright strip of light streamed out from beneath Hank's closed door. I could hear the slow murmur of my wife's voice behind it.

She was perched on the edge of the bed pulling the covers up to our son's chin when I turned the knob. She acknowledged my presence with a concerned look, but I'm not sure my son knew I was there. "Mary sleeps with her eyes half open, and sometimes they roll up in her head," he was saying, taking his thumb out of his mouth and drying it on his choo-choo pajamas.

"Does that scare you?"

"Not if I'm there. If I'm there and she stops breathing I can wake her up again."

She promised him that wasn't going to happen.

"Don't be afraid," Susan said to Hank, brushing back his hair. She may as well have been talking to me. "You let *me* be afraid."

We returned to bed without touching, like strangers, neither of us speaking a word. We lay there in the dark for what felt like hours, silently replaying what had happened to our son. I could feel the tension in the body next to me, and finally she spoke. "Hank was watching Mary to make sure she didn't die in her sleep."

I remember how strange my throat felt.

"It's not just because of Adrian." I winced when I heard that little boy's name. "You know what he told me? He had some idea his grandmother and grandfather Bowman just went to sleep one night and never woke up." I knew she was blaming me. The darkness felt claustrophobic.

Susan sat up. The headboard creaked as she leaned back against it. "You have to explain," she said. "You have to talk it through. Your past becomes your family's past, and the things you don't deal with show up as your children's dirty laundry."

I plastered my arms at my sides like a dart. "I get it," I said.

"Do you really, Lowe? Do you get how long it took me to get over my mother's dirty laundry?"

Her voice was full of such bitterness. We were locked together in a strange motionless dance. I reached out and touched her thigh, finding it warm and pliant. "I'm sorry," I said.

She flopped back down and threw her arms around my neck and pushed her body against me. "Children know when things are being kept from them," she whispered.

A FEW DAYS LATER, SHE TOLD THE CHILDREN EVERYTHING. I WAS LYING IN THE living room reading a biography of Duchamp when Susan sat down and perched on the edge of the couch. She clearly had something to say to me but could not bring herself to speak. "The children and I took a walk down to the lighthouse," she said finally, "I told them about your parents the best way I could."

What did she want me to say? Did she expect me to thank her? I imagined how it must have been, the children tucked on either side of her as they dangled their legs off the deck of the historic lighthouse. "I didn't tell them any specifics, just as much as was necessary. I thought it was best," she said.

"What?"

She sat there poised, biting her lip, and for a moment she seemed to want to add something. Finally, she said, "It's strange, isn't it? So many horrible things happen, and no one has any idea what is best to say."

CHAPTER EIGHTEEN

1962

Not long before Christmas vacation, Cora and I were lying on the floor of her room studying for a test when Mrs. Lessing knocked tentatively, asking if Cora wanted anything from the store. Sitting up quickly, I turned some pages in my history book, trying to look responsible.

I hadn't ever seen Mrs. Lessing leave the house before, and she seemed uncomfortable, as if the outside world didn't suit her. Her hair was gathered in a tight bun, but her coat wasn't buttoned right. It didn't look nearly warm enough.

Cora didn't seem to notice anything amiss, and she rattled off a long list of requests: Wheaties, Skippy, Fig Newtons, candy canes, and a special cream she'd read about in *Seventeen* that was supposed to lighten freckles. My stomach rumbled. I was too hungry to concentrate on studying.

Mrs. Lessing's lace-up shoes, which had been black and shiny earlier that afternoon, were now splattered with white paint, but she didn't seem to care. I tried to work up the courage to say something, to show her I was interested in the things she did. "What were you painting, Mrs. Lessing?" I asked, just as she was turning to go.

"Oh," she said, looking down at her coat and fumbling with the buttons. "Nothing important. Ornaments," and then she was gone.

If it had just been the two of us, Mrs. Lessing would have opened up to me the way mothers and daughters were supposed to with each other—the way they did in the most recent issue of *Life* where Jackie Kennedy was holding Caroline so tightly. Mrs. Lessing might have told me about everything she was working on, about the way the past wouldn't let her go. I would tell her about my mother leaving and how I couldn't stop wondering what I had done wrong. *Nothing,* Mrs. Lessing would say. She'd touch my hair and tell me it was all right. She'd tell me I was important.

"Who won the battle of Hastings?" Cora said, opening her notebook.

I flipped over onto my back, tucking my arms under my head. "I don't know," I said. "Hastings?"

Cora let out a disgusted sigh. "Do you *want* to fail?"

"No," I said. I was past caring about grades, especially in history. Who cared about France when people went missing and were murdered right under your nose and innocent people ended up feeling responsible, paying the price? Mrs. Lessing had created her own sort of prison. "You spend too much time in the attic," I'd heard Mr. Lessing say, to which his wife answered, "But I can't *do* anything else." I wondered if it was easier to be up there, with only her thoughts, if somehow coming down to earth made her think too much about what had happened next door.

When Cora went downstairs to get a snack, I became restless. Trying to stop myself from thinking about food, I wandered into the hall and peered up the attic stairs. The door was open and a shaft of light streamed down, leaving a bright square at my feet. I took it as a sign. Without thinking twice, I went upstairs to turn it off.

Mrs. Lessing's studio was the most beautiful, sad place I had ever seen. Wings were hung on the rough plank walls, some so large they were almost frightening. I went over and touched the feathers, stiff and brittle with paint. Running my fingers over a wire cage, I peered inside, where a tiny red box dangled from a string. In a corner by the small diamond-shaped window sat a globe on a wooden stand; faint with hunger, I knelt down, letting its ridges and latitudes spin beneath my finger. Wherever it stopped was where my mother had gone . . . the Arctic Ocean. I imagined her trapped beneath a layer of ice, her gaze lifeless, her fists frozen where she had tried to break through. *She had gone there to harm herself.* Mrs. Lessing would try to comfort me, to bring me back to the world. And we would hide here in the attic together, sharing stories.

When I found the stack of Christmas presents waiting beneath a folding table, my throat tightened and I began to tear up. I opened a box of beautiful barrettes that Mrs. Lessing must have decorated herself, an illustrated Audubon guide to birds of North America, a store-bought boomerang for Toby, a red wool coat with gold buttons that must have been for Cora. I buried my face in the collar and breathed in the soft scent of department store perfumes. There was that same new smell that still lingered in some of my mother's unworn garments. I tried on the coat and hugged it around me. The inside was lined with a beautiful, soft ivory satin. I felt it slip around my wrists. Outside, the sun was sinking behind the Bowmans' roof, and their house was bathed in purple light. Something about dusk made me hungry for a memory I couldn't quite place. I took off the beautiful red coat and put it back in the box.

I let my hand drift over the feathers and pots of paint on the table, letting my tears fall. There was no one to see. A notebook lay open next to a jar of water where brushes soaked. Mrs. Lessing had drawn a rope down the margin and the frayed end spun into words:

> *You see, I think of my children, I think of the laundry to stop myself from thinking about you. White shirt after white shirt, and how am I able to press them anymore? This feeling has to grow tired and just give up—*

There were footsteps at the top of the stairs, and when I turned around Cora was standing there, staring at me, her pale eyes narrowed, the way they'd when she first saw me outside the Bowmans'. Quickly, I dried my eyes on my sweater.

"You're not supposed to be up here," she said. "No one is."

"Your mother left the light on," I croaked.

Cora crossed her arms. "What's wrong?" she asked, but her tone was suspicious.

My eyes were red, my cheeks streaked with tears. "I don't know," I said, shaking my head, grasping the edge of the table because I felt like I might pass out right there. "Nothing, I guess."

We went back downstairs and I pretended to study, but it wasn't the same. Cora didn't trust me anymore; something had been building up between us.

ON THE LAST DAY OF SCHOOL BEFORE VACATION, I SAW FAYE HALLOCK IN THE hall slipping Christmas cards into lockers. I didn't think to check if she'd given one to me. It was unlikely—she never even wanted to sit next to me in class—but when I packed up my books at the end of the day, a white envelope fluttered to the floor, a white envelope with my name written across it in gold. I couldn't believe it. I didn't show Cora. I kept Faye's card hidden in a secret pocket of my bag like a stolen jewel. My mother would have liked the idea of Faye. Faye was her type of girl, pretty and talkative with her own special flair.

That afternoon, I sat at my mother's letter desk tracing the sequin Christmas tree on the card with the tip of my finger. Faye had made all the dots above the I's into hearts. For a very long time, I sat, trying to copy her perfect, round script in a letter I was writing to Lowell:

Dear Lowell, I would like so much to be your friend. I think there are things we have to say to each other.

But my handwriting was too shaky and strange. I couldn't get it right. Suddenly, it seemed like nothing was ever going to be right, despite all my attempts to make it on my own.

I took my secret fresh package of cigarettes out of the drawer and went outside. The bitter cold seeped through my buttonholes, scraping my lungs. I didn't care. I imagined shedding my coat, hat, and mittens in a pile and just walking and walking and walking into the cold night. I'd lie down in a snowdrift by the old train tracks outside of town and stare up until the stars came together in a single bright light at the end of the sky. They'd find my body like that. My mother would probably feel guilty enough to come back to my father, but I would be gone.

During the evenings, now, my father and I kept to ourselves, curled in on the chill. He often walked from room to room, as if he were looking for something, but he had little to say. My mother went unmentioned for days on end. So did everything else. Our lives had dwindled down to silence and cold. At odd moments we'd find ourselves face-to-face, surprised out of thoughts along dark hallways. Maybe we were both dreaming about Mother on the Riviera or somewhere closer, in pursuit of Starkweather's ghost.

I woke up one morning at the tail end of a dream, sick with dread. Starkweather and Caril Ann had been barreling through the snow in my mother's gold Studebaker, on their way to kill my father. Everything had stopped. Our house seemed caught inside itself, buried beneath a layer of ice. Rising slowly out of bed, I crept down the hall and pushed open my parents' bedroom door. By the dim glow of dawn, I could see my father in his striped pajamas tangled in the sheets, his body curled around a pillow. He lay on his side, his hands tucked beneath his cheek, thin hair grazing his brow. His shoulders rose and fell with his heavy breath. He needed a haircut and a good shave. He didn't look anything like a father. He was a lovesick puppy about to roll over and play dead. I moved through the soft light and knelt down beside the bed, trying to read his dreams. But his face was blank. He shifted away and let out a soft slow snore.

THE NIGHT I FINALLY SAW LOWELL FELT LIKE THE COLDEST EVENING I COULD remember. I stayed around late to help the Lessings decorate their Christmas tree with miniature birds and feather fans tied at the bottom with red ribbon. Mrs. Lessing had collected the feathers for the fans during April and May, when the birds—dark green mallards, mergansers, barn swallows, snow geese, cormorants—migrated from south to north across the wetlands on their way to Canada. If you searched hard at the right time of year, you could find bright feathers hidden in the tall blades of grass, tiny whispers of color that had brushed the sky. Mrs. Lessing had etched some of the feathers with silver or gold, and I could see them shimmering in the light of candles. "They all come at once," she said, as she told the story of the birds' approach. "It's beautiful." But the way she described the scene was so full of longing that it almost hurt to listen. It seemed like Mrs. Lessing herself might fly away.

Mr. Lessing came down from the ladder, where he'd been adjusting the star on the top of the tree, and stood over her, biting his lip, frowning as if not quite sure what to do. He reached down to touch her shoulder. "Corrine—" he said.

But Mrs. Lessing pulled away. I wanted to stay and tell them all never to give her another piece of laundry. She couldn't take it. Her head was too crowded with other things. They should have shown more appreciation. She had picked out the most beautiful gifts.

I wanted to see what would happen, but Cora shot me a look, and I followed her into the sunroom, where she got out the checkers as I strained to hear her parents' voices. But everything had gone quiet. Perhaps they were hugging, or maybe Mr. Lessing was putting his wife to bed with a hot-water bottle and a glass of warm milk to soothe her nerves. Maybe he was rubbing his palm over her back, something I so much wanted someone to do for me.

Outside, the sky was dark. The Bowmans' house loomed like a forgotten ruin beyond the white picket fence. The only light anywhere I could see was our lantern flickering over the table and Cora's round face. We were on a ship, riding the dark waves toward a haunted island, with no land anywhere in sight. I thought of the cat still buried in the sepulchre, its eyes gone white as clouds, and Mrs. Bowman wrapped up in a bedsheet. I thought of her swimming through the dark all on her own.

Cora lined up her checker pieces. "You're the black," she said. "You go first."

I organized my checkers on the board and moved one. "Is your mother upset about the murders?"

Cora sighed. "How should I know?" She moved her checker piece slowly across the surface of the board and looked at me. She knew I didn't want to play. She knew what I wanted to do, but she'd never see why.

I wanted to come to some sort of understanding. The world was so incredibly vast. I got up and went to the window and stared out at the Bowmans' house as a cloud drifted over the moon. All I could see was the skeleton fence, the rectangles of lifeless windows. "What do you think their last thoughts were?" I said.

"Whose?"

I turned around to face her. "*You* know." I was surprised by the insistence in my voice.

"You *think* too much about it," she said as if she were an adult who wanted to emphasize the point of what she was saying.

"Everything's frozen. I can't help thinking it looks like that day when it happened."

"You weren't even here," she said. "They'd taken the Christmas stuff down by then, and there was only a little snow."

"What else do you remember? Did they leave footprints?"

"*I* don't know. What does it matter? Everyone knew who did it anyhow. They had no use for footprints. Footprints were *obsolete*." She sat there looking haughty because she had all the answers. *Obsolete* had been on our vocabulary test last week. Cora had gotten it right.

Suddenly, I understand the kind of boredom my mother had felt. I was so tired of Cora and the same conversations.

Lowell Bowman was what I needed. I opened my bag, pretended to look for a pack of cigarettes, took out a book and then laid Faye Hallock's Christmas card on top of it. When I looked up, I could tell I'd made a mistake. Cora's eyes were so sad. They sparkled in the light from the lantern, like dark bottomless pools. You couldn't help the way you felt about a person, though. I just didn't feel sorry for her. If I were Cora, I would have been a better daughter.

She picked up the card. I watched her open it. She studied it for a moment and then slid it back across the table. Her cheeks went red.

"It's nothing," I said.

Cora stared at the board and ground two checker pieces back and forth between her fingers. "You're different," she said. She chewed on the corner of her thumb, then thrust her hand beneath the table. I wanted to tell her to stop chewing on things, stop *fidgeting*. "All you think about is my mother. I told you that story because I thought you were my friend."

"I was only trying to help her."

"How could you possibly do that? You look in the mirror all the time. When you smoke, you pretend you're in the movies. But you're not. You're like me. You're one of *us*."

I didn't want there to be any *us*.

"Cora—" I said, but I did not have the words to continue. I couldn't give her this one small thing. A shadow moved across her face. A light had gone on in the Bowmans' living room. It was Lowell. It had to be him, home for the holidays. He took off his jacket and hung it over the back of the chair, then ran his fingers through his hair. I couldn't tell the color, only that his shirt was a light shade, a buttondown. I couldn't see his face. I had to get closer. As I approached the window, he peered out into the darkness, like he knew I was there, like he was waiting, then turned around and disappeared out of view. Perhaps he had seen me standing in the lantern light, a far-off figure from a long lost time. Maybe after we got to know each other, he would always remember me this way.

I could hear Cora putting the checkers away. She snuffed out the lantern. The darkness folded us in. "That's him," I whispered.

The air was so still between us. There were all the tiny sounds that made up silence, a whirring, a humming, a pulse.

Then Cora said, "What you really wish is that it had happened to you."

"Oh, for Pete's sake," I said.

"I think you do. And that makes you almost like a murderer yourself. You probably *scared* your mother off." We stood there in the darkness for a moment without moving. I could sense Cora's round outline beside me, hear her breath. I had nothing left to lose. I packed up my bag, threw it over my shoulder, and unlocked the sunroom door.

"Where are you going?" she whispered.

"Home."

"I don't believe you."

It didn't make any difference what she believed. I stepped out into the snow. The cold air cut into my skin, but I didn't care.

"Sue—" Cora said.

I stepped forward through the snow as he passed in front of the window, holding a bottle of something, I couldn't tell what. I only caught a glimpse. As he bent behind the couch, the Christmas tree lights came on. When he stood back up, the glow was soft around him and I walked right up to the fence. A pine tree hummed in the wind. I heard Cora coming up behind me, her boots cracking the frozen crust of snow. Climbing a rise, I stumbled forward and grabbed the fence posts. Cold filled my boots as my feet slipped through layers, last week's fall and all the snows before. When Lowell disappeared for a moment, I moved closer, afraid I'd lose him forever. A moment later, he was back in the frame of the window, flopping down on the couch, with his feet on one arm, his neck resting on the other. His hair was a brown color, straight and short, almost a crew cut, which made him look like what magazines called a man's man. He seemed so close. He opened a book, and I tried to see what it was. I wanted to know what he was reading.

Cora grabbed my shoulder. I lifted myself over the fence. She tugged at my coat. "You *can't.*"

But I could. I broke free and fell forward into a bank of snow by the rose garden. The stars spun above me. I put my face in my hands and rubbed my mittens back and forth across my cheeks. But Lowell Bowman hadn't heard me. He hadn't moved a muscle. The gentle wind in the pine masked any sound. *"Don't think you can come back,"* Cora hissed.

I knew I couldn't come back. I had broken into another world. I had crossed the line, but I didn't care. I was a new person. I was a braver person. There was nothing left to hide behind. I had never been so sure of anything. My cheeks stung with crusted snow, but inside the Bowmans' house the living room light was warm and red, soft as the inside of a heart. My bag hung from my shoulder, heavy and wet. I walked up as close as I dared and hung there, beside the pine, just out of sight. What color were his eyes? What words were inside his head? His feet shifted. Tennis shoes. He tucked up his knees and propped the book on his thighs.

Wet clumps melted around my calves where snow had slipped in. I barely felt it.

Suddenly he threw down the book and stood up. There was impatience. My heart jumped, but I wasn't scared. He wore a blue oxford tucked into belted jeans. He was skinny. I thought, *He must always wear belts.* It was one of those things you knew about a person when you knew him well, like that his socks never matched, or about his underwear patterns, whether they had trains and cowboys or checks and stripes.

Lowell went over to the Christmas tree and took something off a branch, staring down at the palm of his hand. I wanted to know what it was. Something treasured from the old Christmases when the three of them were all together; that had to be it. He placed the object in the center of the coffee table. I came closer, right up the window, trying not to make a sound. I peered over the sill, feeling my heart catch. It was an ornament, bright in color, a large bird with wings painted gold. It looked familiar, like something Mrs. Lessing would have made. He sat with his elbows on his knees, staring, as if he were trying to make it move with his eyes. And then, for some reason, I just knew—the way a person knows things—that guilt was eating away at him. He had no reason to feel guilty. He was right there, strange and private, feeling something the boys at college couldn't possibly understand. But *I* understood how it was to be on your own.

I was desperate to know his thoughts, if he could feel me near the way I had always been able to feel *him.* I came closer. I took off my mitten, watched my hand reach out like something in a dream. I imagined that I was touching him, pressing his cheek with the tip of my finger. He might have thought I was the wind, a ghost, a little chill. I touched the windowpane. My breath left a circle on the glass.

As Lowell looked up and came to the window, I flattened myself against the side of the house and glanced back over my shoulder. I could see him furrow his brow, as he braced both his hands on the glass. He touched the circle my breath had left behind and jerked away from the window, as I stumbled back toward the pine tree, falling forward in my footprints, face down in the snow, the contents of my bag spilling like an avalanche. Ice scraped my tongue. My throat felt stuffed with cotton. I scrambled to pick up my books. Everything was real—the ground, the sky, the footprints—but all of a sudden I didn't want anything to be real.

I heard the patio door open, saw the slit of light in the darkness and the sparkle of snow. There was nothing I could do. My footprints were like craters. I pushed my way along the fence, each step dragging me down, struggling against an impossible undertow. I stopped to catch my breath. I waited for his hands to grab me, to reach out and pull me down into somewhere new. But there was no sound, nothing there. He hadn't followed. I knew I had to have scared him, given everything. He must have jumped at every sound. Not so long ago his parents' murderers had stood on this very same ground.

"Who's there?"

I caught my breath. My feet felt heavy, as if in a nightmare. Forward motion was impossible.

"Who's there?" He stood by the edge of the house, his outline black against the light from the living room. He turned around in his footprints and peered into the darkness. His heart must have been hammering.

I choked on nothing and made my way quickly along the fence, tumbling out onto South 24th Street. A taste clung to my tongue like rusty metal. I hurried in and out of streetlights, my heart pounding in my chest. To snug families in passing cars, I was no one special: just a girl, late for dinner, skittering along with burrs of snow caught to her coat. But inside I had changed. I was an almost criminal, Starkweather's girlfriend, letting love make me crazy. I was following in her footprints, walking that same dangerous ground.

I shed my bag, hat, and coat in a pile by the kitchen door and combed the snow out of my hair like nothing had happened. My father came in holding the newspaper, scratching his head. There were slippers on his feet. I had never seen him wear slippers.

"It's not safe for you to be wandering around after dark."

"Are you worried?"

"I'm your father."

"It's only four blocks."

"A lot can happen in four blocks," he said, tapping the newspaper. "Most car accidents occur within a mile of home. And nobody wears seat belts. The human imagination seems incapable of grasping the concept of its own demise."

"Oh," I said, looking down at my feet, afraid he'd sense I'd been up to no good. But the puddle around my shoes looked sad and ordinary, telling nothing of where I'd been.

My father sighed. "The problem is, your mother doesn't think she'll ever die. She can leave, come back years later, and nothing will have changed."

I studied him for a moment, trying to tell if he'd had too many drinks. His body looked smaller, his head drooping as if it were too heavy to keep up. We both had changed.

I went upstairs and emptied the bag on the floor of my room. Everything inside was damp with snow. A pen had leaked, and left a tiny blue stain on the carpet. I wanted to salvage Faye Hallock's Christmas card, but I couldn't find it anywhere. I checked every pocket twice. My heart lightened, lost gravity completely. I shook books by the spine without feeling their weight.

I had to call Cora. "It's me," I said.

"I saw what happened. He almost caught you," she said. "You're sick."

"Did I leave anything at your house?"

"I don't want to talk to you anymore." I had never heard her voice sound so hateful. And then the line went dead.

Who's there? he'd said. Had he really wanted to know? I could see the gold letters of my name shining like a beacon in the snow where I had fallen.

DAYS PASSED, WITHOUT MOTHER OR ANY WORD FROM CORA. I STOPPED EATing, and tried to forget about what I'd done. I read the newspaper clipping one last time. The pages had yellowed and become thin with so much handling. I examined Starkweather and Fugate closely before throwing the article away, burying it in the bottom of the kitchen trash. I said a strange sort of goodbye to Carol King and Bob Jensen, Moira Dunphey, and Jeanette and Arthur Bowman. I hadn't meant to scare their son. I went up to my room and lay down on my side, feeling as if I'd lost someone dear to me. That night I cried myself to sleep.

ON CHRISTMAS, MY FATHER AND I DROVE TO AUNT PORTIA AND UNCLE Freddy's in Omaha and pretended like everything was all right. But we weren't fooling anyone. Capital Steel was in the red, I'd heard my father tell someone on the telephone, and everyone thought my mother had left because of this. She was kicking him while he was down. They couldn't see how much her leaving had to do with me.

At dinner, Uncle Freddy talked about Coach Devaney and the Cornhuskers' win over Michigan. Claridge, the quarterback, was coming into his own. They were going to be a strong team now, with the rough spots of '61 ironed out. My father agreed. The Huskers had a promising future.

Aunt Portia cornered me in the kitchen when I brought a stack of dirty dishes in from the table. "Puggy," she said, holding me away from her, "you flattened the mashed potatoes under your napkin."

"I wasn't hungry, Aunt Portia."

"You're very thin," she said.

I felt the twitch of a smile on my lips. I stared at Aunt Portia's round figure bulging from beneath her apron, trying imagine the beautiful little girl with the long auburn braids standing in the shade of the elm tree. But there didn't seem to be any likeness to those yellowed photographs. Now her hair was short and gray, her legs thick and stocky as drainpipes. Was it possible for grown women to be jealous of girls? *What happened to you?* I wanted to say.

"Daddy told me you wrote love notes and dropped them all over the house," I said.

"Did he?"

I nodded.

"Shame on him. He made so much fun of me. It was just a game," she said, dismissing the memory with a wave of her hand, but her eyes looked dreamy, far away somehow. "I was such a silly girl with so many grand ideas about the way things would turn out."

"Because of Hans and Elsa?"

Aunt P put the dishes on the drying rack and turned to me. "You can't have silly dreams anymore. You have to take care of your father now. Do you understand what it feels like to lose someone like that?"

I wandered through the newly furnished rooms nibbling peanuts out of silver bowls. I could hear Jimmy Stewart in the den where my cousins watched *It's a Wonderful Life.* My father and Uncle Freddy were smoking cigars behind the white-frosted Christmas tree, blowing great billowy clouds out the window like two boys sneaking cigarettes. I took their half-full drinks off the coffee table and flushed them down the toilet, then put the glasses back on the coasters where I'd found them. The sooner my father finished his drink, the sooner we could go back home.

OUT OF NOWHERE, THE NEW YEAR CAME, AND IT WAS 1963. CORA AND I HAD planned on writing down our resolutions, throwing them into a fire, and sneaking champagne when my father was out. Neither of us had ever had a full drink. But instead, I sat at my bedroom window, staring into the darkness, thinking how strange it was that something so important as an entire year could shift overnight into a great unknown. You woke up, and suddenly it was 1945 and the war was going to end, or it was 1950 and half a century had passed. Or it was 1958 and you would never see your parents again.

Our house was so quiet. Somewhere else, there were sparklers and noisemakers and funny hats. All over Lincoln, people fell down drunk and necked like mad because it was midnight and they wanted to have good luck. They wanted to spend the rest of their lives together. I wondered if Lowell knew who he wanted to spend the rest of his life with. I wondered if anyone would ever want to spend time with me or if my parents were only the beginning, only the first of all kinds of people who wouldn't find me quite special enough to make a difference.

I dreaded the return to school. My mind invented horrible scenarios. Lowell had found the envelope with my name on it and had accused Cora of sneaking around in the dark with her friends. Or, worse, Mrs. Pritchard had found the card and was busy putting two and two together. She had questioned Mrs. Lessing on the subject, having remembered the afternoon a strange awkward girl had wandered into her garden. Yes, it was that day the blizzard began.

I found *Old Possum's Book of Practical Cats* on my grandfather's bookshelf and decided to give it to Cora. It must have belonged to my father or Aunt Portia when they were children, but I wrote Cora's name and *Christmas 1962, Love, Susan* inside the front cover without a second thought. It was the perfect apology. My heart was swollen with generosity. I only had to admit fault to be forgiven.

I got up early and put on eye makeup before school, outlining my eyes carefully, enhancing the shape, making them bigger and soft. Doe-eyed. As long as I looked put together on the outside, no one would be able to guess how I was feeling. Because the liner was my mother's, the color was dark and smoky and gave my face a subtle depth, as if there were worlds of mystery, worlds of experience, behind my eyes. I applied the lines discreetly, not wanting to get sent to the principal for being cheap, like some girls who painted their lips fire-engine red and wore their sweaters unbuttoned too far down. *Seventeen* said the secret to makeup was looking like you weren't wearing any, which didn't seem to be true of the Egyptians, or Hollywood stars. I imagined myself an Egyptian princess, my body becoming tall and angular overnight like one of those ancient hieroglyphics in our World Studies textbook.

When I saw Cora in the hall at school, I lifted my hand in greeting, but she looked right through me. My heart sank. I couldn't get up the courage to talk to her. *Who do you think you are?* she'd say, and I wouldn't have an answer. I'd been stupid to think a book would change anything. Or throwing away that article. I was still the same person. Nothing was any different. Faye leaned against her locker holding her books to her chest, laughing with Steve Bunt, who was handsome and straight-edged, not the sort of boy who would ever be caught dead talking to someone crazy, a window peeper, someone like me.

In English class we read a poem about a sick rose.

Cora had her eyes narrowed at me, tapping her eraser on her desk and staring me down as if to say, *You are the sickest rose I ever saw.*

"What do you think William Blake meant by the sick rose?" Ms. Wimmett asked the class. She had chalk on her nose. Nobody said anything. "Somebody? What is the metaphor?" I pretended to study the poem for the answer, even though I already had one. The sick rose was me.

"Yes, Cora?"

My stomach turned over.

"The rose lost beauty and purity," she said. "Maybe it was corrupted from sticking its nose where it didn't belong."

"Roses don't have noses," someone called out.

I could feel everyone looking at me. For the first time in a month Cora and I weren't sitting together. It was obvious. My cheeks glowed with embarrassment. But she didn't stop there. When Ms. Wimmett asked her to clarify the central metaphor, she said, "*Unholy* love. From an impure heart." Everyone giggled.

Unholy. There was a dark place inside me that had wanted Nils to imagine me naked. There was a strange part of me that pulled me toward windows, that plunged me into places I had no business being, that made me want to do unimaginable things. There was the time I had stolen wine and tried to kiss a dancing teacher, and now my whole body shuddered with fresh embarrassment, as if that very blunder had unfolded only a day before. I was part of the problem, I was part of the deceit, no different from Caril Ann Fugate.

I HAVE NO IDEA WHERE ALL THIS DARKNESS COMES FROM. THE SUN IS BRIGHT, and the sidewalks sparkle, and I am walking down Calvert Street without my coat. My head is so light, I don't touch the ground. There is nothing inside me. I can see from above. A tiny blue thing shakes its fist in the pit of my stomach. This is the cold and hunger.

But I don't care. It is the middle of the day. The sun is impossible. Far away, a distant headlight. I don't know where I'm going.

A tiny dog in a picture window barks and snarls and throws his body against the glass when I pass, over and over, and then I am gone. I don't know where I'm going. I know what I've done, though. I've walked out before fourth period. I've left everything behind. The trees around the golf course claw black streaks in the sky. The land rolls out in an endless white scroll. The ground crunches under my feet. I lie down where the ninth hole might be. The snow stings my back, my arms. I no longer feel my fingers. I don't feel my feet. I don't shut my eyes. The sky is part of another world, blue and spinning like the inside of me.

I turn my head, and someone in a hat is hurrying toward me between the trees. This must be Lowell. Instead, it's a man with big work boots, and he is holding clippers. What will I say? *Let me sleep. I'm tired of feeling so much hunger for so many things. I will never be loved. If a person could see into the future, why would she choose to walk the world alone? I think of killers with girlfriends, and soldiers with letters, and all dead, and I am pretty sure someone must have loved them.*

I watch the clippers thump down in the snow. He smiles and bobs his head. "Hi," he says. He takes off his coat and puts it around me, thick fleece, and it smells like the hide of an animal. The hat is black. The hair underneath pokes out gray. He puts his big gloves over my hands and pulls me up. I am watching this from the outside in; I don't really feel it. I am too tired to resist.

He tells me I am crazy to be out here, without a stitch, and what am I trying to do, kill myself? Do I feel all right? Do I know my name? Do I think I can walk? I walk, but I don't speak. He has his arm around me. He rubs his hand up and down. "I was just cuttin' a loose branch broke from the ice by the thirteenth hole. And then I'm comin' back to the club, and I see you just layin' there. Jesus Christ!" he says. "You scared the hell outa me. What if I never came? You just gonna lay there till spring, little darlin'?"

Little darlin' does not sound like me. It sounds like someone in a song. We walk in silence. The cold hurts. I feel prickles in my fingers because the nerves are waking up. My eyes feel frozen open. My teeth chatter. I am too cold to be embarrassed. My limbs creak. I just want to be warm.

He takes me through the first door we come to, the glass one, in the bar. He tells me rules say he should have brought me around back—he is a groundskeeper—but what the hell? It's the middle of the day. There is a fire in here. It is more important that I am all right. "You sit tight," he says. I hear him at the bar telling Rick the story of how he found me. The way he tells it, it sounds funny, like one of those weird ways married people meet. "She won't give her name."

"I think that's Mr. Hurst's girl," Rick says.

I stare at the flames. He gets me a pail of water to heat up my hands. Want a cheeseburger? I shake my head. French fries? No. The water is cold. "Ouch," I say, and try to lift them out.

"Keep them there." Rick puts his fingers around my wrists and pushes them back down. His wedding band sparkles. There is water in the blond hair on the back of his hands, like dew on grass.

He is a bartender. He knows everyone's secrets. He tells me about crazy times in people's lives when the rug gets pulled out from under them and there seems to be nothing left. They just want to lie down and quit. Who doesn't feel that way from time to time? And when you're young and pain is new, you feel like your heart has been hollowed out with a razor. But the thing is, it keeps ticking. There was this girl in high school, Deidre Lynch, who made him want to die. He felt like jumping off a bridge, but there weren't any bridges. He thought about hanging himself from a tree. Lynching himself. Get it? And there were girls after Dee that made him want to do worse. He laughs. The point is, it's never as bad as you think. We sit in silence. I don't tell him my secret. He pats me on the shoulder and goes to mop down the bar. I close my eyes.

•

MY FATHER HAD BEEN CALLED. HE KNEW WHERE TO FIND ME. HE CAME IN HIS work suit and red tie, his wool coat buttoned wrong like he'd just run out of a meeting. "What in the world happened?" he wanted to know. "I thought you were at school. Are you all right?"

I nodded my head, but I could feel the tears starting to come. I wanted to grab on to my father's coat and slide to the floor. I wanted to give up.

"Thank God Boyd was out there." My father put his arms around me and mashed my face to his chest. His crooked buttons were sharp and cold on my cheek. In the wool folds of his coat, I could smell the wind.

"Everyone hates me," I said.

"You're my girl," my father said. "How could anyone hate you?"

In the parking lot, we stopped to watch the sky turning orange, fading quickly like an extinguished match. He took my hand and kissed my head. "Don't you go leaving too," he said.

CHAPTER NINETEEN

1991

I stood in front of the bedroom window, looking down at the river. The light had all but disappeared; on the far bank, the black shapes of trees brushed the sky. At the gallery, Francesca would just now be closing up, setting the alarm, leaving my collection waiting quietly in the dark.

As the glimmer of a ghost boat slipped through the fog, the image of my wife came to me, sitting in the living room, preparing herself for whatever sort of mood I would bring home with me. I thought about calling her, letting her know that I planned on staying here for a few days, a few weeks; it no longer mattered what I said, she'd know what I meant. But the idea of having to listen to her break down because of something I had done was just too much.

I took off my wedding band and put it on the nightstand, telling myself I didn't deserve to wear it. Part of me had wanted to kiss Jane. I hated myself for that, and yet it had just seemed so much easier to give what wasn't expected. Susan had always expected so much. I had been so grateful for the way she came to me.

Feeling a sudden chill, I took another sip of scotch, assuring myself I could go out and get another bottle as soon as I was finished. But the liquor didn't numb me. It merely traced an icy burn down my throat, making me shiver. Half stumbling, I wandered toward the linen closet to root around for a blanket. The shelves were cluttered with tarnished silver and half-empty boxes full of things that had belonged to Susan's uncle. The very sight of all that junk still packed away here annoyed me, certainly more than it should have.

Pulling a quilt off the top shelf with an unnecessary amount of vigor, I hit a box full of letters knocking it to the floor. Douglas's envelopes spilled out over the rag rug, and I had a mind to burn all that trash. Susan saved obsessively. She could never let go of anything. We had left Nebraska behind and come here without knowing anyone—like reversed pioneers, we had often joked. Yet she had always clung so desperately to every memento.

I remembered her standing in the barn reading her uncle's words, her eyes brimming with tears. It had seemed so gratuitously dramatic to want to mail his old boyfriend those letters. I had been so relieved when she agreed not to do it. Jamming the envelopes back into the box, however, I noticed one that had actually gone through the mail and was addressed to Susan herself. I sat down right there in the hall, leaned my back against the wall, and opened it:

October 3, 1982

Dear Ms. Bowman:

You are so kind to send me Douglas's letter, though *yours* has taken some time finding me as I am now based in Atlanta working for the airlines. So, to answer your question, yes, you did the right thing. As you say, love is not so easy to find, and it is nice to know that someone you once cared about actually remembers. I, in fact, did not know Douglas was sick. To hear he was no longer with us hit me quite hard. When I read his letter, I was sitting in the lounge of the Baton Rouge airport and I found myself right there in public, praying hard he had made his peace.

You ask why I think your uncle did not mail this letter and I'll tell it to you simply: He couldn't come to terms with who he was. It seems that I was the part of him that would always remain a secret. In the end I don't believe he ever told anyone but your mother. So to answer your question, yes, I did meet her once. She was living in New York, working for an artist. She took the train up to Port Saugus to spend the night. I remember her wearing a bright red sweater and a scarf wrapped around her head. It wasn't an outfit any woman could have pulled off, but she certainly got away with it. Your mother tried out recipes on us, burned everything, and stumbled around the kitchen in her heels. We drank quite a lot and lay on our backs looking at the stars. I'm afraid I can't remember much of what we talked about, but I'm sure she must have mentioned you.

You say that difficult times have caused you to question your own importance to those you love. Well, I wouldn't question too much. No doubt you are a remarkable person.

Respectfully,
Michael Downs

Feeling shamed and selfish, I started down to the end of the hall, still holding the letter, and studied the family portrait that Jane had painted. Hank and Mary sat on the bench by the front door, and Susan and I stood beside them with the house in the background. I searched my wife's expression for a hint of all the things she'd been looking for, because surely an artist would sense what I could not. But Susan seemed unworried, absorbed. Her eyes were full of kindness and her arms were wrapped around the children's shoulders so naturally, as if reaching out was something she had never had to try to master. The colors were beautiful, ethereal, almost Renaissance in their conviction. I was the one who looked more ghostly than the others, my features just a little less certain.

THAT SUMMER, BEFORE JANE HAD PAINTED US, I WAS RESTLESS AND ANGRY ALL the time. I had received a phone call from some horrible talk show—*A Current Affair*—asking me to be a guest on one of their episodes about survivors. I had never really considered myself to be one. "No, thank you, I'm not interested," I had said to the insistent and overly sympathetic woman on the other end of the line. She was so smooth and polished. Her tone outraged me. And yet I was still too shocked to sound anything but polite. When I hung up the telephone, I wondered how they had found me and who was to blame. I didn't tell Susan. I just wanted to forget it, and yet I couldn't let myself. How could they have seen it as their right to intrude? Suddenly, everyone was an intruder. It felt like my family was telling secrets. It felt like things were being shoved down my throat.

Spring rain had made the water high, and the spot where the children were usually allowed to swim was declared off limits. They couldn't sit still. Most of the time Susan was there, to take Hank to tennis or golf lessons and Mary to the stables so she could ride Jane's horse Mistletoe or help muck out the stall. After these outings, my wife and seven-year-old daughter would return with the smell of hay and leather and dung caught in their clothes, sharing secretive smiles.

When Susan wasn't there, the children moped around the house complaining about the heat. They wanted to be taken to the public pool, but I had things to do and a lot on my mind. I had made a big sale—a flawless paper-thin Flemish cucumber-colored cup—to the Corning Glass Museum, but summer had slowed everything down and Port Saugus was rather far off the beaten path for major collectors or acquisitions experts from the better-known museums. I was starting to realize that our situation here couldn't be permanent. Sooner or later, we'd have to leave this house where Susan had said she wanted to raise our children.

When she barged into the barn one afternoon to tell me she had decided to ask Jane to paint a family portrait, I pulled out a stack of books and pretended to be absorbed. "What do you think?" my wife said, her face glowing with the idea: the four of us and the dogs in front of the house where our lives together had really begun.

"I think I don't have time to do it just now," I answered, without looking up from a book on ancient bronzes. I guess I was already dreading the idea of telling her we would have to leave.

Susan brushed her hand along the windowsill and frowned at the dust on the tips of her fingers, which annoyed me. "What do you have to do, Lowe?"

I spoke of all the arranging and rearranging that would have to be done in order to get this portrait right, I just couldn't bear the thought. We weren't that kind of family anyway. We didn't look comfortable enough to be preserved for posterity. Maybe no family did anymore. But Susan just stared at me, smiling as if I was crazy.

"Jane paints from photographs. It's not like we have to sit still for five days."

"Don't we *have* a photograph?"

"I want *her* to take it because we don't have a recent one," she said. "And it's important. She'll get the composition right. It'll be something worth holding on to, don't you think?"

In the end I gave in because I knew Susan would quietly persist.

THE DAY OF THE PHOTO, SUSAN HAD SPENT THE MORNING ARRANGING FLOWers, grooming the dogs, and dressing the children. But when Jane arrived early, my wife still wasn't ready. She couldn't find Mary. I helped Jane set up the camera and then took her into the barn to see my objects. She moved with such grace and ease and seemed to notice all the effort I had put into redoing this place, from the floors to the track lighting to the fluted columns I had found in an old stone yard near Balmville, things Susan never took note of.

Through the open window I could smell the grass, just mowed that morning. Susan was by the side of the house, holding the pruning shears and calling for our daughter. The telephone rang and she went to answer it, after which I could hear her soft, restrained laughter and then the dull snap of branches as she began to clip the hedge, the telephone nestled between cheek and shoulder.

"So what do you think?" I said finally, turning away from the window. Jane ran her finger along the edge of a crack in a marble bust of Athena as if she were, by the mere act of touching, stitching that ancient face back together.

"Like a random scoot," she said, her eyes full of something that resembled excitement.

"A random scoot?"

"Picking it all up suddenly and heading somewhere unexpected."

"Ah," I said. "I know what you mean." Lately, I felt that my whole life had been a sort of haphazard journey, unplanned, not carefully thought out, scene after scene unfolding in rapid succession while I stood there watching from the wings. I loved Susan. Of course I always had, but when Jane sat down to examine a gold Roman ring, the fan blew her hair across her cheek, and I wanted to catch the blond strands in my hand and tuck them behind her ear.

There was a strange quiet, and I left Jane with the objects for a moment and stepped outside to see where everyone had gone. Susan was no longer by the hedge, and the telephone receiver had been dropped in the grass. I could hear the busy signal humming like an insect. The sun was blinding, the air thick with humidity, as I made my way across the grass and hung up the phone. Then, sensing that something was wrong, I started across the yard, toward the river, through the tall grass.

As I came up over the wall, I saw Susan and Mary. They were in the river, the current rushing around them, and my wife was pulling our daughter toward the shore. By the time I reached them, Susan was already standing in the shallow water, holding our daughter beneath the arms. Mary's hair strangled her features like a dark vine, but then she started sputtering and coughing, and when the hair fell away from her face I could see her skin was red, her eyes squinting against tears. I wanted to cry with relief. Hank was standing in two feet of water furiously sucking his thumb, tears sliding down his cheeks. "Get back from the river," I said to him, but he just stood there. "Get back, Hank."

I went toward them, plunging into the shallow water in my shoes, socks, khakis in an attempt to help, but they were already out of danger. Susan's wet sundress hugged the ripples of extra weight she had not been able to shed after quitting the cigarettes, and yet I could see the strength of her body beneath it as she carried our daughter, limp and bedraggled, from the current, sat down on the bank, put her arms around her, and held her close. They glittered in the sun like survivors from a shipwreck.

"What happened?" I said, putting my hands in my pockets.

"You almost drowned," Susan said. "Do you know what that would have done to us?" She shook Mary's shoulders.

"Can somebody tell me why she was in the water in the first place?" I said.

"You said Jane was going to make us special in the picture," Mary said to Susan, as if this were explanation enough.

"You broke the rules," Susan said.

"I wanted to be just done swimming."

"That's ridiculous," I said.

Susan gave me a hard look. "She's a child."

"That's not an excuse. Something might have happened to you too."

"Well, what choice did I have? What would *you* have done?"

I had hung up the telephone. I closed my eyes, but I could still see them, my wife and daughter huddled on the shore. I could still see the telephone, and I knew in that moment I was not meant to be a father or a husband; I was, perhaps, not meant to be depended on for anything.

"It's all right," Susan said suddenly, as if nothing had happened. "Let's just get ready for the photo."

"What are you talking about? Look what almost happened."

"Things almost happen every day," she said. "You just go on, Lowell; you pick up and go on."

"You mean, *you* do."

What she did was pick everything up and then pull it apart until nothing was left. I turned on my heels and started off down the edge of the bank, my waterlogged shoes squelching, my pant legs clinging to my itching calves.

"Where are you going?" Susan cried.

I started south, combing the cattails for God knows what. Susan didn't try to follow. I passed the drawbridge, the lighthouse where a flock of geese spread their wings and hissed, trying to keep me from trampling their nests. I made my way along the bank past a washed-up sandal, broken bottles, tossed-up lures.

People in deck chairs squinted at me in the bright light as I marched across the edge of their properties, as if I were no more than a sun spot, a trick of the eye. Perhaps it was my determination that kept them from inquiring my business, the stoop in the shoulders, the hands in the pockets. I was a gentleman on some sort of an important mission, quickly passing suntanning women in bikinis roasting in coconut oil, barbecues, vegetable gardens, dilapidated docks, clouds of boat fuel, and leftover Fourth of July flags flapping in the breeze. I wiped sweat from my brow and kept on going, and yet with each step my wet shoes rubbed my ankles with a little extra vigor, making the emptiness of my every gesture, the futility of my wandering, more and more apparent.

By the time I reached Ed Ryer's house, I was thirsty, and a small group had assembled on the deck for cocktails.

"Is that Lowe Bowman?" someone called out, and I raised my hand in greeting and made my way across the lawn so as not be rude.

"What a surprise," I said, stepping up onto the wooden deck.

"*You're* the surprise." Peg Ryer laughed, but when she saw my state—perhaps it was the shoes, the mud around the pant cuffs—her smile disappeared. "Did you walk all this way?"

"A lost dog," I said, feeling a bit more in control.

"A hot dog?" Ed laughed and clapped me on the back, and I forced out an exaggerated chuckle.

"A beagle, actually. I found some paw prints in the mud and started following them, but so far nothing's turned up." I spoke evenly, trying not to sound unhinged.

"Beagles. Isn't that the breed that follows a scent?" Peg said.

I nodded. "I'm about to give up."

"Then stay for a drink," Ed said.

"Why not?" I said, throwing up my hands in mock exasperation. "Just one."

So I drank two, maybe three cocktails at the Ryers', trying to push away the panic, trying not to think about my family waiting for my return.

It was getting late, and one of their guests offered me a ride home, but I didn't take it. The sun was setting over the roof, the clouds were streaked a smoldering, humid red. I said goodbye and started back along the bank, but when I had rounded the bend in the river, I doubled back down their neighbor's driveway, and headed toward town along the road. I had no desire to go home, drunk and broken. I didn't want to explain what was so impossible to make sense out of: why I had sabotaged the portrait, why the accident with Mary had made me turn away from my family rather than try to protect them. So I headed to town.

I went into Mickey's and pulled up a stool, and when the bartender asked me what my poison was I ordered a vodka tonic, laughing out loud at my choice. "I've always been a bourbon man," I said, shaking my head in disbelief.

"There's a first time for everything," the bartender said, and perhaps sensing I was in need of spilling some story, moved down the bar to unload the dishwasher.

The place was almost empty. A small woman with sunken cheeks shoved quarters in a Keno machine and smacked her palm against the side when the numbers betrayed her. Two men in stiff baseball caps, millworkers maybe, were starting up a game of pool.

The drink went down easily, so I had another and another until things no longer seemed so bad. My daughter had almost drowned, but she had not drowned. Near tragedy had been averted. What more could I possibly have done? I was aware with this last drink that my own body was failing me. I was a stranger to my actions. My eyes wouldn't focus, and when I swallowed it went down hard. I had one last drink and then stumbled toward home along the river.

What must have been two hours seems a mere moment in time. The moon was full over the river. I marveled in its symmetry. I watched the translucent clouds bleed into whiteness, thinking of Jane's paintings guiding me through the clutter as if strings were attached to my legs, and then I fell. I remember knowing how ridiculous it was that my feet would not cooperate, and yet I can't recall feeling any pain when rocks scraped my knees, drawing deep lines of blood through my pants, or the sensation of bending my wrist back against the step of someone's pier.

Then I was at Jane's, knocking on the door and feeling terribly lost. She opened the door a crack, undid the chain, and let me in.

"*There* you are," she said softly.

"There *you* are." I tripped over the edge of the doormat but managed to catch myself. "I ruined the portrait."

"Forget about the portrait," she said. "Where have you been?"

"Walking along the river."

"Does Susan know you're back?"

"Of course," I said, annoyed that my wife had somehow found a way to be present in this moment.

"And are you all right?"

"I'm all right." I followed her gaze down my legs. My khakis were ripped, and I had bled through the fabric. "I could use a drink, though."

"Maybe water."

"Maybe not water. Where's the bourbon? I liked drinking out of those jars." I sat down on the couch.

She seemed to think about this for a moment, whether it would be easier to appease me or try to send me home.

"You're an artist. You should understand excess," I said. "I don't want you to go to any trouble, though. I can get it myself."

"It isn't any trouble." She disappeared into the kitchen.

My head felt thick, my mouth dry, and from the couch I could see the lights of my own house winking as a breeze passed through the leaves. The closeness of it all, that place which had somehow shut me out, only made me more uncomfortable, and there weren't any curtains so I covered my eyes.

Jane came back in, handed me the bourbon, and sat down on the couch beside me. I thought from the color she might have watered down the liquor, but I drank it up anyway without complaint. "That was nice and light," I said, slamming down the jar, which missed the table and fell to the floor. "I've made a mess of things."

"That's all right, Lowell," she said. "Messes have never bothered me," and she patted my knee. "We went ahead with the photo anyway. I'll add you in." With her touch, it all seemed to hit me at once.

I put my head in my hands and ran the tips of my fingers along my brow and then lay down, putting my head in Jane's lap. "I'm sorry. You probably think I'm very presumptuous," I said.

She placed her hand on my shoulder. "I don't think so at all."

"I guess I'm drunk," I said, though I felt as if the liquor were starting to wear off.

I lay there with my eyes closed, trying to think of what to do. I put my hand over my eyes and my shoulders began to shake, and I don't know how much time passed before someone spoke.

"It's OK," she said, but it wasn't Jane's voice, and when I looked up my wife was there, crouched by the couch, running her fingers through my thinning hair. She put her arms around me and pulled me to my feet, and helped me out the door. I had to lean against her to keep from stumbling.

"I haven't any idea what's wrong with me, Susan."

"Nothing's wrong with you," she said, as we wove our way between the trees. "I understand." And then she brought me to the safety of our bedroom, which no longer felt safe. She helped me out of my clothes, sat me down on the bed, and cleaned the cuts on my knees.

"I tried," I said.

"There's no reason to feel guilty," my wife said, and at that very moment I must have fallen asleep.

NEAR MORNING I WOKE UP SOBER WITH A TERRIBLE DARK FEELING. I FELT I had to move around, so I went to get a glass of water. When I came back from the bathroom Susan had the light on and was sitting up in bed, rubbing her eyes.

I sat down on the edge of the bed and put my head in my hands, wanting so much to put my head in her lap. It would have been right to tell her how thankful I was, that I loved her just then. She had saved our daughter. She was trying to save *me.* "I'm a disaster, Susan," I said. "You should leave me."

"I'm not ever going to leave you."

"But you should."

"No," she said. "I'd never leave someone I love."

I READ OVER THE OLD LETTER MICHAEL DOWNS HAD WRITTEN TO MY WIFE, daring myself to imagine what her purpose in writing to him might have been—*I want to know if I'm loved, if I've ever been loved, and now I'm married to a man who doesn't have the answer.*

Six years after those letters were mailed, Susan's mother was buried in Greenwich, Connecticut, beside a man with an Italian name to whom she had never been married. Somebody called Thatcher Hurst to let him know. The old man flew from Lincoln all the way to New York the next day, in spite of his bad health. Susan and her father and I had stood like strangers at the periphery of the graveside ceremony. I had shifted awkwardly from one foot to the other, feeling out of place, wondering why they had wanted to come. But the two of them had held each other and wept beside her grave, as if they had both lost someone who had really been an important part of their lives. Susan told me later it was the irony that had made her cry: Now that her mother was dead, she would finally know where to find her. But I wasn't sure if it had been as simple as that. There I'd been, standing beside her, thinking I should do something, but not really doing it. I hadn't even reached for her hand.

I refolded the letters, tucked them back inside their envelopes, and went downstairs with my drink in my hand. I sat on the couch and put my feet up on the table, feeling dazed. My hands were shaky, as if the absence of my wedding band had somehow thrown off my equilibrium. The fog was thick, the heavy light fading into evening. And though she might never know about it, I finally did what my wife had asked of me. I turned on the lamp, put the shoe box in my lap, and opened the lid.

CHAPTER TWENTY

1958

Charlie was heading us north toward Valentine, on Nebraska highway 2, and I was still his girl. There wasn't anyone else in sight. No headlights. Just the line of the land. I had been resting my forehead on the window, watching the cold world rush by, till I closed my eyes and almost forgot where I was. Charlie woke me up, poking me in the rib. "I saw you," he said. "Don't think I didn't, Caril Ann. It's no fair for you to sleep while I do all the work."

It was enough to make me roll over and pull the covers over my head, only there weren't any covers, just the coat from the lady who lay dead in her beautiful house. I held my hand in front of the heat to move the blood back through, then pushed up my feet and stared for a time at the tips of my shoes. Ice painted pictures on the windshield. "I'll drive for a while," I said finally.

"Now where would we be if I let you do that, Caril Ann, some ditch? You don't even know how to drive. Remember last time?"

"It's different." And then I got to thinking maybe that's where the whole thing started, with me behind the wheel of Charlie's car, spinning on the road, and how if it happened again I could spin back the other way, and nothing would ever be the way it had been.

"You're too young anyway," Chuck said. "It's how come you need me. You're helpless. Like a baby bird."

I looked straight ahead and crossed my arms to tell him no place was worse than where he'd got us. I tried to tell myself I wasn't really mad, though. Charlie was different now, and things weren't always right between us, but I knew he loved me anyhow. I also knew he was afraid; evening was coming on, surrounding the car in a kind of ice-blue shade. It was brittle cold and he had no idea where we would sleep. Or if it was safe to, though this road looked deserted.

We had stayed a while at the big house in Lincoln, lying still in the dark on account of Charlie needing a rest. But I couldn't sleep right with the dead people around, even with him next to me like we were. I tried to stay in one place without moving like Charlie said to, but there was a nasty smell to everything. I sneaked upstairs in the dark, trying not to breathe, and spilled perfume on the carpet, to try and cut the smell. But this was no help so I went into the closet and snipped on the light, and took her ruffle blouse and coat, too, on account of being cold. There was a diamond necklace half sticking out of a box so I put it in the pocket. I didn't feel bad about this. After all, the lady wasn't going to miss it.

Charlie did not notice my new shirt, and I didn't tell him about the diamonds. He and me didn't so much as talk about what happened, we just kept going. We knew what was in the cards. We sneaked out of the house that morning before the sun came up and drove around in the dead man's car for a while, looking for a plan. There were stories on the radio we heard, about all the crazy things me and him did. But they were wrong about one thing. It was not me and Charlie. I never did so much as a thing.

ALL DAY I HAD BEEN DRAWING THINGS I SAW, USING ONLY MY ONE GRAY PENCIL. I'd wished I'd grabbed my colored set, but it didn't matter, most everything being frozen and gray. I had filled one sketchbook already. I tried to find pretty things, like the sand hills covered in snow that made shadows over each other or a naked tree coming up out of the prairie, wearing nothing but white icing. I thought of drawing a diamond even, but I knew it wouldn't shine right. There were sad things too. I did not avoid these because someday I thought maybe I would be an artist, and famous pictures are not always pretty. Some day I thought I'd paint the poor smashed barn cat caught in a puddle like a chewed-up stuffed thing, just north of Broken Bow. Or the burnt-out freight car laughing in the sun. Or Charlie's face, crunched up over the steering wheel. At a roadside gas stop in Grand Island, I drew a picture of his face trying to hide how mad he was over not having money for a full tank. It wasn't his fault, he said. He'd sure done his share. I worked on the picture for a long time, shading even the shadows under his eyes. I ripped out the page and handed it to him. Charlie took it as we sped away. Then he balled up my drawing, rolled down the window, and threw it out onto the empty road. I turned around to watch it go.

I said, "Hey, I worked hard."

He said, "Sweet Christ, Caril Ann, I ain't ugly like that. Stop your dumb drawing!"

I tried not to take it as an insult that he thought my picture was ugly, saying, "How come I love you you're so ugly, then?" I patted his knee, though I was angry. I tried to be real nice. I always did, like it was my job. Sometimes he could be so low. I tried to remind myself I was his one true thing that mattered. I smiled over this fact to keep from crying and tried to forget all the rest. But I couldn't. The car was gray inside with high seats and silvery details, and I fiddled with the radio, flipping by commercials to find a song. There was nothing on about us right then, so I found "Poor Little Fool," and this was good because I was mad for Ricky Nelson. I went drifting off. For a time it was all OK to me.

But soon enough it was getting dark, with the gas gauge almost empty. Outside, a ghost moon hung in a faint blue sky. "Hey!" Charlie yelled, every time I closed my eyes. He pointed at the dash like he couldn't believe what the needle was telling him. "Hot damn fireball, that's *red,*" he said. He looked at me. "What you been doing this whole time while I drive besides dream?" He shook his head to scold me. "Why didn't you tell me we got no gas?"

I didn't say a word. I was hungry, but I would never say it to Charlie.

I did not say that the pancakes we ate so long ago had melted inside me like they had never been. I had not eaten much, sitting there in that library with winter light coming through the window and the deaf maid making those sounds right there in the closet for everyone to hear. Upstairs in the room the lady had told me, *If he loved you he wouldn't do this.* But the lady didn't get it. She couldn't understand. I didn't envy to be her, caught in a balance on the see-saw of Charlie's plan.

Charlie drummed his fingers on the steering wheel. His shoulders were hunched up by his ears. He studied me a moment. Then he reached over and tweaked my arm. "Hello?" Charlie held his hand up to his ear like he was talking on the telephone. "Hello, operator? Can you please connect me to the girl of my dreams?" It was our old routine, but instead of taking the call I rolled my eyes to the ceiling of the car and watched the shadows pass.

Charlie turned fast and looked at me in the dark of the car like he was trying to tell what I thought. I pretended a yawn. Putting my hand in the pocket of the coat I felt the necklace, wishing it would take me someplace else, and looked out the window. We were getting only static on the radio now, voices coming in and out. *A little dab will do ya:* Brill Cream. Vick's. Finally I just turned it off. I wondered if anyone had found that lady yet.

Charlie smacked his palms on the edge of the wheel. He reached over and yanked at the collar of my coat. "What'd you do that for? There might be something on about us."

I shrugged my shoulders. "They're not talking about what *you* did," I said. "No one cares."

Soon the moon turned silver and shone so bright we could see without headlights. We were miles from Valentine yet. Charlie didn't know if we had one gallon left in the Packard or one hundred. Finally, I couldn't help myself. I said, "Maybe you can't do a thing about *this,* but it's just too bad to run out of gas after all the crazy things you got away with, Charlie."

Charlie's breath came out when he spoke in plumes of cold. He turned slow to me in the dark. He said, "The only crazy I ever been is crazy for you, Caril Ann." Tears collected in the pockets of his eyes. I could see them shining. He wiped one away with the heel of his hand and sucked the wet back through his nose.

It had been a cruel thing for me to say. He was very tired. He had done so much. It was cruel because I knew he would never do me harm: this whole thing being for me, he always said, everything back in Lincoln and then all this. After Valentine would come the Pine Ridge Reservation, where Jonny Magpie'd let us drive on through, then a place called Saskatchewan, where we would make our home in peace forever and I had the diamonds to get us going. I wondered if people would understand us up at the end of the world. I had imagined new sights to draw, big antlers to try to get right, and the sun on mountains which I have never seen.

I wanted to throw up my hands and laugh and cry. Sometimes it got so tiresome to make everyone happy. I kissed him instead, to make it up. I kissed him deep. I trailed my pinkie over his blue jeans in tiny circles. "I want to make your babies," I whispered in his ear, on account of there being nothing else to say.

"You're too young to have babies," Charlie said. "That baby would break you clear in two squeezing on out." He didn't blink but kept on staring at the road. His eyes went dry. He looked ahead like I didn't exist.

WE WERE PASSING A TANGLE OF BRUSH WHEN I SAW THE BARN OVER HIS shoulder, just in time. So I pointed my finger and grabbed the arm of his cold leather jacket. The barn rose up dark from under the moon, a little way back from the road. It was a chewed hand with no light and no warmness, and broken boards. Where the land ended in a smooth roll, a house stood with only one porch light. Behind the barn was a fringe of trees. Charlie veered left off the highway, between the bushes, with no word to me for finding it. Real silent, he barely poked his foot to the pedal, like he was trying not to wake the world.

When Charlie spoke it was to justify. "We got no choice. If I have to do it again for a gas gallon, Caril Ann, I'll do it again if it comes to that. I won't care."

"I know, Charlie," is all I said. There was no doubt to me he wouldn't care. He'd blow up the world for a stuffed dog, if he thought I wanted it enough.

Charlie ground the car over ice and we jumbled off the drive behind the barn, into a stand of frosted trees where a tractor laid buried under a hunk of snow that had loaded up on the seat. All this we could see by the light of that moon, and the doors to the barn stuck open a small bit in the ice. Charlie shut off the car, and the dash went black. The world was silent. He got out. There wasn't any wind. Cold air bit me on the face. I put the necklace in the glove box so Charlie wouldn't know about it. He reached in back for the .22. "Get out," he said.

I buttoned the coat and held the wide flaps around me. He opened my door and drug me by the elbow out of the car. Charlie was not usually so rough. He was jittery and bent out of shape. He would be sorry for it later and try and nuzzle up to my heart, only I would push him off. I could do that. I had means to make my own way. I held on to his arm. Charlie and me both slipped on the ice and caught each other like lost lovers. I could see his eyes searching me, dim in the dark. The gun fell against my arm. My hand smacked the barrel. Everything hurts more when the air is cold, and I caught my breath for the nasty bruise. We passed on through, into the barn. It was so dark we couldn't even hope to find a gas can, and I remember the smell of farm animals and the sound of them shifting in their stalls. Pale blue light fell over Charlie's face, and he grabbed my arm.

I shrugged him off. I just walked farther into the darkness like I wasn't scared at all.

He followed after me. He whispered, "Caril Ann. Where are you?" He was no good at seeing in the dark, and somewhere along the way he had lost his glasses. He said, "Give over that coat to cover the window so we can get some light."

Charlie was holding the gun and standing in the middle of the darkness leaning on his bowed left leg. He was appearing a shadow of himself, confused in things he couldn't see. He didn't make a move for me. He just stood there.

"Don't be sore at me, Caril Ann," he said. "I'm all you got." But he was wrong, on account of me having the lady's jewels.

I took off the coat then, button by icy silver button, because Charlie was only wearing the one T-shirt underneath and I felt sorry for that, and the coat wasn't mine to keep anyhow. I tossed it at him. It flapped over his arm, and the buttons clinked the rifle in a happy silver cry. But there was nothing happy about tonight.

Because we did not find any gas after all, because we were tired and hungry and cold, we turned off the light, took down the coat from the sill, and wrapped ourselves up in it. That's when I unbuttoned my shirt and hoped for nature to take its course. We had made it in garages, and in a drain tunnel behind the capitol building, almost on top of the O Street viaduct, in his work truck once, he got so needy. But Charlie didn't want it now. He shifted himself over in a flake of hay and said, "I'm fixed to go up to the house and cause some trouble. There's nothing else to do."

I said, "Later," and he was silent a moment. Then he whispered in my ear. "Caril Ann." His breath was cottony and shallow. "The thing that gives me faith is you. If I go down you'll be there to cry."

"Sure, Chuck," I said. "Shhh."

He nestled his head in my armpit. His eyes glittered at me in the dark like a scared little animal. I wondered if they were tearing. "Do you think I'm mean," he asked, "or just bad?"

I thought for a moment about what he would want me to say. "Bad," I said. "Not mean. Like James Dean."

"No," he said. "It's the other way."

"OK," I said. "Hush." It was cold, but I kept my shirt opened anyhow, and if I had a skirt I would have pulled it up like the other Carol, the one that was dead. I scratched my fingers through his slicked back hair till his chest went heavy with sleeping from under the coat.

I LAID THERE A SPELL, STIFF AS WOOD, LISTENING TO HIS BREATH. THEN I rolled slow from under the coat so as not to shift a thing. The bracelet slid down my arm, cold and tugging at me. The prickly straw stuck in my back and my hair, and I didn't even breathe. But Charlie, he just laid there like a little baby in a patch of moon with his ducktail hair, shoe-polished to hide the red, slopped over his brow. I slipped between the doors fast and smooth as oil. I slipped over the field with the dead cornstalks rustling at the edges, with only the big moon hanging over to watch. I was shivering with my whole body tense and pounding. If he didn't think of me, I would have to think for myself.

I followed that porch light of the house, winking at me with a little dark secret. My body was weak from not eating or sleeping proper in so long, and my hands clutched each other down my pants to be warm. I thought of myself melting over the snow and my cowboy boot prints behind me left like Indian legends, and how people would find them days after we passed safe on through. They would be saying, "Who was that masked lady?" And maybe she would breathe down their necks, and draw pretty little pictures in blood while they dreamed, and leave them on pillows like symbols to find. *S.O.S.: save your selves.*

I moved closer to the house, on up to the back door, a different color than the white wood. I crept with trying not to make a sound toward the house and all those frosty windows. There wasn't a breath, and nothing moved. There were three steps up, and I thought I'd try the door before lifting a window and swinging myself in like a burglar. I pulled back the screen with only a mild creak. The knob turned in my hand. I stepped inside and closed the door behind. I went quiet and leaned up against the wood, my breath held, waiting for some ape-shit dog to come rushing at me. Now I imagined it ruining everything, waking the house with barking and biting. But it wasn't like that. It didn't happen like that at all. Making as if to laugh in my face, some mangy old thing shifts up out of the dark corner and starts beating his tail like I'm the best thing he ever saw. The dog, so old he could barely walk, hunkered over with his nails clicking and licked my hand without so much as a growl. I bent down my face to the bugger and scratched his ear, and we were friends forever.

It was a long dark kitchen I was standing in, with the moon shining through the window and over a sink that had dishes stacked beside it, and an icebox shifting with new electric noises. Me and the old boy padded over to the box like there wasn't a thing to fear. I opened the metal door slowly. I kneeled down and stuck in my head with the dog right beside, my straight hair falling tangled around my eyes, my bracelet twinkling with success. These were real family foods people had long dinners over. Nothing like the lady's high cupboards in Lincoln with her minty fashion cookies and chocolates. Here there was a half-eaten up chicken wrapped in cellophane, a bowl of peas and mashed potatoes, and a tin of tiny gold kernels of corn. There were sweet things too: a jar of pears, runny and sweet, and some chocolate mass on a plate with crust broke in it, most likely pudding pie. I made for this, lifted off its wrapping, and stuck in my finger. I brought the sweetness to my lips, then dipped a piece of crust into the pudding and crunched it. It tasted so good, melting down my throat. I swiped in my finger again and lifted it up for the dog, who was at my shoulder, panting down my neck. He wrapped his grateful warm tongue around it from under his old muzzle. He licked. I patted his head. I whispered, "You love Caril, don't you, boy?"

There was the sound of a chair then, scooting back across the floor to tell me I was not alone. My heart kicked up. My hand smacked the pie plate as I pulled it back. It shattered in globs around my feet. I kneeled there frozen, as the light snapped on.

A man was standing by a wood table against the wall, staring at me as if I had crawled out of his own head and come to life. His hand still rested on the light switch and I did not breathe. He held an alcohol drink up close to his face. He could not let it go in the brief moment, it seemed, but clutched it for a sort of belief in what he saw. He didn't say a word. His hair was tossed over his eyebrows with pieces of gray. The man wore blue pajamas with stripes and nothing over them. It seemed I had waked him from a very deep sleep. The dog was licking the spilled pie splattered around me. There was only the sound of his tongue sliding over my boots.

"Edna always has good taste." The man pointed over at the spotty dog with his drink, as it ran its wide pink tongue along an edge of chocolate. The man let go the wall and put his hand at his side.

My blood went thundering through my veins so much I couldn't hear. He just stood, waiting for me to say something.

I breathed deep. I said, "Edna deserves what she wants," as if I had every reason to be where I was. I moved forward a space from the cold metal door. My foot crunched a piece of plate. "Funny name for a dog." I reached down slow to pat her head without moving my eyes from the man where he stood. I did not act afraid, but I was ready to run if he made a move. My heart was coiled and about to spring. I said, "I thought sure she was a he, she liked me so much."

The man thought I was funny, and I was very pleased for this. He smiled a touch. He seemed to look in my face. This was a good sign he did not know who I was, standing in his kitchen. After all, it wasn't a thing to smile about. I tucked my face behind my hair and peered at him through the curtain of it. "This old dog's my only woman left," he said. "She's the only loyal thing I know." He sat down heavy in the chair and put his drink on the table. He called the dog over and petted her on the head.

"Well, someone must love you a lot to make all that good food you got in there." I said, pointing at the icebox. I looked down. "Sorry I broke the plate." I said this though I had no idea how to explain my being there and sticking my finger in the pie. All I could do was pretend a naturalness.

"I've been waiting for my wife. I've been sitting here waiting two nights for her to come back through that door, dragging her suitcase. I thought sure it was her when I heard the door, but it's just you," he said, as if I was supposed to be sorry for being me, and not his old bag. "Some little girl."

"I'm not so young as I look." I pitched my chest out a little from under my shirt. I swung my hair behind my shoulder. "She wasn't smart to leave you," I said. The man looked up at me from the bottom of his empty glass.

He reached below and picked up a bottle from beside his chair, and stood it in the center of the table. He crossed his legs, looking from the bottle to me like it was a deep mystery we came to occupy that same place. "May I offer you a drink then, madam?" he said with the play of a smirk at the corner of his mouth. He leaned back and kicked a bare foot against the wood leg of the table. It was pale and long as no foot I'd ever seen. The man crossed his arms over his pajamas. The bottle rocked and jiggled. The alcohol rippled. "Do you take bourbon?" He closed his eyes like it hurt too much to see. Then he leaned forward and put his head in his hands.

I brushed the metal back of a chair with my fingers. A doorway spilled my eyes down a warm, dark hall. I imagined his wife moving along it in the night. I imagined her with lipstick, and the city hairdo I have always wanted, pulling a red suitcase quiet over the carpet while he slept. I imagined her closing the door and not looking back, and why would she do that, leave this big warm place, and all of it for what sort of better things? I held one wrist in my other hand and lifted up the cuff of my shirt a bit so the man could see the gold bracelet I wore, so he could see I was not just some tramp spat out of the cold.

"Is your wife making for Hollywood?" I asked. "'Cause that's where I'm headed."

He opened his eyes. He stared at me a moment like I had just appeared, and squinted like he might be upset. Then he let out a huge laugh, and for a minute all the sorrows were gone from his eyes. It was a wonder I could do this for a man so sad. He slapped his hands down on the table like I was the funniest thing that ever lived. I would have painted him in deep blues and a charm. He would have liked it. He would have hanged it on the icebox with a sharp little magnet. The man said, "That's unlikely, sweetheart. My wife's not very talented. Vegas would be more her type of place." He poured himself another drink and slammed it back like a stiff-drinking cowboy, though he was an elegant man with that long nose, those deep eyes, and that light skin. There was a sweet shadow of gray over his chin.

"I've been told I'd be good on television," I said, "but my real talents lie in painting and polite conversation." I got guts up from somewhere, and I pulled up a chair and sat down across from the man. I pushed out my wrist across the table for him to see the bracelet and said, "I got this before I left. It's an heirloom of my family."

He looked down at the shiny gold, never disbelieving I would have it. He took my wrist then in his neat hands. He turned his eyes to my face with a long expression. Then he let go my wrist and poured more from the bottle without taking his eyes from my face. The dark liquid hung below the label.

"Have a drink with me," he said.

"I don't take alcohol," I replied, smiling with a great sweetness I am capable of. I said, "Got any pop?" I shifted my hands under my thighs. I imagined us—the man and me—and how we looked, sitting at the table. We were frozen in the bright frame of the kitchen, a happy little picture in the cold dark night. Outside the wind slammed and tossed dead husks of corn, yawning through the empty hills. Maybe Charlie was shifting in his sleep or grabbing my body for warmness and coming up with a handful of straw. This thought filled me with a wonder.

The man nodded his head, like all he wanted was me happy. He got up, went to the cupboard, and reached down a cola. Then he dropped the bottle. The old dog nosed it along the baseboard, but the man did not make to pick it up. He reached me another and smacked off the cap on the side of the table. There was a force behind his movement, as he put the cola before me with a great flurry and then stepped back. The man ran his long fingers up through his hair and stuck them there an instant. His eyes went strange, and he looked me up and down, sitting in his kitchen like it was the first time I appeared.

He asked, "How did you get here all by yourself?"

I didn't know what to say then. I folded and unfolded my hands around the pop bottle. I said, "I came from Lincoln."

This seemed to be an all-right answer. He put his hands at his sides and cleared his throat. "Is there anyone else I should know about, trespassing on my property?" He didn't seem mad about it, only jealous maybe, like all he wanted to know was where things stood between us.

I looked down into the mouth of my pop, with my hair falling around me to hide the redness in my face, like I would do at school for not knowing the answer. I could feel him watching me, waiting.

Then I looked up at him and straight into his eyes to make him see he was the only one for me. His eyes were brown and soft. They seemed to understand. I shook my head earnest. I said, "No, only me. Cross my heart. I swear."

He nodded his head slowly. He said, "Excuse my impoliteness. Nature calls." He stared down at his feet a moment and went toward the door. He turned his face over his shoulder and looked at me sitting. He said, "Don't budge your pretty body." He smiled at me like a full glass of water in a dry empty desert and disappeared down the hall.

Things were OK with us the way they weren't with me and Charlie. The dead girl with her skirt pulled up didn't matter. I sat tight, sipping pop. I did not think of leaving. There was a thing between the man and me. I knew that now. I sat listening to sounds in the house, the man's footsteps somewhere, and a door closing, the dog's wet nose sniffing the broken plate on the floor. The dog laid down beside my chair with a heavy sigh. She put her gray nose between her two paws. I was wondering offhand what I should do about Charlie and his rifle, but I wasn't real worried yet. He would never hurt me. It seemed far off, the morning when he would wake up, wanting trouble, and me being right beside him like I'd been there all the night, watching the moon through a board in the barn.

The man came back after a few minutes. He paused in the door, a soft colored sketch on a coal-black background. He lifted his fingers to his hair and rubbed them through, watching me sit there, sipping his pop in the middle of the night. I smiled to give him a little boost. I put my knee up on the chair and leaned my chin on it. My hair swayed around my leg. I pulled him over the floor with my eyes. He came over then, to my chair. He had put on socks that drug out from his toes when he walked. The man's pajamas were misbuttoned and rumpled like he had taken them clear off to use the john and put them back on all wrong. He seemed not to know what to do, and me sitting there. It occurred how someone like me could save a man like him. I could put him to bed, pull the blankets to his chin. No one would know the better, me lying here forever, losing myself in the squeak of a brass bed. It was all right with me to make my own choice, to shed Charlie like an old skin for someone who appreciated my gifts, to leave him lying empty on the road, the wind screaming through his teeth for me having gone.

The man looked at me very close. I didn't reach out and squeeze his hand or cry for all the things gone wrong. I didn't throw myself at his feet and beg him to tuck me away in some old forgotten room upstairs. I stood beside him with a realness I have never felt. I balanced on my boot tip. I reached up below his collar, where the buttonhole was skipped. My finger grazed his cheek. His hair fell in his eyes. He looked down in my face, and his lips, very close, smelled strong with a whiskey I wanted to wrap around me like an old blanket, like I was very small. He did not move an inch. I could feel the nearness of that open place between his legs like a target I was not sure of hitting. I had spent nights sleeping in cars or in houses where people were dead. I smelled used by the nasty things I had seen. They hung around me like a bad taste. But I pretended I was the most beautiful woman. I pretended I belonged here. I kept on going. I took the button between my fingers. I pulled it through the hole and whispered in his ear, "Let me straighten you out. You're all messed up."

The man plucked off my fingers one by one. He wove them through his hand. He ran his thumb along the edge of mine. He squeezed the bones tight. He ground them together. He stared into my face. He bent his mouth to the inside my ear. Then he shoved me off. I fell back into a chair. My head hit the table with a shock. "Why don't you get out of here," he told me, "before I call the sheriff."

CHARLIE WAS NO LONGER ASLEEP BY THE WINDOW WHEN I THRUST MYSELF into the barn, cold and shaking. The moon hung over the empty straw like a spotlight. It was matted from where his body had laid. I had no idea how long it had been since I left or how long he had been awake. My whole self went strange with a shaking I could not control. I looked around in the glowing blue darkness of the barn. I wanted to gag all over the ground for ruining everything. I wanted to throw myself up at the feet of the empty sky. The cows shifted and lowed from their sweet heaven of warmness. I started to cry for hating the man and what he did. Little sounds came out of myself like the black poodle I had seen in Lincoln, hiding under the blood-splattered dust ruffle in the boy's room with its neck broke by Charlie's rifle.

It had twisted its head all strange and was mewling in pain. I had been glad of the boy not being there to see his dog like that. I had been glad of his mother too, too hurt to ever see all that we'd done. But there was no reason to have hurt the little dog.

"Where you been, Caril Ann?" Charlie was sitting on a bale of hay, the lady's coat throwed over his shoulders. The .22 was across his lap. I saw the metal by the moonlight, glinting like a surprise for me in the darkness. But it was not aimed on me, so I knew he could not know the whole story of what I had done in the house. He would have shot himself right there for my behavior. So, it was a great responsibility I held, to make it right.

I said, "I went to pee, Charlie." I could not help the crying and the shaking, or my throat closing up, and the sickness in my heart to look at him with that gun, and to think about the grown man shoving me against the chair.

He stared at me and shaked his head. "Where'd you pee, Caril Ann, the moon? You think I'm dumb?"

"No." I cried some more and kicked at the hay bale with the tip of my boot. I could feel the snot running down, and the tears, and how no one right would want me ever.

"Don't lie to me." He said, "Sweet Christ, Caril Ann, do anything but don't lie." He stood up. The gun was dragging like a part of his foot on the floor of the barn. He was not thinking about it.

I knew it might be all right then, that he really couldn't know how bad things were. He was quaking with a madness, but it was not for hating me. "I'm not dumb. I know things about the world you don't know about, 'cause you always have me to save you from them. You got it easy. It's harder for me. Sometimes I hate it."

I fought back my tears. I wiped my nose on my sleeve. I thought a moment about how to fix it. There wasn't any other choice but to love him.

I went over to him, to make him feel strong. My tears were still running down. I felt sick inside. I said, "I went to snoop for gas around back." I held him a minute. He smelled like shoe polish and grease. He was a shell, a boy with bow legs so wide a pig could run through, who everyone teased, and a spray of pimples over his cheek. I buried myself in him and said, "I'm sorry to have left."

He narrowed his eyes and grabbed my hair in his free hand. He said, "You shouldn't have did that, but there's no sense crying." He held me away and looked in my face. My heart was yelling in my ears because I knew this is where I deserved to be no matter how I hated it. He put the lady's coat over my shoulders. I didn't want it anymore, but I hugged it around me. "It's not your fault you don't know how it all works." Charlie petted me on the head. "You don't know better than to play along. I know a thing or two. They try to teach you in school to be nice and fair, but there's no such thing."

"You're right, Charlie." I sniffled.

"People take one look and think 'cause you haul trash you *are* trash," he went on. "It ain't fair."

"I know," I said. "No one's gonna melt the ice off your grave when hell freezes over." Charlie smiled at me for finishing his line. I reached over and kissed his cheek. It was cold, with little bristles of hair, and smelled sour as milk. I looked down and moved my feet in the dirt. I stared at them like they were separate from my own, moving without my thoughts to tell them where to step. I felt sorry about what I had to do now. The gun was heavy against Charlie's thin bow leg. I thought of the man's face inside the house, and how easy it could end up like all the other faces I had seen lately, down the barrel of the gun, down on the clean kitchen floors or in bedrooms surrounded by lace, eyes empty and alone without a hint of pleading to Charlie left, without a hint of who they were or the things they'd done before we stepped on the scene in our bad little boots. This was my price to be paid.

"Is that thing loaded?" I said, pointing down at the gun with my head. I tightened my arms around Charlie like I could ride his bullet through a heart. I wished I was the same girl as when it all started, as when he found me that one day in the tree house crying to myself for all the things gone wrong, and I chose him to love because he chose me. The angriness inside him had seemed closer to something real than anything I knew.

"It is," Charlie said of the gun. "It's ready to go."

"I'm scared, Charlie," I said. "I'm scared he knows we're out here." I had stopped the crying.

"Who's he?" said Charlie.

"I don't know," I said. "The farmer in the house. There's lights on in the house, I saw. I think we're done for." I put my face in his shoulder.

Charlie's muscles were waiting to spring. He held me close. "We ain't done for, whoever he is," Charlie said. He pushed me away and went to combing his hair through his fingers.

It seemed in that second I never had so much as a choice in anything. I felt I would always be paying someone else's price for the things that happened.

I rested my elbow on the window ledge. I looked down at the lady's gold bracelet and twisted it around my wrist. Her diamonds felt very far away. Charlie was pacing around in back, working himself up. He said, "Caril Ann, I think after we do this thing we gotta ditch the Packard."

"I don't want to ditch it," I said, but I was looking out at the moon and he did not hear. The tears started up again with all my heavy thoughts, but Charlie couldn't tell from my voice. I didn't make a sound. I lifted my sleeve to my nose and wiped it around. That's when I thought I saw something, a trace of silver from the bushes that caught the corner of my eye from the dark. A fast motion that caught me in its likeness to Charlie and the way *we* moved together. It was someone—a man—and that's when I first suspected they had found us.

I had not imagined them creeping around in the dark outside a barn on the edge of Valentine, over the rippled land, their feet barely whispering through frozen husks of corn, waiting in the shadows to spring on us from the darkness. That was *our* game. I had imagined it happening right after we left Lincoln, looking back over our shoulders, our necks twisted to meet the shots, or much later, way far outside this state in a world of green where we thought we were free. But you change your choice to suit the situation. This time I could see through to the other side and pick the way I wanted it to be.

I stepped away from the window. I stood against the wall. "Charlie," I whispered. I tried to be still and not panic. I tried to think what to do. I held my wrists together behind me and fingered the bracelet because I didn't want it anymore. I found the clasp and worked my nails to pull it back. The gold tickled my skin as it fell to the cracks.

"What?" Charlie said. "What's wrong?" He had stopped the pacing. I could see his eyes full in the moonlight, looking at me from the corner of the barn.

I did not say a thing then. My voice was stuck.

"Don't be scared," he said. "I got it all figured out."

"No," I said. "It's not that." My heart pounded in my chest. I pointed sideways at the window. I picked up my head. "I want us to keep the Packard."

"Well, we can't," said Charlie. "It's no good for us. And the radio's busted up anyhow."

"Have it your way," I said. My voice never even tremored. I walked away from him, across the barn.

"Don't be sore," said Charlie. "We'll get another."

I didn't answer him. I kept my back to him. I didn't look behind. I was like the magic man at the Lincoln County Fair who pulled the nickel from my ear last August. I was doing my own trick. I felt like that. Anything could happen anywhere. You just had to make a choice and stick to it. I rolled open the barn door, and the dark world spilled out in front of me. In that instant I could see all the way to Valentine. The sand hills rolled up to meet my heart. The lights twinkled. Then the wind bit my eyes and I couldn't see a thing. "Help!" I cried, as loud as I could, to the empty wind. My voice met with a silence. It echoed on forever.

"Jesus, Caril Ann!" I heard Charlie say.

"He's hiding in the barn!" I screamed. I stepped out farther, but then—I couldn't help it—I didn't know what to do. I looked over my shoulder back into the barn to see if he had the .22 pointed my way.

I thought maybe it was over and I was done for, that he had finally had it. But Charlie was standing in the shadows without the gun. He wasn't even holding it. He would never hold it on me no matter what I did. I knew that now. I could see through the dark, his arms held out to me, his palms facing up and empty toward where the sky would be without the roof.

Then lights came at me from somewhere. They yelled for me to get away from the barn. I let go a sob. I couldn't see a thing. I stumbled toward where I knew they must be. I lifted my hands in front of my face to show I had not a thing to hide, not even that bracelet. One officer reached for me. I could feel his hands dig in my arms.

I squinted up in his face. "You don't need to do that. I'm trying to help." But he cuffed me up rough anyhow, like a real killer, though I had not done a thing wrong. I pressed my cheek to his badge, but he wouldn't hold me nice. He pushed me away rough, like a piece of trash, and held me still to see Charlie get pulled from the barn by two more lawmen. Instead of fighting, Charlie was crying, his chin tucked down to his chest like he didn't have a thing left in him. "You goddamn baby," I whispered. "*I'm* not crying."

CHAPTER TWENTY-ONE

1963

I was not allowed out on my own for the rest of January, so I tried to amuse myself at home. I made a snowman in the garden and dressed it in my mother's pillbox hat, and I wandered the house drinking her expensive coffee, listening to Mark Dinning singing about his teen angel. My father called me every day from work to make sure I had gotten home from school safely. For the most part I obeyed him. I liked knowing he cared, but the house felt so dark and small and dreary, I thought I might just disappear. The last Saturday in January, my father went to Omaha for a ribbon ceremony. Before he left, he told me Mother was coming home soon; he could feel it.

"Have you talked to her lately?" I said.

"That isn't necessary."

"How do you know she's coming back then?"

"Seventeen years of marriage." He put on his coat. My father was fooling himself. He didn't know Mother at all. She was too changeable.

"What does the feeling *feel* like?"

"Oh, I don't know." He picked up his briefcase and pulled his hat low like Humphrey Bogart. "Like something is afoot. Like something good is bound to happen." His tie was crooked. I wanted to straighten it.

Do you even know where she is? I wanted to ask. But I knew he had no idea. "I'm tired of staying home all day," I said.

"That's what happens when you behave irrationally. But I'm not getting into it. When Mother comes home you'll be in one piece, not half frozen in some snowbank." He opened the front door. "Be good, Puggy," he said. "If I get back in time, we'll go out to dinner."

I tucked the sweaters I'd been wearing back into my mother's drawers and sat down on the edge of the unmade bed, eyeing the spindly branches of the elm against a backdrop of flat gray clouds. I tried to guess if my mother was somewhere near, staring out a similar window at this same blank sky, thinking about coming home. I closed my eyes and felt around in the dark corners of my mind, trying to sense her, read her thoughts, feel her the way my father said he could feel her. My mother and I had the same blood. It should have been easy. But I had never understood any part of her, except the inexplicable force that had driven her to Nils. Danger. Wanting to be wanted enough to pull everything down. One step sparks an avalanche. Wanting attention from someone can lead you anywhere. Love could fling you out of orbit. There was no controlling how you landed.

Suddenly, staring down at the melting snowman in my mother's ruined hat, I knew I was feeling the way she must have felt. Staying inside this house for another moment where nothing changed and nothing happened was going to kill me. It was a quiet gray Saturday in late January, and I didn't want to be alone anymore. I wanted Cora to forgive me for jumping the fence. I wanted someone to tell me I wasn't so bad. I needed to feel in my heart that I wasn't so bad. I took a bath and brushed my hair till it shone. I put on a little makeup and left the house with *Old Possum's Book of Practical Cats.*

I walked with my head down, feeling that if I looked at anything other than my two feet moving forward, someone would stop me, take me by the shoulders, and walk me back home like a prisoner. I turned the corner and went quickly up the block and stood outside the Lessings' house deciding what to do. South 24th Street was silent. It seemed like everyone had gone away. There were no people outside, scraping ice off windshields or scattering sand on slippery steps, and the Lessings' windows were dark. The garage door was shut. I'd just put the book on the back steps where Cinders had lost his life. Cora would be reminded once again of all I'd done, bravely bearing the dead cat across the garden to the sepulchre. Then she could decide for herself whether or not she wanted to be friends again.

I sucked in my breath and started around the side of the house, crouching low when I passed the sunroom, just in case Cora was sitting there reading magazines or watering the plants. That was her chore. It occurred to me she might have her own reasons for keeping an eye on the neighbors, reasons that had nothing to do with my connection to Lowell. Perhaps she believed in her own connection, maybe she felt her own closeness to what had happened. Cora had once said cars slowed down and people pointed when they passed. I had never seen them, but I didn't doubt it. Everyone wanted to see where something so horrible had happened.

But there wasn't anything for anyone to see. The curtains in the Bowmans' living room were closed; I couldn't make out anything. Lowell would be back at college by now. He had probably forgotten about my lost card, dropped outside his window. Or maybe he had taken it to school with him. Maybe he had spent evenings alone in his dormitory bed unraveling the mystery of my identity or speculating about what his visitor had wanted. *I* didn't have the answer. I had no idea what kept pulling me back.

I went behind the house and studied the Lessings' windows for some sign of life. Through the diamond-shaped pane under the eaves I could see a light on where Mrs. Lessing worked. I imagined her sitting back in a chair soft as a cloud, frowning about an imperfection in something she had made, perhaps the blue of a wing drying more opaquely than she had wanted. Paintings were propped against the walls covered in sheets because Corrine Lessing didn't want to see them anymore. Back when she had painted, the world was somewhere she wanted to be. The days fell in on themselves. The hours tumbled out like ribbon.

I took the book out of my bag and crept up the back steps. My feet crunched too loudly on a fringe of ice, and I slipped, grabbing the railing and pulling myself forward. For a moment, I stood, catching my breath. A breeze kicked up. Hair tickled my cheeks and caught at the corners of my mouth. I brushed it away. I was going to get a haircut, a stylish one that flipped out at the shoulders. It was only a matter of time.

I opened the screen and bent down to prop the book against the door, but the wood gave way against my hand and the book fell forward. The door creaked inward and swung back on rusted hinges. *Practical Cats* slapped the welcome mat. I pulled back my hand. My heart let go. I thought surely I'd been caught, but when I looked up no one was there. The kitchen was dark and still and somehow vacant, as if untouched for years. Perhaps the latch had busted, I didn't know.

A glass had been knocked over on the kitchen table. Though the stem was intact, the bulb had shattered, and wine coursed out over the wood in a violent shock of red. I picked up the book, stepped inside, and closed the door softly behind me. I could hear drops hit the floor, and the sound of them on the cold tile made me want to cry.

I stood there for a moment, unsure what to do. Nothing else seemed out of order, but even so there was a sense of chaos. *What would it be like to find them?* This silence, this stillness would say something wasn't right. And then you went deeper inside and found whatever horrible secrets lay hidden there. Rooms in disarray. Crumpled bedsheets, tipped-over tables, torn shades. Heads twisted at impossible angles. Open eyes that couldn't see. What was it like to come upon someone and know it was too late? While you were tapping your watch impatiently or telephoning, she was struggling for life. Hope rose and fell, deflating like a lung. If you'd really listened to her tone on the telephone, what she was trying to say. *Another time.* It wasn't like her to say such things.

I looked around for a rag. I thought about cleaning up the wine. What else could I do? But suddenly I didn't want to touch it. I didn't want to touch anything. I had no right to be here. *A scrape on the roof.* My heart thudded. *Sliding ice.* I strained to hear any movement, any life, but there was nothing else. Light spilled through a window at the other end of the hall, and I went toward it, as if caught in a spell. For a moment, the sun broke through. Shadows darted like minnows, then melted away. Everything went back to gray.

In the living room the floor was slippery, recently waxed, and the clock ticked over the mantel. Mr. Lessing's collection of antique canes stood upright, untouched in the stand by the fireplace. "Hello?" I said, not loud enough for anyone to hear. I didn't want to surprise someone. It wasn't my place to mount the stairs or find out if anything was wrong.

How would I explain this? It seemed so foolish to be frightened by a broken glass and an open door. Anyway, what could *I* do? There were explanations: the wind, for example. High pressure and low pressure pushed past each other to form tornadoes. Gravity kept things from spinning off the curve of the earth. There was a certain pattern, a scientific code. I went back to the kitchen. Wine had gathered in thin lines between white tiles like blood. I shook off a chill, opened the back door, and closed it firmly behind me.

Inside the house I'd forgotten to breathe, and now I took deep gulps of cold air. I leaned my back against the door, my pulse still hammering in my ears. The air was warming up. A breeze whispered in branches: *Something is afoot.* Ice in gutters groaned: *About to fall.*

And then a sudden movement caught my eye. Someone was by the sepulchre. My spine tingled with the possibility of having been watched. For a moment I thought someone was finally burying the cat. Or maybe it wasn't a person at all, but something had definitely slipped, out there in the back of the garden, and caught itself on the branch of a tree. I could not make it out. The light was opaque, flat, and gray as one shape blended into another, impossible to perceive. There wasn't any snow left in the trees. The branches were naked. I stepped forward. I made out something that looked like wings, fluttering white, then dark underneath. A trick of the eye. I froze with my hand on the railing. A sound drifted from far away, like a whisper you couldn't quite hear. It was a gasp, a sigh, and for a moment I could not tell if it had come from me. The trees themselves seemed to answer. I stepped down from the porch. And then I saw her. My whole body shook with disbelief. Corrine Lessing was out there, clinging to a branch. Gasping, with no one to catch her. There was no one but me.

Don't think. Don't waste time wondering how. Forward through the snow, arms out in front. Feet slipping, knees buckling. Snow whitened. Shapes darkened. I no longer touched the earth. I kept my eyes on her the whole time. I did not think of anything else. *Please, please don't fall.* And then I realized I was speaking out loud. "Please don't fall."

It seemed an incredible distance to reach her. She had heard me. Corrine Lessing's head was turned in my direction. Her hair was loose, longer than I had ever thought possible. I could not read her expression. It must have been so icy. She must have been struggling to hold on. I could not think what to do. I could not think at all. Everything was white. And then I was under her. My foot kicked a bottle against the trunk. Wine streamed out. Red painted the snow.

"Mrs. Lessing," I said. "I'm here. I'm under you." I did not feel that my voice came from inside me but from some incredibly high, unreachable point. It was so thin. I calculated the height. Ten feet? If she fell, she might not even break a bone. It all might be fine. I could hear her breath, loud and ragged.

"Mrs. Lessing," I said. "I can break your fall."

"I don't think so. No." Her voice was so calm.

"I can." I held out my arms. I put them back at my sides. "What should I do?"

"Don't worry."

"I'll get help."

"No."

"Is anyone home?" My voice sounded shrill, ridiculous, hopeless.

"I—really . . . how silly—" She laughed nervously and caught her breath. And her arms slipped. Her whole body gave up, and she tumbled down. Her coat billowed with the slow sound of wind and her hair streamed out like silver wings. I waited with my arms open, bracing against the pain of impact.

The moments were frozen. Time was beautiful, jagged. Everything whittled down to a point. It was in my power to step aside. But this wasn't my choice. She fell toward me and I kept my feet planted, my arms held out. I could be knocked unconscious. My nose might break. None of that mattered. I just wanted to save her.

I caught Mrs. Lessing's coat in my hands. It pulled me down. Her body hit the ground. She didn't cry out. I fell backward with my head against the sepulchre. Everything was weightless. The dark shapes of branches shifted above me. A bit of ice rained down, hitting my nose. My skull throbbed with cold. It was too quiet, so quiet.

But when I sat up, Mrs. Lessing was already on her side by the tree trunk, holding herself up with one arm, staring down at a stain of red in the snow as if it had come from some part of her. For a moment I thought it had too. Then I remembered the bottle. I wanted to tell her it was only the wine, but I couldn't bring myself to speak. I was too embarrassed. A coil of rope had spilled out of the pocket of her black coat, the frayed end dangling in the snow. *An unfinished thought.* I couldn't tear my eyes away.

She looked up, startled, as if suddenly remembering me, and noticed the rope. I felt my face go red. She pushed it back in her pocket and I looked away, pretending not to see.

"It was so silly—I was trying—" She closed her eyes and opened them slowly, as if waking from a long sleep. She smoothed the coat over her green pants and fastened the buttons. I could see her hands were shaking. There was an angry red scratch down the side of her face.

I got up and went over to her. "Let me help you," I said. My voice sounded unsure. I held out my arm and helped her up. Wet snow was matted, wrinkled where she'd landed. I could smell her breath, dry, stale like sickness.

"Susan?" she said, as if she wasn't quite sure of my name.

I nodded, put my arm around her waist, and helped her toward the house. She couldn't put any weight on the right ankle—it was twisted—but her face was blank, almost serene, without pain, as if her mind had crept to a far-off place.

I helped her through the kitchen door and pulled out a chair for her to sit on. "I can hang up your coat," I offered.

"No," she said, and put her hand over the pocket holding the rope. "I'm cold."

How could I have been so stupid? To hide my awkwardness, I filled the kettle with water and placed it on the stove. I put a teabag in a mug. Everything seemed far off, as if in a dream. If I hadn't been there, what would have happened? I didn't want to think about the different ways things could have turned out, but I also felt a little proud. I stood back against the counter waiting for the water to boil. I couldn't figure out what to do with my hands.

Mrs. Lessing touched the spill of wine on the table with the tip of her finger and rubbed it against her thumb. "Did I do that?"

"I can clean it up," I said. I picked out the pieces of glass and threw them away. I got a rag from beside the sink and mopped up the spill.

She smiled, but it wasn't a real smile. It was a sad smile. "You're a nice girl," she said.

I put the cup of tea in front of her and watched as she took a sip. I didn't think I should leave her, not until Mr. Lessing got home. "When is your family coming back?" I said.

She shrugged her shoulders.

"I can stay," I said.

Mrs. Lessing leaned her forehead on her hand and sighed. "I'm just tired. I need to sleep. I'll go to bed." But I didn't want to take any chances. I didn't know what she might do.

Mrs. Lessing pushed back her chair. Her eyes didn't seem to focus on anything. They were dark, without centers, disbelieving. She was beautiful in a fragile sort of way, like a spiderweb, or a lovely broken cup. She stood up and had to brace herself on the table for support. I took her arm and helped her up the stairs.

THE LESSINGS' BEDROOM WAS LIGHT AND AIRY, WITH SHEER WHITE CURTAINS over windows that faced the street. A painting hung over the bed, a scene of gold prairie grass and a tiny cottonwood in the distance etched against a pale blue sky. The scene looked so real you could feel the grass tickle your legs. You could lie down in the shade of the tree, fall asleep to the sounds of insects flitting their paper wings. It would be nice to close your eyes at night and pretend you were inside a painting where nothing moved, where winter was far away and falling snow an illusion.

Mrs. Lessing sat down on the edge of the bed and tried to bend over to take off her shoes, but her back hurt too much, so I took them off for her. The ankle was swollen. "This is silly," she said. "I'm embarrassed," but I was the one who felt most out of place. I'd seen something I wasn't supposed to. I knew too much. I didn't know what to do or say.

Mrs. Lessing unbuttoned her coat and laid it beside the shoes with the pocket holding the rope against the floor. There was no need to be so careful. I'd already seen. She hugged her arms around her narrow shoulders to keep off a chill. I pulled back the covers. She slid between the sheets.

I didn't know where to stand. I put my hands behind my back.

She closed her eyes.

I wanted to keep her company. "Did you paint that?" I said.

"I don't paint anymore. But this one John likes. He won't let me take it down."

"I think it's beautiful," I said. "I wouldn't let you take it down either."

"It's outside Ogallala. Where we met."

"How did you meet?"

She threaded her fingers together on top of the blankets. "He wanted to hunt on our land. But my father wasn't home so he had to get permission from *me*. He came to the door with big boots and suspenders, and he smiled like someone you could trust. No one smiled in our house much." She paused and shut her eyes again, as if she were trying to recall exactly the way it had been.

"Did you know right then you were going to marry him?"

"I didn't know much. I only knew Rosario. I just walked behind this stranger while he hunted—from morning till late afternoon. My feet got tired. I watched him shoot six pheasants, but the dog brought back only five. I found the last one stuck in a bush, with its head under its wing like maybe it hadn't died yet." It didn't seem to make her any happier to remember this. "Later, he said I was good luck. What do you think about that?" She closed her eyes again and hid her arms under the blankets. "You don't need to stay."

I glanced around the room for sharp objects, bottles of pills. I didn't see anything. "I'll get your tea," I said.

WHEN I WENT BACK UPSTAIRS, MRS. LESSING STILL HAD HER EYES CLOSED. I thought she'd fallen asleep, so I put the teacup on the night table and sat down in the chair by the window, wondering how long I should let her sleep. I didn't want to have to wake her up. Maybe sleep was the only place the past turned out differently. Did she dream that the Bowmans were alive again? What did it mean to climb up in a tree in the middle of winter with a rope in your pocket? My mind worked too hard to invent horrible scenarios. Now I only wanted something happy, a story in which Mrs. Lessing would get better.

Mrs. Lessing turned on her side and cupped her hands beneath her cheek. Her eyes were open, red and full of tears, but she didn't make a sound.

"Can I do anything?" I said.

She shut her eyes and put her hands over her face.

"What should I do?"

"I'm so trapped. I can't get out."

"What do you want to get out of?"

She didn't answer.

"If you left, they might never get over it, you know. They love you." It seemed to be what she needed to hear.

"It's never enough. It's my mistake. No one can share that."

"My mother left me. She's been gone three months. My father's upset. I'm not very pleased either. I get scared to go home sometimes, it's so lonely." I crossed my arms. I had no idea where those words had come from. I didn't know what else to say, so I just sat there glaring at the coat.

"Sometimes you want to slither out of your skin, it feels so horrible. All you can do is pound your fists."

"Oh," I said, though I didn't really understand. *I'm always alone. I thought things would be different,* my mother had told my father that night they fought so bitterly about Lucille. "Is that what you were trying to do?" I said.

"I don't know. I don't want to upset anyone." She took a breath, opened her eyes, and looked at me. I couldn't meet her gaze. It made me too uncomfortable. "Please don't tell them what you saw," she said.

But if something happened again? Then it would be my fault. "I won't," I said. "But you have to promise to try to feel better."

"Thank you." Mrs. Lessing turned over and faced the wall. Outside, the light had faded. Everything was still. The sky teetered on the brink of dusk. I felt I had lived a lifetime in one afternoon.

"I was sixteen," I heard Mrs. Lessing say to the wallpaper. "I wanted to run away with Rosario." Her shoulders rose and fell several times, and then her breath went heavy with sleep.

THE LIGHT FELL AWAY. SHADOWS CREPT ACROSS THE ROOM. I LISTENED TO THE sound of her breathing and wondered about her dreams. By moonlight, Corrine followed the trail of a dried up riverbed to the edge of the land. She called the secret greeting, a sand crane, the hoot of an owl. A rustle of grass, and Rosario stood. He'd been there since dusk, waiting for hours.

I sat by the window, waiting for Mr. Lessing. What could I possibly do or say to explain my being there. When I got home, my father might be there. I'd get in trouble all over again, but suddenly that didn't matter. I realized something about my mother; she could not comprehend real suffering. She had always complained about being trapped in our house, but for Mrs. Lessing, being trapped meant so much more. Every time she looked out the window, she remembered that day, the drawn shades, Mrs. Bowman's strained voice on the telephone. She too had inserted herself in the story: *I was meant to save them. I was. I was.* I wanted to cry. Little tears of blood. I thought of the beautiful red coat and wondered if Cora even thought twice about how much thought had gone into choosing it.

Lights turned into the driveway. I could hear a car door slam. From behind the fringe of a gauze curtain, I watched them pile out of the car. Mr. Lessing went around to the back and opened the trunk. He unloaded some bags and distributed them between his children. Toby said something and Cora gave him a little push. The red wool looked nice with her hair. They seemed so happy, without a single idea of what had happened while they'd been gone, without any idea at all of what I had seen. I wondered if they'd ever know, if anyone would ever be told this. I picked up Mrs. Lessing's coat, crept into the hall, and carried it down the stairs. The living room clock chimed the half-hour. Keys fumbled in the lock. I hung the coat on the hook by the back door. I pulled the rope partway out of the pocket. Boots stomped in the foyer.

"Don't be stupid."

"*You're* stupid."

"Your mother's working."

"She's always working."

I opened the back door, closed it softly behind me. I heard the latch click. I stepped into the garden. It was the time of evening when the past seems more vivid and even pleasant memories are heartbreaking. Everything was still, bathed in purple twilight, and the smell of warm fires drifted toward me on a breeze. I felt a sudden chill, though the air had not been so warm in months. Melting ice pelted the drainpipe like falling dimes. I watched the light in the hall turn on, and then someone came into the kitchen. It was my last chance to tell them what had happened. But the dangling rope, I hoped, would speak for itself.

I started around the side of the house, trying not to make a sound. But my feet crunched like teeth on cotton. I wanted to disappear, melt into the night, so no one would ever know I'd been there. I couldn't understand why I felt so horrible after doing something good. I had saved Mrs. Lessing, hadn't I? But I wanted to escape all this sadness. Adults were supposed to be strong. They knew about the world, and yet that knowledge only seemed to make them weaker.

There was a sound. A whisper. At first I thought snow was sliding off the roof, that my ears were playing tricks on me. But then it came again: "Hey." I froze in my tracks, my heart pounding, afraid to look up. The darkness danced with mysterious shapes. Everything inside me moved too fast.

Lowell Bowman was standing on the other side of the fence, watching me. I could see him in the soft light, with his head cocked, leaning up against a tree. He had his arms crossed over his chest, and at the end of one hand the orange ember of a cigarette danced.

He came forward through the snow, put both hands on the fence posts, and stood there staring at me. He took a drag of the cigarette. My legs felt brittle, about to snap. "Come here," he said.

I had to push myself forward. I went toward him with my head down, afraid I wouldn't be able to speak. What if I fell? What if he could read my thoughts, knew I loved him, found it too strange? My heart beat so hard I thought he might hear it. I was so close now I could have touched him. I'd waited so long on the other side of the window; now I didn't have the courage. I smelled the cigarette. I didn't look up.

"I saw what happened," he said. I wanted his voice to be like music. But it was accusing, angry. *It wasn't me,* I wanted to say.

"What was she doing in that tree?" he said.

"Oh." I covered my mouth with my mitten. I looked up and met his eyes, trying to smile like I wasn't afraid. It was getting so dark I could barely see his face. I had never been able to see his face. It didn't matter.

"What's their name? She all right?"

"I can't talk about it here," I said, looking back at the house.

He studied me a moment and put his cigarette out in the snow. "Come over the fence then. Or walk around," he said, moving his finger in a little circle. "Whichever you prefer."

My whole body was shaking, but I managed to put one leg over the fence without incident. When I brought the other leg around, the hem of my coat ripped on a post and pulled me to the ground.

I scrambled up before he could help me and brushed myself off to show him I was OK.

He coughed to hide a laugh. His feet shifted. Oxfords in the snow. That meant he didn't care about ordinary things like ruining good pairs of shoes or ripping coats, things I had to care about now. "I should have had you come around," he said.

"It's just dark."

We stood there in silence beneath the canopy of the pine tree where I had hidden myself to watch him no more than a month before. There was no glass between us this time. Now I was beside him. He wanted something from me. I was the only one who knew what had happened. He cleared his throat. "You're on my mother's roses."

I looked down at my feet and felt the tears come to my eyes.

"I'm kidding," he said, after a time. "We're nowhere near the roses." But he didn't smile. I wasn't quite sure how to please him. He put his hand on my shoulder and gave it a gentle shake to emphasize the joke. I wanted his hand to stay, but he took it off and put it in his pocket.

I couldn't believe he had touched me. After all this time, he had touched me without me having to touch him first.

The Christmas before my grandfather died, Aunt Portia had made a Linzer torte, and when I tried to lick the powdered sugar off the rim of the plate, she'd slapped my hand with the spatula and said, "Good things come to those who wait!" Maybe I had waited long enough. Maybe I was going to have a good thing happen.

"Come inside," he said. "Everyone else went away. They're in Palm Springs." He kicked a chunk of snow, breaking it apart into smaller pieces. I couldn't believe they'd left him rattling around in this house. It wasn't fair. It wasn't right.

"I'll come if you want me to," I said.

"Do you know who I am?"

I shook my head no.

"Then maybe you shouldn't come."

"Why not?"

"I'm a stranger."

Maybe this was the way with college boys. They were clever. They expected you to be clever in return. "Well, you should *tell* me who you are, then," I said.

"I'm Lowe." He had to bend his head a little to talk to me.

I couldn't say anything in return. Susan wasn't good enough. Susan told too much. My voice felt stuck. He was tall, willowy. I smelled cigarettes and, beneath it, the faint scent of beer, something wiser.

I followed him through the snow to the patio door. He didn't say a word. There was only the sound of his footsteps and mine just behind, like a small echo of a bigger voice. Some part of me had always expected it, to meet him, and yet I couldn't believe it was happening. When he slid open the patio door, I held my breath, closed my eyes, and stepped into the place I'd always dreamed of being.

The living room was bigger than it had seemed from the outside, running the entire width of the house. There was the couch where I had watched Lowell read, the round mahogany table where his aunt sat wrapping Christmas presents. There were so many beautiful things here that I had never been able to see: soft-looking armchairs a dusty shade of red and a grand piano by a window that looked out onto the street, which seemed a part of a different world. Everything was real. I imagined Starkweather pacing back and forth in front of the window, keeping guard while Caril Ann slept. I could almost smell it, sick and sweet, the perfume she'd spilled to cover up death. The feeling I had always been able to sense; it was hidden in the drapes, the carpets. I could feel it in the air. A slow black sadness, a collective guilt. We have seen the ugliest parts. These drapes wear the blood of the woman who hung them. We have always known. We walk the thinnest lines.

I was afraid to look at Lowell, so I looked at everything else instead. Here I was. Here he was. It would be so easy to make a mistake, to ruin everything by looking too long at him, by saying something wrong, like I always seemed to do. You had to play games, my mother would say. You had to pretend you weren't interested. The less you wanted him, the more he wanted you back. I knew I'd never play those games right. If he so much as looked at me, he'd be able to see all the things I wanted from him.

"So, what was she doing up in that tree?" Lowell said, running his hands through his short hair. There was intensity to his blue eyes. I imagined tears clinging to the ends of the sad, dark lashes. I imagined wiping them away, saying, *It's not your fault, it's not your fault, Lowe.*

And then I realized I'd seen him before. He'd been in the lobby of the clubhouse last summer, nervously fixing his tie in the mirror. There had been something awkward about his fingers, the way they'd stumbled through the knot, like the whole world was watching. But there was only me, looking up from a magazine, waiting for my father's golf game to end and watching everything.

"Could I have something to drink?" I said. I could feel myself blushing. I stared down at my feet. It was so hard to meet his eyes.

"Sure." When I looked up he was smiling, but I couldn't make myself smile back. I was too nervous. I followed him through the foyer where Mr. Bowman had been shot. My heart pounded. I looked for a stain of blood by the door, some little sign. Nothing. It seemed like someone should have done something to remind us all of what those people had gone through, but I knew Lowell would never ever forget.

In the kitchen, a half-finished sandwich sat on a plate by the toaster. Mustard and mayonnaise jars with knives still in them, empty bottles of cola and beer, littered the counter. There were dirty footprints by the back door. I wondered how long Lowell had been here alone. A vase of sagging purple flowers sat on a wooden table in one corner. The blossoms had grown brown around the edges. Petals lay scattered across the white doily like leaves from a dying tree.

Lowell made no apologies for the mess. He pulled out a chair for me to sit on and went to the icebox. I ran my hand over the wood surface of the table. Starkweather might have sat in this very chair cutting out pictures of himself, composing illiterate notes to the law, but now everything was cluttered, ordinary, disappointing.

"What'll it be?" Lowell said.

"What do you have?"

"Milk, orange juice, cola, beer."

"Beer, please," I said, trying to sound casual.

Lowell hesitated in front of the icebox. He looked over his shoulder. "How old are you, anyway."

"Old enough to drink," I said, pretending to study my thumbnail. "Although I usually prefer wine."

He shrugged and removed the bottle tops with the end of a corkscrew, which I took to be a sign of experience. College boys must do everything with confidence, like passing off a football or moving a girl's hair from her neck. I could barely walk across the room in front of someone I wanted to impress. Lowell sat down in the chair across from me and took a drink of his beer. I watched his Adam's apple rise and fall, that small animal motion. He had seemed so vulnerable standing in front of the mirror at the club, awkward, out of sorts, the way I always felt. I had to remember that. It was something to cling to. How had the world come together like this when just moments ago it had all been in pieces?

"I was about to do something," he said, "but then she let go and I saw you out there, helping her up." He picked at the label on his bottle.

We sat in silence.

"So, are you going to tell me what happened?" he said, after a little while. He was trying to sound casual, but even so I could see it was important, that he needed to know. He put his elbow on the table, rested his chin in his hand, and looked right at me. It would be wrong to mention the rope.

"I just came over to drop something off and I saw her about to fall." I drank more beer to hide my blushing. It made me warmer, more comfortable.

"You're not friends with their daughter, that redhead, are you?"

"No," I said. "Not really. Just school."

"What's your name?"

"Puggy," I said.

"What's your *real* name?"

"That *is* my real name," I said, indicating my nose. I hadn't wanted to point out my nose. It was embarrassing, but then Lowell's wasn't perfect either. Some might have found it too large. I wanted to kiss it. I braced myself for another taste of beer.

"So you popped right out and they took one look at your nose and said, 'My God, that's it!'" He slammed his bottle down on the table for emphasis. "'We'll call her Puggy!'"

"Maybe," I said. "You haven't met my mother." And then I was sorry to have mentioned mothers.

Lowell got up, went to the window, and looked out into the darkness. The sky was electric blue, paler toward the horizon, as if the moon were rising where the sun had fallen. Could he see the tree from that angle? Had he been making that sandwich when he'd seen her fall? How long did he stand there wondering what to do?

"Why was she up there in the first place?" he said, turning around to face me.

"I don't know," I said.

"Why did she get it in her head to climb a tree?"

I shrugged. "Everyone was out," I said, like this was explanation enough.

He came back to the table and flopped down in the chair with his arms crossed over his chest. "I mean, do you have any idea at all why a woman would do a thing like that? That's something a kid would do." But I couldn't let on I knew who he was, that I knew Mrs. Lessing felt guilty about what had happened. I couldn't tell about the rope. It was a delicate balance. I wanted to draw out the story. I wanted to keep his attention. I wanted to say the right thing.

"She's a little crazy," I said. "I went out there and tried to catch her. I barely even broke her fall."

"Did she jump?"

"No," I said. "She fell."

"Did she hurt herself?"

I shook my head. "Not really." The beer made me warm, my words easy. I felt almost pretty at moments. I had all the answers Lowell needed, and he would keep me here as long as I didn't give them to him completely straight. But maybe he didn't want to be alone either.

"So you helped her into the house? You were there for a while," he said. The idea of Lowell waiting for me to come back outside sent chills up my spine. My heart felt light, full of air, about to burst.

"I sat by her bed and held her hand," I said. "I comforted her with funny stories. I waited till the family got home."

"What stories?"

"Embarrassing stories," I said.

I watched him finish his beer.

"Once, when I was younger, I had to go to this dancing class, but it turned out to be just me and the teacher," I said. "He was at least forty. He had a blue fish named Fred Astaire. He taught me the rumba. Do you know how to rumba?"

Lowell shook his head. He looked amused.

"When we were doing the cha-cha, he gave me a flower to hold in my teeth like one of those Spanish dancers. I got swept away on the music and then I kissed him on the neck."

Lowell laughed. "That's a pretty funny picture. How did you kiss him on the neck if you had a flower in your teeth?"

"It dropped on the floor."

"What then?"

"I don't remember. He picked up the flower and handed it back to me. And we continued dancing like nothing had happened."

"I don't believe you."

I felt myself blush. "It wasn't anything worth remembering. I think I went home."

"You told her that story?"

"Well, not exactly. But she's an artist. Artists do crazy things all the time," I said.

"Are you an artist?"

"I don't know yet."

"Yeah, you're too young to know. . . . I doodle. I like to collect things."

"Like what?"

"Artifacts," he said. "The Indians had trade routes all the way from California to Florida. Someone dug a Pueblo kachina out of the Everglades. In Montana, there's a cliff where the Nez Perce used to chase buffalo, and in the grass underneath it there's a rib cage the wind whistles through. If you look hard, you can still find spears, beads . . . arrowheads."

I could see him under the shadow of a cliff in the hot sun, sifting through dirt with long careful fingers. This was Lowell. These were the things he cared about. I wanted to crawl into him. I wanted to know everything there was to know about him. "Have you been all over?" I said.

"No." He pushed back his chair and went to the icebox.

"Can I have another beer?"

"You're barely in high school, right?"

"So?"

"So you're not old enough," he said, smirking. But he came back with another beer anyway and put it down in front of me. "Just don't drink it all," he said.

I took a sip.

"When she was little, I used to tease that girl."

"Who?"

"Next door. I feel bad about it now," he said. "I came home from baseball late one night, and she was sleeping on a cot in the driveway with a weird little bug light on it. I remember her face was this funny shade of blue and she was sucking her thumb. I don't know why, but I took the cot and ran down the middle of the street, rolling it in front of me. She woke up, screaming and crying. I felt bad, so I rolled her back home. I was twelve, so that girl must have been—"

"Eight," I said.

"What? How do *you* know?"

"I guessed," I said.

"My mother just told me not to do it again." He stood up and went over to the sink. "I always got away with everything, I don't know why."

I looked up at him, but he was staring out the window. The light above the counter cast a warm glow across his shoulders. I watched him run his fingers through his hair. I could tell he was thinking about something. "I'm not particularly special," he said. "I'm not going back to college."

"How come?"

"Everyone's—I mean, I'm not . . . never mind." He shook his head.

"Are you going to stay here?"

His brow was furrowed, but beneath it his eyes seemed wide, almost frightened. "They think I've left for school already."

"Where will you go?"

"Egypt, maybe. The pyramids. The Valley of the Kings. I need to ride a camel across the desert." He came to the table and stood over me, looking down. "Hey, come with me. I'll show you the rest of the house." He took my hand, and when I stood my head felt airy. Everything was bright, sharp, a slice of light on a sunless day. I left the beer half finished on the table and followed him through the dining room. The crystal chandelier winked. We went into the foyer. "You know what happened?" he said.

"No. What happened?"

"Never mind," he said, and pulled me up the stairs.

IT WAS A BOY'S ROOM. NOTHING HAD CHANGED. THE BRASS KNOCKER ON THE door was tarnished, but I could still read his name. I took the little handle between my thumb and forefinger and tapped, once, twice, three times. He put his ear to the door—"Anyone home?"—then nudged me inside.

Lowell's room looked out over the street; from this window Caril Ann had watched Mr. Bowman's Packard turn into the driveway. What had she felt, crouched there waiting in the dark? Was it fear? Had it been this desperation, this need? Was I very much different? These same toy soldiers had watched from the case. This same golf trophy—YOUNG PUTTERS, 1955—had sat on the bookshelf as people lost their lives.

Lowell sat down on the bed and leaned forward, resting his elbows on his knees. I sat down too. There was a large gap between us. For a moment, neither of us spoke. We both looked at the floor. The carpet was dark green. I wished I'd taken the beer along, so I'd have something to occupy my mouth, my fingers. Every part of me ached for more. "For a minute I thought you wanted to take me to Egypt," I said.

"That's your fault." He yawned. "You didn't bring your passport."

"Oh."

He leaned his head back and stared at the ceiling. "So this is my room," he said. "The very spot where I always lay, coming up with my brilliant philosophies."

"Like what?"

"I can't explain. It'd be like Greek to you, Piggy Pug."

"Stop." I giggled.

"I'd love to be able to waste away in a Chinese opium den. I'd like to pen a letter to my aunt from a velvet couch and sign it with a puff of smoke." He pursed his lips, as if he were blowing smoke rings, and propped his head against the wall. "I don't want to go to church ever again. I want to be fat, but I can't get fat. I've tried. I ate nine pieces of fried chicken in one sitting. It doesn't work."

"Do you like fat girls?"

"No."

"Then what makes you think they'd like *you* fat?"

"They don't like me anyway. Who cares?"

I like you, I wanted to say. Why couldn't he see that? Maybe he didn't care. Maybe he thought *I* was fat. "Your bed's so small. How do you fit?" I said.

"I said I wanted to be fat, not that I *am* fat." He hit me lightly on the shoulder. He got up, went to the window, and paced up and down. "I have to keep moving," he said.

"Why?"

"I don't know. My legs feel strange."

I followed him into the hall where Lowell's mother had fought for her life. My heart raced. My thoughts tumbled in on themselves. Starkweather said she'd taken a shot, yet nobody had been able to find the bullet hole. *Was it here, or there? Nobody had answers. Nobody knew. The truth lay buried beneath layers of ground.*

He led me to the master bedroom. By the light from the half-open door I could make out a gold headboard, a nightstand, a lamp. And bits of red, shimmering, catching the light. Something magical. A treasure chest spilling out jewels. A ghost woman wearing a cluster of rubies.

My fingers quivered. Light trembled. Blue, like the flash of a camera. A burnt-out bulb. The dark made patterns. When he tried another lamp, everything took shape.

In the corner by a closet, the dress was stretched over a dummy with a white ribbon that said QUEEN AKSARBEN across the chest. Cora and I had seen it through the binoculars, but it was even more beautiful close up. The sequins were red, orange. One person might have spent her whole life sewing them on. This is the dress of a woman up on stage singing in a sultry voice, I thought to myself. A man wouldn't be able to help himself. He'd come out from behind a curtain and kiss her bare shoulder.

Lowell flopped down on the bed with his arms folded under his head and crossed his legs. "That's my aunt's Aksarben ball gown. She doesn't want anyone to forget. She doesn't want anyone to forget anything. But at the same time she pretends not to see it."

"What do you mean?"

He took a deep breath and blew it out slowly. He seemed about to answer.

I didn't know if I should have asked him to tell me more about it. I didn't know whether I should lie down next to him either, take his hand in mine, and tell him I was listening, whatever he needed to say. I wasn't sure I wanted him to spill it all out just yet, to tell me the things I already knew too much about. How could I possibly act surprised?

He shrugged. "I'm not complaining."

I wasn't the sort of person who could console him about chance, about having it all ripped out from under you. It was only that I felt the same way; I just didn't have as much of a reason. People chose not to love me. For Lowell, it wasn't a matter of choice.

I felt full of nervous laughter. Dizzy. I went over to the dummy and pulled a dress strap down over one shoulder. The sequins were cool, shiny little bits of light.

"Very nice," he said.

I giggled.

"You can try it on."

I turned around and looked at him.

He smiled, nodded his head.

"It wouldn't fit. I'm too—"

"You're not," he said.

"I'm too short."

"So what?" He sat up and grinned at me. The idea seemed to please him. "I think you should." He jumped off the bed, pulled the zipper down the back of the dress, and lifted it over the dummy. *A body moving through beads. A gypsy curtain.* "Here." He handed me the dress. "Open the closet door and hide behind it," he said. "I won't look, I promise. Just take off that stupid ribbon." His voice was full of the game. He was excited.

I felt excited too, but what if it didn't fit? No boy had ever seen my bare shoulders, except at the pool, but back then no one had been looking. What if they weren't nice shoulders? What if my stomach bulged?

He lay back down on the bed. "I'm waiting," he said.

I opened the closet door and stepped behind it. There was a full length mirror on the inside. It didn't shield me completely. "Close your eyes."

"OK," Lowell said, and did as he was told.

I fumbled through the buttons on my blouse, and let the cold cotton fall to the floor. I stood in front of the mirror in my bra, my skirt, my stockings, my boots. There was so little between us, half a door, a mirror, no walls or windows. I felt my lungs caving in. Why was I so afraid? This was what I had always wanted, wasn't it? To be in this room alone with him, to have as much attention as he could possibly give. This was my choice.

When I bent down to take off my boots, I peered around the edge of the door. For a brief moment his eyes caught mine.

"Don't," I said.

"I'm not." He closed his eyes again.

I unhooked my bra, and let it drop. Cold air tickled my skin. The hairs on my arm stood up. My nipples felt strange, alive, almost painful.

I stumbled out of my tights. My feet were damp, and I rubbed them over the carpet. Letting my skirt fall in a heap, I stood there for a moment in nothing but my underpants, feeling the air prickle my skin. The underwear was ugly, white and large, but it seemed my hips had changed, rounded out, gently narrowing into the waist. I had a waist, breasts, a nice slope to my shoulders. Even so, the dress wouldn't fit. My thighs were too big. My stomach wasn't tight enough. All that color against such pasty skin. What was I doing? A pulse whirred in my ears. I didn't check to see if he was watching. I didn't want to see the disappointment. My fingers shook. My legs were going to go out from under me. I wasn't ready. For one moment, I closed my eyes and wished to be anywhere else.

"What's taking so long?" he said.

I didn't answer. I picked up the dress, and stepped into it. The fabric slipped over my thighs, my hips. Sequins shimmered like a thousand lit matches, tickled like a thousand fingertips. I put my arms through the straps. The fabric was cold against my chest. I reached behind me and zipped up the back. The dress fit like cool new skin. My body took shape, and I was a mystery. I was sultry. Yes, the straps were too loose. Inches of sequined cloth pooled around my feet. But my body had never felt so sure. I held my hair on top of my head, turned around in front of the mirror, and looked over my shoulder. The back was low. There was a freckle to the left of my spine I had never noticed.

"Let me see," Lowell said.

"It's too long. I need shoes." I dug around on the floor of the closet. In a white shoebox, I found a pair of red silk pumps and put them on. They slipped in the heel, but the fit was close enough. The toes looked sharp, pointed like little trowels. I could walk.

"Come back out here," he said.

"Cover your eyes."

I gathered the extra fabric in my fists, stepped slowly from behind the closet door, and walked toward him. Sequins made a sound against my legs like falling rain. Lowell had his hands over his eyes.

"OK, you can look," I said.

He separated his fingers and peered between them, then took his hands away slowly as if he were unveiling some magnificent treasure. He sat up and raised his eyebrows, and nodded his head. "It fits pretty well." But I could tell he wanted to say more than that. Something in his face had changed. He was noticing me in a new way, a way that no one ever had. No one had ever seen me like this before.

"You really think so?" I asked. The strap had fallen down over my shoulder.

"Really."

I pulled it back up.

My head swam. The light was soft. Beautiful and uncertain. Crouched beneath the sill of Cora's window, this room had seemed like a box, and this dress a jewel tucked safely inside. It was a fantasy we'd never be able to touch. Fancy dresses wouldn't fit. We didn't run fast enough. We were all wrong. But now I was on the inside. I held the jewel in my hand. Everything I had ever wanted came rushing toward me. My whole life pulled me forward. I could see for miles. I could see for years. I was going to be a woman. He would always want me.

"You're pretty." He leaned back against the gold headboard, studying me. "You don't even know it." I imagined him in a smoking jacket, velvet slippers. The prince of a fallen kingdom.

I couldn't help grinning. "It's the dress. I just *became* pretty."

"I know, like a flower." He frowned. "I watched you grow."

"Why are you frowning?" I wanted to know.

He smiled. "Things that grow don't last."

I went to the window and put my hands on the sill and peered into the night. Cora's turtle lamp was on, but I couldn't see her. I was a square of light suspended in darkness. *Are you out there watching?* I put my lips up against the glass and kissed the cold pane. *Can you see me?* On the edge of the stone pool in the garden, the angel blew its trumpet. The killers ran. Bright shapes of goldfish darted beneath a frozen surface. I could feel them, sudden and smooth. Shocks in the dark. Just like me.

Lowell came up behind me, took my hand, and pulled me away from the window. My heart stumbled. "Let's dance," he said.

"There's no music."

"So what?" He spun me around in a little circle. I tripped on the hem of the dress, lost my shoe, and stumbled back against the bed.

He got down on his knee, fished under the dust ruffle, and came up holding the shoe. I took it from him and cradled it against my chest.

"I don't believe you can cha-cha."

I laughed and threw the shoe across the room. It hit the closet door and thumped to the floor. My body felt stiff, strange. Awkward. I lay down on the bed, and Lowell lay next to me. The lamp cast a soft pool on the ceiling. The shade was enormous, a dark shadow, a bat wing. I could hear him breathing.

Lowell put his arm on my shoulder and turned me on my side. Sequins caught on the bedspread, pulled at threads, came free, scattered like little drops of blood. "Look," I said.

"Who cares?"

I lay there staring at him, afraid to breathe. His eyes glittered, but his face was serious. "I've seen her in that tree before."

"What?"

"Mrs. Lessing." He pressed the tip of my nose with his finger. "You know. Tell me why. What was she doing?" I didn't know what to say. My voice felt caught. My heart thudded against bone.

He put his hands around my waist and lifted me on top of him. A line of sequins shimmered where I had lain. There was one in the crease of his collar, a little secret, my secret. A place I had touched. I smelled starch, beer, a breath of smoke. Something else, like sun hitting skin, a gentle sweat. He gathered my hair in his hand and brushed it behind my shoulders.

I decided I never would cut it.

"Tell me," he said. Something magic, a puff of smoke, and I could feel the different parts of his body rising to meet me.

I leaned forward and got up close to his ear. I moved my body against him. "There was a rope in her pocket," I whispered. "She had a *rope*." He shuddered. I could feel every bit of him, his spine, his heart. The tips of his fingers fluttered. His Adam's apple rose and fell, a desperate motion. He wrapped his arms around me and pulled me tight to his chest. I could hear blood drumming through too-narrow veins.

"Was she going to use it?" he said.

"I don't know."

He put his nose in my hair and took a sharp breath. "God." He leaned back against the pillows. His eyes were closed. He seemed a long way off.

I put my head to his chest. "I can hear your heart," I said. "Can you hear mine?"

He opened his eyes, and looked at me. "No. What's it saying?"

I kissed him on the ear. He shifted under me. He slid his tongue down my neck, and my skin came alive. His breath was hot and short. I felt my body opening. Sequins shimmered. Fists crushed fabric. I stepped inside myself, and he was there. Somehow, in this giant world we had come to find ourselves in each other, and still, it wasn't enough.

He lifted himself away and lay down beside me. "I won't do anything you don't want me to do," he said.

I didn't know what I wanted him to do. Red sequins were scattered everywhere like beads from a broken necklace. Everything had tumbled free. I looked down at the dress. It was still all in one piece. I fixed the straps back over my shoulders.

Lowell sighed and rolled over. "I don't want you to go," he said. "But let's just lie here. I'm tired."

"That's what I want," I said. "Just to lie here."

He ran his finger over my shoulder and closed his eyes.

I watched his chest rise and fall. I touched his hair. He didn't move. "Lowe," I whispered, barely moving my lips. He didn't hear me. "I always knew this would happen. I've been waiting my whole life."

I watched the hard angles of his face give way to something softer. I didn't think of Mrs. Lessing or my father all alone, pacing the halls of his father's house tapping his watch, waiting for his family to come home, mistaking his own reflection for the woman he loved. I didn't imagine all the things he'd have to say. I didn't want to go back. I wanted to stay here forever. Lowell's eyelids moved. He dreamed about me, about all the things there were left to do. The night got darker, deeper, and I lay there wondering if he'd heard my words.

CHAPTER TWENTY-TWO

1976

I have learned that love goes away but the things you do during love can't ever go. Like a baby you never wanted in the first place, like the one Leerae was going to have in Community A. Her guy ran off after she got pregnant, and drove her to the stealing. Just like Charlie drove me to all the things we did. He took me off for a steak in that beat-up Ford of his and I never got back. Year after year, I go through these pictures: The Chevrolet with the girl's math book in back, left open on the seat like a great big promise. The fancy Packard. The lights on the lawmen's cars flashing over all the faces. Mother's dark blood, Betty Sue, the picture of that boy the lady had showed and cried over. I can still see it all, though not so clear. Even big things that change you get lost with time. How do you explain what happened in me? I was a girl. He started shooting.

CHARLIE GOT THE CHAIR, WHICH WASN'T ANY SURPRISE, BUT I GOT LIFE WHEN I should have got off. Maybe I was not the best of girls. Maybe I did not always follow the rules. Maybe I should never have let Charlie come in my window that night, but people don't get locked up for that kind of thing. After the sheriff came, me and Charlie both got treated like part of the same thing. We passed the night in separate jails at Valentine, and I couldn't sleep with thinking how sad it was to be stuck in a place with that name. I drew a heart on the cold jail wall and thought about Valentine's Day not being so very far off and how no one had ever gave me a card. I never have gotten one either. People hated me so. They thought I drove Charlie to it. I said no, I did not, so many times I finally just quit.

When the sun came up, we got put in the separate cars again, which was A-OK by me. I never wanted to see Charlie again. There was no place, really, I wanted to look. The lawmen headed us back to Lincoln. Sheriff Meeks said the whole world was waiting for justice. I still didn't believe he meant justice for me. They had taken off my cuffs and sat some old gray-headed baggage right there next to me in the backseat doing her knitting. After a while she had put it away and asked me if I would like to tell her what happened.

"I want to tell Mother what happened," I said. I don't know why, I guess I really thought there was half a chance I'd dreamed this up.

"I'm sorry, that can't be," the old lady said, nice enough.

"How come?" I said. "Doesn't she know?"

The lady gave me a funny look and pushed her glasses up her nose. "Don't you know your mother's dead, Caril?" she said.

"What do you mean, dead?"

"She was killed."

"She was killed?" I could feel my eyes were starting to cry. "Who killed her?"

"Well, you know who, Caril, don't you know who? You were there, weren't you?"

I shaked my head and put my hands in front of my face to hide my eyes and let out a great big sob. "Where's Nig?"

"Who is Nig?"

"Nig. . . ." Yes, it was real. It was all real and there was no going back. "I don't know. I don't know. I got kidnapped." I said it over and over so many times it was true.

The lady handed me a box of Kleenex. Later I got to making little dolls out of the paper to pass the time. After a while, the car holding Charlie had pulled alongside so the lawmen could talk, and there was Charlie in back staring me down. His hair was all messed up and something was smeared over his cheek. He tried to shout at me through the glass, and I had held up one of my little dolls and put it real close to the glass so he couldn't miss it. I took my thumb and my long finger and waved the doll at Charlie. Then I wrang the doll's neck so Charlie could see how I wasn't going to have a problem giving him up.

But the sheriff's old bag said in the court that what I did with the Kleenex "demonstrated a violent nature." She said there wasn't any way she could see I didn't know about Mother getting killed. Either I was putting on an act or I was in shock. *Yes, I was in shock. I was in shock the whole time.*

Mr. Scheele had sat in the plastic chair with spectacles sliding off his nose, trying to capture just what went on. He wouldn't let me forget, even though I told him I had nothing to do with it. "Are you sure that's the way it happened, Miss Fugate?" In the beginning it had made me feel important, a grown man calling me by my second name, like someone was finally going to listen to my side. But after a while I could see he was not on my side. He hoped that if I repeated the story enough, I'd trip and say it was all my fault. I'd go ape and scream, *Yes! I told you a million times how it happened!* and he'd say, *There! Just as I thought. A violent nature.*

> It seems to me there was plenty of opportunity to make a choice, Miss Fugate. You were at your home with Charles for an entire day before the police showed up, and you say that on more than one occasion he went to the grocery store to buy provisions—potato chips. Why did you not then inform the authorities of the situation, if you wanted so badly to get away?
>
> I was too scared of what he'd do.
>
> And when you forced your way into Mr. Lancaster's kitchen just after midnight on the night of your capture, why did you not identify yourself then and direct him immediately to call the authorities?
>
> I thought he would know me. I was telling him with my eyes.
>
> How was that?

But there was no way I could show him on account of looking so hard at the floor. I did not tell him anything more. It is not the kind of thing you can explain, how you love and love till you are all wrapped up in the same skin and have to swallow the same bites and breathe the same cold air, because he chose you and you chose him. And then every one of his choices shrinks up your choices a little more, till you are gone before you realize there was any choice at all.

WARDEN CARMICHAEL CHECKED ME IN. SHE WAS BIG AS THIS STATE.

New commitments are permitted to retain the following items:

One wedding band. I sure as hell didn't have that.

One watch. No, no reason to tell the time.

One commercial religious medallion. I didn't know what that was, but I was pretty sure I didn't have it.

One Bible. No.

Letters. No one had ever so much as written me. Who would write?

Two photographs.

I had given up the shots of me and Charlie, and the picture the lady had showed me in her room of her son and the dog and her husband I kept in my mind. Everything had been so together, everyone in the picture smiling, and a moment later it was all smashed up and ruined, the lady killed, the dog's neck broke, the husband shot dead at the door saying her name, and I had no idea what happened to the boy. She had said he was my age. And maybe the boy was not so different from me now, in having no one and nothing left, not even the dog.

For a year they stuck me in solitary. It was a little room with gray-painted walls other girls had wrote on. There was a heavy door with a diamond window big enough for a face, and a place for sliding my food through like someone had gone and stuck me in a mailbox. I did have my own window with bars to look out over the grass and the fence with the electric wires on top. They let me keep the window open, and I was thankful for this. I never knew the time, but I could tell by the light and by the bell that told the inmates that had some choices what to do. There was breakfast, lunch, and dinner. At night

I would lay in bed and think about what it was like to be outside. But I never could recall the girl I was before Charlie. I would lay there at night and think about the different ways it could have been till it made me crazy. I heard the crickets in the prairie grass and watched the moon out the window, and it seemed to be lighting up all the footprints me and Charlie left behind. I saw futures that never were.

See that boy sliding into second? He would have been my son!

See my grandchild holding a potato chip and making her way across the kitchen floor? She's taking a first step that will never be taken!

Betty Sue, nothing but trouble, hanging around punks at the Capital Race Track.

I was sketching the wedding dress in my notebook when I should have been paying attention, but what did geometry matter when I was going to marry Bob?

Do you think my husband knew I was already dead when he said my name? Did he have any hope?

And I wanted to say, *Don't ask me, lady. I didn't kill him. I was trying to fix the dog's neck so your boy would have something to come back to.* But I couldn't speak. My throat was red and swollen shut from trying to explain.

The only one left who could explain it right was Charlie, and he was about to get the chair. So he wouldn't talk. I begged for someone to let me see him one last time, even though I thought I never would want to see him again. I thought if he saw me, maybe he would feel bad and say how none of it was my fault. But Charlie wouldn't see me and President Eisenhower didn't care. Maybe he never even read the letter I wrote. Or maybe it never got sent. Or maybe it was spelled all wrong and he couldn't make it out, and nobody bothered to tell me.

I waited all day for Charlie to get another stay. But it wasn't just the talking. I thought of his hands touching me all over, his fingers, the face I always knew. I couldn't even draw or eat my food or close my eyes, for everything hanging so much in the balance.

After lights out, I laid there in the dark waiting for someone to come tell me Charlie had spoke. I thought it might happen. There were people who said he loved God now, and there was a time he had swore he loved me too.

And then, just like an answer, someone was there. A key turned in the lock, and the door creaked open and hit cement with a heavy sound. My heart clenched up like a little fist. I sat up in bed and tried to make out who was there. There were keys on a waist and a big dark shape in the moonlight to say it was Warden Carmichael. Her breath came out heavy, and I knew if she got any closer I'd be able to smell it. She did not make to turn on the light. "It's done with. About twenty minutes ago," she said. "Charlie Starkweather's dead." She sounded like maybe this was a great thing, like maybe the world had gone to war, and her side was winning. A little heart that was left inside me drifted away on a gust of wind.

"They shaved off all that red hair and did the sponge," she said. "Then they put on the electrodes—two on the head, one on the calf—and then they flicked the switch."

I didn't want to hear any more about that.

She said how the first shock knocked him senseless and the second fried his brain. Smoke came out of his ears and he soiled himself. The third shock stopped his heart.

"But did he tell them?"

"Oh, he told them, all right."

"What did he say?"

"He wished you were there next to him."

"You mean to talk to?" I said, on account of hoping so much.

Warden Carmichael blew air out through her fat cheeks and said, "He wished that chair was made for two, honey. And he's not the only one that said it. Don't expect any special favors around here."

What special favors had I ever got? My whole life slammed shut. I thought of a flash of light breaking through Charlie's brain and I wondered if he pictured the ways we had loved.

A LONG TIME LATER THEY LET ME OUT OF SOLITARY. WARDEN CARMICHAEL LEFT and Jackie came; she was thin with nice-enough hair and didn't want us to call her *Warden*. There were small changes, but never ones that really mattered. It was true I had some privileges, but it was not like being free. On Wednesdays the van took me to the nursing home, which as far as I could see was not so different from a prison. After lights out sometimes they let me keep up at the drawing in the study room, even though I had run out of new things to draw a long time ago. Sometimes I would stay in the little hood of light an extra hour, pretending to be thinking about a picture, but I was really wondering what the whole world would be like if I ever got out. "Not if, Caril, *when*," Jackie always said, since she believed in us inmates. Jackie believed a woman could change. She had started up the sewing program and reading and the dreaming about the future. In general, this place was a whole lot better. But I didn't know where it would get a person to dream about the future, since all my dreaming with Charlie had only landed me here.

I watched the new girls that came and cried for being here and the crazy ones that went and cried for leaving. The dried-up grass turned green in the spring. There was snow in the winter and weather in the summer, but I never could feel it. When a tornado rolled in they made us walk in straight lines and squeeze in the basement, and we never so much as heard the wind howl. Only doors slamming, and keys locking, and the jokes about how if something happened and sweeped us away, maybe we'd end up someplace better, like that girl with the slippers who got carried out of Kansas. I never once laughed, though, on account of knowing I never would leave. I had come up for parole two times already for good behavior and was told two times I couldn't leave. Soon there was going to be a third time, but I had gave up caring. I had gave up feeling till Leerae dived downstairs like someone swimming and broke her neck with trying so hard to break her baby.

THE WEEK BEFORE IT HAPPENED WAS THE FIRST WEEK LEERAE SHOWED UP. IT was stealing and drugs someone told me, bad ones you shot in your arm, and a baby still inside her with three months left to go. We always knew the new women's stories, though I don't know how we ever heard them. But Leerae was more of a girl than a woman, eighteen, just three years older than me when I had got my sentence.

They had let us out after lunch to walk in circles on the crunched-up grass. There was a frost and winter was coming, but Leerae didn't look cold. She was marching up close alongside the fence with her stomach going up and down, like she was trying to stomp out the baby. I could see something fierce in the way she moved, but this did not bother me on account of never knowing anything that wasn't fierce. She was so lean and, aside for the baby, like a fashion model.

And she dressed like one too, with a coat made out of sheepskin that was the same color as her hair, and dark red pants that went out at the bottom like fancy glasses turned upside down. They had let her keep her clothes, which meant she had not done so bad a thing. Before long she'd be out in the world again. Then she had left off the marching and stood on her tippytoes, trying to reach the wires of the fence. Fat chance. She was tall, but you'd have to be a giant. I wanted to help her. "Don't," I said, thinking someone had just forgot to tell her. "The top part's electric."

She whipped around and gave me a mean look to say I should leave her alone. Her face was pretty but covered in a spray of pimples. "Any other suggestions? Got a coat hanger?"

I had no idea why she would want a coat hanger since the whole of us didn't have any coats here worth hanging. And hers close up was not so nice as I had thought, but used up and dirty, like some old goat tossed in the corner of a barn. "No one's got coat hangers," I said. "It's the rules."

"Well, I don't follow rules." Leerae kicked a stone against the fence, and it made a little *ping*. There was some strange way about her that reminded me of Charlie, and to think of him buried so many years gave me a chill. A white bird with big wings flew out toward the road, and we both stopped to watch it. I had never seen a bird like that.

"What'd you do?" I said, though I should have thought twice about asking since I never would want to tell her what wrong things they thought I'd done.

"I got caught in a mixed-up crowd and I couldn't go home." She told me Jim left her knocked up in Rapid City with no money for rent, and she had to steal. She turned a trick or two and then they busted her. The way she said this was flat and strange, like she had gave up caring. She was the kind of girl the chaplain was going to try to help find God. "And I guess if you were so good at rules you wouldn't be here so long," she said.

"How do you know how long I've been here?"

"Oh, I know. Everyone knows. You look just like the pictures, like no time passed, like you're some kind of spook."

I didn't like her calling me a spook. Time *had* passed. There were wrinkles by my eyes to show it. I had felt every day go by.

"They still talk about it on the outside," she said. "You're the *child girlfriend.*" There were great blue circles under her pretty eyes and a hardness in her jaw.

I certainly wasn't a child anymore. I'd spent a good half of my life at York. I wanted to ask her to take a hard look and think about the things we do as children and if they deserved to be forgiven and forgotten like Jackie had told me. After all, I was not so different from her in *getting caught in a mixed-up crowd.* And I had never so much as thought about turning a trick.

It made me sick to think about me and Charlie still being talked about at every supper table in every town, because maybe they were still saying the same old thing: that I was a part of killing the lady since I had stole from her. But not saving is not the same as killing, no matter how you look at it.

"Well, stories you hear aren't always true," I said.

"Right," Leerae said, and kind of laughed. She watched a transfer van drive too fast down Recharge Road. There was nothing else moving anywhere I could make out, no mark to separate the plains from the sky. When she turned back around I could see a wetness in her eyes that looked to be tears.

There didn't seem to be anything worth saying, so I started to walk away. "A lot of us should never have been born," she said, and punched her fist on the baby like an exclamation point. I knew how she felt. I did not believe in reasons for everything.

"You don't want to hurt your baby, though," I said, on account of knowing how it felt to hurt Mother's baby, even though I had not been the one to stick in the knife.

"It doesn't matter anymore," Leerae said of the baby. "It's hurt enough already."

She stood there a second still as salt and then a funny look crawled up over the edge of her face, and her skin went white behind the red spots. Blood was running out from her nose, and all the toughness in her was running out with it. It spilled in two red trails that went between her fingers down her wrist and inside the sleeve of her coat. Red was painting the grass, petals that had ripped off from a flower, and she went down on her knees and put her arms out like she was making to gather them. I wondered how it was blood kept following me. I kneeled on the cold ground beside her. I took my hands and tilted back her head like how the orderly did at the nursing home. "Don't touch me," she said, but I didn't listen. We kneeled there for a time, and after a while the bleeding stopped.

LEERAE WAS NOT GOING TO LET HERSELF BE SAVED. THE GIRLS WHO SAW IT happen said there was no way you could predict it. When Leerae had got to the landing, she put her arms at her sides and dived down the stairs with a sureness of being shot from a cannon, like someone was going to catch her. But no one was there to catch her. The guard had stumbled after her but couldn't get a hold, and Leerae had landed at the foot of the stairs with her head against the wall and her neck all twisted and you could tell from her eyes right then she had died. I didn't want to hear any more about it, but everyone was whispering. *Eyes like blue skies all clouded up. Even a pretty girl like her wasn't happy.*

I wondered if the baby had died right when she died, or if it struggled for a little while, trying to make sense out of the quiet dark. I thought of all the people I had seen before they were killed and how they had tried to make sense of it too.

I didn't want to leave my room anymore. I wouldn't go to the nursing home. I laid down on the bed and painted pictures in my mind out of light that was making different shadows on the wall. All the ghosts were there, but they had no voices left to say what really happened, just lips that moved without a sound. *Jeanette,* he said, because he loved her. She had gave me a chance. She told me there was always a choice. But it hadn't seemed to me there was *ever* a choice.

ALL THOSE YEARS LATER WHEN THE PAROLE BOARD LET ME OFF AND JACKIE told me I was free, I really didn't care. She said, "Isn't it wonderful, Caril?" But I didn't feel one bit wonderful. I looked out at the flat ground on the other side of the fence. It went on forever, and in my case forever was a pretty bad thing. Forever I'd have to live with it: what I did or what I didn't do, depending on how you looked at it.

"You know," Jackie said, and put her arm around my shoulders, "it's not my job to say whether you are guilty or not, but it's my job to say when you are rehabilitated."

"Am I?"

"There isn't any question in my mind you are rehabilitated."

But I did not feel the least bit *rehabilitated.*

"There are certain services we offer that will help you get on your feet again."

"I don't want any services, Jackie."

"I wish you would, Caril. These services are meant to protect you." But I didn't feel like being protected.

Jackie took me to her office and gave me the box full of the things I came with. Before I opened the box, I looked down at my clothes and they were not so different from the ones I showed up in—*I was a spook.* I didn't have any need for the old things in that box, but I opened it anyway because I was supposed to. But there were new clothes inside, my size, on account of Jackie knowing me better than anyone else. She had gone to Grand Island and bought me green pants with a flare and a coat that looked to be made of white leather with a trace of fur around the collar. "Jackie," was all I could say on account of being so shocked by her kindness. "Leather?"

"It's not really leather. It's pleather."

It looked enough like leather to me. I put it on and pulled it close around me. "Thank you," I said.

She nodded her head and told me how great I looked, and I wondered if there would be anyone else to ever think so.

I turned around in a circle 'cause she wanted to see me happy.

"Your sister is coming to pick you up in York?"

I nodded my head at her.

"Why not here?" I did not tell her my sister wasn't coming at all, that I hadn't so much as called her. I hadn't seen Barbara since I had got here, and I was pretty sure she wouldn't want to see me now.

"I want a walk," I said. " I haven't really walked anywhere in a long time."

Jackie took me down the hall and held open the door, and a rush of cold came in to meet me. I knew all the girls would be watching from the windows waiting to wave, and maybe it would give them a little hope to see me leave. Suddenly I couldn't move. My feet felt stuck in one place.

"Go on. You've got a whole life left," Jackie said. But I had already passed half my life in here.

"What are they going to say, Jackie?"

"Who cares what they say? You can change your name, and eventually they'll forget."

But I didn't think anyone was ever going to forget.

"You know, Caril, the world forgives," she told me, and touched my arm like the lady in Lincoln. I wasn't so sure about that either. How could parents forgive for the children that got taken? And how could the boy forgive the way I let his mother and father get killed? She had told me his name. And I knew his age, on account of its being the same as mine. Sometimes I wondered where he was, but I never would want to know anything more than that. I was too afraid he didn't come out right. Maybe he came out like me.

The sky was gray and the road was gray, no different really from the walls I had left. I walked along the side for a while, crunching snow with my boots, leaving my footprints. I wished I could brush them away. I wondered about all the different places I had seen on maps, and if there was anywhere someone wouldn't know my story. The town of York was five miles. When I got there, I would take a bus west and make my way to a lake because I had never so much as been to one. I knew there was a lake made of salt in the state of Utah, where Salt Lake City got its name. I heard there was so much salt, it washed up on the shore and stayed, like something spat up from a great big ocean. I would head in that direction because it was something, and I had no more reason than a lake full of salt to head anywhere else.

CHAPTER TWENTY-THREE

1991

I came home for Christmas vacation in 1957, from my first semester at boarding school. Instead of letting me watch kids dance across the television screen or organize my collection of Indian arrowheads, however, my mother insisted I take a piano lesson with Miss Voight. "I don't want you to forget everything you learned," she said. "If you don't practice you'll lose all that ground"—only I'd never gained any ground to begin with. "You're just not practicing enough," my mother would always say, as if she hadn't heard me protest. "You have the fingers. Miss Voight says you have those long piano fingers."

"Football is what these fingers are for," I said, not wanting to be any sort of sissy boy.

My mother had tried for years to play the piano, shaking her head in frustration every time her heavy rings slipped over the white keys. Her fingers jangled discordant notes into the air as I stood on the lip of the living room step, transfixed by her failure. Moira was the only one who called what my mother played music. She would dust the piano while my mother practiced, but Moira was almost stone deaf and liked the vibrations the hammers made beneath the lid. "Jeanette, I feel beautiful music," she'd say haltingly, as I tried not to laugh.

My mother finally gave up the piano. Instead, she went to the Lincoln Symphony regularly. She took up a black opera singer named Barbara because she claimed the sound of her voice made her feel at peace in her own skin. "I'm living vicariously," my mother would sigh. She traveled everywhere to see Barbara perform: Chicago, Minneapolis, even New York. She'd meet her backstage with flowers and come home the next day almost in tears. "Barbara's life has been so hard it breaks my heart," she had said once, because an opera had not been well attended. "For someone like Miss Voight who's had everything and is so attractive, success comes easily. It isn't fair."

"Miss Voight," my father said in a strained tone, "is not traveling to New York to play piano, Jeanette. She's giving lessons in Lincoln."

"She will be soon enough. She's still so young. And then she won't want to give Lowell lessons anymore. She'll forget all about him." My mother pressed her lips together. "Just you wait."

So I waited. I had waited two years for Miss Voight to forget me, to leave me alone, but here I was at fourteen, between Christmas and New Year's, with the doorbell ringing and Miss Voight standing in the snow on the front step, wearing her purple hat and her enormous purse over her shoulder, with music sheets sticking out. When I opened the door to the cold air and ushered her quickly inside, Miss Voight threw her arms around me, and something felt different. I could feel her body, tight and smooth beneath the layer of her baggy coat. "Lowell," she cried, pressing my nose into her collarbone so I could smell the dusky perfume hiding there. I quickly threw my arms around her and squeezed. Then I thrust my hands behind my back.

My piano teacher told me she'd missed me and asked if I'd been practicing.

Yes, I wanted to say, but all I could do was stand there.

"No, he hasn't," said my mother, coming down the stairs carrying something shiny for her New Year's party. "He hasn't even opened the lid. He's been doing nothing but looking at the new television since he got home."

"I've been playing football," I said.

"No, you haven't," said my mother. "He hasn't. He doesn't even play football! His eyes are like saucers. Look at him!"

My face went hot. In those days, I felt that my mother was always embarrassing me intentionally, trying to transform me into her trick-flipping lapdog, something to be poked fun at in front of other people. I couldn't stand it. I put my hands at my sides and stared down at the carpet. Miss Voight's heels were impossibly high. I wondered how women could walk in shoes like that as I followed Miss Voight into the living room, watching her ankles balancing on red stick-like heels. My father always said that the future of a woman's beauty lay hidden in her ankles. If her ankles were fat, the woman wouldn't age well. If they were thin, she'd get prettier every year. Miss Voight's ankles were slender and delicate as a racehorse. I imagined myself pinching her tendon between my fingers and running my tongue up and down it as she flexed her feet against the pedals.

I sat down beside her on the bench and banged open the lid too hard. I felt all wrong inside, afraid she could read my thoughts, see the invisible string in my head pulling my lap to hers. Miss Voight had done something different with her hair, which looked deep red and glossy. I wanted to press down her curls and feel them spring back against my piano fingers. Miss Voight pulled a music book out of her bag. For a moment, I couldn't even lift my hands to play, and when I finally did my fingers were clumsier than they had ever been. Every time I played something wrong, Miss Voight gave me a little sideways hug which only made things worse. "You're just rusty," she said.

"He's just bad." My father was standing in the doorway in his coat and tie, home for lunch. He put down his briefcase and walked up behind us. "He has no interest or feel for it, really."

"Maybe it's me," volunteered Miss Voight. "I've barely been teaching at all." My piano teacher turned away from me and looked up at my father as if he were the star on top of the tree. "I've been practicing for a concert in Chicago."

"Wow. That's just terrific," said my father, rocking back on his heels. "That's swell! We'll have to come and see it, won't we,

Lowe?" He hadn't ever gone anywhere with my mother to see Barbara, though she'd asked him to more than once.

"Please don't trouble yourself," Miss Voight said, blushing.

My father told her it was no trouble at all. Then he invited her to our party and asked her to play "Auld Lang Syne."

"I've always found New Year's disappointing." Miss Voight squinted when she spoke, as if she were looking straight into the sun. "I never have anyone to kiss."

"Well, our party has never been disappointing," my father said, shooting me a wink.

I narrowed my eyes at the sheet music in front of me. I had always found my parents' parties disappointing, adults making the rotations, talking to me awkwardly, until I had discovered the pleasure in draining the remains of their drinks. After that, everything had seemed funny. I traded gushing compliments for secrets with housewives. I had switched all the music to my Platters and Skyliners records so I could dance with the ladies to the love songs, pressing my cheek to the greatest cleavages in Nebraska.

Miss Voight had a way of hanging her head and biting her lip at the same time, and I imagine her resorting to these usual gestures as my father leaned down and plugged in the Christmas tree bulbs. When he left the room and I continued to play, Miss Voight no longer noticed my mistakes. She looked out at the snowflakes drifting down into the street, the Christmas bulbs flashing against the window, transforming her face into some beautiful blue angel. Clearly, my failed attempts at the keyboard no longer seemed to trouble her.

I prayed Miss Voight would come to my parents' New Year's party. For days it was all I thought about. I felt all hot inside, strange, hopeless, frustrated. I kicked the dog, and once she bit me. I endlessly studied my different expressions in the mirror, trying to master a way to look older, wise beyond my years. I wondered what I'd possibly ever be able to give her.

Every year for their wedding anniversary, which fell just before the holidays, my father told my mother he loved her by presenting her with a piece of jewelry, always engraved in script with the date of their wedding: *December 10, 1937*. For their nineteenth anniversary he had given her a bracelet with emeralds and diamonds set in platinum from Marshall Field's. Now, for their twentieth, she had received the necklace to match. This year, my mother had given my father a gold pocket watch with a picture of the three of us and Queenie, my mother's poodle, dangling from the gold chain. This annual exchange was proof enough to me of my parents' love, of something profound between them I'd never be able to touch.

My mother was no longer a pretty woman. Perhaps she had never been exactly. But when she put her sparkling new diamond necklace around her neck, and the matching bracelet from the year before on her wrist, and descended the stairs in her green New Year's dress, I could see why my father had given her such precious stones. Her eyes seemed large and full of emotion, her cheeks flushed from the heat of the kitchen as she oversaw the preparations. "Get her out of here," I remember her saying to me in the kitchen, as she thrust the black poodle in my direction and pressed the heavy necklace against her skin to make sure it was still in place. "Take her upstairs and close her in my room. She'll just get stepped on."

I carried Queenie upstairs and dumped her on the pink rug in my parents' bedroom. She scurried under the bed and peeked her sharp muzzle out from under the dust ruffle. I noticed muddy prints on the arm of my shirt; the dog had stepped in something wet. Staring at myself in the full-length mirror on the door of the dressing room, I tried to straighten myself up, combing my hair back from my forehead and trying to puff it up, more like Frankie Avalon's. But it wouldn't stay that way no matter how much I wetted it; it just fell flat. No girl had ever taken me seriously. In ballroom dancing at the country club the beauties always whispered in my ear about the boys they really wanted to dance with and stared past me when I cut in during the multiplication dance. I was that sort of boy.

I stood up straight in the mirror and rocked back on my heels like my father would do when he laughed in that free and easy way women loved, holding one wrist in the other hand by his belt buckle. Outside my parents' bedroom window, the night was blue and soft with falling flakes. It had been a white Christmas that year.

The snow kept falling. I could hear cars rumbling toward the house, see headlights waver and flash over deep drifts. I went over to my mother's bureau and opened her jewelry box. Digging through the silver and gold, the earrings, brooches, and strands of pearls, I tried to find something Miss Voight would love, a piece my mother would never miss. A gold bracelet, simple and elegant yet slightly exotic, studded with different-colored pieces of stone or glass, looked like it would do the trick.

I imagined myself pulling Miss Voight aside and pressing the bracelet into her palm, saying "Merry Christmas, love." Her face would light up with joy as she hugged me—no, pressed her red lips against mine. The doorbell chimed. I smoothed out the bracelet, thrust it in my pocket, and ran downstairs.

I waited a solid hour and a half for my piano teacher to arrive, my mother's stolen bracelet burning a hole in my pocket, my chest puffed up with the importance of secrecy. Finally Miss Voight did arrive, all by herself, looking beautiful in a black dress with red heels and red fingernails, her hair piled on top of her head. I was lucky enough to open the door for her. That was my job, and I did it with what I liked to think of as style.

But before I could say anything, my father was right behind me with a glass of champagne. "There you are," said my father to Miss Voight. "Watch out for this one," he warned, beaming as he tousled my hair. "Last year I caught him sneaking the dregs of everyone's drinks!" My father laughed. He helped Miss Voight remove her coat and thrust it over my arms as if I were a hook; then he grabbed a glass of champagne from a passing tray and presented it to her. She didn't even look at me.

They were both gone, into the crowd. I remember the candles burning softly, the Christmas tree lights flashing blue as they did every year of my childhood, the clinking glasses, the scent of cheese puffs clashing with cologne. I remember how people kept touching my mother's necklace admiringly. I could see them bending over and examining the emeralds and diamonds in the candlelight as my mother thrust her neck out from the green collar of her dress for them to see more clearly how much her husband loved her.

In the den, I hung Miss Voight's coat on the rack with extra care, removing a strand of red hair from her sleeve and wrapping it around my finger for safekeeping. I buried my face in the wool and clutched it in my arms as if I were hugging my piano teacher.

It was close to midnight, and my job was to pour the champagne into the rows of glasses by the bar. People were eyeing the clock. My father took out his pocket watch every few minutes and announced the time. Miss Voight sat down at the piano and people gathered around her. I pushed my way through the bodies to see her better, hoping she'd look at me or say something that would make my offering to her seem justified—more forgivable, I suppose. I wanted her to tell everyone that she was here because of me. I thought how well her black dress looked with the lacquered wood of the piano, and how beautifully the red poinsettias caught her hair. But then my father bent over Miss Voight, putting one hand on the lid of the piano, the other on the small of her long, straight back. Then he traced his finger in a tiny circle over the fabric of her black dress—an almost invisible gesture rippling like a chain from the tip of my father's finger through Miss Voight's hands and into my chest. For a moment I wasn't sure what I had witnessed.

As my piano teacher began to play and my father pulled back, I pushed between the bodies, feeling hot, sick, confounded, that bracelet sagging like a dead weight in my pants. All my effort seemed futile. I did not see my mother anywhere. I looked up at the faces, wondering if anyone else had seen my father and Miss Voight. But every expression looked blurred by drinks and cheer and suddenly older, sagging and ruddy, as if my parents' friends were aging, disappearing, coming closer to death right there in the living room. I don't remember the song my piano teacher was playing. I'm not sure I even noticed. As I thrust myself between shoulders and arms and sagging breasts, I was overcome by a heart-wrenching sensation, something on the fringe of excitement that made my eyes swim and my body tingle.

I opened the cellar door against the pantry light and plunged into the cool purple heart of the basement to collect myself, to get my head together while the party churned above me. I was no longer frightened of the sheet-covered furniture and old lamps looming like statues in a house of wax. Something inside me had changed. Frustration, maybe lust, had replaced fear. But when I turned the corner around the stairs, I saw my mother sitting on a case of champagne. Her face was in her hands, her dress fanned out over the box like a bell. When she looked up at me through the shadows, my heart jumped. She'd been crying; I could see the tears shining in the stream of light from the half-open door, the diamond necklace sparkling. I could hear music and laughter, and far away the sound of Queenie's futile barking made everything seem more still and quiet in the cellar, more ghostly, a world apart. My mother reached out her hand to me. I couldn't take it, too afraid she'd somehow found out what I'd intended to do with her bracelet. I just stood there staring at her. Her former dignity seemed like a formal outfit, quickly discarded.

"Lowe," she said. "Come here." So I went to her and stood over her, but I didn't know what she wanted. She reached out and patted my leg. "I'm so glad you're a boy," she said, clutching her arms around herself and hugging her bare shoulders to keep away the chill. She touched the necklace against her skin. It must have been cold. "When women get old, men don't love them anymore, no matter how they pretend to. They're like crows attracted to bright objects. It's a fact, Lowe. Remember that when you grow up."

I didn't know what she wanted me to say, so I said nothing at all. I didn't even reach down and touch her or try to offer her a bit of comfort. I just stood there frozen, staring down at the top of my mother's head, vowing to myself to return the bracelet I had stolen. Then, upstairs, the noisemakers started cranking, and the horns blew, and my mother's words were lost in the commotion. The new year was upon us with all its magic, anticipation, and innocence. I wondered if Miss Voight had found someone to kiss.

Three weeks later, when the minister came to get me out of history class and sat me down on the headmaster's couch to tell me that my parents had been murdered, that my father had been shot and pushed down the cellar stairs, that my mother had been stabbed, that there was evil in this world only the Christian heart could conquer, I could not cry. I could not feel. Believe. When he escorted me back on the airplane to Nebraska, all I could do was press my forehead to the cold window and look down through the clouds at the frozen lakes and endless flat drifts and the snow coming down all across the land that had been my home. I thought of the necklace my father had given my mother and of the last time I had seen it, twinkling in the darkness of the cellar at me like a thousand winking eyes.

I LIFTED THE FLIMSY LID OF THE CARDBOARD BOX, CERTAIN NOW OF WHAT IT held. My mother's diamond bracelet and necklace lay nestled deep inside, shimmering in a cradle of tissue paper. I held the necklace up to the light, and it sparkled as hopefully as the first time she'd worn it. Next to it was my father's gold pocket watch, their wedding bands, and the bracelet I had almost given Miss Voight. I tested the weight of the watch in my hand, letting the chain slip past my fingers, remembering the way my father had showed off the picture of us inside the lid to anyone who would take the time to look. And everyone did. He was the sort of man who gathered a crowd. Running my thumb around the smooth curve of my parents' wedding bands, I knew I was glad to have these small tokens, however imperfect their love had been.

I don't know how much time passed before the sound of tires on wet gravel jarred me. Though I couldn't see the driveway from the living room window, I was quite sure a car had pulled in. I thought I could make out the sputter of an engine and then an impenetrable silence. Putting my mother's necklace back in its tissue paper, I rose to my feet. I thought of course that Susan had come, that she had shown up as she always did.

But it wasn't Susan. Standing by the window, I saw two dark figures coming down the path toward the house. They looked to me like they didn't want to be seen. Maybe they were intruders who came here regularly: an abandoned summer house. It could not have been easier. They looked almost like children. One had his arm tossed over the other's shoulders, and I thought I heard laughter.

The intruders stepped up onto the porch and out of my view. In my dark corner, I heard them fumbling with the door, which I had left unlocked. "Weird," one of them said in a hushed voice, as they slipped through the door. And then louder, another voice: "Is someone here?"

I took a breath and stepped from the shadows to meet them. "You bet someone's here," I said firmly. The girl gasped and the boy stepped in front of her. I fumbled for the wall switch. As the light came on, the boy stared from beneath the hood of his blue raincoat, his eyes wide in his narrow face. He lowered two duffel bags slowly to the floor, and the girl stepped out from behind him. It was my daughter.

"Dad," she said. "What are you doing here?"

I almost wanted to laugh, but it was more complicated than relief. In spite of my anger, in spite of her nerve, I wanted to hug her. At the same time, I was embarrassed at having been found out. "My God, Mary, don't you think I should be asking *you* that same question? And who's this?"

"Jack Hinnman, sir." The boy stuck out his hand, but I didn't take it. His face turned red and he dropped his arm at his side. In different circumstances, I might have given him credit for trying.

"You're news to *me*," I said. "I don't recall hearing anything about you."

"Everything's news," my daughter said, biting her lip and suddenly grabbing the tip of her thick dark braid. She was wearing too much lipstick. What had my daughter and this boy come here to do, drugs? Was he going to liquor my little girl up with the intention of taking advantage of her in the blue room with the clouds on the ceiling? "Take off your coats. Stay awhile. Apparently that is what you were planning anyway," I said. "I'd like an explanation."

They unzipped their raincoats but left them on and stood there shifting their feet by the doormat. My daughter looked at the floor.

"It was my fault," this Jack character tried to explain. "I wanted to get out of the city, and I thought we should come here. Mary said it was your real home. I was going to cook dinner. That's all." He was older than Mary, but it didn't seem by very much. He had that awkward look, the same one that had plagued me as a boy when I'd grown so much in one summer that I hadn't had time to get used to my limbs. But his face was much better looking than mine had ever been. He had one of those square jaws that meant he'd get what he wanted.

"Why should I believe you?" I said.

"Because it's the truth," Mary answered.

The boy took off his hood, revealing a small silver hoop in his ear. I was quite sure I didn't like whatever it stood for.

"Just so you know, I respect your daughter," he said. "I think she's amazing."Mary's face lit up for just a moment, in spite of all the embarrassment and anger she must have been feeling, and I could tell that what Jack said had taken her by surprise and pleased her. His words pleased me too, in a way he couldn't have known. I was glad to know my daughter felt she belonged somewhere.

"I'm assuming your mother doesn't know about this," I said to Mary. "Where does she think you are?"

"Where does she think *you* are?"

"I think we should discuss this in private," I said.

"What about Jack?"

"Jack can wait."

Mary looked at the boy, and he nodded eagerly. She clenched her jaw and followed me down the hall.

In the living room, my daughter and I stood there, staring at each other in the soft lamplight. "Where does your mother think you are?" I said.

"At Neeley's."

"Has Mom met Jack?" I said.

Mary nodded. "She likes him."

I sat down on the couch and kneaded my forehead with my fingers.

"So, what are you going to do?" she said finally.

I shook my head. "This is unacceptable behavior."

"Why? Because we don't want to stay in the city and get drunk like everybody else?" She stared pointedly at my glass of scotch.

"Yes, it's a drink," I said. "It's a glass of scotch. But I'm your father, and I don't really feel that I should be the one explaining."

"As if."

"Excuse me?"

"You never explain anything, Dad."

"Listen, it's not—"

"I know," my daughter said softly, which surprised me. She came farther into the room, took off her raincoat, and put it down on the piano bench. Her shirt was too tight, almost like a leotard, hugging her small chest, her delicate rib cage. She turned around and studied the old piano. Briefly, as she passed, I saw her reflection in it. She was so small, so frail. She didn't eat enough. Last year her soccer coach had called to tell us that Mary would have to spend most of her time on the bench if she didn't put on some pounds, and my daughter *had* gained weight, but it seemed somewhere along the way she'd lost it again.

"Hey, you were playing," she said suddenly, running her fingers along the piano keys.

"Not exactly," I said, "just knocking around." When she turned to face me again, there was an intensity to her expression, an inexplicable radiance, and it struck me how oddly beautiful she was. She resembled Susan's mother more than either of us, and yet she was more serious and quiet than Susan said her mother had been.

"This boy, I don't doubt that he's nice enough," I said. "And he probably likes you quite a bit, but I don't approve of you coming here with him. You're too young to be on your own together like this."

"See, I don't think I *am* too young. I don't see it that way at all."

"No," I said. "I suppose you don't. And why should you listen to *me*?"

Mary sat down and, with her silence, acknowledged the truth in what I had said. But the look on her face suggested that her opinion of me might be less harsh than I had imagined. "Are you going to tell Mom?" she said.

I couldn't think of what to say.

"I think you're not," she said hopefully. I didn't want to disappoint her. Something between us had shifted. We had a secret between us. Her eyes sparkled as her mother's had when, so many years ago, she'd stepped out from behind my closet door wearing

Aunt Clara's glittering ball gown. I remembered that same expression five years later, when, coming down the steps of the university library, Susan had caught sight of me leaning against the bicycle rack with my hands in my pockets. She'd dropped her customary cigarette and stopped in her tracks, her eyes lighting up. "*You* again?" she'd said.

"You'll like Jack," Mary said, her black hair shining in the dim light. Without thinking, I reached up and touched my palm to the crown of her head. In return, she gave me a funny little half-smile, then caught sight of the shoebox, and leaned over the coffee table so she could look inside. "What's this?" she said, pulling my mother's necklace out of its tissue paper cradle and holding it up to the light like a shimmering snake.

"That was your grandmother's necklace," I said.

"It's so pretty," she said, and turned it over to read the inscription. "What's December tenth?"

"Their wedding anniversary."

I spread out my parents' belongings on the table for her to examine. She touched the matching bracelet, the wedding bands, rubbed her fingers over the stones in the gold bracelet I had tried to give to my piano teacher. Opening my father's pocket watch, she stared at the face as if she were hungry for something, as if she could decipher some bit of information from the hour at which the hands had stopped. She examined the oval picture of me, my mother and father, and Queenie pasted on the inside of the lid before snapping the watch closed and putting it back down on the table. She sat back in her chair and looked down at her hands.

"This is the necklace she took. And that bracelet," she said, pointing at the one I had almost given my piano teacher.

"Who?"

"Caril Ann Fugate." I felt as if a tiny sharp little pebble were scraping at the inside of my heart. "They found the bracelet on the floor of a barn," she said.

"I didn't know," I said. "Who told you this?"

"Hank got a book and we both read it. Are you angry?" she asked.

"Did you find what you were looking for?"

She shook her head. "It didn't tell us what we really wanted to know."

"Which was?"

"What they were like."

"Why would you want to know what they were like?" I said. "They were inhuman."

"Not *them.* Your parents."

At times I could barely remember my parents myself. I had hidden them away. Their faces had almost faded from my mind, and yet particular memories were vivid. At times the sounds of their voices still came to me, bringing tears to my eyes at surprising moments, though I could hardly recall the funeral on that snowy day when it seemed the world had stopped. What would my children be able to tell *their* children about *me*? *He was always a mystery. We never really knew him. He just packed his things and left.* I had played so little part in their upbringing. Susan had been the one to get down on her hands and knees with them. She had bought them paints, decorated the house with their drawings, comforted them in the middle of the night, read over their school applications before sending them off. I had been too afraid of getting close to something that wouldn't last.

I tried to think of something special to tell Mary, just for her, something she would always be able to hold on to.

"My father had a tweed winter coat that he always wore when they went out. It smelled of cologne and smoke," I said.

Mary smiled.

"He ate shredded wheat every morning even though we had Moira to do the cooking. He was the kind of man everyone wanted to know. He was the president of Provident and Federal Savings, a good businessman, but he was also interested in other things. He took me everywhere. They wanted me to know the world was bigger than Lincoln."

I told her about a small collection of Mayan artifacts in my father's possession that had been donated to a museum when he died, about how he had inspired me to set up my own displays of things in the basement. One evening, my father and I came back from one of our semiprecious stone adventures, and my mother was standing by the door biting her lip. She'd never seemed to care about what we came back with, but when we unwrapped the agate and jet rocks and spread them out on the kitchen table for her to see, she picked the stones up and examined them closely in the light, exclaiming about how perfect they were. "Why don't you go add them to your displays, Lowe," she said.

"Right now? Before dinner?"

"Yes," she'd said, "right now. Immediately," and all three of us had raced down to the basement together. Under a sheet she had hidden a stone buffing machine—for turning our finds into jewelry. She was so proud.

"Where did you pick this up, Jeanette?" my father had wanted to know.

"Oh, I have my ways," she said, and he picked her up in his arms and kissed her on the neck.

I described to my daughter how we would make the jewelry together. I would stand between my mother's knees and hold the stone and then my mother would put her hand over mine and guide it over the buffer. And though nothing ever came out the way we had planned, there was excitement each time in the possibility that it might.

My daughter seemed to hang on this little story. She listened to me with her dark eyes as if she were reading instead of hearing, running my memories over in her mind, savoring every word. "Were they happy?" Mary wanted to know.

I thought about this for a moment, about what was the right thing to say. "For the most part, but then there were moments when I suppose they weren't. Everyone's life is full of a certain amount of those moments."

Mary looked down at her hands. "Are you here because Mom kicked you out?"

It was a reasonable thing to assume—Susan should have kicked me out long ago—but I was caught off guard anyway, almost hurt. It had never occurred to me that Susan might have been fed up enough to *want* me to leave. "No, I don't think so," I said.

"Then why are you here?"

"I came to get the jewelry," I said, "and to do some thinking."

"Are you getting divorced?" She made it sound so mutual.

"It's more complicated than that, sweetheart," I said. Somehow I felt cast off in that moment, with no mooring. I wasn't sure anymore that I wanted to end up this way.

Mary's face looked troubled, and I wanted to soothe her. "It'll be all right," I said. "Don't worry."

I left her alone with Jack and went outside with my drink and the box of my parents' belongings, letting the screen door fall softly behind me. The rain had stopped, but the clouds were still thick, obscuring the moon. The air smelled of damp leaves and the chill of fall. For a moment I stood there in the shadow of the house, watching my daughter and this boy move around the bright kitchen, getting things ready for dinner. She was standing by the sink washing out a pot, and he came up and put his hands on her shoulders and kissed her forehead. My daughter tried to whip him with the dish towel.

Through the trees, I could see a light on in Jane's upstairs window. Her soft dark shape moved through its glow. She was perhaps unpacking her suitcase, hanging her husband's paintings, settling in for a life alone. I felt a strange chill, a dark uncertainty. I made my way across the lawn and lowered myself to the cement lip at the edge of our property, my feet dangling over the Hudson River, holding a drink as the sky grew even darker. Beside me sat the open box, my parents' lives packed neatly away.

I tried to imagine what Susan was thinking, but it was impossible. I didn't have a clue. She was strong and independent. Why *should* she want me back? I imagined her at home, in our dusty apartment, drifting through the empty rooms, convinced now that everyone had left her. She runs her hands across the untouched bedclothes and removes her ring the way I have shed mine.

A breeze carried the scent of rain, and the leaves whispered their ancient stories. An animal rustled through the cattails. The lighthouse flashed, and though I couldn't see the structure around the bend from where I sat, its beam lit the riffles in the current like jewels. I was sure of something.

• • •

I LEFT MARY AND JACK IN PORT SAUGUS AND PULLED ONTO THE THRUWAY, heading south toward the city. The dash cast a ghostly glow over my naked hands as I clutched the wheel hard, afraid to let go. I sped down the vacant wet road late into the night with my parents' things beside me—his pocket watch, her necklace, and bracelets, their wedding bands—thinking how close all these treasures had come to meaning nothing. I passed New Paltz and Plattekill. But at Newburgh, I found myself pulling off at a Hess station, plagued by a sudden change of heart. I was nervous now, uncertain as to whether or not I could deliver what was required of me. Standing in the parking lot, gathering strength from a half-dozen packages of peanut butter crackers, I noticed a woman wearing a dirty pink sweatshirt with a piece of paper stuck to her moon boots. Opening the door of a smashed-up minivan, she reclined the seat and settled in for the night. I thought of our apartment, of Susan's warm body, which I hadn't touched in so long. She didn't deserve to spend her life alone, and though there are no guarantees of anything in this world, I was quite sure now that I didn't want to lose her.

On the road again, I sped past Vails Gate, a pack of truckers traveling in tandem. The sign for the artist colony at Storm King glowed fluorescent in the pool of my headlights. When I got closer to the city, I paid my toll and sped into the glittering skyline, buses and off-duty taxis weaving around me, every light in each building crying something different, my wife waiting somewhere deep within that restless heart.

I parked the car and nodded my head at Eddy when he opened the front door of our building. I didn't try to explain myself. I stepped into the elevator as Saint Thomas's bells struck midnight and watched the floors slip by me one by one, the oval light bouncing from number to number.

The apartment was silent, blue and dark, still and shadowed, as if time had stopped. There was not a sound from the city below. I put down my suitcase in the foyer and took my mother's necklace out of the box, feeling its weight against my fingers, the silver clasp draping around my wrist. I went to my wife's closed door. I put my hand on the brass knob, turned it, and stood there on the threshold peering into the dark room. For a moment, as my eyes adjusted, I didn't see her. Panic set in. How ironic it would have been to find her missing. But there she was after all, tangled in the comforter, sleeping soundly in the dim light from the window, her mask over her eyes, her knees curled up to her stomach, dreaming peacefully, I didn't dare guess of what.

I tiptoed into the room. I sat down slowly on the edge of the bed, trying not to breathe. It wasn't until then I noticed she'd cut her hair. Straight gray-flecked gold brushed the edge of the blanket. Somewhere during that day she'd decided to be rid of it and now the hair was short, just above her jaw. I put my legs up on the bed and pressed her body to me, thick and warm with the smell of sleep. I bent my knees to fit my wife's position and ran my arm under the blankets and around her waist. She shifted and murmured sleepily into the pillow, "You're home."

"Yes," I said. "Shhh." I took my mother's diamond necklace in both hands, leaned up on my elbow for support, and slipped it carefully around my wife's neck, fastening the clasp.

"What are you doing?" she whispered. I put my finger to her lips, and lay there in the half-light, watching the small stones glitter.

CAVAN COUNTY
LIBRARY

ACKNOWLEDGMENTS

I wish to thank my Nebraska relatives, Bud and Ann Sidles, for their encouragement and blessing. To my mother, Stark Ward, for sharing her stories and reading mine. To my father, Michael Ward, for his generosity in allowing me to explore this delicate material. Thanks to Kevin Canty, Brettne Bloom, and Sims McCormick for their careful reading and advice. To all the MFA students and professors at the University of Montana who suffered through this manuscript in the early stages. To Will McCormick for his astute reading, generosity, candor, and support.

To those who aided my research: Chad Wall at the Nebraska State Historical Society, Mark Nappelio and Ann Sidles, who dropped everything each time I called.

To Barbara Ganley at Middlebury College who encouraged me to write in the first place.

To Michael Curtis who discovered my stories and made them shine. To the late Michael Kelly, an inspiring presence, who took the time to offer encouragement when it was needed most.

To my agent Rob McQuilkin who went far beyond the call of duty and believed in me from the very beginning.

And a special thanks to my editor, George Hodgman, at Henry Holt for understanding what I was trying to accomplish and without whose brilliant work and tireless dedication, this book would not have been possible.

ABOUT THE AUTHOR

Liza Ward was born in New York City and holds degrees from Middlebury College and the University of Montana. Her stories have been published in *The Atlantic Monthly, Agni, The Georgia Review,* and thc *Antioch Review.* Her work has also been selected for the *2004 O. Henry Prize Stories* and Harcourt's *Best New American Voices 2004* collection. In 2004, she attended Yaddo. She lives in Massachusetts.